Space in the Heart

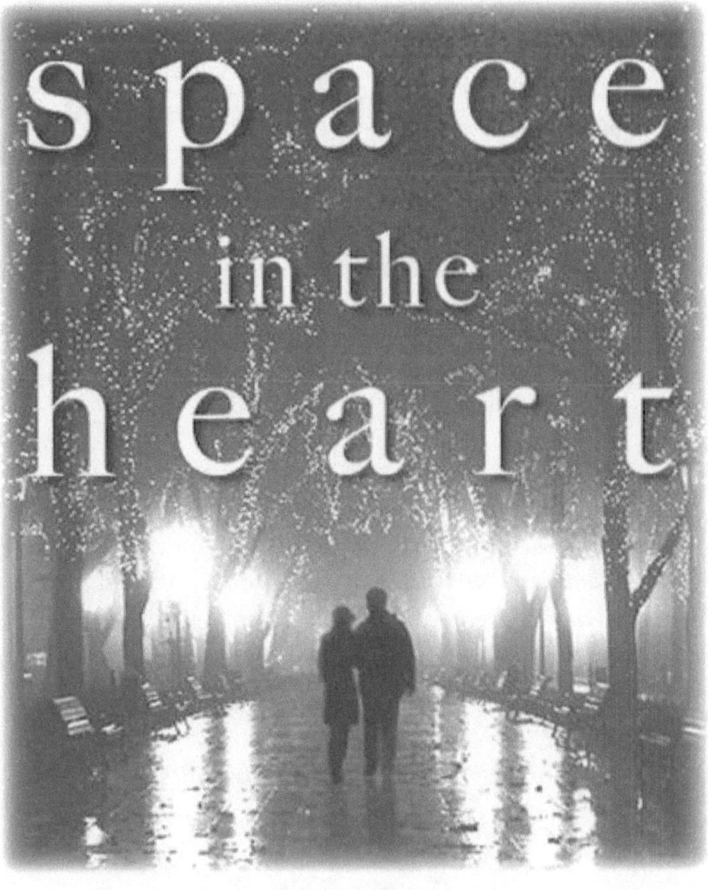

space in the heart

RODNEY WALTHER

Redstone Ranch Press

Publisher's Note: This is a work of fiction. Names, characters, places, and incidents either are the product of the author's imagination or are used fictitiously, and any resemblance to actual persons, living or dead, events, or locales is entirely coincidental.

Cover Design by j allen fielder

ISBN-13: 978-0982944639
ISBN-10: 0982944632

PRINTED IN THE UNITED STATES OF AMERICA

To order additional copies, visit the author's website at
www.rodneywalther.com

For Dad,

who taught me how to be a father

SPACE IN THE HEART

Chapter 1

September 1999

Inside her darkened car rushing along the highway, Celeste kept replaying their argument. He'd been so confident standing there in the driveway, reassuring her that her father was going to be fine, that it was okay to be concerned about some chest pains but not to freak out.

"He's my father," Celeste had said. "I need to be there."

"Just wait until morning," he'd told her as she bundled Zoey into the car seat. "Come on, babe. Driving late at night is a terrible idea. Who knows what might happen?"

Then she'd snapped back about how he was so busy with his new job that he wouldn't miss them anyway, and to just shut his mouth and put the luggage in the car. The argument was burned into her memory, and she knew that each of them would need to apologize when this whole ordeal with her dad was over. Why did people who loved each other say such hurtful things?

She lifted an arm and wiped her runny nose with the sleeve of her shirt, then blinked back tears that threatened to blur the lights of an oncoming eighteen-wheeler.

Normally she enjoyed this four-hour trip from south

Houston through Central Texas, staring out the window at the landscape. She always liked cruising past old farms with cows grazing in the pastures, past high-end ranches with fancy wrought-iron gates and game fencing, and past the rolling hills and limestone outcroppings west of Austin. That's where the Texas Hill Country began . . . and where she grew up.

But this trip had been miserable. After pulling out of their driveway, Celeste had fought tears for at least an hour, alternately frustrated with her overprotective husband and frightened for her father, who'd been rushed to Austin's Heart Hospital earlier in the day. Once she reached the outskirts of Houston, where she usually enjoyed the change of scenery, a thick bank of clouds had rolled in, obscuring the sky and threatening rain. Now the dashboard clock read close to midnight, and Celeste realized she hadn't been able to see anything along the road in a couple of hours, save the occasional stab of headlights. The world outside was as dark as she felt.

Mild whimpers sounded from the backseat, and Celeste gently shushed her child, hoping Zoey would settle back to sleep. She was a good sleeper, always had been. Within a week of bringing her home from the hospital, Zoey would go down by nine and stay asleep—with the exception of a midnight feeding—until five in the morning. When she was asleep, she was an angel. But when she woke up, especially if it wasn't her idea, she could be very demanding. Or as Celeste's mom had soft-pedaled it, "independent."

Just then her cell phone rang and she lunged for it, cradled in the cup holder of the center console, praying the ringtone wouldn't wake Zoey. *It's him*, she thought. She pressed the talk button. "Hi, honey."

But the call was from her mother. "Your dad's fine. The hospital ran some tests. He didn't have a heart attack and his enzymes look good. We're driving back to Johnson City now."

"Shouldn't they keep him overnight? He was having chest

pains." Celeste could hear the strain in her voice.

"It was probably reflux. Honestly, I think your father just gorged himself on enchiladas at lunch. He was burping nonstop until a couple of hours ago."

"I'm almost to Austin."

"Celeste." Her mom said the name softly, and Celeste could almost see her patting her lap and opening her arms to offer a comforting hug. "You didn't need to drive up here. You should have at least waited until morning." And that produced an image of her husband standing in the driveway, both hands pressed to the hood of her car, saying the same thing.

"Can I stay with y'all tonight? I've got Zoey with me."

"My daughter and my grandbaby? Seems like we should go to the hospital more often. I'll get your bedroom ready. See you soon. Be safe."

Celeste hung up, breathed a sigh of relief, and considered calling home and telling him the good news. But her world was in perfect harmony right now—Dad was healthy, Zoey was asleep, and he was probably asleep, too. *Just enjoy the trip*, she thought. There would be plenty of time to tell him later.

She continued to press on toward Johnson City, the rhythmic thump-thump of her tires slowly lulling her into a semi-catatonic state until she drove past a dead skunk and its foul stench flooded the car and snapped her back to full alert. When she peered through the windshield to get a sense of how far they still had to go, she didn't recognize the area anymore. "Oh, come on," she said to herself. "There's no way I'm lost."

Just then, she heard rustling sounds from the backseat. She adjusted the rearview mirror to see Zoey's outstretched arms shudder a bit and then drop back down onto her chest. With a sharp pull, the girl tugged the light blanket from her face and blinked several times. Celeste smiled into the mirror. "You awake, Pookie?"

Zoey rubbed the back of her hand across her nose and let out a wide yawn. "Momma?" she said, her voice sounding confused.

"We're driving, remember, to see Meemy and PawPaw." *Of course, I have no idea where the hell I am.*

Zoey pulled at the straps of her car seat, then stretched—Incredible Hulk style—to attempt an escape. When she failed, she whimpered in protest. "I'm hungry."

"It's okay, sweetie. We can stop. You need to go potty?" But Zoey's whimpers had already turned into a high-pitched squeal. Celeste shushed her. "We're just gonna go a little bit more, I promise." With the sound of Zoey's cries filling the car, she tried to see where she could pull over. Not on the shoulder—too dangerous. If she could find her way to Austin, there were plenty of options. At this point, she would settle for a gas station.

The screams were at ear-splitting levels now. Celeste had no idea if Zoey was hungry, wet, or simply tired of being cooped up, but her hysterics were becoming contagious. She wanted to yell into the back seat—*Shut up, already!*—but also knew that would make matters worse. "Come on, Pookie," she begged.

Topping a hill, she could see a smattering of lights in the distance. Even from a mile away, she could make out the logos mounted on thick poles: Exxon, Shell, Burger King. Relieved, she flipped on her blinker. She reached back and patted Zoey on the leg. "We're here, baby."

After pulling into the Burger King parking lot, Celeste unbuckled Zoey from the car seat, grabbed the diaper bag and her purse, and walked toward the entrance with the girl settled on her left hip. As she approached, she saw a woman inside the restaurant moving toward the door. She wore a striped blue polo and BK cap and wielded a large keychain. "No!" Celeste called and rushed forward, but she was too late. The woman had already turned away.

With Zoey fiddling with the loop earrings Celeste had put on in the morning, she stepped to the door and tried the lever. "Please. We need to use the restroom."

A guy dressed in an identical BK uniform strolled by with a broom and long dustpan. "You have to use the drive-thru," he said, pointing to his watch. "It's midnight."

"Come on," she pleaded. "It's only eleven fifty-five." She felt a slight tug on her ear, and Zoey leaned close and barked, "Momma!" Celeste ducked and half-slapped at the tiny hands waving near her ear. "Cut it out, Zoey!"

She whistled to draw the attention of the workers, but they either didn't hear her or were ignoring her, so she knocked on the door. Nothing. She mumbled under her breath and cut her eyes to the two gas stations. The Shell next door was dark and shuttered, and from the glow of the Burger King she could see the Shell station's collapsed roof and its outside cinder-block wall covered in oily, black residue. The Exxon across the street wasn't much better. It looked disgusting from the outside, garbage overflowing its Dumpster, paper swirling around its gasoline pumps as if a tiny trash tornado had struck the place. Burger King was her only hope.

She turned back to the restaurant's door and Zoey started to whine. "It's okay, Pook—" Celeste began, but a brilliant flash of pain struck her mid-sentence. She spun to Zoey, who looked at her with a startled expression, a loop earring clutched in her fingers. A tiny sliver of flesh hung from the fourteen-carat gold circle.

Celeste's knees buckled, but she somehow managed to keep her balance and set Zoey down without dropping her. After a moment, she brought a hand to her ear to inspect the damage. When she pulled the hand away, it was bright red. Waves of nausea cascaded over her.

"Watch me, Momma!" Zoey shrieked as she performed what appeared to be a kind of touchdown dance for having yanked off Momma's earring.

Even through the pain, Celeste couldn't help but smile at her little girl—she was just so innocent. She reached out to catch Zoey's arm and retrieve the jewelry that moments ago had been fastened securely to her own earlobe, but a sudden movement at the corner of the building stopped her. A figure appeared from the dim shadows, a disheveled man in ratty clothes. He staggered toward them, his head jerking from side to side, his right hand bouncing against the brick wall. Celeste heard what sounded like buzzing, then realized this homeless guy or meth freak—or both—was humming to himself.

She grabbed up Zoey in her arms and banged on the restaurant door, her fist leaving bloody splotches on the glass. "Seriously, let us in!"

She cast a quick glance back toward the man, but the sidewalk along the building was empty. It was as if he'd disappeared right into the wall.

Her stomach lurched. This trip had been a terrible idea.

Chapter 2

May 2011

Garrison Sterling ran a gloved hand along the surface of the four-foot rocket model, feeling for spurs and cracks. He'd been working on it for more than a month, and everything needed to be perfect before he delivered it to the science museum in Waco. Illuminating the gleaming white surface of the orbiter with his flashlight, Garrison considered how truly beautiful the space shuttle was.

Just one flight, he thought, for probably the millionth time since he received his acceptance letter from NASA. Just one flight into the dark expanse of space, one chance to experience the rumbling liftoff from a launch pad, to circle the planet and gaze down on her continents and oceans, to float weightless. But that *one flight* had never been in the cards for him.

He examined the silvery, ribbed surface of the main engine thrusters, slightly wiggling them to make sure they'd hold up to minor bumps. He confirmed the position of every decal and the color of every painted line, because he knew that details mattered. And then, as he always did for every handmade model of the space shuttle, he inspected the grey-tipped delta wing of the orbiter, lightly running his fingers along its leading edge as if checking for foam insulation damage.

In the quiet of his workshop, surrounded by spray paint cans of every imaginable color, organization bins for PVC pipe fittings, and a movie poster of *Apollo 13* on the wall, Garrison paused to remember his friends.

He'd worked with them all, of course. The American public didn't know the crew's names—Husband, McCool, Anderson, Ramon, Chawla, Brown, and Clark—until they perished in the sky over East Texas, but Garrison had long known them on a first-name basis. Because he'd trained with them. Because he'd originally been slated to fly with them.

A drop of sweat fell from the tip of his nose and landed on the orbiter's payload bay doors. He quickly wiped it off and blew on the shuttle's surface. This was not the time for mistakes.

His cell phone buzzed, and then Elton John's *Rocket Man* filled the silence. Garrison fished the phone from his pocket.

"Mister Garrison?" the female voice asked.

"It's Mister Sterling. Garrison's my first name."

"Oh."

After an awkward pause, he said, "Can I help you?"

"You're the Mister Garrison with the telescope?"

He took a deep breath and gritted his teeth. "Garrison's my first name," he repeated. "My last name is Sterling. And yes, I have a telescope out at my weekend ranch. I'm sorry, ma'am, but what do you want?"

"This is Kelly from Scope World. My boss said to call you. There's a sales rep from Meade Instruments at our store today."

Garrison remembered the last conversation he'd had with the store manager—Tucker something-or-other—back when he'd bought his equipment. Tucker had told him all about the parties where local astronomy enthusiasts gathered to swap stories and to gaze at the stars. And he'd mentioned the astronomy convention, too—last year's was held in San

Antonio. Neither of those ideas appealed to Garrison, who wasn't big on crowds. But when Tucker mentioned that manufacturer representatives occasionally visited the store, demonstrating the latest models of telescopes and accessories, Garrison had relented and scribbled his phone number on a business card.

"Sales rep brought a lot of new telescopes," Kelly said. "We've got them set up across the store. There's this really sweet sixteen-incher with ACF optics and GPS, plus a wireless controller. Sure wish I had one of those."

"I . . . I really don't want to drive up there."

"Tucker thought you'd want to know. Everything's thirty percent off today."

"Appreciate you calling, but . . ." Garrison looked to the corner of his workshop, which housed his latest engineering marvel: a custom-built motorized chair that looked like a crude version of NASA's centrifuge trainer. It was supposed to swivel and recline and would be perfect for viewing the night sky once he had installed all the components. "Kelly," he said, "did the sales rep happen to bring any astro binoculars?"

"Let me check."

As Garrison waited, he thought about what it would be like to finish the project for his daughter. He'd been tinkering with the binocular chair off and on, and if he put his mind to it, he could finish the darn thing.

"Okay, Mister Garrison—I mean Mister Sterling. He says he has lots of astro binocs. But the rep's only going to be here until three."

Garrison wasn't sure what to do. He could order the high-powered binoculars online, but then he'd never get a chance to look them over first. Just the thought of driving to a crowded store made Garrison's shoulders tense.

"We're open until six today," Kelly said.

Garrison swallowed hard. "How busy are you?"

The telescope store was tucked into a strip mall near The Galleria and flanked by an upscale nail salon and a Lebanese restaurant named Al-Amir that had, according to the sign in the window, "The Best Hummus in Houston." Garrison sat in his van with the engine off, garlicky odors from the restaurant permeating the vehicle's interior, and listened to his long-time inner voice. *Go home. Too many strangers around.*

His neck muscles tightened, and suddenly his chest felt the same way. Another panic attack was coming on. As much as he knew those feelings were irrational, it didn't change the fact that they were real. He nervously watched the front door and then blew a controlled, measured breath to bolster himself. *This is for my little girl*, he thought, and hustled from his vehicle to Scope World's entrance, passing through a pungent cloud of Middle Eastern spices on his way.

When he stepped inside, he could no longer smell Al-Amir. That was probably because the telescope shop, which resembled a semiconductor cleanroom more than a retail storefront, was outfitted with a series of industrial-strength air purifiers. He let his scientific mind ponder on the physics of removing airborne particulates, calculating how long it might take to recirculate the air in the entire store. Those kinds of mental exercises always seemed to help him wrest back control and calm his nerves.

He scanned the room and saw at least fifty telescopes, refractors and reflectors mounted on heavy tripods, dotting the clean grey carpet around the perimeter of the store. They looked like old friends. He wandered the store, past thick glass cases containing eyepieces and lenses and filters, then past gleaming glass cabinets containing microscopes and binoculars. On one side of the store, in front of a wall-to-wall poster of the lunar horizon, a phalanx of jet-black catadioptric telescopes stood guard.

A smile spread across his face. He remembered the day he and his daughter had finally affixed his "cat" to its concrete pier. They'd etched their names and the date on the star shack wall, and later that night, under an inky black sky, they'd played with the telescope for hours.

"Can I help you, sir?"

Garrison jumped at the sound and turned to see two men walking toward him. The first man, dark and tall, had an angular face and a sharp chin. Wearing a sport jacket, he pulled a wheeled catalog bag, and Garrison thought he looked like an undertaker on a house call. Walking behind the undertaker was Tucker, the store manager, decked out in a Hawaiian camp shirt and khakis.

"You like those cats?" Tucker asked, pointing to the line of telescopes. "We can get you hooked up."

The two men drew closer, and that old feeling of being uncomfortable around strangers reared its ugly head again. Garrison took a step back and brushed the leg of a tripod, causing it to shake.

"Watch out!" called the undertaker. "Be careful. Those are expensive."

Garrison's eyes flashed to the tripod, then to the two men who'd surprised him. "Sorry," he said, moving toward the front door. "Just . . . browsing."

"Oh, I didn't recognize you there, Mister Sterling. I heard you might drop by. Are you feeling okay? You're looking kinda pale."

Garrison shrugged. "I'm fine. Can you show me your astro binoculars?"

"Anything specific?"

"High mag, an aperture of at least fifty. They're for my daughter."

"We have lots of models with those specs. But you should know that astro binocs are heavy. How old is your daughter?"

"Almost fourteen."

"And she likes stars? That's sweet. I'm sure we have a pair that's perfect for her. You know, it's not every day you find a teenager who likes doing things with her mom and dad."

Garrison forced a smile. He never knew what to say when someone mentioned his wife. For a while, he used to correct people with something to the effect of "I'm a single dad," but that turned awkward more often than not, as people tended to become nosy. The truth was even harder to explain: she died a long time ago.

He hated the term "widower," but there was no escaping the cold, hard facts. There wasn't a wife in Garrison's world, not even a girlfriend, although the idea of meeting someone special was a dream he still held on to. His life revolved around his daughter. If she was happy, he was happy.

As he returned to the counter to inspect various models of large aperture binoculars, the ones designed especially for stargazing, he found himself more comfortable than when he first came in. Just being around telescopes had a calming effect—one good night of viewing the stars often cleared his mind—but he knew the real reason he was no longer nervous. He was thinking about his daughter. For a teenager smart enough to operate a telescope and program its autoguider, she didn't have any equipment to call her own. She was going to be thrilled with her gift.

He ended up choosing a pair of 25x100 binoculars with multi-coated optics that were designed for magnifying planets and star clusters and able to be mounted on his still-unfinished binocular chair. "Here you go, Mister Sterling," Tucker said, handing him a plastic bag with the large box inside. "You coming out to George Bush Park this Saturday?"

"Uh . . ."

"Everybody's meeting at six to grill burgers and set up their equipment. Jim's trotting out his big Dobsonian." He handed Garrison the credit card receipt. "Forecast is for clear skies. Bring your family. It'll be fun."

Hanging around a bunch of strangers in the dark was not Garrison's idea of fun. "Sorry, Saturday's my daughter's birthday."

A look of comprehension slowly dawned on Tucker's face. "Oh, I remember your daughter. She's in a wheelchair, right?"

Garrison nodded.

"She's fourteen now? Wow, time sure flies. You ought to make her birthday special. Join us."

"I'll think about it," he lied. As he left the store and made his way through a fragrant cloud of garlic, onion, and what was probably roasted lamb, Garrison decided he would do something special for her birthday. First, he'd finish that binocular chair. Then he'd give her this new pair of binoculars, enjoy a nice birthday dinner in their cabin, and spend the night at the star shack.

Just him and Zoey.

Chapter 3

Zoey drummed her fingers on the arms of her wheelchair, willing the school bell to ring. "What if my dad says no?"

Cara Reynolds shook her head. "Why would he? It's just a sleepover. My mom will spread out air mattresses in the music room downstairs. We'll sleep there. Dad is setting up our new TV tonight. You're gonna be so impressed. It's ginormous."

Zoey thought about the television she had at home, probably four years old by now, and felt secretly jealous of Cara. Her best friend always had the latest gadgets, courtesy of a father who was a bigwig in the airline industry, and the cutest fashions, which her stay-at-home mom bought from the trendiest boutiques in Houston. "Your parents are so cool," Zoey said.

Cara made a sour face. "I can't stand them. All they do is argue."

"At least they let you do fun things. Not like my dad." As much as Zoey loved him, he absolutely drove her crazy with his overprotective attitude. And with her mom long gone, that meant her dad was on the job 24-7. *My father and my smother.*

The bell rang, followed immediately by the sound of chairs being pushed back, but Zoey knew better than to make a rush for it. There wasn't any need to get caught up in the crowd of kids running for buses or their parents' cars. Her ride would be there, waiting patiently for her . . . as he had every afternoon since her first day of kindergarten.

"Let's get outta here," Cara said. "I have to head home in a few minutes. Did I tell you my mom's picking up Maverick from the vet?"

Good grief. Zoey was getting tired of hearing about Cara's new Labradoodle. Her folks had bought the designer dog from some out-of-town breeder last week, and now they were finally bringing it home. Cara hadn't been able to shut up about it.

"Can you believe my folks paid three thousand bucks for a dog?"

"Wait. Seriously?" Zoey had been bugging her dad for years about getting a dog, either a service animal or just a friendly companion. She would have been happy with a two-dollar mutt from the shelter.

"Actually, it was my mom's idea. She and my dad had a big argument about how much he was spending on golf, and the next thing I know she was calling dog breeders." Cara slung her backpack over a shoulder and cruised right out of the classroom, while Zoey had to push hard just to keep up. Cara laughed. "Hurry up, slowpoke. I need you to run interference for me."

They entered the hallway, and Zoey wheeled around a bunch of students to get in front of her friend. She used to watch reruns of *Saved by the Bell* and *Boy Meets World* and had wanted to believe those shows portrayed typical school life. But her suburban middle school was no sitcom. Sure, there were the jocks and the brainiacs and the band geeks—that was her—but her middle-school caste system was more layered than that. It consisted of an entire continuum that ran from the Populars to the Invisibles.

And for a girl in a wheelchair? Well, there was a special category for her.

When she and Cara exited the building, they immediately headed for the tennis courts. It was their secret hideout, a place where they occasionally held conversations after school without fear of interruption.

It was also the place where Zoey could let her imagination run wild. Behind the privacy fence screen, she could picture herself at Wimbledon, running around a court on muscular legs, diving to reach a hard return, curtsying to royalty after her match. Far from the bullying world of middle school, she could be normal there.

But today the tennis courts were occupied.

"What the heck?" Zoey said.

"I bet it's tryouts for next year's tennis team."

Zoey grimaced—of course it was—and felt an empty ache in the pit of her stomach. She gave her chair a hard push and veered right, toward a bench on the court's perimeter. "I don't even know why they hold tryouts," she muttered.

Cara walked up to the fence and peered through the black mesh fabric. "I see Reshma. She told me she was trying out."

"She didn't say anything to me." It wasn't as if she and Reshma Kumar were besties or anything, but they did occasionally eat lunch together.

"There's a bunch of kids out here," Cara said. "Eric Finco, Allison Cleary, Tiffany McAdams."

"Ugh. Not the Populars." Back in elementary school, Tiffany McAdams had been a gap-toothed girl in pigtails who liked to wear oversized Disney t-shirts and flowery skorts. Now Tiffany and her friends were the self-appointed arbiters of what was considered stylish on campus. Zoey couldn't stand their little clique. "Ignore them, Cara. Let's talk."

Cara shrugged, then came over and joined her. While Zoey sat in her wheelchair next to a concrete bench, Cara sprawled across it, leaning back on her arms like that girl silhouette on truck mudflaps, her blond hair blowing in the breeze, her tan legs stretching out, her curvy chest jutting up.

"I forget what you told me," Zoey said, looking the other way, "what kind of dog are you getting?"

"Labradoodle. It's a hybrid."

"Like a Prius?" She realized immediately how utterly stupid she sounded. "I mean, that was a joke."

Cara rolled her eyes. She sat forward and reached her arms overhead, her fingers linked together. "I should have tried out for tennis."

"What? You don't even like sports. I remember when—" Zoey stopped and looked closely at her. "Did you dip dye your hair?"

Cara tossed her head. "Yeah, with Kool-Aid. It's the big thing now. Haven't you heard?"

"Why didn't you tell me?" For whatever reason, Cara was being flakier than normal, and Zoey couldn't understand it.

"Jeez, Zoey, are you trying to be my mom or something?"

"No, it's just—"

"Ooh, can you see Tiffany?" Cara said, cutting in. She pointed toward the tennis court. "That is a seriously cute outfit. I think she bought it just for tryouts. See how it shows off her boobs?"

Zoey winced. She didn't like it when Cara talked about things like that.

"I think Tiffany has the biggest ones in school," Cara continued. "Bigger than Allison Cleary's, that's for sure. And guess what? Allison stuffs her bra. I saw some tissue peeking out after gym. Did you know that?"

"Um . . ."

Cara pushed her breasts together, which made her look like one of those women in a beer commercial. "My mom thinks I'm going to be a D-cup just like her. What are you, Zoey? An A? Or more like an A-minus?" She cackled at her own joke.

The truth was that Zoey was far from joining that world.

She reflexively glanced down at her own chest, embarrassed to admit she was still wearing a training bra. She knew the term was "late bloomer," but she so badly wanted to grow up, to be treated like an adult. Yet she hadn't even gotten her period.

"Well, I need to go," Cara said, grabbing her backpack. "Mom and Maverick will be home soon. Don't forget to ask your dad about the sleepover." She began walking away, toward the nearby subdivision where she lived in a mansion beside a golf course. The last thing Zoey heard was, "Did I tell you my folks paid three thousand dollars for him?"

All by herself now, Zoey closed her eyes and tried to ignore the happy shouts coming from the tennis courts. Even though the Populars had invaded her sanctuary, she still liked being out here, alone with her thoughts, the hot sun baking the nape of her neck.

She dug inside one of the wheelchair pouches for her dog-eared copy of Shakespeare's *Romeo and Juliet*, required reading for her English class. When she eventually finished— and she knew the tragic end of the story was coming soon—she would be one step closer to the goal she'd set two years ago: reading twenty-five classic works of literature before her freshman year of high school.

Her list began in sixth grade with *Little Women* (wonderful!), *Animal Farm* (reminded her of school), *Lord of the Flies* (school again), and *The Count of Monte Cristo* (just like the movie). Her favorite had been Tolkien's *Lord of the Rings*, but that was probably because she had watched all the DVDs.

The tennis teams were playing doubles now. Zoey could hear the steady thwack of racquet against ball, the occasional grunts—almost always from the boys—and the whoops of players celebrating a point.

She tried to ignore them by opening her book, but after re-reading the same page four times, she knew Shakespeare didn't stand a chance. Her fingers curled around the paperback, and she dropped it in her lap. Pushing closer to the fence, she watched with envy at all the activity taking place on the other side. She didn't feel like reading anymore—she felt like swinging a racquet.

But playing tennis was one of those dreams that would never come true, like participating in marching band or being the first woman to win Daytona. Like meeting the perfect guy and walking down the church aisle to marry him. Like having a mom around.

Zoey eventually tired of the tennis tryouts and returned to the story of Shakespeare's teenage lovers. She hoped she would eventually fall in love with someone like Romeo, a guy who cared so much that he would rather die than lose her. She hadn't met her true love yet, but held out the possibility that she would. Or was she just kidding herself?

Suddenly the gate to the tennis courts flung open and crashed against the fence. She flinched. Tiffany McAdams rushed out without looking and slammed right into her wheelchair. The collision caused Tiffany to fall back and land on her rear, where she let out a yelp.

"What are you doing out here?" Tiffany snarled. She stood and smoothed her tennis outfit, glaring at Zoey the whole time.

"Sorry. Are you hurt?" It was one thing to be looked down upon by the Populars. Provoking their queen was tantamount to suicide.

More kids appeared through the open gate and gathered behind the girl that their eighth-grade class had voted *Most Beautiful*. Tiffany wrinkled her nose in disgust. "Where's your short bus? Aren't you supposed to be with the rest of the spazzes?" When Zoey didn't reply, Tiffany pushed past and muttered, "Get out of my way, Bulldozer."

Zoey sat there open-mouthed and ashamed as the other students began to laugh.

Garrison swung his van into the parking lot at five-fifteen. He would have gladly picked up Zoey right after school as usual, but she had begged him during breakfast to let her stay late and chat with Cara. He hadn't been excited about the idea.

The buses were long gone, and only a handful of students waited around under the awning next to the parking lot. He didn't see Zoey—she was supposed to be waiting for him.

His jaws clenched and his fingers squeezed the steering wheel. As he inched the van forward, he scanned the sidewalk through the passenger window. The only people he saw were a knot of boys throwing a Frisbee and a redheaded girl lying on a concrete bench, her eyes shielded by the crook of an elbow.

The uneasiness he'd felt at the telescope shop had subsided on the drive home, but now it was back. He steered the van into the fire lane and hit the brakes so hard that his seatbelt automatically locked up, pinning his shoulder against the seat. He rolled down the window and blasted his horn twice. "Zoey!"

The redhead gazed his way. "You looking for Zoey Sterling?"

"Where is she?"

"I saw her a few minutes ago in the band hall."

Garrison forced himself to breathe. She's fine, he thought. Probably just talking to some of her friends. He stepped out of the van and strode to the cafeteria doors, entering the school building as a kid exited.

When he passed the choir room, he heard crying in the distance. It was Zoey. He broke into a sprint and headed for her voice. Rounding the corner into the band hall, he saw a door ajar to one of the practice rooms. He threw it open.

She was sitting there by herself, her face in her hands, her shoulders trembling.

"Zoey?"

His little girl, the one who'd dealt with so much pain, looked up at him from her wheelchair, tears streaming down her face. "They call me Bulldozer!"

Chapter 4

"Who calls you Bulldozer?" her father asked.

Zoey rubbed her eyes, the tears still seeping from beneath her fingers. "Never mind, Dad, it's not a big deal."

"I don't believe that and neither do you." He knelt in front of her chair, his hands resting on her knees. "Who calls you Bulldozer?"

She could tell by his tone that he was prepared to escalate the issue. The last thing she needed was for school administrators to be dragged into this.

"It's just kids being stupid," she said, sniffling, trying to regain her composure.

He studied her, his blue-grey eyes searching for the truth she didn't want to share. After a moment, he leaned forward and kissed her on the forehead. "Don't let the mean ones drag you down, Pookie." He reached into her lap and gently removed her denim backpack, adorned with glittery stars and a keychain built from tiny alphabet beads that spelled her name. Then he stepped behind the chair and whispered, "Let's go home."

Her tears slowly dissipated as they traveled through the Fine Arts wing, but she wasn't able to shake the humiliation that had caused them. For years, she'd been someone whose differences were right there in the open. Even though she occasionally ran across nice folks who would clear a path in the hallway or open a classroom door—some people had proper manners—more often than not, fellow students gave her the stink eye. Some jerks would even run up behind her and jump on the wheelchair's push handles, riding her as if she were a shopping cart. Then there were the clueless who gaped and pointed at her, the hilarious ones who called her names, and the vast majority who simply looked through her as if she were invisible.

She could understand why her dad didn't like being around people.

When they passed by the school trophy cases and beneath a banner that read *Caring About Character*, he asked, "Are you excited about turning fourteen?"

She shrugged. Fourteen was one of those ages that didn't seem very interesting to her. Last year had been good—she'd finally become a teenager. And everyone she knew was eager to turn fifteen and obtain a driving permit. Sweet Sixteen would come next, followed by R-rated movies at seventeen and everything else at eighteen. But fourteen? Big effing deal.

"I thought we could leave for the ranch right after school lets out on Friday," her dad said.

"But Cara wants me to come to her house Friday night."

"No, sweetie. Saturday's your birthday—"

"Really, Dad?" she snapped. "You don't think I know that?"

He pulled back on the chair, stopping it. That was the thing about a wheelchair—whoever was driving had complete control. The chair spun around and he pointed a finger at her. "Don't cop an attitude, young lady."

"It's not fair that you plan my weekend without even talking to me. I don't want to go to the ranch." Zoey was lying, of course. She loved going there with her father, spending weekends in the rustic cabin, stargazing in the observatory they'd built together. Just not this weekend. Not on her birthday.

"Cara's parents invited me," she said, exaggerating a bit since this was a plan she and Cara had cooked up themselves only today in English class.

"No one called me."

"Because it's just a sleepover! Jeez, there aren't going to be any boys there, if that's what you're worried about."

His mouth twisted to one side as if he were processing the information. "We'll talk about this later."

She crossed her arms, not speaking to him the rest of the way through the school building but allowing him to push her chair. When they exited, Zoey discovered the sidewalk wasn't as empty as she'd hoped. Four boys in sweaty t-shirts leaned against the school building. She knew they played football on the eighth-grade "A" team, and she recognized the guy with a Frisbee as the hunk rumored to be going steady with Allison Cleary. Two girls from the top band sat on a concrete bench, smacking their lips and blowing huge pink bubbles. And coming across the parking lot were a dozen or so players with tennis racquets in their hands. Zoey suddenly wanted to be anywhere else.

She raised a hand. "Hold on, Dad. I . . . uh . . . forgot something in my locker."

"Let's get you in the van, and I can run back inside."

"No." Zoey reached her hands outside the chair and pinched the rims. Her wheelchair stopped abruptly and she felt a *whoomp* as her father collided against the handles. "I'll get it, Dad. I know what I'm looking for. Why don't you pick me up at the front parking lot? It's reallysomuchcloser."

She could hear how fast she was talking but couldn't help herself. Completing the awkward transition from wheelchair to the van's front seat was always a big production, and today she didn't feel like doing it in front of everyone. When her dad stepped to the side, she turned a one-eighty and rolled back inside the school. She paced herself for a few seconds until she rounded the corner, then pushed liked crazy to get away.

Cruising down the hallway, Zoey wondered what she could do to convince her dad to let her spend the night with Cara. He was just so stubborn. Maybe she'd wait until dinner—he always seemed more relaxed at home.

She was headed toward the front entrance when she remembered that she actually had left something in her locker: a worksheet folded neatly into her foreign language textbook. She needed to pull at least a B on the assignment or she was in trouble, because Spanish class was kicking her butt. She opened her locker and retrieved *En Espanol!*, and knew she would be staring at that book tonight and learning absolutely nothing . . . or else she was going to have to break down and beg Cara for help.

The weird thing was that Spanish hadn't always been so tough. It had been fun memorizing the words for family members, parts of the body, and household objects. Nouns weren't hard. Adjectives, however, were a totally different story, especially with the whole feminine-masculine agreement nonsense. She had learned a few: Tiffany was *bonita*, Señor Alvarez was *gordo*, and she was *paralizada*. And the Populars were, well, *popular*.

Her cell phone vibrated, and Zoey fished it from the custom holster her dad had fashioned for her on the chair's arm. She recognized the vibrating signal as an incoming text message. And she knew the worry wart who'd sent it. *Am in front. Is there a problem?*

She scoffed and stuffed the phone back into its holster, not bothering to send a reply.

As he stood in the kitchen, Garrison went through the routine of preparing dinner but kept finding himself distracted by thoughts of Zoey, who had barricaded herself in her bedroom. For most of her life, she'd handled difficult situations with a steady composure, even a certain grace. Not much fazed her. But then she'd hit puberty, and emotion became her currency. After talking with her, Garrison didn't know whether he should get involved with this "Bulldozer" situation at school or whether she needed to work matters out on her own. One thing was clear, though: someone had really gotten under her skin.

He opened a bag of farfalle pasta and dumped it into boiling water. Chicken pesto was Zoey's favorite meal, and she especially liked it when he prepared it with his homemade sauce, a concoction of toasted pine nuts and extra virgin olive oil and fresh cut basil, along with his secret ingredients: cilantro and a splash of lemon juice. This was the meal he'd intended for her birthday celebration, but after seeing her mood at school, he figured sooner was better than later.

He took a set of tongs out to the grill and removed two chicken breasts, then came back inside and began slicing the meat into thin strips. All he'd need to do was toss them into the cooked pasta along with his pesto sauce and some freshly grated Parmesan cheese, and all her problems would disappear.

Yeah, right.

Maybe he couldn't fix her troubles at school, but he certainly needed to do what he could to make her birthday memorable. He sat down at the kitchen table and opened a spiral notebook, the best way he'd found to keep his thoughts organized. Goal number one: finish the binocular chair.

He wasn't worried about mounting the heavy binoculars— the bracket system he'd designed would work fine. And he wasn't worried about the chair itself, because its aluminum plating and upholstered seat would support even him. But the motorized seat control had been a thorn in his side since he'd conceived of the idea.

The chair was supposed to swivel smoothly and recline gently, allowing for easy viewing, but it always seemed to shudder and jolt when it moved, like a rollercoaster pulling away from the platform. He knew he could fix the problem—and he *needed* to fix the problem—but it might take a couple of long days and nights. If he was lucky, he could knock it out by Friday. If he was lucky.

He focused on the problem at hand as he sketched designs for improving the swivel mount, including a random idea of using the sprockets of a bicycle. Before he knew it, he had filled five pages with notes and drawings. Satisfied, he leaned back in his chair and took a deep breath.

The distinctive fragrance of basil pesto drifted into his consciousness, and he suddenly remembered he had pasta cooking on the stove. He cut his eyes to the wall clock and mouthed a silent profanity. The pot had been boiling for forty-five minutes.

He dumped the pasta into a colander and stared at the shapeless mass. What once had been little firm bow-ties was now a heap of rubber bands. Muttering, he shifted to the pantry to find another package of pasta. He didn't need to spend much time looking—he knew he'd already used their last one. And he couldn't even improvise with spaghetti, rotini, or basic egg noodles because they were out of those, too.

"Hi, Dad," Zoey said, coming into the kitchen. "Dinner ready yet?" She'd changed into a yellow t-shirt with the image of a toothy beaver on its front, the kitschy logo of a Texas truck stop named Buc-ees. It had been an impulse buy during their San Antonio mini-vacation last summer, the first time he'd ever seen Zoey pull her teenage *drama queen* act. She rolled up to the kitchen island and stole a slice of chicken. "I'm hungry."

Garrison looked to the sink, where the farfalle pasta strings hadn't yet slithered through the tiny holes of the colander. "How about we try something new?" he said cheerfully.

Zoey turned up her nose. "You never try anything new."

"Well, necessity's the mother of invention. You've heard that phrase before, right?"

She rolled her eyes. "About this weekend. I want to spend time with Cara."

Garrison pitched the soggy pasta into the trash can. "Don't you see her every day at school already?"

"This is different," she said with an air of exasperation. "It's a sleepover Friday night. So, can I go?"

He hated being put in this position. Zoey knew she wasn't allowed to spend the night elsewhere—too much uncertainty and difficulty with her wheelchair. It wasn't fair to Cara's folks or anyone's parents to deal with the needs of a girl who was paraplegic. "I've got an idea," he said. "Invite your friend to the ranch."

Zoey scoffed. "She's from Mallburbia. I doubt Cara would be interested in seeing our little star shack in the country. And no offense, Dad, but you're kind of . . ." She hunted for the right word. "Intimidating."

Crossing his arms, he replied, "Thanks. That makes me feel special."

She ignored him and took another slice of meat. "You're making chicken pesto? I thought that was gonna be for my birthday."

"It was, but—"

"So this is going to be, like, my crappiest birthday ever?"

He balled his hands into fists. If Zoey would just listen to reason, life would be so much easier. But no, she was emotional and impulsive, traits she'd inherited straight from her mother. When he looked at Zoey, she was sticking out her tongue. He threw up his hands. "Why are you being so dramatic?"

"Because you're being a total pain in the—" She growled in frustration. "No birthday dinner. No sleepover. No dog—"

"Please, not the dog again. We've discussed that."

"Come on, Dad. I'm gonna be fourteen. I'm growing up and you're still treating me like a kid."

She was so demanding, he thought, bristling at the idea of rewarding her insolence. He wasn't going to compromise his principles just to get a little peace and quiet. And he darn sure wasn't going to get a dog. Okay, maybe Zoey was getting old enough to spend one night away, but there was also a reason their family had rules.

When it came down to it, all he wanted was to be a good father. But did that mean holding fast to his positions or yielding to her wishes? His stomach churned as the doubt nagged at him. What was he supposed to do?

Your dead wife would know, his inner voice chimed in.

Garrison ran a hand across his mouth and swallowed hard. "Fine," he said, unsure if he was making a huge mistake. "You can go on the sleepover."

Chapter 5

Piercing, high-pitched beeps from the bedside alarm clock bore into the brain of Danica Cortez. She groaned and pulled the covers over her head, but the insistent beeping continued. *Just a little more sleep*, she thought, pressing the snooze button and rolling onto her side.

Nine minutes later, the beeping started up again.

"Ugh," she muttered and smacked her hand down on the alarm. She checked the time—two-thirty—and dragged herself out of bed. Even though she'd been a weekday news anchor for more than three years, she still hated waking up in the middle of the night.

With the energy of a zombie, Danica slogged through her morning routine. She poured a cup of coffee and microwaved a bowl of oatmeal—enough energy to keep her going through two hours of live broadcasting but not enough calories to change the size of her clothes.

From the kitchen wall came the song of a white-throated sparrow. Danica sipped her coffee and glanced up at the bird clock her mom had given to her as a birthday present. One more hour until she needed to leave. *At least it's Friday.* She dropped her head, unexcited to spend the next hour selecting an outfit and applying makeup.

The outfit was the easy part. She opened the door to one of her two master walk-in closets and surveyed its contents. All of her professional clothes hung neatly on satin padded hangers, blouses arranged by color just like she'd learned from her mentor at her first job. Danica knew better than to open the door to her other closet, the one that held her regular clothes and that was intended for the "man in your life," as the real estate agent had once told her. There hadn't been a man in Danica's life in a long time, so that closet was cluttered with everything from her personal life. Such as it was.

She sighed and selected a long-collared cerulean blouse over solid-black camisole, with a pair of coordinating black slacks. The slacks were never an issue—no one could see those behind the anchor desk—but the blouse had to meet a stringent set of requirements established by Eyewitness9's executive producer: professional-looking; free of any patterns or prints; and flattering to her features, which she took to mean "look sexy but not slutty."

Danica hit the switch next to the sink, and five million watts of artificial light washed over the bathroom. She opened her mouth in a toothy smile and stared into the mirror, inspecting her skin like some sixteen year old looking for overnight pimple eruptions. "These are your good years," her mom had told her last summer at her thirty-third birthday party. "After the acne but before the wrinkles and grey hair." Then her mom had whispered in her ear, "Danni, it's time to settle down and get married. You need to start making me some grandbabies."

As Danica smoothed foundation on her face, she considered how much easier life was when she'd been a field reporter. Sure, she'd still needed to wear makeup, but not to the same extent. For a profession that prided itself on revealing truth, the use of heavy makeup seemed the ultimate irony.

She brushed on some dark bronzer—"Look more Hispanic," her producer had told her—and inspected the results in the mirror. Through the makeup, the only features she could distinguish were the ones her parents had passed on: the wavy, raven hair and dark eyes of her Sicilian father; and the tiny dimples in her cheeks, just like her Irish mother. *Mom probably wouldn't even recognize me like this*, she decided, then realized with a pang of sadness that today marked six months since Mom had died.

Danica began decorating her eyes and mused about her mom, a woman whose persistent optimism had been sorely tested throughout her life. Together, the two of them had tried to sustain the family through the difficult times, but now with Mom gone—with everyone gone—Danica was on her own. She had managed to keep herself busy at the station, often working late to check out story leads, trying to stave off the loneliness. She wasn't always successful.

As Danica was applying a strip of false lashes to her right eye, the bathroom suddenly plunged into darkness. "Are you kidding me?" she said.

She waited a few minutes for the power to return. It didn't. She rummaged through the other closet for some regular clothes, because she never donned her broadcast outfit—*her costume*—until she finished her makeup. Then she called Jerry Tomlinson, her news director and the most nocturnal person at the station.

"My power's gone out."

"And I should care because? . . ."

"Because right now it looks as if I got dressed in the dark. Which I did. This is a heads-up, Jerry. When I get there, I need to use the makeup room. And I don't want to hear any crap about how I look."

"Get here as soon as you can. Lots of news this morning."

"Really?" Even though Danica hated her morning routine, she did enjoy the process of news gathering, of writing and editing stories, of discussing what was important to viewers. Yet these days it seemed she'd been turned into another teleprompter-reading, journalism-lacking telegenic cutie. She wanted to be the hard-hitting reporter known as Danni Cortez, not "Houston's number-one morning anchor, Dah-nica Corrrrrrtez!"

"There's a two-alarm fire near the Galleria and there's been a shooting outside a nightclub on your side of town."

"Is that all?"

"What do you mean?"

"That's not real news. That kind of stuff happens every day in Houston." She sighed. "Forget it, I'm just cranky. I gotta go." She hung up, tossed her makeup in a bag, and crawled into her car.

Danica flipped on the low-beams and hazard lights before pulling out of her driveway. A white blanket of fog had fallen overnight, a byproduct of Gulf Coast moisture and pre-dawn cooling. She couldn't see more than fifty feet.

The fog always reminded her of when she was a little girl. Her folks owned a cottage on Fidalgo Island, north of Seattle, and Danica used to walk with her mom to the ferry terminal, to watch the tourists in line for the San Juan Islands.

One day when she was seven or eight years old, Danica begged to go whale watching. It was summer, the time of year when the resident orca pods regularly cruised the strait, so her mother relented and they rode the ferry across to the big island. As the two of them sat on the cliffs above Lime Kiln Point, scanning the horizon for telltale whale blows or dorsal fins appearing in unison, a dense fog began to roll in.

Soon they couldn't see the water, let alone any whales. Cloaked in a cocoon of white mist, the two of them lay on a cotton blanket, Danica's head resting on her mother's lap, which hardly existed anymore due to her pregnancy.

"I can't see anything," Danica said. "It's like we're in a cloud."

"Well, honey, we kinda are."

Danica could feel the moist air on her skin and could hear the rhythmic waves lapping the shore and the faraway call of a bald eagle. After a moment, she asked, "Do you think heaven's like this? You know, all peaceful and white?"

Her mom shushed her softly and caressed Danica's cheek with a delicate hand. Then she ran her fingers through Danica's hair, soothing her as if she were an infant. That was the day her mom had wept the whole way back on the ferry and recounted stories about the grandfather Danica had never known.

At the main intersection leaving her south Houston neighborhood, far from the cliffs of Lime Kiln Point, Danica stared through thick fog to check for oncoming cars. She pulled onto Space Center Boulevard, the long artery running north of NASA. She'd left home later than she'd wanted, and she still needed time to finish her makeup. If traffic was backed up due to the low visibility, she was going to be screwed.

But so far the road was empty, which actually seemed to make the outside world even more ominous. It was as if the fog had swallowed up everything. She slowed the car and muttered to herself. Driving in the middle of the night, especially in bad weather, was another reason she hated being a morning anchor. That's why her promotion to prime time, promised for a couple of years already, couldn't come soon enough.

Off to her left, she could see the glow of runway lights for Ellington Field, the long-time military airport that now served NASA and handled small commercial aircraft. The place was like an old friend, a landmark that greeted her every morning.

As she rounded a curve east of the airport, a large, slow-moving shape appeared in her peripheral vision. Her mind registered it as an airplane, even though it was enveloped in a shroud of white. She'd seen airplanes land at Ellington lots of times, but somehow this seemed different.

She looked out to her right and watched the plane descend from the sky, its landing gear deployed, its wings shuddering violently. Its engines growled a throaty rumble.

The plane's too low. "Pull up," she said, giving voice to an inner thought. "Pull up!"

Danica couldn't believe what she was seeing. The fog seemed to push down on the plane, as if the sky were smothering it with a pillow. A line of trees at the edge of a field reached up and tore off a wheel, and the plane tilted. Its left wing struck the tree canopy and sheared off.

The nose of the plane hit first, and the rest of the fuselage tumbled over it like the world's worst cartwheel. Debris littered the air.

Danica felt the shockwave and heard her car windows rattle. She yanked the steering wheel to the right and hit her brakes, fearing the crash would spill over onto the road. "Oh, shit!"

As the plane broke apart, red and yellow flames shot out from the fuselage. What was left then exploded, illuminating the sky with a brilliant orange fireball.

Danica steered her car to a stop beside the crash site. She jumped out and stood in the road, looking both ways so she could flag down a passing driver. A few seconds later, with no one in sight, she abandoned the idea.

Not knowing what else to do, she clambered over a barbed-wire fence and ran toward the smoking remains of the plane, while her fingers tried to wrest the cell phone from her pocket. She automatically punched some numbers, and a familiar voice answered.

"Eyewitness9 news desk."

She pounded the phone against her head. *What was she thinking, calling the station?* She hung up and dialed 911. "I need help. I just saw an airplane crash!"

"Where are you located?"

The question engaged something deep inside Danica, and all her journalism training and on-scene reporting gave her instant clarity. "An airplane went down. Not a jumbo jet. Maybe a charter. It crashed east of Ellington Field approximately . . . a mile and a half."

"Can you see where it landed?"

"It didn't land—it crashed! Send ambulances and fire trucks to Space Center Boulevard, north of Clear Lake and east of the Beltway. Hurry!"

Danica hung up and dialed the newsroom again. When no one answered by the third ring, she realized she couldn't just stand there and wait, not for the police or the firefighters or her colleagues at Eyewitness9. She had to do something.

Through the choking fog, Danica couldn't make out anything but burning wreckage. She moved cautiously toward it, fearing another explosion. Intense heat radiated from what had been the front half of the plane. She extended a hand to shield herself.

Farther into the grassy field, more wreckage was strewn about. Her brain processed the images of jumbled metal and told her that she was seeing an engine, more fuselage, and the plane's tail. *How could anyone survive this?*

A duffel bag that had obviously been ejected from the plane lay in the grass, but Danica didn't see it until she tripped over it and fell onto her knees. She glanced back to the road, hoping to see emergency vehicles, but she was all alone. Stumbling to her feet, she ran toward the back half of the plane, the only section not engulfed in flames. "Anyone there?" she called, and squinted through a gaping hole in the wreckage.

Something—*someone*—moaned in response.

Danica froze at the sound but knew what she had to do. She took a steadying breath, braced her arms on each side of the open fuselage, and lifted herself up. Once inside, she was enveloped by total blackness. "Where are you?" she called, crawling along the aisle, patting the seats on either side to find survivors. But all the seats were empty. Finally she felt a bare leg and shook it. "Tell me where you're hurt."

No answer. She pulled out her cell phone to illuminate the darkness.

A woman sat motionless in the seat, and the first thing Danica could see was a broad swath of tattoos all over the woman's body. A tiger with thick stripes and bared fangs seemed to be crawling down her left arm, while her right arm was covered with a garish field of colorful skulls. A large scorpion was wending its way up her neck and below her ear.

Danica cast the light on the woman's face—it stared back, mouth agape and eyes wide. A necklace with a large teardrop-shaped emerald hung around her neck. Danica reached out to check for a pulse, but the woman's head rolled to the side. Metal shrapnel had lodged in her neck and skull; her body was practically decapitated.

Danica clamped a hand over her mouth and stifled a gag. She crawled past the woman and called, "Who's here? Say something."

A moan sounded from her left.

She climbed over a seat and found a man locked in his seatbelt. She shone her lighted cell phone at him and saw a bone protruding from his upper leg, his left arm flailing. A sheet of blood poured from a gash on his forehead, down his cheek and onto his shirt. He coughed and turned toward her, his famous face unmistakable.

Danica gasped. "Senator Hartwell?"

Chapter 6

The man Danica recognized as a United States senator—the guy she'd voted for—slumped forward. She lifted his head and could see that his eyes had rolled up. He was still breathing, but unconscious.

A strong odor that reminded her of an old kerosene lamp flooded the cabin. Danica recognized the danger—they needed to get out now. She quickly checked the cabin for other passengers but didn't find any. They were running out of time. If the fuel ignited, they'd be dead.

Danica unbuckled the seatbelt around the senator's waist and thrust her shoulder under his arm. His limp body sagged against hers, and she began to haul him from his seat. He was a big guy, but carrying him over her shoulder wasn't as difficult as she'd expected. Apparently, whatever adrenaline that had been released when she witnessed the airplane crash had now been replaced with some sort of super-adrenaline.

When she reached the place where the aircraft had torn apart, she tried to pull him through. He wouldn't budge. The stench of fuel was overwhelming and she was desperate to get out of there, so she readjusted her body and thrust him higher. But he was stuck, as if the plane didn't want to give up its claim on him.

"Come on!" she yelled, looking back as she heaved once more, finally noticing that the man's leg was caught on something. She reached back and discovered his exposed leg bone was lodged against a metal seat support. Bile rose in her throat with the realization that while she'd been pulling on the senator, his femur had been banging against the plane.

When she landed on the grass, she could hear the sound of sirens in the distance. *Oh, thank God.* She reached her hands under his arms and dragged his still-unconscious body away from the plane. Then she decided to make another run for more survivors—maybe she'd missed someone. But before she could take a step, a thin string of fire shot toward the wreckage. Acting on instinct, she fell onto the senator and covered him, burying her head into his chest.

A second fireball ignited, and Danica could see orange behind her closed eyes and feel a blast of heat across her back. As she slipped into unconsciousness, she remembered lying across her mother and dreaming of whales and of being swallowed by a cloud.

The man moved beneath her, and Danica's consciousness returned. "Senator Hartwell," she said, pulling onto her knees. "Can you hear me?"

"Where is she?" he mumbled. "She wasn't supposed . . ." His voice faded and his eyes closed once more.

Danica shook his shoulders. "Stay with me, Senator."

A fire truck and an ambulance arrived simultaneously, their flashing lights piercing through the fog. Firefighters spilled from the truck. Danica stood and waved her arms. "Over here!"

The next half-hour was a blur. She sat on the curb, an oxygen mask over her nose and mouth, a paramedic closely watching her. Danica pulled the mask away and asked, "How bad?"

The paramedic's eyes darted to the wreckage, and he shook his head. "Just one survivor." He placed his hands over hers and manipulated the oxygen mask back over her face. "Ma'am, you really should go to the hospital."

She turned to see firefighters foaming down the front half of the plane, the intense flames refusing to yield. *Just one survivor.*

"Ma'am. The hospital."

Danica shook her head and tugged off the mask. "I'm supposed to be at work." She pulled out her phone and dialed the station. "Jerry," she said, her words slurring, her world suddenly spinning. "Hold on . . . whoa, I don't feel so good."

"Where are you?" he barked.

"I don't think I can come in today."

"Don't give me this bullshit, Danica. We've got a huge story going on right now. A plane just crashed."

"I know." Her head was dizzy. "I'm here."

"You're where?"

Her mind flashed an image of the airplane falling from the sky, and the enormity of the situation snapped her back to full awareness. "The plane crash. I saw it. It happened right in front of me."

Jerry was silent for a moment. Then he said, "This is great."

She shook her head, sickened by his excitement. "No, it was horrible."

"Pull yourself together. Our truck is on the way. I need you to tell the viewers what happened. I mean, holy crap, you were right there!"

She stared over at the wreckage. *Just one survivor.* "I tried so hard."

"What do you mean, you tried?"

"I tried to save them, but I couldn't." Tears streamed down Danica's cheeks. "Is Senator Hartwell gonna make it?"

"Hold on, are you telling me that Senator Joe Hartwell was on that plane?"

"I had to climb in and pull him out."

Jerry gasped. "Danica, this is . . . this is very important. Rocky's coming on the live truck. Don't talk to anyone else but him. This is *our* story."

Danica sat shivering under a blanket when the first news vehicle rolled onto the scene. A blonde named Barb Edwards bounded out the open door and rushed over to a fire engine. Barb was new to the business, with only two years as a reporter for Channel Five, but she'd already been lighting up the Internet message boards with her golden curls and tight-fitting blouses and calendar photos from her days as a swimsuit model.

Barb pulled one of the young firefighters aside and was chatting him up, standing close and touching his arm. The Channel Five photographer set up quickly, and before Danica knew it, Barb was already talking to the camera. "We're on the scene of an airplane crash in south Harris County," she said. "Approximately twenty minutes ago, this plane—" Barb gestured to the still-burning wreckage. "We're still trying to gather the details. But as you can see, this plane exploded in midflight."

Danica scoffed. The plane hadn't exploded in the air—it had crashed onto the ground and then burst into flames. She hated when reporters got their facts wrong or, worse, when they made up stories because they didn't know the facts. And Barb Edwards was notorious for shooting from the hip.

When Barb finished, she looked around as if someone were going to hand her an Emmy. Then she saw Danica. "God, is that you, Cortez?"

Danica pretended she didn't hear her.

"Looks like Channel Five beat you guys to the big story again."

Danica whipped her head around. "Yeah? At least we don't go out and make up stuff."

"Speaking of makeup," she sneered. "Are you seriously gonna do a stand-up looking like that?"

Danica was about to give Barb a piece of her mind, but just then the Eyewitness9 microwave truck arrived, and following in its exhaust fumes, the crews from two other networks. Barb cast a dismissive glare before strutting away.

Paulo Rosales, the burly Eyewitness9 photojournalist who always tried to speak Spanish to Danica, got to work immediately raising the mast. Rocky Campbell walked over and squeezed her shoulder. "How are you doing?"

She blew a long breath. "Jerry said to talk with you about the crash."

"You sure you're okay?"

"I'm fine. Let's do this." Danica wanted to go back home and crawl under the covers, pretend it was all some bad dream. She unconsciously reached toward her neck and thought about the dead, tattooed woman. The woman had looked like her, with light brown skin, but younger.

Rocky pressed the microphone into her hands. "Jerry wants you to report the story."

"Screw Jerry. He has no idea how awful it was."

"That's what you need to tell everyone." He folded his hands around hers. "God knows I'd love to do this story, Danica. A major plane crash. But it's not my call. This is your time. That's why they pay you the big bucks, right?"

She offered a wan smile. Rocky was one of the good guys in the business. "Give me a few minutes to clear my head."

"I'll get a towel," he said, gesturing. "Your face is, uh . . ."

"I don't care about my makeup."

"We're ready," Paulo said, flipping on a bank of portable lights. He gave a sharp whistle. "*Ahora mismo.*"

She rubbed her dirty palms against her jeans and then took an IFB from Rocky and inserted it into her ear. Soon she could hear Jerry's gruff voice yelling at someone in the control room. "Give me some goddamn graphics! The feed's up. Is Danica ready?"

"I'm here. But you really should let Rocky—"

"Okay, Mitch will throw it to you from the studio. Ten seconds. Everybody, on your toes!"

Danica gathered her thoughts, wanting to relay the truth of what happened but not wanting to share the gory details. When she heard her prompt, she began speaking to the camera. "Here's what we know, Mitch. Just before four o'clock this morning, a jet attempted to land at Ellington Field. But it fell short of the runway, clipping some trees before it crashed into a field." Her last word drifted away as the scene replayed in her mind.

Paulo adjusted his camera from the wreckage back to Danica, but she just stood there mute, her mouth moving but no words coming out.

"Danica," Jerry said into her earpiece. "Tell 'em you were there!"

She could feel her pulse racing and her breath quickening, the effects of shock taking hold. She always prided herself on her professionalism, her ability to remain objective in the midst of chaos, but she was on the verge of losing it. Her eyes cut away from the camera to Rocky, who stood at Paulo's side.

You, Rocky mouthed, pointing at her. *You can do it.*

She nodded and cleared her throat. Pulling out her cell phone, she said in a steady voice, "Contrary to reports from other stations, this plane crash actually occurred at three fifty-six this morning, a little more than forty-five minutes ago. I know this for a fact because I placed a 911 call at three fifty-seven."

"There you go!" Jerry exclaimed.

"I was driving to the station this morning, traveling north up Space Center Boulevard. The weather was extremely foggy. And I witnessed the plane crash." She could sense heads turning toward her. Her hands gripped the microphone as if it were a lifeline, and suddenly she understood the way out of her own fog.

She pointed at the wreckage. "The plane split into two sections. The front half exploded on impact. That's the fire you see over there."

"Say something about the survivors," Jerry said into her ear.

"Follow me this way," she said, walking toward a strip of yellow tape that wrapped around a speed limit sign and was tied to the mirror of a fire truck. "In the distance is the other half of the plane. It's about a hundred yards away, and you can see that it's still engulfed in flames."

"Survivors!" Jerry's scream was so loud that she had to yank out her IFB.

"Only one person survived the crash," she said calmly, knowing that not only was she telling the viewers what they needed to know but also that Eyewitness9 had just scooped every other station in town. She paused, allowing the extent of the tragedy to sink in. "We're not sure of the total number of passengers and crew members, but I can tell you firsthand that Senator Joe Hartwell was pulled from the plane and transported to the hospital."

An audible gasp came from the mass of news people and emergency workers. "Were you the one who saved Senator Hartwell?" someone shouted.

She nodded in response, then felt annoyed with herself for interrupting her own report. "To repeat," she said, "breaking news from south Houston—Senator Joseph Hartwell was seriously injured this morning in an airplane crash, which occurred in this grassy field on the outskirts of Ellington Field."

As she continued to report on what she'd seen, a crowd began to gather on the other side of Paulo and Rocky. Reporters from competing stations were writing in notebooks, and cameramen were focusing their equipment on her. This was all so surreal. She had to get this over with. "We'll keep you updated on this situation in Clear Lake," she said, preparing to throw it back to Mitch in the studio, "but for now, this is Danica Cortez, Eyewitness9." When Paulo finally lowered the camera, she felt a flood of relief.

Microphones suddenly appeared in her face, and cameramen blinded her with lights. "Did you really pull him from a burning plane?" . . . "Did the senator say anything to you?" . . . "How badly is he injured?"

She put up a hand. "Please. I've pretty much said everything I know."

"How do you feel," someone called, "about being a hero?"

Ignoring the question, Danica climbed into the news truck. Rocky opened the other door and sat beside her. He poured coffee from a thermos into a metal cup and handed it to her. "You do realize we're gonna have to keep reporting from the crash site all morning, don't you?"

"I want to go home."

"I know you do."

"But I'll stay."

"I know you will." He threw an arm around her. "Jerry wants you to record a one-on-one interview with me. Networks are gonna want to talk with you, too. *Reporter Saves Senator*— it's a hell of a story."

Danica didn't feel like talking anymore. Her muscles ached. Her mind was numb. She leaned back, eyes closed, trying to let it all go.

Yet her senses betrayed her. She could smell the oily smoke permeating her clothes. She could hear the metal groaning as it burned. The worst part was what she could see in her mind's eye: ghastly images of a doomed plane struggling to climb, a sheared-off wing glowing red and orange, and an emerald necklace hanging around a woman's partially severed neck.

Chapter 7

A s Zoey sat at the kitchen table, plucking out her favorite colored marshmallows from a bowl of Lucky Charms and pouring the bland cereal pieces back into the box, she decided she couldn't wait to get to school. Tomorrow would be her actual birthday, but today—Friday— she'd be receiving the full celebrity treatment. She wondered what Cara had planned. Of course there was tonight's sleepover, but there would also be the obligatory locker decorations, homemade cookies, and gifts. Zoey popped a pink heart and a blue diamond into her mouth, hoping her dad would drive her in early. Yeah, today was going to be fun.

She flipped on the TV, musing about the sleepover and wondering if she'd finally get a chance to watch an R-rated movie for once in her life. Absently scanning the channels, she paused when a red *Breaking News* banner flashed at the bottom of the screen. She stuck another Lucky Charms marshmallow on her tongue but didn't close her mouth.

Something big was happening.

As image after image was displayed on the screen, Zoey couldn't believe what she was seeing. According to the news anchor—a guy who resembled her father, with a strong jaw and a kind smile and a touch of silver above his ears—an airplane had crashed just before dawn.

"This is the first daylight view of the crash site," the anchorman intoned in a deep voice. "These pictures are from our Eyewitness9 helicopter flying over the scene."

When the camera zoomed in on the wreckage, Zoey could make out the skeleton of a downed plane. Plumes of smoke rose from the twisted metal and drifted above the treetops.

The station displayed a map on the screen, indicating the crash had occurred east of Ellington Field. Zoey cocked her head. *This happened in Clear Lake? Holy crap.* Was that the loud boom that woke her up this morning?

The news anchor's eyes darted off-camera and he lifted a hand to his ear. "We're sending it back out to the field. As we've been reporting, Eyewitness9's own Danica Cortez is being regarded as a hero this morning. She called in the crash to authorities and singlehandedly pulled Senator Joseph Hartwell from the wreckage."

Zoey watched with rapt attention as the reporter recounted how the plane came apart and how she happened to be there to rescue the injured man. What a brave lady, Zoey thought, and wondered how people were able to summon the courage to perform such heroic acts. She backed her wheelchair from underneath the table and rolled toward her father's bedroom. "Hey, Dad," she called. "Have you heard the news?"

"I'm getting dressed."

"A plane crashed near our house."

"I'll be out soon."

A few minutes later, Zoey was sitting in the kitchen and watching the news again when her dad walked in. "Do you know about the plane crash?" she asked.

"What plane crash?"

"Here in Clear Lake. Some politician. A news reporter saved him."

He took a long look at the TV, then grabbed the remote and clicked it off. "You know how I feel about you watching that stuff."

"I know, but—"

"News stations," he sneered. "All they do is profit off people's tragedies. They can't get enough death to satisfy 'em. Bunch of vultures."

There wasn't much that made her father angry, but he couldn't stand television news. He'd once told her that he'd witnessed the first shuttle explosion during his high-school science class, and fifteen years later happened to see the second hijacked plane hit the South Tower. Those were certainly traumatic, but Zoey knew her dad's aversion to news people stemmed from something far more personal.

From long practice, she knew not to push matters—there were certain subjects that were off-limits with Dad. This was one of them. Smiling sweetly, she asked, "Are you going into NASA today or do you get to work from home again?"

He smiled back. "It's a pretty good setup, don't you think? I'm staying home today." He grabbed a bowl from the cabinet and filled it with Lucky Charms, then cast a knowing look at her. "How's your breakfast?"

She looked into her bowl, where a rainbow of colors swirled in the milk, and then into his, where a single green clover sat perched on a mound of crumbled oat bits. "I have to get to school early," she said, changing the subject. "I've got a project." Which was technically true—she had a History project due next Thursday—but this was one of those times where she found a little fib to be useful. He didn't need to know everything about her life.

By the time her father had pulled into the middle-school parking lot, all Zoey could think about was how amazing her birthday was going to be. In some ways, it was a shame that it fell on the weekend, but her best friend had planned to make it a big two-day celebration. "Dad," she said, "you're still cool with me sleeping over at Cara's tonight, right?" He frowned, and Zoey knew that it meant he wasn't happy about it but wouldn't fight her. She flashed a smile. "Thanks. You're awesome."

He edged the van along the curb and then went around to help her. Having been in a wheelchair for practically forever, Zoey could easily transfer on and off. But her dad liked to hold the chair for her and spot her in case she fell.

She hadn't fallen in a long time.

After opening the door, she placed her limp legs out of the vehicle. She heard the air brakes of a school bus and turned her head. Soon a crush of kids began to pour from the bus, with Allison Cleary and Tiffany McAdams leading the charge. Zoey paused a moment—no need to draw attention to herself.

"Forget something, sweetie?"

"Give me a minute." She pretended to rummage through the backpack in her lap, all the while watching the bus in her peripheral vision. The bus door eventually whooshed closed. With the dexterity of a trapeze artist, Zoey held onto the van's grab bar and swung her body out, sliding into the wheelchair.

Her dad looped her backpack over the chair's handles. Giving her a quick kiss, he uttered the same parting words she'd heard her entire life. "Love you."

Without even a wave, Zoey took off for the school building. Three minutes later, she sat and stared at her locker. No one had taped wrapping paper across its front, no one had written feel-good messages in glitter pen, and no one had strung a mylar balloon that read "Happy Birthday." She opened the locker slowly, half-hoping that streamers and confetti would fly out. But the locker was the same as she'd left it.

A peal of laughter sounded from behind her, and she swung her chair around, sure that a surprise welcome was on its way. It was only Tiffany and a smattering of Populars, and they gathered in a circle some ten feet away. Zoey pretended to stay busy at her locker, not wanting to make eye contact, but couldn't help overhearing them.

"My dad gave them to me yesterday."

"They are so cute! Are they real diamonds?"

"Obviously. And check out my new bag. It's Coach."

Zoey grunted in disgust. What a bunch of spoiled snobs. She figured Tiffany's father must be one of those Disneyland Dads who showered their kids with gifts, trying to buy affection. God, she couldn't stand these annoying clones and their shared shallowness.

Yet as self-indulgent and cliquey—and mean—as the Populars were, Zoey couldn't help but envy how many friends they had. Her only friend was Cara . . . and she wasn't even around.

Zoey cut her eyes to the Populars, partly wishing someone would invite her over and partly wishing the whole group would spontaneously combust.

"What are you looking at?" Tiffany snapped. "We're trying to have a private conversation." Then she turned to her fangirls. "Let's get out of here. I smell loser."

Zoey suddenly found herself alone in the hall. No balloons. No fancy decorations. No friends. She gnawed at her bottom lip—no one was going to see her cry.

She sat through first period in a daze. *How could Cara have forgotten? Does she hate me?* When the bell sounded, she raced into the hall and toward her second-period English class, where she and Cara always sat next to each other in the back of the room. She was rolling so fast that two kids had to leap out of her way.

But Cara wasn't in English.

All Zoey could figure was that Cara was sick. That would explain her not decorating the locker. Oh no, she thought, what about the sleepover? Was that going to be cancelled, too? That would totally suck if that happened. She needed to text Cara between classes and see how she was feeling.

As Ms. Pettigrew droned on at the whiteboard, Zoey scrawled in her spiral notebook, not interested in hearing about Shakespeare's *Romeo and Juliet*. She'd already seen the movie—the one with the gorgeous Leonardo DiCaprio as Romeo—so it was easy to tune out Ms. Pettigrew's lecture. The next thing she knew, her teacher was towering over her. "What do you think, Zoey?"

Her mouth went dry as she tried to piece together snippets of phrases that had seeped into her brain: "Montagues and Capulets," "ill-fated lovers," and "dramatic irony." But she didn't have a clue what her teacher had asked.

"I . . . uh . . ." She met Ms. Pettigrew's gaze, and her eyes darted down to her notebook. There between the doodles of hearts and balloons were the words "Worst Day Ever" and "I H8 School."

"Is everything okay?"

"Um, sure. Of course." Zoey slammed the notebook closed.

Ms. Pettigrew eyed her closely. "You're friends with Cara, right?"

"Yes, ma'am."

"Would you remind her about the essay due Monday? I don't extend deadlines due to unexcused absences."

Zoey nodded, confused, and then the bell rang. As she rolled out of the classroom, she wondered what the heck Ms. Pettigrew had been talking about. Unexcused absence?

In the hall, she saw Reshma Kumar, one of her band friends who occasionally hung out with her and Cara. "Maybe we can sit together at lunch today," Zoey suggested, feeling a keen sense of isolation. "Cara's out sick."

"Didn't you see her Facebook?" Reshma said, her accent very British with no trace of her native India. "Cara's not sick."

"I don't understand."

"You mean she didn't tell you? She's playing hooky. Her dad flew her up to Dallas."

Chapter 8

With a gentle push, the binocular chair began to turn counterclockwise. Garrison had been designing and fabricating and testing the components for days, and this was the first time Zoey's birthday present had swiveled smoothly.

Now all he had to do was finish the binocular mount and attach the chair to its base. The whole thing would take three hours or so. And he could do that tonight while Zoey was sleeping over at her friend's house.

Garrison allowed himself a smile. He couldn't wait to see Zoey use her new chair out at the ranch. He'd already hatched a plan for unloading it and moving it to the star shack. He had no illusions of surprising Zoey—the binocular chair would take up most of the van's rear—but if he was lucky, he could set it up, mount the binoculars, and attach a bow while she was otherwise occupied.

An alert sounded from his computer, so Garrison wiped his hands on a rag and stepped over to read his email. The incoming message was from Anita Holmquest, the director of the McLennan County Museum of Natural Science. She probably wanted to follow up on the model he'd been building for the museum, a four-foot space shuttle replica that was going to be the centerpiece of an exhibit on Baylor University's only graduate to have piloted a shuttle.

Call me ASAP, the subject line read. The body of the email was blank. Before he even had a chance to respond, his phone buzzed.

"Hi, Anita. Just got your email." He dropped into the chair and felt a warm rush on the back of his neck. Anita Holmquest was one complicated woman. To the aerospace community, she was a genius and a tough project engineer. To Waco, she was family, the daughter of a Baylor University Regent and the hand-picked director of the city's fledgling science museum. And to Garrison? Well, he'd been mulling on that one for a long time. The two of them had been colleagues, rivals, and—for a brief period—lovers.

"You still working on my shuttle?"

"Almost done," he replied, not bothering to tell her that it still lacked its booster engines and orange fuel tank.

"The ceremony is in three weeks. I'm getting nervous."

"It'll be ready. Trust me."

She sighed. "I trust you. In fact, you're the most trustworthy man I know."

Uh-oh. He could hear the gears turning in her head. "I'll complete the shuttle over the weekend," he promised. "And I can drive it up there on Wednesday."

"Wednesday? That'll be perfect. We have a Regents meeting the next day. I'd love for them to meet the man I've been raving about, the famous astronaut-turned-artist."

At the mention of the word *astronaut*, Garrison's gut clenched. He may have been in the program, may have even been slated to fly, but he'd never spent a single minute in space. And as for being an artist, he was just a guy interested in rockets, someone with an eye for detail. My Great Adventurer, his wife had called him. More like the Great Pretender.

"Let me take you out Wednesday night," Anita said, no trace of question in her voice. "I can't wait to see you again. Been too long."

Garrison fidgeted in his chair, recalling how intense their three months together had been. He didn't want to complicate his life with a relationship. Especially now that Zoey was a teenager. "Maybe another time. This has to be a day trip. Zoey's still in school."

Anita paused on the other end of the line, and Garrison could almost hear her gathering words of pity. "Of course. Zoey. I forgot."

"I have a lot of responsibilities here, Anita. Can't just do what I want when I want."

"You know that's gonna change one day. When Zoey grows up and . . ." Her voice trailed away, then suddenly brightened. "Well, it was great talking with you. See you next week. It'll be fun."

He mumbled a goodbye and stuffed the cell phone in his pocket. *That's gonna change when Zoey grows up*. As he turned away from his desk, he knew that even a fully functioning, swiveling, reclining binocular chair wouldn't help his little girl become independent.

She'd always need him.

By noon, the road east of Ellington Field was jammed with rubberneckers. The ambulances had left a few hours ago and only a single fire truck remained.

Danica and Rocky stood in the shade of a live oak, a hot wind blowing in from the Gulf, the fog long gone. With the temperature crawling into the low nineties, Danica could feel sweat rolling down her back.

She'd been on unpleasant locations before: inside the hellhole of a damaged hotel while Hurricane Ike barreled through Galveston, behind a crack house to interview an addict who claimed to have sold drugs to a Houston city councilman, waist-deep in brackish water and raw sewage after New Orleans flooded. The summer heat she could handle, just not the smoke rising from the plane's wreckage. It tasted like death.

Rocky adjusted his collar and cleared his throat. He counted down from three and then held out his microphone. "Could you walk us through how you came to rescue Senator Hartwell?"

Danica didn't respond right away. She'd been answering the same question all morning, to Matt Lauer on *The Today Show*, to Robin Roberts on *Good Morning America*, and to the morning anchors on CNN and Fox News. Everyone wanted to hear the feel-good story—in fact, the CNN producer had told her, "No one wants to hear about dead bodies, so let's just concentrate on the bit about you rushing into the burning airplane."

"Danica?" Rocky said.

She reached out and covered the microphone. "Please."

"I know you're exhausted. You've been going nonstop all morning. You need something to eat?"

"No." She trudged over to the news truck, yanked open the passenger door, and crawled inside. Leaning out the window, she told him, "I need to go home and shower. We can do your interview later at the station, I promise." Then she glanced back at the crumpled, smoking fuselage. "But I can't spend another minute out here."

Rocky didn't say anything. Instead, he opened the lift gate and began to pack his gear. "You are gonna have to get out of the truck, though."

"I already told you—"

"If you want to go home," he said with a smirk and jabbed his thumb toward the street, "I think you should drive your own car."

She flashed a sheepish smile, crawled out of the front seat, and gave him a hug. "Rocky, you're the best."

A minute later, as she trekked to her car, she noticed a pair of uniformed police officers headed in her direction. Drawing closer, she saw a look of recognition cross one man's face. This was the last thing she needed. She steeled herself and kept on walking. "Hi, officers," she said, trying to be polite.

The younger cop nodded back, but the older one—the guy who recognized her—elbowed him and muttered, "Don't talk to her."

"Who is she?"

"TV chick." He scowled at her. "She's bad news."

Danica kept her mouth shut, not wanting to escalate matters, and wondered when the hostility would ever go away. She'd spent years trying to mend fences with the local police, had even been the one to uncover massive fraud by the hedge fund manager overseeing their pension fund. Beat cops should have been thankful she'd shone a light on the embezzlement that was taking money away from their families.

Yet cops, especially the old-timers, still hated her.

She couldn't seem to escape her past, even though it had been years since she landed her first TV job, since she investigated corruption in the District Attorney's office.

Since Sergeant Andrew Quinn was murdered.

Chapter 9

T he last thing Zoey needed was an interrogation from her dad, so she'd given him the silent treatment on the ride home from school and then disappeared into her bedroom to sort everything out. Although there wasn't much to sort out—the situation was obvious. Cara had blown her off, hadn't even bothered to return a single text. Staring at her phone for the hundredth time, Zoey decided that being with Dad was better than being alone, so she wheeled into the kitchen.

He was standing at the island stirring a pitcher of lemonade. When he saw her, he gave her one of his *concerned father* looks. "Want to talk about anything?"

"Nope." She rocked her chair forward and back, the wheels squeaking softly in response.

"Need me to check the pressure on your tires?"

"I'm not sleeping over at Cara's," she declared flatly.

"Oh, change your mind?"

She rolled her eyes. He was so clueless sometimes. "Cara wasn't at school today. She went on some stupid vacation with her dad."

"I'm sorry, honey. You sure?"

"You think I'd make this up? You think I'd rather hang out

with you than my best— my *former* best friend?" She wheeled closer and nudged him with her chair. "I want to get out of Clear Lake. Let's go to the ranch tonight."

He dropped onto a barstool and studied her, a move she'd always appreciated, him getting closer to her level, treating her as an equal. "We'll go tomorrow, like we planned. I have things to do tonight."

"Like what?" she snapped.

"In my workshop."

"Come on, Dad, you're always messing around with stuff in there. Can't your stupid rocket wait another day? You know it's never gonna fly, right?"

His jaw clenched and he glowered at her, his usual signal to stop the backtalk. But she didn't care right now. "Why do you have a workshop, anyway? Oh yeah, it's your place to get away. From the whole frickin' world."

"That's enough. Stop acting like a baby."

"This from someone who plays with dolls. I mean, your little models. You're the one who needs to grow up. God, I hate you." She spun her wheels in opposite directions and then zipped down the hall to her bedroom, slamming the door closed behind her.

She jammed her wheelchair against the bed, set the brakes, and lifted herself to the edge of the seat. As she'd done thousands of times, she leaned forward and pivoted on her outstretched fist, guiding herself onto the bed.

Lying there, she thought about how stubborn her dad was, how inconsiderate Cara was, how hateful all the kids at school were. Everyone was so mean. No one cared about her.

Then she remembered what she'd told him: *I hate you.*

Who was she kidding? She was the mean one. No wonder no one wanted to be friends with her. She covered her face with a pillow and began to sob, realizing her loneliness was her own fault. Eventually, she cried herself out.

An hour later, Zoey emerged from her room with a new

attitude, thanks to the long nap. "I'm sorry about before," she told her dad.

"Feeling any better?"

"I'm sorry for what I said. Can we go to the ranch?"

"Let's talk about that after dinner. What do you want me to make? I was thinking goulash or maybe tuna casserole."

She crinkled her nose. "Can we just go out to eat? Call it my birthday dinner."

"You know that going out's not my thing, honey."

That was an understatement. She could count on one hand the number of times they'd visited a restaurant since Christmas. "Someplace quiet," she suggested for his benefit. "Just the two of us. Please?"

They compromised with dinner at the local Sonic, hamburgers and tater tots and cherry limeades all consumed in the comfort of the van's front seat. She could see her father's eyes darting from windshield to side mirror, his nerves keenly on edge.

When his eyes met hers, he gave her a reassuring smile. She knew how much stress an outing like this was for him, yet he was still making the effort. "Thanks for trying to make me feel better," she said. "This is nice."

He offered a wan smile. "I'm enjoying it, too." A dog barked, and Garrison's head turned sharply. Then he shrugged. "Well, enjoying it in my own way."

Zoey looked through the side window to see a scruffy brown-and-black mutt walking alongside the restaurant's dumpster. It sniffed the air, probably sensing all the edible garbage, and barked when a loud pickup rolled by. "Look, Dad," she said, lowering her window. "I bet he's hungry."

"He's probably exploring."

"I'm gonna give him the rest of my food. I'm done eating." She began ripping the remaining portion of her hamburger into small pieces.

"You're not supposed to feed strays."

The dog sat down and began scratching an ear with his foot. When he finished, that one ear was flopped over on itself. He was so cute. "Maybe he's lost. We should check his collar."

Her dad turned the key in the ignition. "Okay, sweetie, let's head on back."

"What about the dog? We can take care of him, at least until we find out who his owner is." She couldn't stand the thought of this poor dog having to scrounge for his food from people's garbage. He needed a home where someone would love him and take care of him. In an instant of clarity, she knew that this little guy was all alone . . . and in need of a friend.

Her father backed out of the parking space and drove over to where the dog stood. He lowered the window and whistled. "Here you go, boy," he called, tossing out some tater tots and the torn pieces of her sandwich. He turned back to her. "Don't get any ideas."

"But he's—"

"No," he said, and steered out of the parking lot.

By the time they were almost home, she couldn't hold it in any longer. "Why are you so mean?"

"I know what you were thinking, Pookie. But our family doesn't need a dog."

"You don't care about anything I want."

He gave a deep sigh. "I do care."

"You say no to everything." When he didn't reply, she tried to sound more adult. "You know, if we had a dog, it could help me with my wheelchair, maybe bring me my shoes and my backpack. Don't you want me to be more independent?"

She could see his fingers tighten on the wheel. "This is a conversation for another time. Not today."

"Today sucks," she muttered as they pulled into their driveway. "Can we at least go to the ranch tonight?"

"No. It's getting late."

"But—"

"Listen, Zoey. It's too dark to drive. Way too danger—" He

stopped mid-sentence. He kneaded his hands together and twisted the gold band on his left ring finger. Something was bothering him, and she knew it was more than his usual anxiety around being out in public.

"Are you okay?"

"I should have tried harder," he whispered from his dark reverie, but she couldn't understand what he was talking about. "Maybe things would have turned out different."

Danica rolled over in bed, frustrated that it was Saturday morning and she wasn't sound asleep. When she'd crawled into bed last night after the longest day of her life—reporting from the crash site, doing satellite interviews with evening cable programs, and finally appearing on her own station's ten-o'clock news—she had figured she'd be sacked out for hours.

All it took was a nightmare about being chased by a headless woman with tattoos to bolt her wide awake.

I might as well get up, she thought, knowing she had a tennis date in a couple of hours anyway. Her usual routine was to log in to her computer and check her phone first thing every morning, but all the emails and text messages had proved too annoying, so she had decided to go without technology since late last night. To her surprise, she actually liked it.

Selecting a tennis skirt and matching blouse from her closet, Danica knew that tennis with her best friend might be just the tonic to get her mind off everything that had happened. Samantha Jachowicz, whom Danica had called Sam ever since they roomed together in college, was now her regular tennis partner, although their matches were becoming less frequent due to Danica's job demands. Sam hit a mean serve. Danica had the better ground game. It didn't really matter.

When Danica arrived at the public tennis courts near the shore of Clear Lake, she fixed her dark hair into a ponytail and slipped on a white visor sweatband. She hadn't applied any makeup, as she hoped her plain face would provide some anonymity, but she did open a bottle of sunscreen and rubbed the lotion across her arms, legs, and face. That was another directive from Eyewitness9: don't show up with a sunburn.

She swung her arms to loosen her shoulders, stretched her quads and hammies, and practiced serves into the fence, but after what seemed like half an hour, Sam still hadn't arrived.

Something was wrong. Sam was never late.

Danica retreated to her racquet bag for a towel and her cell phone. Forty-one missed calls since yesterday. More than a hundred text messages. Danica shook her head in amazement and dialed the phone. "Sam, where are you?"

"Didn't you get my email? Or my text?"

"Sorry, I turned everything off. Anything wrong?" Danica instantly thought about Sam's parents, who still lived in Poland and were dealing with a variety of health issues. "Are your folks okay?"

"Everyone's fine," Sam replied. "I've been trying to get hold of you since yesterday and ask how you were doing. Guess you're too famous for me now."

"Yeah, right. Are we meeting or what?"

Sam gave one of her mock groans. "So, yesterday I was packing up stuff to donate to the library. Dropped a huge box of books on my foot."

"Oh my gosh, are you okay?"

"My big toe's so swollen I can't even wear a shoe. I assume you're at the tennis courts?"

"Uh-huh." Danica wiped her face with the towel and peered into the bright sky, where the sun glowed like a heat lamp.

"Maybe you can find someone there to play with you," Sam offered. "I know what you need—some young stud to trade strokes with."

Danica rolled her eyes. "You're impossible."

"Hey, I'm not the one who's single and celibate."

"Bye, Sam." Danica frowned as she tossed the cell phone into her bag. Now what? She didn't want to go back home and stare at her empty house, especially now that her muscles were warmed up. Running around a tennis court was exactly the kind of activity that relaxed her—something about all the endorphins—but she couldn't do it by herself.

As she leaned against the fence sipping a bottle of water, she heard the whirr of helicopter rotors and looked to the sky again. One of those Life Flight helicopters was flying low, and it brought back memories from yesterday morning, when all those news choppers buzzed overhead like a swarm of wasps.

So much for tennis taking her mind off the airplane crash.

Garrison steered the van onto NASA Road 1 and headed east, past the Johnson Space Center and along the shore of Clear Lake. The morning had gone as well as he could have hoped, especially with Zoey in such a great mood after eating her special birthday blueberry waffles. The evening's plans were going to be simple, just the two of them at the star shack. With astronomy blogs predicting clear skies, a new moon, and an excellent view of Saturn, Garrison knew that stargazing conditions would be ideal.

"Where are we going, Dad?"

"Told you. It's a surprise." Maybe it was his training in the space program or his days as a Boy Scout, but Garrison liked to be prepared. That's why he'd hatched a backup plan for her birthday in case things didn't work out with the binocular chair, which he'd stayed up until three in the morning to finish. He gave himself a mental high-five.

"We're going to Kemah Boardwalk!" Zoey exclaimed. "Oh my gosh, I want to ride the rollercoaster. They'll let me, right?"

"I thought you might like this instead." He turned into Clear Lake Park and found the closest handicapped space next to the tennis courts.

"No way!"

"You don't think I pay attention? I've picked you up a dozen times at school outside the courts. And you're always recording stuff from the Tennis Channel." He reached behind him and pulled out her present, an awkwardly-wrapped tennis racquet. "Happy birthday."

She squealed and ripped it open. "This is so cool!"

When they found an empty court, Garrison realized he was officially out of his element. Although he knew the basics of tennis—he'd played some intramural matches in college with his dorm buddies, had even followed Wimbledon and the U.S. Open when the Americans used to be good—he hadn't been on a tennis court since Zoey was born.

Before they even started playing, he could feel his t-shirt sticking to his back and see rivulets of sweat running down his arms. What had he been thinking? Zoey had never done this before, and here he was trying to teach her in almost-ninety-degree heat.

He began by positioning her wheelchair facing the net. "You want to see your opponent," he explained, "plus it'll give you room to swing your racquet. Remember, you get two bounces."

"What if I don't need two bounces?"

He sighed. "Do what I showed you. And don't forget to follow through." Then he ran back across the court to pick up a tennis ball and instantly regretted his decision not to buy himself a racquet as well . . . or more than three tennis balls. "Here we go," he called. "Forehand." He lobbed a tennis ball across the net, and it clanged against the front of her wheelchair.

"Come on, Dad. Make it a good throw."

His next throw was perfect, flat and medium-speed. It landed on the other side of the court and bounced up beside her chair, within reach for Zoey. She didn't swing.

"Why didn't you hit it? That was perfect."

"You said it's supposed to bounce twice."

He clenched his fingers into tight fists. She was just like her mother.

"I'll explain it again," he said, gesturing. "Tennis in a wheelchair is no different than regular tennis. Same court, same net, same equipment. Only difference is that you're allowed two bounces to hit the ball."

"So I can hit it after one bounce?"

"Or volley it in the air."

"Then why didn't you tell me that?" she snapped.

"I just don't understand you these days, Zoey." He shook his head. He wanted her birthday to be enjoyable, but it seemed she was going out of her way to be contrary. "Let's try this again. It'll be fun, I promise."

Garrison retreated around the net and in his peripheral vision noticed a dark-haired woman standing alone. She was leaning against the fence, underneath what passed as shade, dribbling a ball against the court surface and eyeing the two of them. Garrison looked away, embarrassed by the scrutiny. He picked up their last tennis ball, squeezing it tight in his fingers, and blew a hard breath. "Ready?" he called to Zoey through a forced smile, then tossed it to her, flat and hard.

This one hit her in the head.

"Ow!" she yelped. She threw up her hands and flung her racquet, skipping it across the concrete surface and into the net. "Screw this."

That caused something to snap inside him. "Hey! Don't you dare treat my new racquet—your racquet—like that." He dashed over and picked it up. There was a deep scratch along its tip, and when he looked closer, he could see scuff marks on the frame. "Is this the way you say 'Thank you'?"

"Thank you for what? For dragging me out here in the heat? For making me look like an idiot?"

"How about 'Thank you for playing tennis with me'?"

Tears welled up in her eyes. "Can we just go home?"

Garrison felt a stab of guilt, knowing he'd screwed up their outing, screwed up her birthday. Zoey's posture told the entire story, slumped shoulders and bowed head. He shouldn't have been so hard on her. He poured ice water into a towel and draped it on the back of her neck. "I know it's hot out here. You're being a real trouper."

"This is a stupid game."

He closed his eyes and tried to let her angry words wash by. *Let it go*, he told himself. *Don't escalate the argument.*

"How's it going?" a voice called from behind him.

Garrison turned and saw the dark-haired woman bouncing a ball in the air with her racquet. She flipped up the ball and caught it with her left hand, then slid it smoothly into the pocket of her tennis skirt. There was something graceful, beautiful about her.

"I'm sorry," he replied. "What did you say?"

The woman adjusted her visor. "Do you need a hand?"

Chapter 10

G arrison's initial reaction—as always—was to tense the muscles of his neck and shoulders. A simple hello from a stranger could trigger it. He might be pushing a shopping cart in the grocery store, jogging along the secluded path near their home, or pumping gas at the local Texaco. "Hey, mister," was all it took for him to bring up his defenses, to break into fight-or-flight mode.

But something about this woman led Garrison to sense she wasn't a threat. She gave a nod and a friendly smile, and he could feel his shoulders relax, his back muscles unwind.

She knelt down in front of Zoey. "Hi, I'm Danica."

Zoey turned her head, obviously still in mid-pout and unwilling to grant forgiveness for being dragged to the park.

"Want to hit a few?" the woman said. "I'm here by myself."

He saw Zoey sneak a sideways glance and uncross her arms.

"Didn't mean to intrude on you guys. If you want, feel free to use my equipment. I have a spare racquet and plenty of balls."

Garrison thought for a second. The woman—*was her name Danica?*—seemed nice enough, but that didn't mean they needed her hanging around. "Actually, I think we're about to leave. You ready, sweetie?"

The same girl who moments ago had all but given up on tennis was now swinging her racquet in imaginary forehands and backhands. "I'm Zoey," she told the woman, then pointed at him. "He's my dad. You said you're here by yourself?"

The woman shrugged her shoulders. "My friend didn't show up."

Zoey nodded. "I've got a friend named Cara. She ditched me, too. It sucks. You play tennis?"

Danica dropped her racquet bag alongside the net. "Since middle school. Even used to play with someone in a wheelchair. If you want, I could share some tips."

"That's okay," Garrison said, "we don't need any help." Knowing that sounded ungrateful, he added, "But we appreciate the offer."

"Dad?"

One glimpse of the pleading look on her face and he caved immediately. If Zoey would have asked him to drive to Hawaii for a pineapple, he would have done it. "Just for a few minutes. But no more tantrums."

Danica clapped her hands together. "Then let's rock and roll." She fixed her gaze on Garrison and then shooed him with her hands. "Would you give us some room?"

He took two steps back.

"That's not what I meant. Zoey and I are gonna need some space. How about you . . . uh . . . stand outside the fence?"

Who does this lady think she is? "I think I'll stay here."

"But how can she teach me tennis if you're in the way?"

Danica shrugged at him. "Your call."

All he'd wanted was to give Zoey a chance to learn tennis. He looked over to the pretty stranger. Even though it wasn't what he'd planned, maybe this woman could help. After all, she'd mentioned playing with someone in a wheelchair. "Ma'am," he said, "do you know what you're doing?"

She frowned. "I'll let you know if I need anything."

He retreated to a bench outside the court, which he quickly

abandoned in favor of standing at the fence, his fingers curled around the wires. Straining to hear their conversation, he cupped his hand behind his ear. "Forget what your dad told you," he could hear her say. "Wheelchair tennis is about using the chair, not the racquet."

She was as stubborn as Zoey.

Normally he wouldn't have allowed himself to be sidelined like this, but something about Danica set him back on his heels, kept him a little off balance. Maybe it was her forceful personality, the way she wouldn't take no for an answer. Maybe it was her honest smile. Or maybe it was the way she looked in a tennis skirt, an item of clothing he now believed was seriously underrated.

He shook his head. *Concentrate.*

He listened as Danica molded Zoey's fingers around the racquet grip. "Thumb goes on the rim," she explained. "Pull the racquet to your wheel and push. You gotta explode to the ball." Danica stepped back. "And . . . now."

With over a decade in her chair, Zoey was an experienced driver. So at Danica's signal, she blasted forward with two strong pushes.

"Pivot left," Danica said without explanation, and Zoey released her racquet hand and braked with her free hand. She spun left, and Danica dropped a tennis ball. The racquet whipped through the air and smashed the ball across the net and past the baseline.

Garrison stood open-mouthed.

"That's what I'm talking about!" Danica hollered. "It's all about movement. See how you moved into the shot—great power, by the way—and then had enough momentum to get ready for the next ball? Excellent!"

Zoey nodded, a wide grin plastered across her face.

When he saw that smile, that wonderful smile, Garrison could feel his spirits lift. For the next fifteen minutes, he stood outside the fence as Danica showed her how to cross left and right, how to not drop the racquet as she pushed, how to turn into a forehand. He was proud of his little girl—when she put her mind to something, she could do anything. But the more Danica contradicted what he'd been trying to teach, the more annoyed he became.

Danica ran Zoey through a drill where she wheeled along the baseline, spun, and then wheeled back to where she started. Zoey was doing great, flying from one side of the court to the other, but it sure didn't look safe to him. At one point, one of her wheels tipped up, and he thought she was going to tumble over. Seconds later, she turned the wrong way and banged hard against the fence. Her racquet clattered onto the concrete.

"Zoey!" He jumped over the bench and bolted inside the court area. "Are you hurt?"

"I'm fine, Dad," she said, bursting into a fit of giggles. "Told you he's a stress monkey."

"She's getting tired," he told Danica.

Danica tossed another tennis ball toward Zoey, who yanked hard on her wheel, turning the chair sharply. She hit the ball over the net, past the opposite court, and over the cyclone fence. "Home run!" she whooped and raised her arms triumphantly.

"Are you through?"

Danica stood at mock attention, her eyes darting from Zoey to him, her mouth squeezed tight as if she were suppressing a smile.

"Don't mind him," Zoey said. "He hates it when I'm having fun."

Danica gave her a high five. "I'm having fun, too. You don't know how much I needed this today." She dabbed Zoey's face with her towel. "Why don't you go sit in the shade for a few minutes and cool down?"

"I'm fine. But I do need to go to the bathroom. Do you know where they are?" Danica pointed to a dull-grey concrete structure a hundred yards away, "Okay, I'll be back in a bit."

After Zoey left the court area, Garrison glared at the woman. "Look, ma'am."

A strand of dark hair had come loose from her ponytail and fallen across her face. She blew it out of the way. "Call me Danica."

Garrison cleared his throat. "Maybe this wasn't such a good idea."

"Who peed in your Cheerios, Mister? Zoey's having a great time. Frankly, she's pretty talented. Quick learner. And she navigates her chair like a pro."

"So that's why she ran into the fence and almost fell."

"Wow," she said, shaking her head. "You're blaming me."

"We were having fun until you barged in." Which wasn't exactly true, but that wasn't the point.

Danica crossed her arms, and he could see how tan and athletic she was. "I watched the two of you," she said. "Neither of you was having any fun."

"Excuse me?" he said through clenched teeth. He'd gone out of his way to make this day fun for Zoey. He was being a good father, a hell of a father. How dare Danica criticize his parenting abilities?

She unzipped her racquet bag and began shoving in her equipment. "Just calling it like I see it." Then she picked up her cell phone and examined it. She blew an exasperated breath. "Crap, it's my stupid job. I gotta go. Would you say goodbye to Zoey for me?"

He nodded, but couldn't help thinking he hadn't been this worked up in years. Danica was getting under his skin the same way Celeste used to. He took a deep breath. Trying to be polite, he told her, "I do appreciate you taking time with Zoey. You didn't have to."

Her eyes met his. "I know. I wanted to."

He watched as she grabbed her stuff, exited the court, and strode out to the parking lot. Part of him wanted to see her gone, but part of him didn't mind standing there and arguing with her. She'd completely flustered him, and he couldn't understand why. He was usually able to keep his emotions under control.

Waiting for Zoey to return from the bathroom, he killed time by juggling the three tennis balls, a skill he'd mastered in college. As each ball traveled in a sweeping arc from hand to hand, he fell into a relaxed, steady rhythm. His mind drifted to images of Zoey: her joyful reaction upon opening her gift, her excitement to spend time with him, her graceful movements on the court. Then an image flashed of Danica. He dropped a ball.

For some reason, he looked out to the parking lot again. She was still there, sitting inside her car and talking on a cell phone. She had undone her ponytail, and now her face was half-hidden by a dark curtain of hair. *Why won't she just leave?*

He checked his watch. Zoey never took this long. He could feel his chest tighten and his breathing increase, and he knew he'd feel this way until she came back. He tried juggling again, but that didn't help. He waited five more minutes, actually setting the lap timer on his phone to measure the seconds.

This wasn't normal.

As he wrestled with what to do—barge into the women's restroom or wait in frustration outside—he had another idea: ask someone to check on Zoey.

He scanned the tennis courts. Four teenage boys goofing around. Two bald men, each wearing a sweatband across his head. They couldn't help.

Which left only *her.*

When Danica saw Zoey's father headed her way, she was tempted to back her car out and take off. But the cell signal was better here than near her home, probably because of the proximity to NASA, and she was waiting on a call back from the station.

She rolled down the window. "What do you want?"

"Could you do me a big favor?"

"Good Lord."

"No, please. Zoey's been gone for a while. In the restroom." He rubbed a hand across his jaw. "I know the chair can slow her down, but I'm kinda concerned."

Danica remembered how he'd overreacted when Zoey ran into the fence. "She's probably hiding. Doesn't want another argument."

"Maybe. But could you check?"

His face was earnest and caring, and Danica actually felt sympathy for the guy. Probably a divorced father who only saw his daughter on the weekends. But he seemed genuinely concerned about her. "What the heck. I wanted to say goodbye to her anyway."

"Thank you."

Danica left him standing there and walked to the restroom, one of those ugly cinder block buildings that probably cost the city all of thirty bucks to build. She stepped inside and could see the far stall was occupied and the other toilet had been wrapped with a plastic garbage bag and labeled with an out-of-order sign. She could see the wheels of Zoey's chair under the stall partition.

The wheelchair rattled against the door, and she was flooded with memories of Mario. His dark, wavy hair. His mischievous smile. The way he used to bang into walls after his muscles lost their strength.

Danica hesitated, not wanting to disturb the girl's privacy, then finally said, "Zoey? I have to go to work. It was nice meeting you."

Muffled sobs sounded from the stall, and Danica could hear the spinning of a toilet paper roll. "Zoey?" she repeated.

Gulping, panicked breaths came from behind the partition. "Danica?" a meek voice asked.

"You okay in there?"

"I'm bleeding!"

Chapter 11

O h, my God, Danica thought. Had Zoey's crash into the fence been worse than it seemed? Or had she fallen off her wheelchair?

Danica tried the stall door, but Zoey had fastened the lock, so she began pressing her shoulder against it. "How bad are you hurt?"

"I'm not hurt. Please don't tell my dad."

It took a second for the reality to sink in, but Danica finally understood the delicate situation. "Do you need some pads?"

Silence, and then a whisper. "I don't know. It's my . . . first time."

"Oh, no. Your mom explained things, right?"

More silence. "I don't have a mom. She died."

Danica took a deep breath and attempted to summon the composure she'd been able to muster in the past, in the aftermath of gruesome traffic accidents, the school shooting in Beaumont, the plane crash.

"Do you have any toilet paper in there?"

"It's empty."

"Listen to me, Zoey. You're gonna be okay. I'll help you through this."

She dashed outside and located the men's restroom on the

other side of the building. After a moment's hesitation, she rushed in. A man turned from the urinal and startled when she hurried past.

In the lone bathroom stall, a roll of paper hung from a heavy-duty rod next to the toilet. She tried to jiggle it free. It wouldn't budge. So she yanked it from the wall, the rod snapping in two. With the roll of paper in hand, she flew out of the stall and past the man, who stood at the mirror slack-jawed. She pointed at him. "Don't ask."

She went into the women's restroom and handed Zoey the roll of toilet paper underneath the stall door. She remembered how scary her first time had been, so she calmly explained the basics of feminine hygiene and reassured Zoey that everything was perfectly normal. "I have some stuff in my car," she told Zoey.

"Don't go."

"It's exactly what you need. I promise."

Danica threw open the outside door, the sunshine momentarily blinding her, and ran headlong into Zoey's dad.

"What's wrong?"

She put a finger to her lips and shushed him. "Follow me." When they were out of earshot, Danica explained the situation. He was duly mortified.

Shaking his head, he said, "I knew it was only a matter of time. She's fourteen today."

"On her birthday? That's no fun." She rummaged through a bag and selected various products Zoey might need. "We're gonna be a while, I think. Don't ask a lot of questions. She's pretty upset."

He nodded. "Thank you, Danica."

She felt a pang of guilt for what she'd thought about the guy, that he was a selfish father in the middle of a divorce. But it was clear he was a widower, and even though he seemed overprotective, she could understand where he was coming from. "I'm sorry, I didn't catch your name."

He extended his hand. "Garrison. Garrison Sterling."

After the strangest thirty minutes of her life, Zoey emerged from the bathroom feeling transformed. She had finally joined the club. Now she was like all her friends.

Danica was waiting for her outside, but Zoey didn't see her father, which completely surprised her. He was usually hovering nearby. "Have you seen my dad?"

"He said he was gonna take a walk around the park. You need to call him?"

"God, no." This was one topic she could never discuss with her father. "All the girls at school have had their period. I didn't think I ever would."

"Everyone worries about their first time. You okay?"

Zoey nodded. "Could we go somewhere and talk? You know, woman to woman?"

They found a picnic table under the shade of a live oak, and Zoey could see the reflection of sunlight on the waves of the nearby lake. Walking down a gravel path in the distance was her dad, holding a tennis racquet in his hand.

She asked Danica all the questions she had either forgotten the answers to or never knew to ask. And Danica patiently answered every one in a no-nonsense manner, with no judgment or embarrassment. "Can I ask you something else?" Zoey said.

"Sure."

"Well, my dad—he doesn't understand this stuff. And I don't have any aunts or grandmas to check with. If I need to, could I talk to you again?"

"That's up to your father." Danica's phone rang. "Sorry. Let me take this real quick . . . You want me to cover? . . . Five and ten? . . . I guess so." When she hung up, she forced a smile. "Work."

"You need to go?"

"In a bit. You mind if I ask you something? How long have you been in a wheelchair?"

Zoey had fielded the same question for years, sometimes with embarrassment, sometimes with defiance, sometimes with sadness. But she'd never told anyone the whole account as she understood it. "It's a long story."

"Not trying to pry. Just wondering. I had a brother who used a wheelchair." Her eyes misted over. "His name was Mario."

"Tell me about him. I want to know." Zoey heard the rattle of a metal gate and glanced up to see her dad walking toward them. Oh, no. "A little longer, Dad. Please?"

He stood with hands on hips, his usual pose. "Five minutes." Then he headed over to the restroom.

After he left, Zoey said, "Tell me about your brother."

"Like you said, it's a long story."

They stared at each other, the discomfort growing with each passing moment. Zoey knew that time was running out, and she was afraid of losing her new friend. "I want you to teach me tennis," she blurted out.

Danica took Zoey's hands in hers. "That would be great. But it's pretty complicated. I've got this job with crazy hours."

"I'm flexible. And school's almost out."

Danica blew a deep sigh. "I don't know. Your dad doesn't seem to like me."

Zoey had to laugh. "My dad doesn't like anybody. He's a world-class grumpazoid. Can I call you sometime?"

Danica seemed to ponder things and then eventually surrendered her phone number. "Don't tell your dad."

"Deal. Next time we talk, you can tell me about Mario. And I'll tell you how I ended up in this wheelchair."

She felt her chair move slightly and heard someone clear their throat. It was him.

"You know we don't talk about that stuff, Zoey. That's

ancient history. And no one else's business." He drew his mouth tight, his lips hardly visible.

"Dad, don't be rude." She hated it when he got all weird around people he didn't know.

Danica stood and said, "Well, it was great meeting you, Zoey. I hope you have a happy birthday." She gave Zoey a hug and whispered, "You're right. He really is a grumpazoid."

Zoey was still smiling when Danica left. She thought it hilarious that Danica could grasp the truth about Dad in such a short time, especially all the ways he could be frustrating.

Yet Zoey wasn't frustrated herself anymore. She really had enjoyed her morning. And it had all been his idea. "Thanks for playing tennis with me," she told him.

"You bet." He gently laid the tennis racquet in her lap.

"Why are your hands wet?"

He wiped his hands on the front of his shorts before grabbing the chair's push handles. "Restroom didn't have any towels." As they traveled along the sidewalk, she heard him mutter, "No toilet paper, either."

Chapter 12

Celeste pounded on the door of the Burger King. A bloody film coated the glass, but in its reflection she could see the damage to her torn ear, could see the panicked expression on her own face. "We need some help!" she pleaded, squeezing Zoey's hand tightly, not wanting to let go.

Seconds later, a teenager in a BK uniform appeared. His eyes grew wide as he gaped at them. With shaking hands, he unlocked the door.

"Oh, thank you," Celeste said, rushing in, breathless. "I need to use your bathroom." She managed to lug Zoey and her gear down the hall, but a minute later returned to the counter. Tears of frustration ran down her face. "You're out of toilet paper."

"What happened to your ear?"

Celeste tossed the diaper bag onto the counter and began rifling through it before finding two diapers. She unfolded one and pressed it against her head. "I look terrible, I know," she said, scanning the waiting area for a highchair. When she saw one, she dragged it across the restaurant floor, along with the diaper bag. She carried Zoey on her hip.

Exhausted, she flopped onto a molded seat attached to a

table. Now there were two Burger King employees standing behind the counter, the older woman who'd locked the door and the teenage boy who'd unlocked it. They were staring at her.

She needed to call Garrison, tell him what had happened. She dug in the diaper bag for her phone. It wasn't there. *It's in the car.*

Glancing nervously through the pane glass windows, she decided she wasn't stepping outside if that homeless guy was still wandering the parking lot. She'd stay here if she had to.

Everything's gonna be fine, she told herself. *Relax*. She exhaled and took a long look around the restaurant. The two employees at the counter had gone back to their duties. On her right was the children's play area, basically a pit filled with hundreds of brightly colored plastic balls. To her left were the rest of the tables, all vacant except for one.

A man in his fifties, with silver hair and wire-rimmed glasses, studied her as he sipped a cup of coffee. "You gonna be okay?" he called.

She half-waved to him, but Zoey, who refused the highchair, suddenly crawled off her seat and peered into the play area. "Momma? I want there."

"No, Pookie. Momma needs to rest." Celeste reached into the diaper bag and looked for some Goldfish crackers. But there weren't any, another casualty of their mad dash from Clear Lake. She laid her head on the table, the diaper now serving as both pillow and Band-Aid, and watched her little rebel walk over to the ball pit anyway, dragging the diaper bag behind her.

"Watch me, Momma." Zoey stood on the top step with a mischievous grin on her face, and then dove with a squeal into the sea of colored balls.

Celeste had to chuckle. At least one of them was having a good time.

"Hungry?" a gravelly voice said, and Celeste turned to see

the silver-haired man holding a tray of food. "Maybe something before you hit the road?"

"How did you know—"

"You're driving alone with your kid and you pull into this place in the middle of the night. I'm guessing *road-trip-from-hell*."

Celeste thought about Garrison, how he'd warned her that the trip was a bad idea. She ached to hear the sound of his voice.

The man set the tray down on the table. It was filled with a kid's meal, a Dutch apple pie, and a large soda. She considered the man who'd brought it—for some reason, she knew she could trust him. "Thanks."

The man pointed to the play area. "She's a cutie. How old?"

"Not quite two and a half. She's a handful." She looked over to Zoey, who was amusing herself by tossing red and yellow balls at the Lucite wall.

He gestured to her head. "What happened? Cut yourself?"

"Lost an earring. My daughter yanked it out." When Celeste pulled the diaper away, the man grimaced.

"Use direct pressure," he told her. "Squeeze the earlobe. Let me get you some napkins."

After applying pressure to her ear for more than five minutes, Celeste finally allowed herself to believe she wouldn't bleed to death. She sipped Diet Coke through the straw of her large cup, and nibbled at the French fries in Zoey's meal. A pile of blood-soaked napkins lay heaped on the adjacent chair.

She thought about their ridiculous argument, how she and Garrison had wounded each other with their unkind words. And she thought again about her cell phone. When she got back in the car, she'd call Garrison. She'd tell him how Zoey had injured her, and he'd want to rush straight to Austin to take care of her—he was a loving husband, after all, even though he sometimes ruined things with his sharp tongue. And she knew they'd apologize to each other and forgive each other and reaffirm their love for each other. Because that's what you did when you were married.

"Excuse me."

Celeste looked up to see the Burger King kid, probably a high schooler based on his whisper of a mustache, holding a trash bag filled with half-eaten hamburgers, greasy French fries, and sandwich wrappers. Wires from a hidden music player in the boy's pocket led to tiny headphones in his ears. "If you're done with anything, I can take it." He shuffled his feet and stared awkwardly at the tile floor. "Ma'am, we're real sorry about locking you out. It's company policy."

She gathered the napkins, some stained red and some dotted pink, and dumped them into his trash bag. She smiled warmly, wanting to take pity on the kid—Javier according to his nametag. "Don't sweat it, Javier. You were just doing your job."

"Yes, ma'am. Where's your kid?"

She turned and could barely make out Zoey lying on her back in the ball pit, waving her arms as if making a snow angel, sinking deeper into the mass of plastic balls. "Swimming," she said with a smile.

He held out his trash bag and spun it, then tied the plastic to itself in a wide knot. "If you need anything, let us know. You folks can stay as long as you want." He dug a keychain from his pocket, then moved to the glass door entrance. "I'm gonna take this trash out," he called to the woman standing at the front counter.

"Hurry up."

Javier exited, locking the door behind him, and Celeste turned to watch Zoey making her snow angels. Thank goodness she had Zoey along to keep her smiling.

A minute later, Celeste heard the door open again. "Alma," the boy called, pulling the headphones out of his ears and letting the cord drape around his shoulders. "An animal's gotten into the dumpster."

"Then you're gonna have to clean it up. I'm sorry, Javier, but it's just the two of us tonight. Lock the door behind you."

Javier nodded and stuffed his earbuds back in place. He extracted the keys from his pocket again, but this time they fell with a jangle to the ground. When he bent over, the door flew open, smacking him in the forehead and sending him sprawling across the floor.

Celeste couldn't believe what she was seeing. Javier lay on the ground, blood streaming from his head, his arms flailing.

A man burst through the open door, the same homeless man she'd seen earlier. He had a dark jacket. He had a wild look in his eyes. And he had a gun.

Chapter 13

D anica ran across the parking lot and yanked open the glass door of the Eyewitness9 building. She wouldn't be on the air for well over an hour, but she needed time to clear both her head and the mountain of email messages. That had been something she planned on doing after playing tennis with Zoey and before meeting Sam at her apartment, but then she'd passed out on the couch for two hours instead.

At least she'd finally gotten some sleep.

She stepped to the front desk and flashed her badge to the guard, adhering to the new security protocols laid down by station management. What a bunch of worriers, she thought. What were they afraid of? That viewers might storm the studio because "Weather Wizard" Steve Postic blew the forecast?

"Congratulations, Ms. Cortez," the burly guard said with a grin, not even glancing at her badge. "Everyone's been talking about you."

Danica offered a wan smile and hurried to the elevator. She had hoped that all the attention on her—the interviews and the coverage from other stations—would fade after a few days. Wait a minute. Today was Saturday. The plane crash occurred less than thirty-six hours ago. That's what she got for running on no sleep.

Upstairs she found Kathy Hammett, Eyewitness9's executive producer, standing near the assignments desk. Danica waved to attract her attention. "Tell me again why I'm supposed to be here?"

"Dennis is sick. Food poisoning, they think. His wife had to drive him to the emergency room."

"Yeah, I saw your message. But I also saw Frank leaving on the elevator. He could have worked tonight." Decisions on *who-goes-where-and-when* were essential to the news business, but Danica still found them aggravating. Besides Frank DeNicola, there were also two reporters in the building—Alyssa Chao and Shawntea Williams—who occasionally pulled spot anchor duty. Any of them could have covered the evening broadcasts. "I just don't get why it had to be me."

"You know why. Fans love you. You should see all the phone messages and emails that have been pouring in since yesterday. That usually only happens when we screw up."

Danica scoffed. "Can we talk? Privately?" She gestured to a glass-enclosed office known as the War Room, the aptly-named place where anchors, reporters, and producers met to discuss newscasts. Danica had fought her share of battles there, usually arguing for a focus on more investigative pieces while others insisted they should stick with the daily gore. Kathy presided over the chaos.

With more than twenty-five years in the business, including eight as anchor of the city's top-rated newscast and nine as Eyewitness9's executive producer, Kathy Hammett was a legend in Houston news. She hadn't been on the air in almost a decade, mostly due to the fact that she had gained fifty pounds after her husband died. Back when the camera loved her, Kathy was the face of the station. Danica knew that if anyone could empathize, it would be Kathy.

When they were alone, Danica said, "About this anchor

position . . ."

"I know," Kathy said, throwing up a hand. "Your contract's up soon and you're thinking about your career."

"That's not exactly what I—"

"Trust me, we want you in the anchor chair. Monday to Friday, six and ten. I think it'll happen, too. Especially after this latest story."

"That's what I want to talk about. I hate being treated like a marketing brochure."

"Not true, Danica. You're one of our best anchors."

Her hands balled into fists at her side. "I saw the promo they're running. *Danica Cortez—Houston's Hero.* Look, I happened to be part of a story instead of merely covering it. What's the big deal?"

"It's national news. You're a celebrity."

"No," she replied, gritting her teeth. "I'm a journalist."

Back at her desk and still irritated about being trotted out as some kind of rock star, Danica pored over her email. Most were congratulatory notes from viewers—her favorite kind— and she breezed through those quickly. The political messages, with subjects such as "Only commies save commies" and "You should have let him die," went straight into her trash folder.

One weirdo had even sent her a nude photo and asked for a date. "That would be a *No*," she said, pressing the delete button and hoping the oddball didn't eventually graduate to stalker.

She knew of women in the business who had been so freaked out by such emails that they had quit. Or had stopped going out in public. That wasn't going to be her, though. She wasn't going to overreact just because her inbox contained a photo of some guy's crotch.

With only forty-five minutes remaining before airtime, she

went to grab a cup of coffee and check her makeup. In the coffee bar, she almost bumped headlong into her news director, Jerry Tomlinson.

"How's it going, Danica?" he asked in a voice that was simultaneously eager and whiny. The last time she'd heard that voice was when he'd been screaming in her earpiece. "Great stuff with the plane crash. I've got an idea. It's right up your alley. You know, investigative crap."

She selected an eco-friendly cup from the cabinet and filled it from a pot of what the station called coffee. "I'm listening."

"You should check out that plane's manufacturer. There's gotta be some shortcuts they took. Expose their incompetence or whatever."

"You do know that the plane crashed in heavy fog, right?"

"Maybe the air traffic controllers were asleep or drunk. Maybe they were supposed to issue some fog warning. Or—get this—what if it was an assassination attempt?"

Jerry had a wild look in his eyes, and she knew he was going to be bugging her for a while . . . or at least until the next high-profile story came along. In some ways, they were kindred spirits, with a shared passion for delivering the news, except he cared less about the truth and more about creating a "kick-ass broadcast," as he liked to say.

"I'll check it out. Thanks." But she had no intention of pursuing Jerry's suggestions, as the guy was notoriously off the mark when it came to story ideas. Sure, he could cover them, but he lacked a critical characteristic for a news person: instinct.

She left Jerry in the coffee bar, where he continued to bend the ear of someone else about another of his conspiracy theories, this one involving the IRS. Then she touched up her makeup and returned to her desk. Thirty minutes before air.

As she sat sipping coffee, her cell phone chimed with an incoming text. She'd already cleared her messages earlier and didn't want to lose control over those again, so she checked her phone. The message was from Zoey. *Thanks for playing tennis with me.*

Danica smiled. She'd been having the same thought herself ever since arriving at the station and finding herself confronted by the same old work aggravations. In the span of two hours this morning, she'd realized that demonstrating tennis to a complete stranger—and then helping her through one of life's most delicate situations—offered a sense of peace that often eluded her.

Her eyes landed on a desktop photo of her brother, the one she'd taken of him at Yosemite. He was in his wheelchair and pointing up at the granite cliff called El Capitan, boasting he would climb it one day. But that damn disease had won out.

This new girl was like Mario, tough and full of life. It didn't seem as if anything could hold her back. Except maybe her father.

The man—*was his name Garrison?*—had been so annoying, butting in and arguing with her, but there was still something about him that had resonated in her head all morning.

Garrison was ruggedly handsome in a way that reminded her of old movie cowboys, and for her friend Sam that might be enough. But Danica understood that looks weren't everything. From her own experience, she knew that handsome guys walked out when times got tough. Her dad was handsome. So was her college boyfriend.

Danica texted Zoey back, telling her how much fun tennis had been and wishing her well. After pressing the send button, she knew that would be the last time she'd hear from Zoey. A too-familiar feeling of melancholy rose in her chest.

Then she thought about Garrison. It was tough to admit, but when she'd woken up from another nightmare at home, her first thought had been to reach out for him. *Pull yourself together.*

Kathy Hammett suddenly appeared by her desk. "War room. Now."

"What's up?" she replied, her mind still filled with thoughts of Garrison and Zoey.

"Breaking news. We're gonna have to change the broadcast."

Danica gave a deep sigh. This was the part she hated about local news: corpse reports. It seemed all they covered were glorified obituaries: murder/suicide in a quiet suburban neighborhood, deadly shooting outside a bar, major freeway accident with fatalities. She could argue about this until she was blue in the face, but she wanted to pursue stories that led somewhere other than to a grieving relative.

"Let me guess," Danica said, "Drive-by on the northeast side."

Kathy ignored her and yelled out to the assignment desk. "Lindsay, I want another two crews on this. Is the chopper up yet?"

Danica jerked, and an adrenalin surge hit her system.

"There's a fire on the Ship Channel," Kathy explained. "Explosion at a chemical plant. Authorities have already issued a shelter-in-place. No one knows how bad things are."

"And we go live in fifteen minutes."

"Which makes me glad that you're in the anchor chair instead of Frank. Put on your tap shoes."

When the red light of the robotic camera turned on, Danica lifted her eyes from the papers on the anchor desk and gazed directly into the camera's lens. "Breaking news just in from the Ship Channel," she said, the tone of her voice deadly serious. "A chemical tank has exploded and authorities are unsure of the danger posed to the community. As you can see from the images provided by Eyewitness9's Air Team hovering over the scene, firefighters are battling the blaze, which began more than half an hour ago."

She spent much of the broadcast balancing reports from the field and the news helicopter, as well as absorbing comments from Jerry talking nonstop in her ear. She'd recap the events for viewers, then move on nimbly to another aspect of the story. And through it all, she felt incredibly energized and focused.

After they returned from a final round of commercials, Danica delivered the newscast's closing segment. "In tonight's Parting Shot, we're going to leave you with images of a fire burning on the Ship Channel. We'll have updates on this major story during our ten o'clock broadcast or as events warrant." She allowed her tight lips to dissolve into a smile, then gave her signature sign-off, deviating only a bit. "Have a good *evening* . . . friends."

The camera light turned dark. "Don't anyone go too far away," Jerry announced from the control room. "If anything changes on this plant explosion, we might cut into network programming."

Danica pushed through the soundproof doors of the studio and headed back to her desk. She passed Kathy, who gave her a thumbs-up and said, "See? Celebrity *and* journalist. Good job."

As much as she hated to admit it, Danica had actually enjoyed the rush of the broadcast. Juggling the reporters' accounts and narrating a story that wasn't served up on a teleprompter really jazzed her. She wondered if the station's website already had the video feed online.

Danica sat at her desk and typed in her computer password. Another email appeared in her inbox. The sender's name was Senator Joseph Hartwell. The message listed a phone number and two words: *Call me.*

Chapter 14

Danica screwed up her face and re-read the cryptic email. *Call me.* As much as she wanted to speak with the injured senator, to reassure herself that he was indeed recovering and to wipe away images of his bloody face and gruesome leg, she didn't believe the email was real.

Someone had to be playing a joke on her. Maybe it was her friend Sam, who always saw an opportunity for humor in odd places. Or maybe it was one of Danica's competitors—someone like Barb Edwards might stoop to that level.

She shook her head and deleted the email.

"What are you doing in today?" came a familiar voice from behind her. "I thought you were taking it easy."

Danica scoffed. "You know me, Rocky. Miss Lazypants. Nah, they called me in to ride anchor tonight. You headed out to cover the fire on the Ship Channel?"

"Something even more exciting. I get to edit a piece on the new baby giraffe at the zoo."

"Sounds like Pulitzer material."

He shrugged. "Just doing the work. What about you? Still fielding congratulatory calls from the President and the ghost of Walter Cronkite?"

"Very funny. I—" She cocked her head, remembering the strange email she'd received. Had she just deleted an email from the most-discussed person on the planet? "Can I let you go, Rocky? I've gotta get back to something."

Danica quickly navigated to her email trash folder and found the note. *Was it really him?* The return email address contained the senator's name, but anyone could have forged that. The body of the email was short and sweet. A ten-digit phone number, with a Houston area code.

She punched the numbers into her cell phone but held off on pressing the call button. *I need to find someplace private,* she thought, and grabbed a pen and a notebook and headed for the War Room.

A man answered on the sixth ring. "Who is this?"

If she had indeed fallen for a sick practical joke, she was going to kill someone. She peered out the glass panels of the War Room to see if any colleagues were spying on her. This would be the perfect prank, of course, because everyone knew how much she respected the senator. During his last election, someone had taped up one of his campaign signs on her cubicle wall and drawn red hearts all around his name.

"Is this Senator Hartwell?"

"Uh . . . thank you, nurse." His voice sounded far away. "Tell my wife to go grab some dinner in the cafeteria. No, I'll be fine."

Danica cupped her free hand over her other ear, trying to make out his words. "Senator, can you hear me?" Suddenly she was back in the plane's wreckage, shaking the barely conscious man, saying the same thing.

"This is Danica Cortez of Eyewitness9."

The man cleared his throat. "Of course, Miss Cortez. Thanks for calling."

She couldn't believe it. She was actually talking to Senator Joseph "Call me Joe" Hartwell, the popular two-term U.S. Senator and the man she'd voted for. With a folksy voice that reminded everyone of Andy Griffith, he even had an "aw-shucks" persona that resonated with the electorate.

"How are you doing, sir? It's an honor to speak with you."

"You, too."

Her mind was racing. This was the highest-profile newsmaker in the country right now. He hadn't even delegated the task of making contact to one of his assistants. He had contacted her. This phone call was going to make for a great story.

"I understand you've had surgery on your leg," she said. "What have they told you about recovery? Is there a timetable?"

"Please, no questions. Just wanted to express my deepest gratitude."

"That's very kind, but—"

"You're a brave woman, Miss Cortez. Not many people would react like you did. It must have been very frightening."

As if on cue, her mind served up a maelstrom of horrific memories. In her mind's eye, she could see the plane emerging from the fog and clipping the trees. She could see the initial fireball and the roiling smoke. She could see the lifeless eyes of the dead, tattooed woman.

"It all happened so fast," she said, shaking her head. "I didn't have time to be afraid. But what about you? Can you at least give me an update on your condition?"

He lowered his voice. "Can we go off the record?"

She grimaced. "If you really need to." Loud knocks sounded on the glass door, and Kathy poked her head in.

"We need the War Room. And we need you, too."

Danica covered the mouthpiece. "Five minutes? I'm on an important call."

Kathy was standing there with her arms crossed, tapping a foot. "I hope it's the frickin' president of the chemical plant, because we can't get jackshit for information from anyone out there."

"No, it's . . ." For some reason, Danica didn't want to share the fact that she was talking to Senator Hartwell. So she listened to her gut and repeated, "Five minutes."

Kathy reluctantly closed the door, and Danica returned to her cell phone. "I apologize, Senator."

"Not a problem. Again, this is off the record."

"Yes, sir."

"My office will be issuing a statement, but I can tell you my injuries ain't gonna kill me. Thank God it was only a broken leg and a concussion, a few cuts and bruises. But I don't need to tell you. You were there."

"Uh-huh."

"Tell me what you remember," he said. But this folksy Andy Griffith voice reminded Danica not of good-ol'-boy Andy Taylor of the Mayberry sheriff's office but of the *more-than-he-appears* Ben Matlock of an Atlanta courtroom. This was the voice she remembered from watching reruns with Mom, who always liked to point out just when "Mister Matlock" was about to trick the defendant into saying something incriminating.

Tell me what you remember. It was such an odd response. Most folks she interviewed after a trauma wanted to talk about anything but the incident itself. "Maybe we shouldn't talk about that," she replied. "Can we go back on the record?"

"I'd just like to know what you saw. No one here will answer my questions."

"I didn't see anything." She didn't want to make him feel worse than he already did. There was nothing to gain by spelling out those horrors: watching the plane disintegrate, discovering a dead body and then the senator's own broken body, staring at the burning fuselage and knowing that a woman was being cremated before Danica's very eyes.

"Really?" he said with an edge in his voice that made Danica uncomfortable.

"I don't remember anything. Honestly, it's all a blur."

He was quiet on the other end of the line. "That's probably

for the best, anyway. It was nice talking with you. Again, thank you for being so darn brave."

"One more thing, Senator. We should really sit down for an interview."

"Most definitely. In the future, though. After I'm fully recovered."

"But—"

"Thanks again, Miss Cortez."

She could sense him pulling back, and she knew this once-in-a-lifetime opportunity was slipping away. She had to do something. "I know you're injured," she said, "but let me interview you in the hospital. One on one. Just think what kind of sympathy you'll get from people."

"By people, you mean viewers."

"Better than that, sir. Voters."

Two hours later, the Ship Channel story had turned into a dud. There had been an explosion, but only of a single vessel containing propane. No ethylene oxide had been released into the atmosphere as first feared. Fire safety personnel had extinguished the blaze, and the shelter-in-place had been lifted. Everything was back to normal.

Danica led the broadcast with the explosion but spent less than two minutes on it. She cruised through the remainder of the stories: a double slaying in the Montrose area, the discovery of a body in a bayou, and a protest march against teacher pay cuts. They ran a clip of NTSB investigators standing in the field where she'd been the previous day. Then she threw it to Steve Postic for weather.

While Steve delivered the weather in front of the Eyewitness9 chroma wall, she listened to the director in her ear. "Danica, stand by," Jerry said. "Senator Hartwell has just released a statement. We've got it on graphics. Let's do this now, before sports."

The red light came on again, and Danica paused for the *Breaking News* animation to play. "And now an update on yesterday's plane crash that seriously injured Senator Joseph Hartwell. He issued a statement today."

I am deeply saddened by the events of yesterday morning. Please join me in praying for the families of the five people who lost their lives: pilots James Poldrack and Greg Briscoe, Christopher King and Carlos Reyes of Genetechnologix Corporation, and my chief of staff and very good friend, Arnie Fletcher. I want to thank the doctors at St. Luke's Hospital and Ms. Danica Cortez, who put herself in harm's way to save me. Thankfully, my injuries are not life-threatening. I expect a complete recovery and will soon return to Washington to work on behalf of the citizens of Texas. God bless you all.

Sure that she had misread the senator's statement, Danica looked again at the monitor. But the graphic disappeared before she could examine it. Confused, she sat at the anchor desk without saying anything.

"What are you doing, Danica?" Jerry barked in her ear. "Sports!"

"Uh . . . that came from the Senator's office. And now on to Hank Neff with tonight's scores."

When the camera was off, she shook her head and muttered, "That can't be right."

"What did you say, Danica?" the voice in her ear replied.

"I think I read it wrong. How many people were on that plane?"

"Six. The senator was the only survivor."

Danica's head was racing. Hartwell had paid tribute to only five victims. All men. She couldn't shake the image of the gape-necked woman inside the wreckage. Why hadn't he mentioned her?

SPACE IN THE HEART97

Chapter 15

G arrison turned off the paved farm-to-market road and onto a gravel path barely wide enough to accommodate the van. This last five minutes of the drive to their ranch, located outside the Central Texas town of Cat Spring, always seemed to make the previous two hours bearable. Passing under a canopy of live oaks and bull pine, he opened the van's windows and breathed in the fragrance of pine needles and the clover-like scent of Bahia grass. "Don't you love that smell?" he told Zoey. "Must have rained recently."

She ignored him and said, "When we get to the cabin, I want to take a nap."

"But you slept the whole way here."

"Tennis kinda wore me out."

IIe had hoped their drive would provide an opportunity to discuss what had happened this morning. Although he wasn't looking forward to talking about cramps and hormones and female stuff—their first discussion about sex had been hopelessly awkward—he knew a conversation was necessary. But Zoey had been zonked out ever since leaving Houston.

When they reached the ranch entrance, a nondescript metal gate in the middle of a long run of barbed-wire fencing, he got out and unlocked the padlock. He placed his hands on his hips and leaned back, popping each vertebra to shake off the effects of the long drive. Peering up, he could see wispy cirrus clouds feathered across the vast blue expanse and two long contrails that crisscrossed the sky. He couldn't wait until darkness fell.

At the cabin, Zoey wheeled inside without a word. Garrison stood at the rear of the van, contemplating how he was going to move the binocular chair. If he'd known any of his Cat Spring neighbors, he could have asked them for help, but he didn't. That meant he would have to unload the binocular chair from the van the same way he loaded it: by himself. As a test, he lifted up the chair's base, his arm muscles straining under the weight. *I can do this.*

He squatted and put his arms around it. Then he backed up slightly, easing the bulky chair out of the van. With a grunt, he lifted it and began to turn, but it was too heavy. The chair's base bounced off the rear bumper and dropped onto the driveway, almost landing on his foot. Something metallic ricocheted across the concrete.

"Son of a—" he muttered, and reached down to pick up the loose metal. It was a stainless steel hex bolt, sheared cleanly in half. He turned it over in his fingers and, out of habit, imagined how much force it must have endured before breaking.

With a frustrated sigh, he began to examine the chair, hoping against hope that nothing was broken. It soon became clear that although the binocular mount was still intact, when he swiveled the chair, its smooth 360-degree action was gone, replaced by a wobble and an annoying clicking sound. "Stupid chair," he said, running a hand across his forehead. How was he going to fix this before tonight?

Maybe he could find a replacement bolt or at least a functioning substitute somewhere in the cabin. Then he'd need time to make the repair . . . which was possible only if Zoey slept for a couple more hours. It was worth a shot.

He came back into the cabin and found Zoey sitting on the couch, her empty wheelchair next to her. "I thought you were asleep," he said.

"With the racket you were making?" She pointed up at the TV. "Check it out, Dad. See who's on the news."

He frowned. "The news? We've talked about this. You know how I feel. Pop in a DVD or something. But don't watch—"

"It's Danica."

He turned and looked up. On the screen, a brunette with light mocha skin and gleaming teeth was speaking from behind an anchor desk. Before he could process the image, the shot changed to a helicopter view of a massive fire. Then the scene changed back to the studio, and Danica was speaking directly into the camera.

Garrison stared at the TV, finding it hard to believe this was the same woman they'd seen at the tennis courts. She looked so different, with her dark hair down instead of tied in a ponytail and with wavy curls that lay on her shoulders. Even in high-definition, her skin didn't reveal any blemishes.

"Doesn't she have beautiful eyes?" Zoey said, twisting her fingers through golden brown hair. "I wish I looked like her."

He dropped into a seat next to his daughter. The station was covering some sort of fire. Danica appeared off and on, and he couldn't take his eyes off the screen.

Eventually the newscast broke for commercial. After the usual promos for Texas-sized pickups and a local furniture store that "saves you money!" the screen showed smoking wreckage strewn across a field. Garrison assumed it was an update on the senator's plane crash. But it wasn't a news story—it was another commercial, solemnly narrated by a deep-voiced man.

A plane crashes in Houston. And Eyewitness9 is there, first on the scene, first with the truth. Now the nation discovers what we already knew. Dah-nica Corrrrtez, whose courage helped save a U.S. Senator, is a true American hero.

Garrison and Zoey turned to each other. "Holy crap," he said.

"Oh my gosh, I saw this yesterday. I didn't know it was Danica. She was right there when the plane crashed. Then she dragged the congressman—"

"Senator—"

"Yeah, senator . . . from the plane. Wow, Dad, she's pretty amazing."

He sat transfixed, watching the woman on the screen as Zoey's words slowly seeped into his consciousness. *Pretty. Amazing.*

With great effort, Garrison was able to place a carpeted dolly underneath the binocular chair and haul it into the cabin's workshop. He searched every bin and drawer of his workbench for something that would stabilize the base—he didn't care if the thing swiveled as long as it would safely hold Zoey. But after half an hour, he had to give up. He'd just have to show her the chair and explain how it worked.

"Zoey," he called upon entering the cabin. "Want to see your new birthday present?"

No reply.

"Wake up, sleepyhead," he said as he walked into her bedroom. But the bed was still made, the country plaid comforter and pale blue pillows untouched.

He threw open the front door and stepped onto the porch. "Zoey! Where are you?"

Their cabin was built at the edge of a dense forest, a dark pond stocked with bluegill and mudcats to the west, a small homemade observatory they called their *star shack* in a broad clearing to the south, and a phalanx of cedars and oaks wrapped in thick yaupon underbrush blocking passage to the north and east. The most obvious place for her to go was back up the driveway, toward the pond. Shielding his eyes against the setting sun, he scanned the western horizon. But all he could see was a great blue heron standing guard at the water's edge.

He glanced south, past the van, where a trail connected the cabin to the star shack a hundred yards away. The trail was made of hard-packed decomposed granite—that had been Zoey's suggestion, because she thought concrete would ruin the natural view. Even though the path was wheelchair accessible, the decomposed granite wasn't the friendliest surface for her, especially when it was wet. Garrison stepped around the van for a closer look. Two grooved indentations—more like ruts because of the recent rain—ran the length of the trail.

With a warm southern breeze in his face, he set out along the trail toward the star shack. The only sounds came from stones crunching beneath his shoes and squirrels skittering in tree branches. When he reached the halfway point, the landmark cedar tree that Zoey had adorned with goofy fake eyes, he could actually feel his blood pressure decrease.

When he and Celeste bought the ranch, three years before Zoey was born, they thought it would be a nice place to go on the weekends. The wooded land and primitive cabin offered sanctuary from the hubbub of city life, an opportunity to draw closer to nature, and a place to reaffirm their feelings for each other.

Now that it was just him and Zoey, the ranch—and the observatory they'd built together—had become even more important.

Rounding the final bend in the path, he saw Zoey up near the star shack, on the forty-by-forty concrete patio outside the building. She was wheeling back and forth, pushing hard and pivoting on a dime. And in her right hand was a tennis racquet.

"Hey there, Serena!"

She stopped in mid-swing. "What?"

"Serena Williams. You know, the tennis player. She and her sister Venus—"

"I know who she is." She laid the racquet in her lap and crossed her arms. "Twenty-five acres and I can't find a space for myself. Weren't you busy messing with your rocket thing?"

"It's not a rocket. Something better. I'll show you later. Mind if I watch?"

"I'm just practicing stuff that Danica showed me."

"I figured."

She waved her racquet toward a picnic table that sat beside one of the largest pines on the ranch. "Go over there. And don't tell me what I'm doing wrong."

Garrison thought about arguing with her but decided against it. He sat at the picnic table and watched her race from side to side. "I can get some tennis balls if you want," he called.

She paused briefly but didn't acknowledge him. So much for having a nice conversation.

After ten minutes of watching her work up a sweat, he lay back on top of the picnic table and gazed upward. The sky, now lavender, was dotted with pink clouds that reflected the setting sun. Soon the clouds would turn orange and the forest would settle in for its nightly slumber.

And the sky would come to life.

He could still remember the first time his dad explained the miracle of astronomy. They'd gone camping together—along with a hundred other Boy Scouts and their fathers—to Pedernales Falls State Park in the heart of the Texas Hill Country. At nine years old, Garrison was a city kid from Plano who didn't know a meteor from a meatball.

After the evening campfire and before lights-out, Garrison's dad led a handful of scouts to an outcropping with a full view of the winter sky. Back in the suburbs of Plano, Garrison had seen stars, but nothing like what was visible above him. Thousands—millions—of brilliant lights shined and sparkled, and all he could think was that he was watching angels looking down from heaven. Then his dad began pointing out the constellations and asterisms: the Big Dipper of Ursa Major, the W-shaped Cassiopeia, and Orion with his three-star belt.

That's the night Garrison fell in love with science and nature. And the first night he'd ever said a prayer of thanksgiving for the beauty around him.

"Dad, wake up."

He slowly opened his eyes and yawned. "Did I fall asleep?"

"The sky's getting cloudy. Not gonna be a good night for stargazing."

"Don't be silly," he said, sitting up. He cupped his hands around his eyes and peered into the night sky. "What is it, ten o'clock?"

"Eight-thirty. Bunch of clouds rolled in the last hour or so."

He hopped down from the picnic table. "Come help me prepare the telescope."

Zoey put on a pouty face but followed him over to the star shack. "By the time we set things up," she said, "we won't be able to see anything."

He ignored her and opened the door, then turned on the nighttime switches. Warm red light glowed from rope lighting underneath the cabinets and from a colored incandescent bulb above the computer desk. With red light bathing this area, he could barely see the big telescope mounted on a concrete plinth on the other side of the room.

A smile spread across his face. The only thing he enjoyed more than watching stars and planets was tinkering with his equipment ahead of time, planning the observing session, configuring the tracking software, setting up the CCD imager. He gunned up his computer and loaded a star chart. "Have you thought about what you want to track tonight?" he asked her. "Saturn's pretty awesome right now. Just above the star Spica in the southeast. Spica's in Virgo, remember? Will you locate that for us?"

"I hope you won't be mad, but I don't feel like messing with the telescope."

Garrison's smile disappeared. "But that's why we came up here, right? And tomorrow morning we can get up early and see the conjunction of Mercury, Venus, and Jupiter."

She sniffled. "Please, Dad."

In the faint red glow, he thought he saw tears streak her face. "What's wrong?"

"Can we just go outside and lie down?"

"Of course, sweetie." Garrison powered down the computer and moved to the closet, where he pulled out two chaise lounges. Then he followed Zoey through the door. He unfolded the patio chairs and placed them on the concrete. "Ready?" he asked. When she nodded, he gently lifted her from the wheelchair and placed her onto the chaise lounge, then slipped into the one next to her.

As they lay there underneath the increasingly cloudy sky, Garrison tried to gather courage to start the conversation.

"Big day today, huh?" When she didn't respond, he said, "Tennis sure was fun. Danica said you're a quick learner. She was very impressed." He continued to stare into the sky and watched two more stars disappear behind clouds. "Did you know you have another birthday present?"

He explained to her about the binocular chair, told her how he'd spent nights putting it together, and described how he'd dropped it on the driveway. "I can fix it, though. It's gonna be awesome. I promise."

She moved her hand out to touch his. "Thanks, but—"

"You're disappointed, aren't you? I'm sorry, honey. I really tried to fix it."

"That's not it."

"Then what?"

She drew an audible breath. "Danica told you?"

"Yeah, she said you were really good at tennis." As soon as the words escaped his mouth, he realized that wasn't what she meant. He swallowed hard. "I mean . . . yes, she told me."

This was the moment he'd been hoping for all day, an open and honest conversation with his daughter. But now he found himself mute. He turned his head to look at her. In the glow of red light that slipped through the star shack's window, he could see that she was smiling. Which brought a smile to his own face.

"It's pretty cool, isn't it?" she said. "Your little girl is growing up."

"Yeah," he said vacantly. His memory flooded with images of Zoey: an infant lying in her crib, swaddled in a receiving blanket; a toddler racing around the living room before tumbling into the sharp edges of the brick fireplace hearth; a young girl sitting in her new wheelchair, trying to learn how to drive it.

He'd spent his whole life trying to shield her from a brutal world. Now she was on her journey to becoming an adult and he didn't know the first thing about how to protect her.

"Stars are almost gone," she said.

He fixed his gaze upward, a lump forming in his throat. "You were right. Way too many clouds tonight. Want to head back to the cabin?"

"No. I like it out here." She inhaled deeply, then softly exhaled. "Is this what it's like to feel weightless?"

Garrison knew exactly what she was talking about. There were times when he lay back on a chaise lounge, the silent forest surrounding him, the darkness tempered only by pinpricks of starlight or by the wash of moonlight, and he could imagine his body drifting above the earth.

He'd experienced actual weightlessness before, of course, aboard a KC-135 Stratotanker that NASA used to train its astronauts. Before he was assigned to the Columbia flight, he rode the Vomit Comet numerous times as part of his instruction. Each flight consisted of the pilot executing parabolic zero-g maneuvers, and every forty seconds or so, he'd float in the cargo area and turn somersaults and execute training exercises.

With a perfect record of never throwing up, Garrison had been regarded as a shoo-in for selection to a flight crew. When the call came to be part of STS-107, the ill-fated Columbia mission, he couldn't wait for his opportunity to experience weightlessness in space.

Then Celeste died.

When the memory of Celeste entered his head, it was as if the zero-g aircraft had gone nose-down on its elliptical path. He was no longer floating in a dreamy space world, but rather hurtling downward, pulled by an unseen force, only to crash back to earth.

Trying to push away thoughts of Zoey in her wheelchair and Celeste in her casket, he squeezed his eyes closed. And found himself immersed in a terrible darkness, the one that often threatened to overcome him, the one that almost succeeded when he once turned to drinking.

"Weightlessness is overrated," he mumbled.

"What did you say, Dad?"

"Nothing."

"But I heard—"

"Don't worry about it. I'm just upset by this weather. Everyone was predicting clear skies."

"At least it was sunny this morning. Tennis was fun."

He opened his eyes, but found himself still deep in blackness. "Uh-huh."

"And Danica's nice."

At the mention of her name, Garrison could have sworn he saw a little star flash between the clouds.

"She's gonna teach me tennis."

He clenched his jaw. That was the one thing he'd been afraid of when he took Zoey to the tennis courts, that she'd want to take up the game. "I don't know about you playing tennis," he said.

"Don't do this to me again, Dad."

"Do what?"

"Show me something interesting and then take it away."

He scoffed. "You spend a few hours playing tennis—"

"And I love it. That's why Danica's gonna be my coach. Because she cares about making me better."

"We'll talk about this some other time."

"All you care about is making sure I don't have any fun. Everything I do is something you map out for me."

He gritted his teeth. "I said we'll talk about it later."

The two of them lay there without saying a word, staring up at a starless sky, the space between them as great as the space above them.

Then it began to rain.

Chapter 16

A clap of thunder rattled the bedroom windows, and Garrison bolted awake. Disoriented, it took a few seconds to realize he was in the cabin instead of his Clear Lake home. He crossed the room and, drawing a hand to the blinds, peered through the gap between the slats. But he couldn't see a thing.

He glanced over to the alarm clock and flinched when he saw the time. He stared at the numbers, willing them to be anything but 4:07—the same gut-punching time as years ago, when an emergency phone call had woken him during a heavy thunderstorm.

Rain pelted the windowpane beneath his palm, the percussion on the glass sending vibrations through his fingertips. A flash of lightning filled the sky, and for the briefest instant, Garrison could see sheets of rain swaying in the wind like some sort of flag.

On the driveway stood Celeste.

He gasped and fell back, his heart lurching in his chest. He could hear the wind howling and moaning through the trees. *It's not her*, he told himself. *Can't be.*

He stood there shaking, clad only in a pair of pajama pants and a single white sock that hung loosely from his right foot.

And he could remember the words of his therapist: "Confront your fears, Garrison." Dr. Claiborne had always been calm and reassuring, but Garrison knew that the man could never appreciate what it meant to wake up with night terrors, to have your dead wife emerge from the other side to accuse you, to live with the crippling guilt.

With an unsteady hand, he grasped the cord for the blinds and yanked it down, just as lightning flashed again.

There was nobody outside.

He collapsed back onto the bed, trying to will the image of Celeste away from his mind. But each time he closed his eyes, she'd reappear. *Am I going crazy?*

After ten minutes of lying there, his breath rapid and shallow, adrenalin surging through his body, he decided to get up and check on Zoey. Rising to his feet, he brought a shaky hand to his forehead and wiped his brow.

He padded out of the bedroom and down the hall. At Zoey's door, he slowly turned the knob, not wanting to wake her. But after opening the door, he realized there was no need to worry. She was sacked out beneath the covers, her empty wheelchair beside the bed. The storm hadn't bothered her at all.

Lightning flashed again. Zoey turned her head from one side to the other and mumbled something unintelligible, then fell back asleep. He watched her for a few moments, a reassuring calm slowly enveloping him. Now he could try to get some sleep.

Three hours later, when sunlight peeked through the window, Garrison blinked open his eyes and rolled out of bed. Glancing outside, he realized the rain had stopped. Which meant everything would be okay again.

He showered and dressed, thinking about everything he needed to do before heading home, each thought pushing the memories of that long-ago horrific night further back into the recesses of his mind. Stepping into the workshop, he spied the broken binocular chair by his workbench and made a mental note to search for the correct size bolt at home. Then he pulled on a pair of waterproof mud boots and stepped outside to check on the star shack.

He crossed the driveway and looked south down the trail. Dotted with pools of standing water, it looked more like a stream than a trail. He took one step and then another before realizing his boots had sunk in a full inch.

That was a stupid thing to do, he thought, and wondered if he even needed to go inspect the star shack. After all, he was pretty sure they'd buttoned things up like they were supposed to last night. He stepped out of the muck, his mud boots making a disgusting sound. Then he turned back toward the cabin. But thoughts nagged at him: maybe he hadn't secured the door, maybe the strong winds had knocked something onto the roof.

With a shrug, he looked south again. Better check.

Walking beside the muddy trail in the high grass, he scanned the surrounding area for signs of storm damage. A few branches lay scattered on the ground, but surprisingly that was the extent of the destruction. The star shack itself turned out to be in perfect condition. No leaks, no lights left on—it was as if the storm had never occurred.

The telescope in the middle of the room, mounted on a concrete pier that extended deep into the ground, towered like a sentry. "Sorry, big fella," Garrison said. "Maybe next time."

He was about to leave when he saw a black object sticking out of a trash can near the door. An umbrella, he figured. Wondering if the rain might return, he reached down to grab it. But it wasn't an umbrella. Stuffed into the trash can was Zoey's new tennis racquet.

Confused, he pulled it out and examined it. Nothing broken as far as he could tell, the strings and grip in seemingly perfect condition. Maybe Zoey had simply set it there when they'd gone inside. He tucked it under his arm and exited the building, then locked the place up and headed back toward the cabin.

"Dad!" Zoey cried in the distance.

He jumped at the sound of her voice. Something was wrong.

"Dad!" Her voice was urgent, insistent.

Garrison raced toward the cabin, his stomach churning. He knew that tone too well—she either was hurt or needed help. Rounding the final turn in the trail, he saw Zoey sitting in her chair, its wheels sunk into the sodden earth. "Are you okay?" he called.

"I can't move it."

He ran to her side, tossed the racquet onto the driveway, and kissed her head. "Don't worry. I'll help you."

"No need to freak out, Dad."

"I'm not freaking out." He stepped behind her and pulled on the handles. The chair wouldn't budge. "You got the brake on?"

"Seriously? You think I'm stupid?"

He yanked again, to no avail. "Zoey, what were you thinking? We got maybe three inches of rain last night. You can't drive your chair through mud."

"You *do* think I'm stupid!"

"Honey," he said, making a final heave. "It's stuck."

"Well, that's just great."

"Let me think for a second." He squatted to examine the wheels and inspect the muddy ground. The engineer in him knew exactly what was going on. "The reason the tires won't move is that there's just too much weight on them."

"Now you're calling me fat!"

He dropped his head and sighed. Standing, he said, "Look at me, Zoey. I'll pick you up and take you inside. Then I'll free your chair. No big deal."

She crossed her arms. "This is so ridiculous!"

He bent down and put an arm under her thighs and another around her back. "Ready?" he asked, then grunted and lifted her from the seat. His feet slid sideways in the slimy mud, and for a moment he thought he might drop her, like the binocular chair, onto the ground.

"See?" he said, forcing a smile, even as a stab of pain shot through his lower back. "No big deal." He carried her into the cabin and laid her on the couch. Then he went back and rolled the chair out of the mire, mud flying in every direction.

By the time he hauled the chair back onto the driveway, mud covered the entire circumference of the wheels, including the brakes. "This is gonna take all morning," he grumbled.

"Dad!" she called again, and he recognized this tone as well. He'd heard it a number of times, especially in the past two years. This was her *I'm-pissed-off-and-I-demand-your-attention* voice.

"I'm cleaning your chair," he called. "I'll come in when I'm done." He turned on the water spigot and pointed a spray nozzle at the tires, taking care not to shoot water into the seals.

When he bent over to inspect the brakes, he felt another twinge in his back.

Taking care not to make any sudden movements, he wiped down the aluminum frame with an old towel, dried the seat cushion, and even squirted some WD-40 into the front casters and rear axle. He wheeled it back to the cabin and opened the front door. "Good as new—" he said, but the words choked off when he saw Zoey.

She lay on the couch, an arm covering her eyes, softly sobbing. "Leave me alone."

"What's wrong?" he said, then noticed the dark stain on the sofa beneath her. "Oh, God. I'm sorry. How can I help?"

"You can't, Dad," she blubbered. "You don't understand."

He looked at her lying there and felt utterly useless. For years, he'd been able to soothe her tears when she became angry or sad. But now she was growing up. He didn't know what to do anymore.

She looked up at him, her eyes glistening with tears. "Please, if you want to help, you gotta let me do this myself. I just need my chair."

He nodded. "I'll be outside. Holler if you need anything. Anything." He stepped toward the door, then turned back to her. "I love you, Zoey."

Sitting on the porch, he stared out on the lake as he tried to suppress every urge to run inside and help. But she wasn't a little girl anymore. Her problems were bigger now.

What had he been thinking? Zoey gets her first period and instead of acknowledging it, he pretends nothing happened and drags her out to the ranch. He was such a screw-up.

What kind of place was this for her anyway? Maybe he should just sell the ranch and accept the fact that rural property and wheelchairs didn't go together. After all, Zoey didn't even like coming up here anymore.

He wished Celeste were here. She'd know what to do.

When Zoey finally emerged from the house a half-hour later, dressed in a fresh set of clothes, he could tell she was still feeling down. "I packed the van," he said. "Just give me a few minutes to grab my clothes and we can head out. Why don't you stay here on the porch and enjoy the view? I saw a couple of snowy egrets out on the lake earlier."

She nodded but didn't respond.

He wanted to reach out and hug her but figured she might prefer being left alone. "Well, let me know if you see anything interesting." Then he disappeared inside, quickly retrieving items for the ride home and gulping down two ibuprofen for the growing pain in his back. When he returned to the front porch, he saw that Zoey had moved out onto the driveway near the van. She was holding her tennis racquet. "Oh yeah," he said. "I found that in the star shack. You must have forgotten it last night."

She looked up at him, her face pained. "This was the worst weekend ever."

The words gutted him. He'd planned such a special weekend for her, hoping she'd particularly enjoy the tennis, the binocular chair, the stargazing. "I wish you knew how sorry I really am."

"And I don't want to go back to school. They all hate me there."

He winced. Zoey didn't often feel sorry for herself, but when she did, her devastation was profound. "You're just dealing with a lot of stuff. Getting older. Your body, uh, changing."

"Daddy?" she said, calling him by the name she always used when she was low. "Why did God put me in this stupid wheelchair? Was it . . . was it to punish me?"

He tightened his hands into fists. If anyone needed to feel guilty for Zoey being in a wheelchair, it was him. He still couldn't believe he'd just stood there in front of Celeste's car and let them drive away. What kind of husband does that? Everything that had happened to his family was his fault. Not Zoey's.

"Daddy, are you okay?"

For years, he'd tried to suppress that horrible night. But he could still remember every detail, from the moment Celeste learned of her father's illness to the 4:07am phone call from Officer Farragut of the Austin PD. And he could still remember those last conversations with Celeste, practically word for word. Their discussion about the dangers of driving after dark, which had escalated into an argument about how much time he was spending on his NASA training. The ultimatum he'd laid down and that she'd rejected.

Everything was burned into his memory.

"I'm going to Johnson City," Celeste had said flatly as she turned the key in the ignition.

His cruel final words still haunted him. "I don't care where you go," he'd told her, his hands pressed to the hood of her car, angry that she wouldn't listen to reason. "As far as I'm concerned, you can go to hell!"

Go to hell.

That's why Zoey was in a wheelchair. God had punished him—was still punishing him—for his shameful, cowardly words.

He pulled the fist from his mouth and could see blood trickling from the knuckle of his index finger. Kneeling beside a perplexed Zoey, he took her hands in his. "You didn't deserve this."

"What's wrong, Dad?"

"You're the most amazing person I know. I'm so proud of you." He touched the tennis racquet in her lap. "You know, not many people can do what you did yesterday, playing tennis from a wheelchair."

"I'm a freak. That's what everyone says."

He swallowed hard. "I hate seeing you so sad."

"Why did you get this for me anyway?" she said, pointing the racquet at him. "I'll never be able to play."

Zoey was wallowing now, and he was afraid she'd spiral even further downward. He had to do something. "I know how much you like tennis," he said. "I promise to take you to the courts anytime you want. And I'll get a racquet, too. It'll be fun."

She shook her head and mumbled, "That's not what I want."

"Then what, honey? What do you want?"

"I already told you. I want Danica to teach me tennis."

Garrison groaned, remembering how he'd felt when that woman had butted in yesterday: annoyed, ignored, jealous. For practically all of Zoey's life, he was the only person she ever wanted, the only one she ever needed. And even though she was changing before his very eyes, that didn't mean they need someone else in their lives. Especially an outsider.

"But she'd never do it," Zoey said. "She's too pretty, too important, to be with someone like me."

"Don't talk like that."

She paused a moment, then absently swung her tennis racquet at her side. "Would you call her, Dad?"

"Who? Danica?"

"Would you? I'm nobody special, but she'd listen to you.

You're an astronaut."

Former astronaut, he thought. Who never flew in space. Like that would impress a celebrity like Danica. "I don't think you need someone messing up your routine," he told Zoey. "You just need to get out and have a little fun."

"Forget it, Dad. It was a dumb idea." She slumped her shoulders and gave a deep sigh. As she rolled toward the van, she muttered, "Who'd care about *me* anyway?"

Garrison wanted to say something but held his tongue. He couldn't stand to see her like this. She lifted herself into the van without saying a word, he stored her chair in the cargo area, and they drove away.

During the entire trip back to Clear Lake, Zoey sat there brooding. He was at a complete loss. She rejected every father-daughter outing he suggested, from a tour of the Blue Bell creamery to an evening on the Kemah Boardwalk, and completely shut down when he mentioned possibly seeing a therapist. But he couldn't merely stand by and watch her pull away from him. Like Celeste had done.

As he rolled Zoey's problems around in his head, every possible answer kept circling back to Danica. She was the one Zoey wanted to hang out with. She was the one who'd seemed to bring a little joy into Zoey's life. But what if Zoey called her and Danica turned her down? His little girl would be devastated.

No, he couldn't allow that.

Easing off the freeway at the Clear Lake exit, he glanced over at Zoey. Even though her eyes were closed, tears leaked from behind her lids and ran down her face. Two hours on the road and Zoey was still heartbroken.

He steeled himself, knowing that his only choice was the thing he feared most: talking to a stranger. He'd have to call Danica.

Chapter 17

What a great day, Danica thought as she stepped into the kitchen. A familiar bird song sounded from the wall clock, and she whistled along with it, thrilled to be waking up when the sun was directly overhead instead of beneath the horizon. There was nothing better than twelve-and-a-half hours of uninterrupted sleep. Sundays were the best.

With her stomach growling, she considered making a quick lunch run but didn't want to deal with getting dressed and putting on her makeup. Instead she started a pot of coffee and opened the pantry to find something to eat.

As usual, the pantry held nothing of interest. Two boxes of cereal, some chewy granola bars, instant pudding. She crinkled her nose as she picked up a can of tuna, not really wanting to go to the effort of preparing a full-blown lunch. She didn't have many options, though, as the freezer and refrigerator were mostly bare as well. So she ran the tuna through the electric can opener and emptied its contents into a bowl. Then she boiled an egg and found a couple of condiment packets—mayonnaise and sweet relish—and combined it all together.

Effobee, her mom had called it when Danica was a little girl. Her favorite meal, which Mom prepared at least once a week, had always sounded so exotic. She used to pretend she was European royalty as she ate the petite triangular sandwiches, which Mom fancied up by cutting away their crusts and adorning them with brightly colored toothpicks. Eventually she moved away to college, far from Mom's cooking, and had been disappointed to not find any effobee in the dining hall. "No, Danni," her mom had said, laughing, when she'd called home for the recipe. "It's just plain old tuna fish. Not effobee. F.O.B. Fish on bread."

Danica finished mixing the tuna and blew out a long breath. After two days of doing live reports and network interviews, some effobee might just hit the spot. She spread the tuna across two slices of stale wheat bread and took a bite as she flipped on the television. When Senator Hartwell appeared on the screen, propped up in a hospital bed, she practically choked.

"Thank you, Senator," the MSNBC anchor said. "And we wish you a speedy recovery." The video cut back to the studio, where the anchor now faced camera one. "Again, the news from Texas. Senator Joe Hartwell, hospitalized since last Friday's plane crash that claimed five lives, expects to be released from the hospital in the next day or so. On Tuesday, he'll deliver the eulogy for Arnie Fletcher, his former Chief of Staff who died in that tragic crash. And he expects to be back in Washington next Monday when the Senate returns from recess. It's truly an amazing story of recovery."

Disgusted, Danica powered off the TV. She shook her head and pointed at the black screen. "That was supposed to be my interview. You suck, Hartwell."

She opened a can of Pringles and dropped one of the saddle-shaped crisps onto her tongue. Hartwell sure was a piece of work. Only yesterday he'd promised her an interview, but then he'd changed his mind. Maybe he'd been lying to her the entire time. Typical politician. And to think she'd voted for the guy.

As she ate her sandwich and potato chips, she remembered yesterday's phone call with him. He'd seemed so grateful, a stark contrast from his public persona as a sharp-tongued, tough-minded politician. Then she imagined him trapped in the plane, blood rushing down his face, his leg bone sticking out—just a regular guy in the middle of a horrible situation. Who was the real Joe Hartwell?

There was only one person who could help her sort through this. She reached for her cell phone and thumbed the numbers for Samantha Jachowicz.

As the phone rang on the other end, Danica kept thinking about the plane crash. The sound of twisting metal. The sight of a dead body covered in garish tattoos. The awful stench of everything burning: jet fuel, trees, and what must have been human flesh.

Sam finally picked up. "Hey, Miss Popular," Sam said cheerily. "You making time to talk with the common folk?"

"Can you come over?"

"What's wrong? You sound stressed."

"It's this plane crash. I need someone to talk to." She realized how insensitive that sounded, especially considering the hours Sam had spent with her at the hospital, holding her hand as they awaited results from Mom's cardiologist. Sam was more than *someone*—they were best friends. "If you're busy, I understand."

"I'll be there as soon as I can."

"Thanks, Sam."

Danica hopped in and out of the shower, threw on a t-shirt and a pair of jeans, and pulled her hair back into a ponytail. One of the biggest reasons she liked Sundays was that she didn't have to spend an hour and a half applying studio makeup.

She grabbed her laptop from the kitchen table and carried it into the living room, where she plopped onto the leather sofa and folded her legs underneath her. The smell of freshly brewed coffee wafted in from the other room, but she stayed focused on the task at hand: learning more about Senator Hartwell. For the next thirty minutes, she googled articles about the popular politician and read dozens of profiles on him—some glowing, some scathing. Most focused on his political views.

Senator Joe Hartwell was something of an enigma in Texas politics: a Democrat in the reddest of Southern states, a man whose folksy demeanor and strong pro-business policies had earned him accolades from both sides of the aisle. He had a pretty wife who'd immigrated into Texas—legally—from Central America, plus two brown-skinned kids that seemed to help curry favor in Hispanic districts. And Hartwell's business acumen was rivaled only by his humanitarian efforts and his passion for rebuilding inner cities to raise up the poor. Most people considered his upcoming reelection a no-brainer.

Her research produced nothing but more questions, which she noted on a draft document titled *Need Some Answers*. Why had the man acted so strange during their phone call? What had he been doing in Las Vegas? Why were they landing at four in the morning? Who was the woman with skulls down her arm and a scorpion up her neck?

The doorbell rang, followed immediately by a knock, and Sam opened the door. "You really should lock the house." When they met in college, Samantha was less than two years removed from her native Warsaw and still spoke with a slight Polish accent. The occasional hard-d was the only remnant of her heritage.

Gone was the plain, mousy girl that Danica first met at Berkeley. These days, Sam decorated herself with purple highlights in her short, blond hair and seven stud earrings in each of her ears. And gone was Sam's shyness. Yeah, that was long gone.

Danica glanced up and saw her friend hobbling through the door. A walking boot covered Sam's left foot. "I'm such an idiot! I forgot you were hurt. You should be home resting. Is it broken?"

Sam raised her fists in celebration. "Cracked it right down the middle of my big toe. Don't worry about it. Figured I could feel sorry for myself over here as much as in my own apartment." She limped into the living room and took a seat in the recliner, then reached down and tore open the Velcro straps on her boot. "Can I have some of that coffee?"

Danica returned with two steaming cups, placed them on the end table, and then gently inserted a pillow under Sam's foot. When her friend seemed comfortable, she took her own coffee cup and sat on the sofa. "Have you been following this story about Senator Hartwell?"

Sam looked at her quizzically. "You're kidding, right? I can't turn on the TV without seeing your goofy face. Look everybody, it's Dah-nica Corrrrrrtez!"

"Puh-lease."

"You're so popular, I probably ought to take this coffee cup home and put it on eBay." Sam mimed pulling a slot machine handle. "Ka-ching."

"This isn't about me. It's about the plane crash." Saying the words triggered yet another unwelcome flashback, a memory of stumbling from the wreckage and then being knocked to ground by the concussion wave.

Danica rubbed her temples. "Something's seriously messed up."

"I'll tell you what's messed up. My college roomie's probably gonna be profiled on CNN—"

"Would you cut it out?" Danica snapped. She exhaled to steady herself, then said, "I'm sorry. I just get tired of this whole media circus."

Sam held Danica in her gaze as she lifted the coffee cup to her mouth. She seemed to consider saying something, but instead took a sip.

"What?" Danica said.

"Nothing. Forget it."

Danica's cell phone rang and she scowled at it. "I want to bounce some ideas off you—" she told Sam, but paused as her cell phone continued to ring, distracting her. "What the heck was I talking about?"

"Go ahead. Answer it. Who knows? Might be Anderson Cooper. Or that cute George Stephanopoulos."

Danica shrugged apologetically and picked up her phone. She didn't recognize the number but knew it was local. She answered, and a man's voice said, "Miss Cortez?"

"Who's this?"

"Sorry for bothering you. I got your number from my daughter's phone."

It was bad enough when people stopped her in the grocery store or interrupted her at a restaurant. Now she was getting phone calls at home. "I'm busy right now."

"Remember Zoey Sterling from the tennis courts? I'm her dad."

Oh, yeah. The sweet girl who reminded her of Mario. And the man on the phone—she searched her memory—was Garrison. "Wait," she said, "is everything okay with her?"

"Yeah, mostly. Thanks for your help yesterday." He fell silent, and she thought she'd dropped the connection. After a moment, she said, "Um . . . I have a favor to ask."

And there it was. The worst part about being a public figure. Can I have your autograph? Will you come speak to our organization? May I take your picture? She'd even had complete strangers approach her for a date—maybe Garrison was one of those.

"I've never seen her like this," he continued. "Sad and moody and . . . well, that's not your problem. But she really liked learning tennis from you."

Danica mumbled vague agreement while peering at her laptop display, which was playing a video of the crash scene, shot from a helicopter. A handful of people in white jumpsuits and half-face respirators were combing through the wreckage. The phone in her hand slipped down her cheek as the footage rolled.

". . . so I was wondering if that would be okay. What do you think? Danica?"

She heard her name and lifted the phone back to her ear. "I'm sorry. Please tell Zoey hello for me."

"But you didn't answer my question."

As she looked at the wreckage, she finally comprehended the scope of the accident, where the pieces of fuselage had fallen and where she'd been at the scene. She gestured to Sam and pointed at her computer.

"Hello?" he said. "Are you there?"

"I gotta go," she said in a rush and hung up, still staring at the image on the screen.

She knew Hartwell had been avoiding her. Now she knew why.

Chapter 18

"Who was that?" Sam asked. "On the phone?"

Danica scoffed. "Some guy I met yesterday."

"Ooh, a guy. About time."

"Forget him. You gotta see what I found." She carried the laptop over to the recliner and held it up to show Sam. "Recognize this?"

"Yeah, that's the crash site. What about it?"

She couldn't believe she hadn't caught it before. In all those stand-ups she'd delivered from the field and in all those voiceovers she'd looped inside the studio, she'd never realized exactly what had happened. Suddenly everything made sense. In her mind's eye, she could see the crash unfold again, the plane breaking apart at impact, her crawling into the fuselage and touching the dead woman's leg, and then everything bursting into flames.

"See that?" Danica said, pointing at the screen. "The front of the plane. No wonder those people died. There's hardly anything left."

"I can't imagine how you crawled inside that."

"I didn't. Maybe because it was so damaged, I don't remember. I know I ran toward the trees. And crawled into the rear of the plane."

Sam looked at her strangely. "Can't be. I watched Senator Hartwell's interview this morning. He said he was sitting next to Arnie Fletcher up front and that they'd grabbed hands when the plane hit the trees. It's the last thing he remembers."

"That piece of shit," Danica snapped, then shut the cover of her laptop so hard that she had to open it back up to verify she hadn't cracked the screen. "I know where I was. I crawled over a wing. Hartwell's lying through his teeth."

"Hold on, Danni. You're getting all worked up for no reason. Maybe he's just confused."

Danica's phone rang and she glared at it. Zoey's father was calling again. She pushed a button to send him to voicemail. "You know, Sam, that's what I thought at first, too. But Hartwell knows the truth." She took a deep breath. "And so do I."

"What are you talking about?"

Lacing her fingers together, she tried to decide what she could tell Sam. This was bigger than a simple plane crash. Of course she trusted her, but if this story got out prematurely . . .

"Danni, what's going on? Tell me. I'm your best friend."

And Sam *was* her best friend. She'd been by her side since college, especially through the hard times: being cheated on by her boyfriend, being blamed for the murder of that cop, attending the funerals of Mom and Mario. Through it all, Sam had been her rock. And she deserved to know everything.

"There's the back half of the plane," Danica said, enlarging the image on the screen. "It's completely burned up. But who cares, right? Everyone was up front. Except that's total crap. I pulled Hartwell out of the rear section, from this pile of incinerated debris."

"But why would he?—"

"And I saw someone else on that plane. Seated near the senator. A woman."

Sam turned sharply. "What do you mean you saw a woman?

Was she? . . ."

Danica nodded. She could still see the dead woman's head lolling to the side, practically decapitated, the fancy necklace barely hanging on. "There's only one reason for Hartwell to lie. Because he didn't want anyone to know this woman was on the plane." Danica was pacing now, like a lioness. "But I saw her," she said, her voice rising. "And he's not gonna get away with it!"

"You've lost me, Danni."

"That woman was . . ." *Who exactly?* She balled her fists and pressed them to her temples. What seemed so clear a moment ago was slipping away. "Dammit, I'm confusing myself."

"Start at the beginning."

Danica spent an hour going over everything with Sam: the facts she knew, the questions she couldn't answer, the next steps she needed to take. Once she'd laid out the whole story, she realized how uncomplicated it really was. Hartwell had been cheating on his wife, and now he was lying to cover it up.

"You know the worst part?" Sam said. "He has all this sympathy going for him."

"Oh, he knows how to play the media, that's for sure. Hospital bed interview and everything. I can't wait to bust him."

"Why don't you just tell someone where that woman's body is?"

Danica remembered the massive fire that had burned all Friday morning. Her eyes darted back to the computer screen, where the airplane debris looked more like the remnants of a bonfire. "Anything in there got cremated," she said with an air of resignation. "Maybe there's some trace DNA, I don't know. They probably weren't looking for anyone after they retrieved the five bodies they expected to find."

Sam looked crestfallen.

"Don't worry," Danica said. "I'll get to the bottom of this."

"You know it'll end up being his word against yours."

"So?"

"He's a U.S. Senator and now a crash victim. And you're . . . well, never mind." Sam gave a wan smile. "I know one thing. If you can crack him, this story's gonna be huge."

Danica was way ahead of her. If Senator Hartwell had smuggled a mistress or some hooker onto the plane, revealing that secret would certainly end his political career. But she needed to tread carefully. Exposing the truth could put her in the crosshairs of some of the most powerful people in the nation.

"This is why I became a journalist," she told Sam. "To uncover facts and not let officials get away with lying. To make a difference."

"This is gonna be a hell of a career maker."

"I don't care about that."

Sam burst out laughing. "Oh yeah, I forgot," she said sarcastically. "You don't care about the money or the fame."

"I don't."

"Look, I love you to death, Danni, but don't kid yourself. You eat it up when people pay attention to you."

"What's your point?" Danica said, annoyed.

"It's a juicy story. Do what you do best. Take the bastard down. Just don't . . ."

"What?"

Sam stared solemnly into her eyes. "Don't forget who might get hurt."

The words struck Danica like a gut punch. She knew exactly what Sam was talking about. "This is different than the Wiesler story. And you know it."

"That's not what I'm saying."

Danica rubbed her temples again, her mind swimming with bad memories. For twelve years, she'd tried to forget her first big story. The one that brought down a corrupt assistant district attorney named Blaine Wiesler. The one that launched her career. The one that cost police officer Andrew Quinn his life.

She'd vowed to never let that happen again. "Hartwell's gonna answer for this," she said, her voice almost a whisper. "But if anyone gets hurt, it'll be his fault, not mine."

"You're not still blaming yourself for that cop getting killed, are you?"

Danica fell silent. She thought about all the times in therapy where she'd broken down in tears over the ordeal and the times she'd yearned to pick up the phone and beg forgiveness from the cop's widow.

Whether it was the Quinn debacle, Mario's untimely death, or her dad's abandonment of the family for a pot-smoking, twenty-something stripper, Danica knew the easiest way to deal with her sadness was to ignore it, to power through to the next story.

"What I need to do," Danica said, finally, "is figure out who that woman was." She looked into Sam's eyes and forced herself to smile, as if the red light on a news camera had suddenly come on. "And you're gonna help me."

"I have an idea," Sam said, lowering the foot of the recliner. She fastened the Velcro straps on her walking boot and stood. "Let's get out of here. Go shopping. Clear your mind for a couple of hours."

"I'd rather stay here."

"And wallow? I don't think so. Here's the deal. I'm making the rest of the decisions today."

Danica rolled her eyes. "Oh, I see how this works."

"The way I figure it, you owe me."

"How's that?"

"Well, I've been forced to watch those dumb 'Dah-nica Corrrrrrtez' promos for the past couple of days. The least you could do is buy me a new purse."

Danica chuckled and her phone rang again. She answered it without thinking.

"Um," a man said, and then he cleared his throat. "This is Garrison Sterling. I'm sorry for bothering you."

Oh, right. Him again.

"Please don't hang up." His voice trailed off, then he took a deep breath. "I have to ask a favor."

"Hang on a second." Danica covered the phone and told Sam, "It's this guy again. Can you pretend to need me so I can get off the phone?"

Sam placed her hands on her hips. "A man calls you out of the blue and you want to get rid of him? Honey, there's a difference between playing hard to get and building a wall. Talk to him." Then she pointed and said, "Remember, I make the decisions today."

Danica frowned at Sam and lifted the phone to her face. "Sorry, I'm back."

"Zoey had a terrible weekend. Except for Saturday, when she spent time with you. Is there any chance you could carve out a couple of hours to teach her some tennis?"

In a perfect world, she would have loved hanging out with Zoey. But his timing was terrible, especially given her job responsibilities and the magnitude of the Hartwell story. "I'm not a tennis coach."

"I know. Maybe just one time? It would mean the world to her."

Danica remembered Zoey's big smile on the tennis court and her look of gratitude in the bathroom, and felt pleased she'd been able to help the girl in some small way. "But why me?"

"You saw me out there. I was trying my best." He sighed. "You two seemed to hit it off."

"That's sweet, but I've got this job that has me working all hours."

"I've looked into it. Tennis is one of the few sports that allows Zoey to be a normal kid. She'd practice anytime you want. She's home from school every day at four. Maybe you could surprise her. I'll text you our address."

"It's not that simple." *Jeez, can't this guy take a hint?*

"Danica, I mean, Miss Cortez—"

"Danica's fine. I just don't think I should make promises I can't keep."

"I want Zoey to be happy. You could really make a difference."

His words echoed in her head. *Make a difference.* That was her reason for studying journalism in the first place, the reason for taking a job at a local TV news station, the reason for volunteering at a food pantry.

"Danica, I have to be honest. I'm kinda desperate here."

She covered the phone again and looked to Sam. "He wants me to play tennis with his daughter."

"The girl in the wheelchair you told me about? Go for it."

"I wish I could, but . . ." An image flashed of seeing Zoey for the first time, moping and sulking after playing with her dad, driving around the court as if she hated being there. Then she pictured the look of unabashed joy on Zoey's face the first time she drilled a forehand and the secret smile they had shared after Zoey smacked the ball over the fence. Of course she wanted to help—she was just too busy.

Sam studied her. "You know what I think? This girl reminds you of Mario." Danica flinched at the mention of her brother but knew her friend was right. "I know you played tennis with him," Sam said softly, taking her hand. "And I know how much you miss him. Danni, I think maybe you need this girl even more than she needs you."

Danica twisted a finger around a curl of her hair, pondering what Sam had said. Then she raised the phone and cleared her throat. "Let me think about it."

Chapter 19

Brimming with confidence, Zoey rolled through the front entrance of her school on Monday morning. For the past couple of years, she'd always been the slow-to-develop one. Even though her breasts were still too small to attract attention, a big change had happened over the weekend. Zoey Sterling had joined the club.

Traveling past the trophy cases, she saw a knot of young girls, flat-chested sixth graders who still looked like they were in elementary school. "Hang in there," she wanted to shout, "your time is coming."

She couldn't wait to find Cara and tell her everything. Although she'd already forgiven her for cancelling the sleepover—Zoey totally understood how difficult a dad could be when he got an idea in his head—she was still hurt by the way Cara had failed to keep her in the loop.

As Zoey zoomed up the hallway, all she could think about was this past weekend, playing tennis and getting her period, each for the first time. No one knew about it, of course, except for Danica, who seemed nice for a total stranger, and Dad, who had been so tongue-tied he couldn't bring himself to talk about it. With no mom to confide in, she knew that her best friend might be the only one who'd understand.

Cara's first period had occurred more than a year ago, and Zoey never heard the end of it. Apparently the occasion was akin to the arrival of the Pope, and Cara's mother had recognized—no, celebrated—her daughter's "graduation" by whisking her off for a spa treatment in the Galleria and, later, buying her a cute blouse and the latest iPhone.

"Don't you think that was a little over the top?" Zoey had wanted to ask Cara the next day, especially since the grand event would repeat itself a month later. But she'd held her tongue and even commiserated when Cara endured cramps and had to lie down in the nurse's office.

Zoey wasn't looking forward to the bleeding and the bloating—"the killer bees," as Cara called them—but knew it had to be better than feeling like she was the only girl who would never become a woman.

And now she had.

She rounded a corner onto a long, wide hallway and spotted Erik Finco ahead on her right, standing near the lockers and laughing with some other jocks. A head taller and more muscular than other boys his age, Finco—everybody called him Finco—was loud and obnoxious. But he always seemed to have guys and girls listening to his every word.

He'd never given Zoey a second look.

Students moved through the hall like carpenter ants, lugging backpacks and armfuls of books, steering clear of Finco and his buddies. As Zoey drew closer, she noticed a stray ant, a boy she recognized from her English class, walking up the hallway close to the lockers before finding himself blocked by the group of jocks. The boy shuffled left, then right, looking confused when they matched his movements.

Then Finco shoved him to the floor.

Zoey tried to stop, but the boy was right in front of her, his arms reflexively covering his face, and she couldn't help it. She banged into his legs and rolled over his foot.

One of the jocks high-fived Finco. "Two losers for the price of one. Good job, dude."

Zoey glared at them. "Stop being mean."

Finco smirked. "Ooh, I'm so scared. What are you gonna do? Kick me in the nuts?"

"Someone ought to," she muttered.

The boy who had fallen, Lucas Hardesty, placed a hand on Zoey's wheelchair and raised himself from the floor. His eyes met hers, and she could see thankfulness and embarrassment flicker across his face.

"Look, her little dork buddy is standing up. Five bucks he pissed himself."

Lucas moved behind the wheelchair and leaned down. "You okay?" he whispered. When she nodded, he said, "Come with me."

A minute later they reached the library, Zoey having taken over the pushing once they turned the corner. Lucas inspected his backpack for damage, then brushed dust from his blue jeans.

"I'm sorry I ran over you."

"Not your fault," he replied, bending the temples of his wire-rimmed glasses back into place and polishing them with the hem of his t-shirt. "Those guys are jerks."

Lucas Hardesty was one of those eighth graders who'd accomplished more in his middle school career than many of his peers would during their entire lives. He was a straight-A student, a member of the yearbook staff, and the best trombonist in the band. But none of that mattered, because the Populars had deemed him a non-person.

Just like her.

"One day," he said, "I'd like to get back at those d-bags."

"Don't sink to their level, Lucas. You're better than those guys. Everyone knows that."

He seemed to contemplate what she'd said, shrugged, and gave a crooked grin.

And Zoey noticed for the first time that Lucas Hardesty,

self-professed math geek and band nerd, the only boy in English class who actually read the assignments, a guy she'd basically ignored since third grade, was kind of cute.

"Hey, there," Cara called, peeking her head from behind Zoey's locker door.

"You're back. How was Dallas?"

"Oh my gosh. You won't believe what happened to me at Six Flags."

"I had a big weekend, too—"

"There's this boy. Jeffrey Throckmorton the Third or something. Anyway, Jeffrey's from Arlington and he's a sophomore. He has a driver's license and everything!"

Zoey's shoulders slumped. She had seen this look in Cara's eyes before. From the first day they'd met two years ago at band camp, when Cara spent the entire lunch break telling about their family vacation to Yellowstone, which included not one but four separate sightings of black bears, Zoey knew that when Cara began talking, it was best to step back and let her finish.

"You should see Jeffrey. He's crazy hot. I met him in line at the Shock Wave. He was wearing this badass Slytherin t-shirt, and I swear he looked just like Draco Malfoy."

"Wow," Zoey mumbled, not knowing what else to say.

The tardy bell rang and Cara scowled up at it. "I've got so much to tell you."

"Me too," Zoey said, but Cara had already spun on her heels and was headed toward the classroom door.

When Zoey rolled into the room, Ms. Pettigrew was messing with video equipment. Today they would begin watching a film version of *Romeo and Juliet*, the one with Leonardo DiCaprio and Claire Danes in the lead roles. She couldn't remember how many times she'd seen the movie—three seemed about right—

but she still liked it, especially because everyone spoke the original Shakespearean dialogue. Not to mention she absolutely adored Leonardo DiCaprio. The first time she saw him as Romeo, which was a week after she watched *Titanic* on DVD, she spent days writing *Mrs. Leonardo DiCaprio* and *Leo + Zoey* all over her notebook.

The monitor turned blue, and Zoey realized she had only a small window of opportunity before the film started. "Hey, Cara," she whispered, leaning toward the desk next to her. "On my birthday, I got my—"

"See?" Cara interrupted, shoving her phone at Zoey and flashing a photo of a long-haired blond guy that looked like exactly like Draco Malfoy. "This is Jeffrey. Mad hot, huh?"

Zoey frowned. She never could get a word in edgewise with Cara, who always seemed to one-up her on everything. She was last chair clarinet; Cara was first chair. She was struggling in Spanish; Cara spoke it at home. Plus, Cara had a home on the golf course and two parents. It wasn't fair.

"I had an interesting weekend," Zoey whispered urgently. "Guess what happened?"

A throat cleared in front of the room. "Miss Sterling, do you have something to say?"

Zoey gulped and looked up to see Ms. Pettigrew, her face pinched in disapproval.

"If you have something important to share with the class, go right ahead. Because apparently my rules do not apply to you."

A wave of heat rose in her face and on the back of her neck. "I'm . . . I'm sorry, Ms. Pettigrew."

She could feel the stares from other students and was glad she hadn't spilled her news in public. Feeling as self-conscious as she had on her first day of kindergarten, when all the other kids murmured and pointed at her, Zoey wished she could just disappear.

The lights eventually dimmed and the movie started. Zoey sagged into her chair and let out a huge breath. She laid her head in her hand, her elbow propped on the wheelchair's armrest. And thought about Romeo and Juliet.

They weren't much older than she, of course, teenagers destined to be together but kept apart by their warring families. Her favorite scene in the film was the first time the lovers meet, when Romeo spies Juliet through the glass of an aquarium, runs after her, and steals a kiss. That would be so romantic, Zoey thought, being kissed by someone as gorgeous as Leonardo. She sighed.

But Romeo and Juliet's big kiss was a bit further along in the movie, and Zoey didn't care for all the blood and gunfights in the early scenes, so she let her eyes drift from the screen to the darkened classroom. Ms. Pettigrew sat doing paperwork, a couple of girls communicated using sign language, a boy lay asleep at his desk.

Then she saw Lucas.

His head happened to turn in her direction, and their eyes momentarily locked on to each other. He flashed a lopsided smile. She felt an unexpected flutter in her stomach and quickly looked away. After a moment, she summoned the courage to glance his way again.

"Watch the movie, Miss Sterling."

Zoey's eyes whipped to the screen and stayed there a solid five minutes—she was sure any further attempts at eye contact would get her into more trouble. But she needed to know whether the moment between them had been an accident . . . or something more. She raised her eyes to the teacher, hoping she'd be distracted.

Ms. Pettigrew was staring right at her.

With a sigh, Zoey gave up and turned back to the movie. But soon it grew boring because Leonardo wasn't onscreen. Her eyelids grew heavy. She stifled a yawn. And eventually the voices of Capulets and Montagues faded into background noise.

A sharp elbow from Cara woke her up. "Nap time's over."

"What?" she said, confused. The fluorescent lights were so bright that she had to shield her eyes. After blinking her pupils back to normal, she realized the room was half-empty.

"You're lucky Ms. Pettigrew didn't see you. She already busted Tommy. Of course, he was snoring."

"Where's Lucas?"

"Come on, let's get out of here. I want to tell you about Jeffrey." She grimaced and pointed at Zoey's face. "And wipe that drool from your chin. You look like a retard."

In the bathroom, Zoey watched as Cara checked out her makeup in the mirror. Cara wore a lot of makeup these days, especially around her eyes, and Zoey thought it made her look different . . . and not in a good way.

"So you met some boy?" Zoey said.

"Jeffrey is not a boy," Cara huffed. "He's mature." She pulled back the collar of her blouse to reveal a red mark on her neck. "See? He gave me a hickey."

"Oh my gosh. When did you—"

"While we were waiting for the big rollercoaster. I guess we got carried away."

"Where was your dad?"

Cara rolled her eyes. "Who cares? Jeffrey and I were having fun," she said, smiling as she ran a tube of strawberry-scented gloss over her lips. "I let him touch my boobs."

Zoey couldn't believe what she was hearing. What had happened to her best friend, the girl who just three months ago had been worrying about her UIL audition? Now she was acting all weird and slutty. At the same time, Zoey knew she had to support her friend, even if she didn't understand her.

"I asked Jeffrey to come visit me this summer."

"You're kidding, right?"

Cara put her hands on her hips and gave a disapproving stare. "You wouldn't understand. Jeffrey really cares about me. He's texted me, like, twenty times since I got home."

That was enough for Zoey. "I gotta go. Or I'll be late for my next class."

Exiting the bathroom, Cara said, "Hey, didn't you want to tell me something?"

Zoey looked at her best friend, unsure who she even was anymore. "Never mind. I'll tell you at lunch."

"Yeah, about lunch. I'm busy."

Zoey did a double-take and lifted her hands off her rims. Cara was going to screw her over again? Maybe she shouldn't have been surprised, but she was. Cara had left her hanging on Friday, had been gone all weekend, and now she was blowing off lunch. It was almost as if Cara didn't care how hurtful she was being.

Around the corner, Tiffany and her friends suddenly appeared, reeking of heavy perfume and arrogant condescension. "Yuck," Zoey said. "It's those stupid witches again. Know what I mean?"

Cara didn't reply.

Zoey's eyes darted to where her friend had been. Cara was gone. She must have seen the Populars coming and booked it out of there. A little easier to do when you're not in a wheelchair.

A loud cackle rose from the approaching girls, and Zoey lowered her head. If she stayed invisible, they would simply leave her alone. So she pretended to rummage through her backpack.

When she finally looked up, her mouth fell open.

Cara was with *them*.

Chapter 20

G arrison arrived at NASA half an hour early, planning to go straight to his boss's office. If he could brief Chip on his findings ahead of time, maybe he wouldn't get stuck in the project status meeting. He proceeded through the security gates and swung his van into the parking lot, a wide span of concrete that could have passed for the moon's surface, considering the number of potholes it had.

For fifty years, NASA had called Houston home, and its Johnson Space Center campus of a hundred-plus buildings was not only a testament to mankind's capacity to reach for the stars but also a reminder that 1960s architecture was incredibly boring. Garrison appreciated functionality as much as the next person—maybe even more so—but the cold, repetitive design of the NASA buildings reminded him of a prison.

Standing in front of Chip's closed office door, Garrison ran a finger over the engraved nameplate and felt a pang of envy for his old buddy. The celebrated Alan "Chip" Chipperfield turned heads wherever he went at Johnson Space Center. He stood six-foot-three—almost exceeding the maximum height requirement for shuttle astronauts—and sported a head of perfect hair and a mouth of perfect teeth. He was the kind of television-friendly astronaut that NASA liked to trot out to the public. And he was well-known for his flashy lifestyle, which included a trophy wife and his ubiquitous red sports car, anything from a Corvette to a Mustang to a Viper. Garrison had seen that one in the parking lot.

Anyone would be jealous of a guy like that. But Garrison had a deeper reason.

For years, Chip had been like a brother. The two of them shared a friendly rivalry going back to their early days as members of the same astronaut class, *The Sardines*, always competing with each other, always trying to one-up each other. Back when Garrison earned his seat on Columbia, his celebration had been that much sweeter because he'd beaten Chip to the punch.

Eventually the tables turned, and he could only watch as Chip landed the dream assignments. First, there was the mission specialist role on Atlantis. Garrison had done his best to be supportive but couldn't shake his disappointment. After Chip performed an extended EVA during his second flight, Garrison had presented him with a model of the Space Shuttle Endeavour, the first one he'd ever built.

It was supposed to have been the two of them, Butch Cassidy and the Sundance Kid, rocketing into space. But Butch Cassidy had been grounded, and the Kid had zoomed along without him, performing the final servicing operation on the Hubble telescope during his third flight and then being selected to the committee studying the space shuttle's replacement. Now Chip was program manager for the Houston division of the James Webb Space Telescope program. His ego "no longer fit inside the payload bay," as Anita Holmquest was fond of saying, but he had always treated Garrison right.

Ever since the tragedy, Chip had been there for him, first spearheading a collection for Zoey's future education in memory of Celeste, then pulling strings to assign Garrison to only Houston-based projects, and even arranging a free trip to Disney World. Chip may have had a Texas-size ego, but he also had a Texas-size heart. And he was Garrison's best friend.

"Come in," Chip called when Garrison knocked. "Long time, buddy," he said, gripping Garrison's hand with an eager handshake. "How's Zoey?"

"She's good," he replied, knowing that Chip had no comprehension of what parenting involved, considering he was on wife number three and still childless, apparently by mutual agreement. "You don't need me for the status meeting, do you?"

"Hold that thought. I gotta hit the head. When I get back, I've got lots to talk about."

Chip rocketed out the door, and Garrison found himself alone. He sat at Chip's round conference table and waited. He played a bored game of thumb war with himself. He played Sudoku on his cell phone. He wondered how he was going to fix the binocular chair.

Eventually, he let his gaze drift through the room's floor-to-ceiling windows. One of the consequences of working at NASA was that sometimes project teams were exiled to buildings on the edge of JSC's main campus, which Garrison didn't mind so much because there were fewer people to interact with. And because he had a great view of the area he'd called home for fifteen years.

To his east, at the edge of Clear Lake, he could see the landmark Nassau Bay Hilton, the hotel known not only for its great height but for its parking lot, where satellite news trucks had gathered in the aftermath of Hurricane Ike and where infamous murderess Clara Harris had once "accidentally" run over her cheating husband—three times—with her Mercedes-Benz. But Garrison remembered the Hilton more fondly as the place where he and Celeste had spent a romantic weekend during the last months of her pregnancy.

Farther east, light poles towered above the tennis courts of

Clear Lake Park. He instantly thought of Zoey and their terrible tennis outing over the weekend. All he'd wanted was to be a good dad and let her have fun on her birthday. But not a single thing had gone right.

He wondered how she was feeling, so he reached into his pocket and checked his cell phone. No messages.

Garrison felt of twinge of unease. She'd promised to text him by noon, and he was still second-guessing his decision to let her attend the Spanish Club outing. Even though she'd assured him the school would transport everyone to and from Lupe Tortilla, he didn't like the idea of not being there to help.

That's it, he thought. He could shuttle her to the Mexican restaurant himself. And if she didn't mind, he could even wait around in the van until she was finished. It was such a solid plan that he couldn't understand why he hadn't thought of it before.

He started punching the numbers to call her, but the office door suddenly flung open. It was Chip's administrative assistant. "Garrison, there you are! You're late. Everyone's waiting for you in the conference room."

He pocketed the phone and frowned. He'd have to call her later. The status meeting wouldn't go on that long.

Three hours later, and Garrison was still stuck in the same project meeting, half-listening to the video teleconference that had begun a few minutes ago. He kept glancing down at the phone in his lap, hoping Zoey would text him back. It was so annoying when she stayed out of touch, and he sometimes thought she did it on purpose.

Teenagers. Did anyone know how to raise them?

His parents did, except they were long gone. His colleagues were all divorced or single, or they were dinosaurs like Henry Choate, who was so old that his teenagers may have watched

Neil and Buzz walk on the moon. The only person who'd seemed to forge any bond with Zoey—Danica Cortez—had flaked out on him, not even bothering to contact him since yesterday's telephone conversation.

And that was a shame. For the past day, he kept finding himself thinking about her. Danica had been the only one to bring a smile to Zoey's face . . . and to his own face, for that matter. There was something beautiful about her and not just that she was possibly the most attractive woman he'd come across. But he had to accept the fact that her intersection in their lives was a one-time thing.

"Bullshit," a voice said through the teleconference speaker, and Garrison raised his eyes.

The grainy video screen showed a bunch of suits sitting around a table, NASA administrators from the Human Exploration and Operations Directorate. "Need . . . schedule impact . . ." said a stern-looking man onscreen, but half the words were getting chopped out and it sounded like he was talking inside a tin drum. Garrison could make out the words "quality" and "slippage" and "jeopardized," which made his stomach do loop-de-loops. The last thing he needed was for Washington bean-counters to muck things up.

Then the audio dropped away completely.

"This is such a waste of time," said the guy on his left, a ruddy-complexioned man fated to have a quadruple bypass one day. "We lost the connection again."

Chip stood and crossed his arms. "Then fix it, Ed. And I don't want to hear any complaining when they get back on the line. They're the ones with our balls in their hands. I don't want to give them any reason to squeeze."

No one dared mention the rumors, but bigwigs in Washington were supposedly having serious concerns about JWST's budget and schedule. Even though the Houston team was hitting every milestone, there were reports that the whole program might be defunded. It was the same kind of disquieting talk Garrison had heard before, when President Bush announced the end of the shuttle missions. He felt a twist in his gut.

"I can't reestablish audio," Ed said, finally throwing up his hands. "It's not a problem on our end."

"Message them," Chip said. "Tell them I'll reschedule the meeting. And apologize for the technical problems. The rest of you—I guess we're done."

Garrison closed his spiral notebook and pushed back his chair.

"Not so fast," Chip said. "I want to talk with you. My office."

"Take a seat," Chip said, motioning to his conference table, the one made from quilted maple that he had surreptitiously "acquired" when he landed his current position. "We haven't talked in a while."

Garrison didn't like it when Chip wasn't flashing his trademark smile. "What's up?"

Chip sighed. "End of an era, man. Can you believe there's only going to be one more shuttle flight?"

"Thirty years. Blink of an eye." He could barely remember Columbia's maiden flight with Young and Crippen, which occurred back when he was in middle school, although he'd followed every single flight since the Challenger disaster.

"Glad it's gonna be Atlantis, though." Chip gave a rueful smile. "She was my first. Took my space virginity."

Garrison studied him, confused by his buddy's sudden nostalgia. "I didn't think you were the sentimental type."

Chip cleared his throat, then pulled at the collar of his shirt. "I was just wondering. Have you thought about what you want to do after this project?"

"Are you trying to tell me something?"

"It's been great working together again. Just like the old

days. Butch and Sundance, remember?" He reached up and lifted the Endeavour model from its shelf. "You gave this to me after my first flight."

"Actually, it was your second. Now tell me what the hell is going on."

Chip scrunched up his face. "They're transferring me to Goddard."

"The mother ship?" Located in Maryland, a few miles from Washington, D.C., Goddard Space Flight Center was a major NASA research lab and the management hub for the James Webb Space Telescope program. Their truncated videoconference had been with Goddard senior management. "Hold on," Garrison said, the hollow in his gut returning. "What's gonna happen to our work at JSC?"

Neither of them said anything, then Chip finally took a deep breath. "Maybe you should check around. See if another project interests you. You'd be perfect for the Mars rover. Or you can transfer to Goddard."

The last thing Garrison wanted was change. "I'm staying here until they lock the doors. Wait, are the rumors true?"

Chip shook his head. "Congress is still jacking around. The only saving grace is that Senator Hartwell didn't die in that plane crash this weekend. You heard about it, right?"

He nodded.

"If Hartwell had been killed, we would have been screwed. Can you imagine Senator Phillips heading up the Appropriations Committee instead of Hartwell? She'd take all our money and funnel it to California." Chip placed the model of Endeavour in the middle of the table. "I don't know what's going to happen, but you and I have been together a long time. I thought you'd want a heads-up."

His mind was swirling. Was his job actually in jeopardy?

Chip ran his fingers along the shuttle model. "You know, this is much better quality than that crap everybody else sells. I love all the details, like the way the main engines gimbal away from each other. You've got an artist's eye."

Garrison scoffed. "At least if I lose my job, I'll have something to fall back on. Me and my little cardboard sign. Will build models for food."

"I'm serious, Garrison. There's a market for stuff like this. How much is that museum paying you for that big shuttle you're building?"

He shrugged. "It's a favor for Anita."

"You gotta be kidding me. They should be paying you, like, a few thousand bucks."

"Well, they are paying for materials."

Chip raised an eyebrow. "What happened to the Butch Cassidy I knew, the brash guy who could ride a centrifuge all day long without puking? He wouldn't have let people take advantage of him."

The words cut Garrison to the quick, but he didn't say anything. A lifetime ago, he'd been that risk-taking outlaw, but that was before his wife was murdered and his daughter was turned into a paraplegic. Watching Butch and Sundance jump off a cliff may have seemed cool in the safety of a darkened theater, but in the harsh light of reality, Garrison understood that taking risks was simply irresponsible.

"So," he said, "you're moving to Goddard. What does Janet think?" Janet was wife number three in the Chipperfield marriage carousel, and if Chip cheated on her like he'd done with his first two, Janet would be ex-wife number three as well.

Chip shot him a look that said *you-really-want-to-go-there?* and steepled his fingers in front of his face. "I talked with Anita Holmquest this morning. She called me from Waco. She's worried."

"Stay out of my business, Chip. I've got everything under control."

"I'm gonna do you a favor. Take the next three days off. Think of it as comp time for all those hours you've been putting in. Finish your model and think about what you want to do after this project."

"I don't need to—"

"Three days," Chip said, crossing his arms. Then his face softened. "Go find Butch Cassidy."

Garrison climbed onto the treadmill in his workshop and selected his usual cardio program. Within a few minutes, he had settled into a hard uphill pace. He tried to concentrate on anything other than work—the expansive starfield poster he'd mounted on the wall in front of him, the various rocket models he'd already completed and the ones still planned, the binocular chair he still needed to fix—but his mind kept coming back to Chip's news.

What would happen if everything fell apart?

A decade ago—even five years ago—he had been one of the top engineers at NASA, their resident expert in advanced polymers. Ever since, as he hopped from one project to another, a new wave of engineers had joined NASA and its subcontractors, armed with skills he'd never have a chance to acquire. Now he was tasked with performing risk analysis and project autopsies, figuring out what had gone wrong instead of coming up with solutions himself. Maybe Henry Choate wasn't the only dinosaur anymore.

That's right, Garrison. You're not the man you used to be.

He bumped the treadmill speed up to seven miles an hour, as if trying to run away from the inner voice. But no matter how fast he ran, he couldn't get away from the truth. He needed that job.

Still clinging to your little fantasy? Working at NASA doesn't make you an astronaut.

He hit the stop button and leaned against the treadmill, his head in his hands. If he did get laid off, he didn't want to end up staring at the walls of this place, listening to the dark urges of his inner voice. But he didn't want to go pound the pavement and look for a new career either. No, what he wanted—what he needed—was for things to stay the same. Safe and predictable.

He left the workshop and headed toward the kitchen, needing something to quench his thirst and rebuffing his inner voice's suggestion of something alcoholic. As he passed through the hallway, he surveyed the photos lining the wall, some at eye level but most lower so Zoey could see them. He touched the glass of a family portrait they'd had taken a couple of months before everything happened, wishing he could turn back the clock to the time when his life actually was safe and predictable.

The doorbell rang in the distance. Not wanting to talk to some salesman, he ignored it. Then the doorbell rang again, followed by a loud rapping on the glass.

He rounded the corner and looked out.

There stood Danica Cortez.

Chapter 21

Garrison closed his eyes and took a deep breath. For the past day, his hopes for breaking Zoey out of her funk had rested on Danica. Now here she was, on the other side of the door.

He swung it open and was greeted, not by her smiling face, but by the sight of her rear end, clad in a turquoise tennis skirt. She was bending away from him, her hands rustling through a tennis bag, and he couldn't help but smile. "Hello?"

She spun around, flustered, and tried to smooth down her skirt. "I hope this is a good time," she said, straightening her matching tank top.

Her breasts swelled as she pulled on the fabric of her tank, and he found himself momentarily distracted. His opened and closed his mouth, forgetting what he was about to say.

"I know I should have called you back," she said. "But you texted me your address and said to drop by anytime." She frowned. "My fault."

He waved his hands. "No, no, don't worry about it. I'm glad you're here." The words came out as simple platitudes, but the truth was that he was thrilled to see her. Ever since their telephone conversation, Danica was all he could think about. He wondered why she'd been so willing to lend a hand to someone she didn't know, and why she'd been out playing tennis a day after rescuing someone from a burning plane. She seemed too good to be true. Earlier today, he'd flipped on the morning news for the first time in forever just to convince himself she was real.

"So, can I see Zoey?"

"Of course. Come in and I'll tell her—" He stopped with the sudden realization that Zoey was away on her field trip.

Danica got a quizzical look on her face. "Something wrong?"

"Um . . . Actually, Zoey's at school. Well, sort of."

"I'm confused. Is she here or not?"

He grimaced. "No."

"Well, today was really the only time I had available. I'd hoped we might get in a little tennis before I had to head home. I've got an early-morning job."

"You're on TV."

She pressed her lips into a tight smile. "That's right." Then she stepped back off the porch and said, "Tell Zoey I'm sorry I missed her."

He knew that if Danica walked away now, she'd never come back. Which meant he'd disappoint Zoey once again. "She'll be home soon," he fibbed, knowing it would be well over an hour before he needed to pick her up. "Please. Come in."

"You sure I'm not interrupting?"

He thought of the shuttle model that needed final assembly, the binocular chair that needed a design fix, and the dinner that needed to be prepared. Five minutes ago, he was happy to spend his afternoon working on those. Now they didn't seem to matter.

He swung open the door and made a sweeping gesture. The phrase "*Mi casa es su casa*" came to mind, but not only did he think it sounded dorky, he thought she might take it the wrong way. Instead, he said, "Come on in." Then he ushered her into the family room, her tennis shoes making little squeaky noises as she walked across the hardwood floor. He averted his eyes from her tennis skirt.

"Nice house. Not many one-stories here in Clear Lake."

He nodded, unsure of what to say. When he and his wife originally moved to the area after he was accepted into the astronaut program, they had lived in one of those two-story McMansions with four bedrooms, a game room and a media room, with everything located upstairs. But Zoey and stairs were obviously incompatible, so within six months of Celeste's death and Zoey's injury, he'd had to pack up one home and find another, all the while wondering why he was even sticking around Clear Lake.

"You been playing tennis a long time?" he asked, trying to steer the conversation to a more mundane topic.

"Since before high school. And then in college. Had a scholarship that helped pay for my undergrad."

"I kinda figured. But how do you know about wheelchair tennis? Is that a new thing?"

"I used to play with my brother," she replied softly. "His name was Mario. He had muscular dystrophy."

He could see why Zoey had taken such an instant liking to her; she was obviously a gentle soul. "That's a cruel disease," he replied. "I'm sorry."

She raised a fist to her mouth and took a couple of deep breaths through it. "May I use your restroom?"

"Sure. Down the hall. Second door on the right."

As she disappeared from the room, he rubbed a hand across his chin. Had he upset her? He sure hadn't meant to. As he tried to think of ways to make her feel more welcome, he glanced around the room and realized how untidy it was. Normally he kept the place neat and organized, but he'd been spending most evenings in his workshop and now the house was a mess.

"Where are you?" she called from the other room.

"In the kitchen. I'll be right out." *Pull yourself together*, he thought, then took two glasses from the cabinet and filled them with ice and lemonade, just as his mom had taught him. "Lemonade turns strangers into friends," she used to say. He smiled at the old memory.

"I love these photos," Danica called out, as if she'd somehow sensed he was thinking about his mom.

A decade ago, after he and Zoey moved into the new house, his mom and dad came and lived with them for three months. Dad took care of mowing the lawn and doing odd jobs around the house, while Mom cooked their meals and washed their laundry. Having Mom and Dad around actually made the horrific ordeal somewhat bearable.

One day he came home to see his mom hanging a series of framed pictures in the hallway. Her eyes were puffy and brimmed red, and it was clear she'd been crying a while.

"I'm not sure about this," he'd told her, motioning at the wall.

"I know it's hard, honey," Mom said, "but Zoey deserves to see pictures of her mother. Of her family." Her bottom lip quivered, and she began to weep.

For the sake of his mom and Zoey, he decided to keep all the pictures as she'd hung them, except for the one of him and Celeste at their wedding and his official astronaut portrait. He'd removed those and placed them in a box at the top of his closet, unwilling to face that pain every day.

"Would you like something to drink?" he called to Danica.

"I'm good. Just looking at all these pictures."

He laid the glasses of lemonade on the coffee table, then checked his watch to see when he'd need to leave to pick up Zoey. Would Danica stick around in the interim?

Laughter flowed from the hallway, a sound that was generally foreign in the house. "Where did you take this? Disney World?"

He gave an unhappy grunt. That was the other photo he should have taken down.

When Zoey was nine months old, Celeste convinced him

that it would be cute to have some Winnie the Pooh pictures taken of her. Celeste had always been a big Disney fan—that's where they spent their honeymoon—and she'd decorated the baby room, not with any of the major characters like Mickey or Minnie, but with Pooh and his friends.

The morning of the photo shoot, Celeste snuggled close to him in bed. "Could you do me a teeny tiny favor?" she whispered into his ear.

And that's how he'd been scammed into having professional photos taken of Zoey wearing a cute Tigger costume, as Celeste posed behind her as a life-size Winnie the Pooh and he crawled on all fours in a furry, purple-and-grey Eeyore costume, complete with tail and droopy ears.

He dashed into the hallway to cover the picture with his hand. "Please ignore that. It was taken a long time ago."

"It's adorable."

"I've poured you some lemonade." He began walking back to the family room, but she didn't take the hint to follow.

"I really like the way you hang these pictures low on the wall. My family used to do the same thing."

The low-hanging pictures had been his mom's idea. Practically every photo was level with his waist, and she'd hung them that way to let Zoey see them better. At first he thought it looked odd, but he eventually came to realize he preferred looking at the span of empty wall instead of the photos beneath.

"Tell me about this one," Danica said, pointing to a collage of some fifteen snapshots that Celeste had put together only a month before she died.

A Sterling Year – 1998 was printed carefully across the bottom of the matte surface, and the frame held important snapshots from the year: Zoey learning to walk, Celeste posing next to her new car, the three of them standing in front of colorful hot air balloons on the NASA campus. There was a picture of him crossing the finish line at the Houston

Marathon, taken back when he was twenty pounds lighter.

"My wife . . . she liked doing that sort of thing." He didn't mention that Celeste had vowed to put together a collage every year so that their kids could see family history come alive on the walls and not tucked away in some scrapbook. And he didn't say that Celeste only lived long enough to frame 1997 and 1998.

"Excuse me for prying," Danica said, her eyes cast down, her cheeks blushing pink. "Just the habits of a news reporter."

Although he'd watched her on TV, he hadn't pegged Danica as the reporter type. Reporters were the people who'd hounded him in his driveway after Celeste's death, the newspaper columnist who'd wanted to interview him for an in-depth piece on the victims of random violence, the obnoxious TV guy who'd shown up at the hospital as Zoey was in surgery and tried to browbeat him into going on camera. Reporters were scum.

Although he wanted to give Danica the benefit of the doubt—she was probably nothing like the vultures that had pursued him—he certainly didn't feel like talking about Celeste anymore. He turned and headed back to the family room and could feel Danica trailing behind him. Sneaking a peek at his watch, he still had forty minutes before Zoey needed to be picked up. Maybe having Danica hang out here was a bad idea.

But what were his options? Allow her to leave and totally screw up his chance to make things right with Zoey? No, it would be better to deal with some awkwardness for a while.

He handed Danica the glass of lemonade and motioned for her to sit down. "I happened to see the news. Seems you're some kind of hero. Congratulations."

She managed a smile and shrugged her shoulders.

"We were just talking about it at work," he continued. "Senator Hartwell's a big supporter of NASA."

"You work at NASA?"

Back in the old days, he'd let that sort of question hang

there, give it a dramatic pause and then reveal he was an astronaut, just to watch the questioner's eyes widen. But he wasn't an astronaut anymore, hadn't been one in eleven years. "I'm an engineer," he said. "Mechanical. Material sciences. That kind of thing."

She nodded as her right hand slid into her tennis bag and pulled out a phone. She cast a surreptitious glance at it while sipping her lemonade. "When is Zoey gonna get here? I really can't stay long."

"Maybe half an hour."

"Half an hour?" she yelped, her voice an octave higher. "I thought you said she was coming home soon."

"It's not that long. And it won't take me but ten or fifteen minutes to pick her up."

"Wait a second. You mean a bus isn't dropping her off? Then why am I even here?" She grabbed her tennis bag and rose from the couch. "You made it sound like she was gonna come in the door any second. Respect me enough to tell the truth, Garrison."

"That wasn't what I . . . If you'd let me explain . . . Never mind, I just thought it would be great for you and Zoey to hang out today."

"Well, she's not here, is she?"

He shuffled his feet. "I guess not. I'm sorry. I should have been straight with you."

"I gotta go." She yanked a set of keys from her tennis bag with such force that they flew from her hand and shot straight toward Garrison's head. He ducked, and the keys clanged off the wall and fell with a jangly thud to the floor.

"Don't leave mad," he pleaded, and for some reason an image flashed of Celeste backing out of their driveway, flipping him off. "Please."

"Do you have any idea how frustrated I am?" She scooped the keys from the floor.

He clenched his fists at his side, trying to keep his own

frustration at bay. "At least let me walk you out."

Danica squeaked across the wood flooring toward the front door. She put a hand on the doorknob, then paused. "I do understand why you wanted me to stay."

"I just want Zoey to be happy."

She exhaled a deep sigh. "You know, I wasn't being straight with you either. Today's not my only available day. My afternoon schedule isn't that full."

"I'm not trying to lay a guilt trip on you."

He reached out instinctively and touched her arm, his fingers lightly brushing against her skin. A tiny charge of static electricity arced from her skin to his, and although his scientific mind understood that electrons were simply flowing to reach equilibrium, his emotional subconscious couldn't help but offer another theory: there was a spark between them.

"Maybe I could come by sometime when Zoey's actually here. How does tomorrow look?"

He stared at his hand, still resting on her arm, then pulled it back as if he'd just touched a hot stove.

"Tomorrow?" she repeated. "Zoey will be at home, right?"

Zoey. He shook his head, trying to clear it. "Y-yes," he stammered. "Four o'clock. Wait, make it four-fifteen. I don't want you to show up and she's not here."

Danica shook her head in mock annoyance. "Four-fifteen."

They exited the house together, and Danica strode to her car. She popped her trunk and tossed the tennis bag inside. This is finally going to work out, he thought. This was the perfect birthday present. He couldn't wait to see Zoey's face, to have her squeeze his hand and thank him and tell him how awesome he was.

Just then, his cell phone buzzed with a text message: *Back at school. Where are you?*

This'll be great, he thought. Maybe Danica would wait a few more minutes. He waved his arms and shouted, but she'd already crawled into the front seat. He whistled sharply, something his dad had taught him to do as a kid, but she didn't look his way. Then her engine turned over.

"Dammit," he muttered. A few lousy seconds and she might have hung around. Disappointed, he pressed the key fob and heard the van doors unlock. He figured he might as well head over to school and pick up Zoey. When he turned toward the van, his mouth fell open. He wasn't going anywhere.

The van had a flat tire.

Chapter 22

Danica started the car, then took a moment to scroll through her phone's email. Nothing from the senator's office, even though one of his assistants had contacted her at lunch to invite her to a press conference at the hospital the next morning.

She understood that her presence was only a public relations ploy by Senator Hartwell's reelection campaign, but since she'd been unable to speak with him directly in two days, she figured she might as well take advantage of the opportunity. Maybe she could conduct a brief interview before his discharge, get him on the record and then confront him with his lies.

Her foot depressed the brake, the transmission slipped into gear, and she rotated her head for a final over-the-shoulder safety check. She startled as a figure appeared in her window.

"I need your help," Garrison shouted.

Lowering the window, she said, "You scared the crap out of me."

"Zoey's waiting at school, and my van has a flat tire. Any chance you could—"

"Are you serious?"

"Look." He jabbed his thumb toward the driveway. One of

the van's rear tires was completely deflated, its rim practically resting on the concrete. "Her school's less than five minutes away. And don't worry, your car will work fine. We can store her wheelchair in the trunk." He offered a shy smile. "I really appreciate it."

"Get in."

It wasn't like her to let a stranger into her car, but there was something about Garrison that made her feel completely at ease. Maybe it was how earnest he seemed. Or how awkward he acted. Or maybe it was the sensation she'd felt when he'd touched her arm.

He climbed in next to her. "Thank you, Danica."

The timbre of his voice was like honey, and she suddenly became aware of his scent: a combination of fresh earth and leather, the fragrance of a man comfortable in his own skin.

"Sorry about your flat tire."

"I'm not. Some things are meant to be. I'm just glad you're not pissed at me anymore."

"Who says I'm not?" she said, chuckling.

As they drove through the neighborhood, they chatted about their first time together on the tennis court. She couldn't believe it had only been two days ago. She also couldn't believe that this was the same man who'd been pouting outside the fence.

"Seriously, Garrison," she said, shaking her head. "Who goes and plays tennis with only one racquet?" He laughed in response, and she joined in. "When that tennis ball bounced off Zoey's head, and then she threw her racquet . . . I tell you, I was totally cracking up."

A Texaco station appeared in the distance, and her laughter suddenly fell away.

"Take a left up there," Garrison said, his voice seeming distant.

Her hands began to shake, even though she was gripping the steering wheel as tightly as she could. *Not again.* She allowed her car to decelerate and pulled it to a stop at the red light.

Then she cast a nervous glance to the north, out the passenger window.

She'd stopped at this intersection practically every day, always turning right to take a shortcut to the beltway. The last time she'd turned that direction was Friday morning, when the weather had been so foggy she could barely see the handful of oncoming cars, could barely see the Texaco sign at the corner, could barely see the airplane as it tumbled from the sky.

Her eyes squeezed shut. She tried to think of anything else, but the disturbing images from that foggy morning kept pushing their way to the front of her mind. This was just like her nightmares.

"Are you okay?" Garrison asked, and she opened her eyes just as the light turned from yellow to red. He followed her gaze out his window. "That's where it happened, isn't it?"

She pressed her lips tightly and swallowed hard. This is exactly why she'd been taking another route to work the past few days, just to avoid this feeling.

"Wanna talk about it?"

"Nope."

The traffic light turned green again, and the driver behind her immediately laid on the horn. She drew a deep breath and pulled into the intersection, then quickly accelerated to forty miles an hour, trying to put distance between her and the catastrophe, between her and those memories.

A minute later, her breathing had become regular again. Her jaws no longer clamped together. She drove past a bank and dry cleaners, then past a donut shop and a Starbucks. This was the life she was familiar with, boring and suburban. When a two-story brick building appeared soon after, she said, "Is this where Zoey's gonna attend high school?"

"Yeah."

"In just a few months, right?"

"Don't remind me."

She passed the school's entrance and could see metal bleachers flanking a grassy field. "I remember thinking how fun high school was going to be. Football games, marching band, Friday nights. Zoey probably feels the same way."

"I guess."

"It can be kinda scary, though. Especially for girls. At least it was for me. When I was her age, we relocated to a new neighborhood, so I didn't know anyone. To top it off, my mom had just started her job, so I had to sign myself up for classes."

"All by yourself?"

"Mom couldn't take off work."

"What about your dad?"

She scoffed. "My dad walked out on us twenty years ago."

When she was thirteen, just after Mario's diagnosis, her dad packed three suitcases and drove away one Saturday afternoon to "find some happiness." She never knew what happiness he was searching for, or if he ever found it—and she didn't think his fling with a skanky college girl counted—but she stopped caring about him when he did the same about her.

"I admire anyone who sticks it out when times get tough," she told Garrison. "Like you. Gotta be hard raising Zoey all alone."

"It's not so bad. I'm used to it. We have a pretty good routine."

"I don't mean to be rude, but why is Zoey in a wheelchair? Is she sick?"

He shook his head. "It happened a long time ago."

"Car accident?"

"Something like that," he said, his expression pained. "Look, that's her middle school. Pull in and drive around back."

It was clear he didn't want to talk about why Zoey was in a wheelchair, and she could respect that. She felt awful for questioning him, but she also knew that if she could understand Zoey's past then that would make things easier. Besides, she thought, it was always better to know the truth.

Up ahead on the sidewalk, Zoey was sitting in the shade of a pecan tree. Her head was bent forward, a paperback book covering her face.

"Do me a favor, Danica? Stay in the car and let me talk to Zoey first?"

"You want to bag some brownie points with her. I completely understand." As she pulled her car to the curb, she thought about how different Garrison was from her own father. Here was this guy who'd been through an unspeakable tragedy, yet he was doing everything in his power to make his daughter happy.

"Back in a minute," he said, stepping out of the car.

"I'll wait for your signal." She cleared her throat. "Um, Garrison?"

"Yeah?"

"Zoey's lucky to have a dad like you."

"Where is he?" Zoey muttered, setting down the copy of *Romeo and Juliet* on her lap. She checked her phone again—Dad hadn't replied to her text message. Had he forgotten the time?

That would be just like him. The one time she needed him around, he was busy fiddling with one of his projects. Too bad he wouldn't stay that distracted when she tried to gain any small measure of independence. She'd seen her fair share of helicopter parents, but her dad was more like one of those top-secret "black helicopters," ever vigilant, always ready to swoop in.

She wiped her face to dry the sweat and thought about the horrible day she'd had. Visiting the school nurse had been embarrassing. Listening to Cara drone on about her new boyfriend had been annoying. But going on the field trip to Lupe Tortilla and sitting at the end of the table—all by herself—as a dozen other students laughed and chatted farther down, had been humiliating.

It all started because they brought the wrong bus. Everyone in her Spanish Club was whining about standing outside in the heat, and when the wheelchair-friendly bus finally came, no one even wanted to talk to her anymore. Then when they got to the restaurant, everyone ran inside and claimed the best seats. By the time the bus driver lowered her wheelchair and she rolled inside, the only available place at the table was next to her Spanish teacher, Señor Alvarez, whom she disliked because he had yellow teeth and always acted creepy. When she finally flagged down the waiter to get something to drink, he was bringing out everyone's food.

"Why didn't you order anything?" Señor Alvarez asked when everyone began diving into their enchiladas and fajitas.

A boy mumbled something she couldn't hear, and the table erupted in laughter.

Zoey lowered her eyes and dipped a tortilla chip into the bowl of salsa. "I'm not hungry," she murmured.

Only one thing had kept her day from being a complete disaster: talking with Lucas Hardesty. If he were a member of the Spanish Club, her field trip would have turned out differently. He would have waited with her at the bus, and he would have saved a place for her at the table. Because he was a nice guy. She couldn't wait to visit him the next day in English class before Ms. Pettigrew fired up *Romeo and Juliet* again.

"Hi, Zoey," her dad said, strolling up the sidewalk.

She frowned. "You're late."

"Paperwork said you weren't coming back until five-thirty."

"I told you this morning. Five o'clock. Can we go?"

He walked behind her wheelchair and began pushing it. "How was your field trip?"

She swatted an arm behind her. "I can do it, Dad."

"I know. Just trying to be nice. I've got a surprise for you."

"What, are you gonna install GPS on my chair?" She yanked the chair to one side and took over the pushing. Then she scanned the parking lot, which was sparsely filled with cars. "Where's the van?"

"About that. So, the van has a flat tire."

She hoped he wasn't going to deliver another long-winded monologue on the dangers of driving. "Look, Dad, I'm tired. I've had a long day. Cara was a total pain, and if you tell me you walked here from the house, I'm gonna scream.'"

"Stop being so dramatic."

Of all his phrases, that was the one that really pushed her buttons. Anytime she had a legitimate gripe, he would whip out the *drama queen* card. But he was the one who'd left her at school all alone. She could bitch if she wanted.

"How's your homework load tonight?"

"Ugh. I can't wait for school to be out. Because I'm—" She stopped and stared through the windshield of a green sedan parked at the curb. Could it be—?

Danica Cortez stepped out and smiled broadly. "I heard that someone was looking to play a little tennis."

"You remembered!" Zoey rolled down the wheelchair ramp and hugged her around the waist.

"Danica just dropped by the house," her dad said. "Wasn't that nice?"

"This is so awesome."

"It's all your father's doing," Danica said, nodding toward him. Then she whispered, "Maybe you should tell someone thanks."

"You're right," she squealed. "Thank you, Danica!"

Back at the house, Zoey went inside while her dad stayed in the driveway to change the tire. He'd pulled his usual party pooper act, suggesting tennis should wait until the van got fixed, but this time she didn't mind. She could have some one-on-one time with Danica.

She rolled into the kitchen for something to eat because her stomach was still growling. "You want anything?" she asked Danica, reaching for an orange in the fruit bowl.

"I'm good."

"Wanna see my room?" She spun her chair and led Danica through the family room and down the hallway, past a bunch of photos she rarely looked at anymore. She bumped open the door and led Danica inside. "Don't mind all the clothes on the floor. It's pretty messy. At least that's what Dad says."

"I've got a confession," Danica said, dropping her voice to a conspiratorial whisper. "Mine's just as messy."

Grinning, Zoey rolled to her bed and made the transfer, peeled the rind from her orange, and lay on the comforter, her head propped up on an elbow. "Tell me what it's like to be on TV. I want to be famous one day."

"Trust me, you don't want to be famous."

"That's gotta be better than everyone ignoring you. Right?" She broke off a wedge of orange and popped it in her mouth.

Danica sighed. "Mind if I sit down?" she asked, gesturing to the wheelchair.

"Yeah, no probs."

"I remember what it was like to be your age. Everyone feels like they don't fit in."

Oh, God. Zoey did not want to go down this road. Between her teachers and her dad, who was king of the lecturers, she'd heard all the standard-issue speeches. She fell silent and studied Danica, who was absently rocking back and forth in the wheelchair, her hands sliding on the rims with a practiced touch. "You really know what you're doing with that chair," Zoey said.

Danica stopped mid-rock. "My brother had one."

For some reason, this surprised Zoey. She rarely ran across

anyone in her same situation. "Your brother was in a wheelchair? Mario, right?"

"Yeah, Mario. You remembered his name, I'm impressed. I used to goof around with him in his extra chair. We raced each other around the house. I got pretty good at it. But . . ."

"But what?"

Danica bobbed her head as if she were trying to recall the story. "I haven't been in a wheelchair in years. Not since college."

"Why's that?" As soon as she'd asked the question, she winced, realizing the obvious. "I'm so sorry, Danica."

"That's okay. He'd been sick for a long time." She took a deep breath. "He was your age when he died."

Danica looked like she might cry, and Zoey couldn't help but feel a deep sadness for her new friend. Sensing Danica must have seen a bit of Mario in her, she said, "If you're wondering, I'm in a wheelchair because I got paralyzed. I'm not sick or anything."

"Yeah, your dad told me."

"He talked with you about what happened?"

"He cares about you a lot."

"You don't understand, Danica. My dad is, like, uber-protective of me. I'm totally shocked he'd share that. Did you know he freaks out when he's around strangers?"

"Freaks out?"

"We don't go to restaurants anymore. We can't go to the mall. It's so frustrating. I want to get out and live my life, but he's afraid to let me go. I mean, I love him, but he can be a real nutburger sometimes. I'm talking double-meat-with-cheese nutburger."

Danica spun the wheelchair in a tight circle. "I like you. You're so full of life."

Zoey beamed. No one had ever talked so nice to her before. She sat up and leaned against the wall, then pulled her legs over the edge of the bed. She bit into another slice of orange, the juice dripping down her chin. This conversation was exactly what she imagined a sleepover with friends would be like, discussing deep subjects and sharing secrets.

"Can I tell you something?" Zoey said.

"You bet."

"My best friend Cara doesn't know this, and neither does my dad. You can't tell anyone."

Danica nodded, then pantomimed zipping her mouth and locking it with a key.

"So," Zoey said, "today I met a boy."

Chapter 23

Immediately following Tuesday morning's newscast, Danica rushed to the world-renowned Texas Medical Center for Senator Hartwell's noon press conference.

According to the email exchange with one of his flunkies, she was supposed to sit in the front row and wait for the senator to ask her the first question. She couldn't wait.

She walked into St. Luke's Episcopal Hospital over an hour early, thanks to the light traffic on the freeway and a heavy foot on the accelerator. The press conference was slated for the Denton A. Cooley Building, an airy and spacious addition to St. Luke's that was named after the famous heart surgeon. After comparing the room number she'd been given against the number on the engraved sign, she pushed open the door.

The place was already crammed full of people. In the back of the room, TV cameras lined the wall. Up front, a row of tables was covered with at least a dozen microphones, each wrapped with a mic flag sporting the logo of a local or national news network.

"Excuse me," she said to a man wearing an official-looking hospital badge around his neck.

"Like I already told everyone," he said, "They'll get here when they get here."

"Isn't this supposed to start at noon?"

"Honey, I don't know where you get your information, but this was scheduled to start at ten-thirty." He checked his watch. "And it's supposed to be over by now."

"I'm Danica Cortez with Eyewitness9."

"I don't care if you're frickin' Katie Couric. Just close the door and find a seat."

Confused, she wandered to the front of the room and scanned the line of chairs, each occupied with a reporter scribbling on a notepad or playing with a smartphone. "I'm supposed to be up here," she said. "Anybody sitting in a reserved seat?"

Barb Edwards of Channel Five scowled at her. "Check your tickets, sweetie. You're in the luxury boxes. Back there. Along the wall."

Danica surveyed the room, looking for anyone who might be able to help. She recognized her competition: reporters from all the local channels and a couple of national news correspondents. They wouldn't do anything for her. And she had no idea what Thomas Smullen looked like, the guy from the Senator's office who'd emailed her.

Maybe she ought to hang loose until the press conference was ready to start. Hopefully someone from Hartwell's staff would recognize her and escort her to a more prominent location. Armed with a plan, she found an empty spot on the side wall, somewhat near the front of the room, and leaned against it.

"Danica?" came a surprised voice from her left. "It's me, Cheryl Turquette. I mean, Cheryl Butler. I'm married now."

"Wow. Long time." Cheryl used to be a city beat reporter for the *Austin American-Statesman* back when Danica landed her first gig out of college, and they'd crossed paths on more than one occasion. Danica gave her a hug. "Still in Austin?"

"Still in Austin. Now I'm a political blogger. Of course, we all know about your career. Sounds like you're lighting it up big time here in Houston."

Before she could respond, a man stepped to the microphones. "Sorry, folks, but it's gonna be a few more minutes." A collective groan rose from the crowd. "Hey, it's a hospital. Gotta learn to be flexible."

Danica checked the wall clock—straight-up eleven—and tried to process what had happened. Had someone intentionally misled her about the start time? That didn't make any sense. This Smullen guy had contacted her, had even asked her to sit up front to ask Hartwell the first question. The simplest explanation had to be that they'd decided to move things up, and she just never got the message.

"I knew you were too bright of a star to be stuck in Austin," Cheryl said. "I saw your interview the other day on *Good Morning America*. If you ask me, you'd do a better job in that chair than any of them."

"Uh-huh," Danica mumbled absently.

"There were all sorts of rumors when you left. That you got sick, that another station offered you six figures, that you got fired after your piece on the District Attorney's office. Any of that true?"

Danica didn't want to rehash her time in Austin, didn't want to talk about the past. "Sorry, I've got a splitting headache. Just need some quiet time for a few minutes. Nice seeing you again." She closed her eyes, wishing Cheryl would find someone else to talk with.

And memories of that big story came flooding back.

A dozen years ago, Danica landed her first job as a reporter, only a month removed from life at Berkeley, where she'd served as editor for *The Daily Californian* and as unpaid gofer for Al Gore's Presidential campaign. Armed with a journalism degree and a passion for seeking and speaking truth, she took a job in Texas at a medium-sized TV station. And because she considered journalism more a calling than a job, she earned barely more than a teacher.

She almost quit three months in, though, because she was bawling her eyes out every night when she came home, after covering nothing but stories of tragedy. An elderly woman who shot her husband when his Alzheimer's had progressed beyond her ability to cope. The apartment fire that left twenty families homeless, including a blind single mother and her twin baby girls. The newlyweds who perished on Lake Travis. Once, after interviewing a disconsolate widow live on the air, Danica drove home feeling disgusted with herself and drained an entire bottle of wine.

So much heartache. So much despair.

One day, the station received a tip from a caller about some alleged irregularities in the Travis County District Attorney's office. Her producer mentioned it offhand after a meeting.

"I'd like to check this out," Danica told him. "At least it's different than our usual stories."

"Gotta be honest with you," he replied, scratching the back of his neck. "I don't think it'll amount to anything. Sounds like a pissed-off employee and normal office politics."

"But if it's not . . ."

"Don't go all Woodward and Bernstein on me, Cortez. Follow up with the person who called in the tip. Let me know what you find out."

Over the next couple of weeks, Danica tried to figure out what was going on at the District Attorney's office, in between doing stand-up reports about bar shootings and traffic accidents, plus a puff piece on a water park for dogs.

Tracking down the woman who'd called in the original tip had been easy. Getting her to repeat accusations about the county's second assistant district attorney proved more difficult. Danica had to call five times just to arrange a conversation, which finally took place in a Waffle House on the south side of Austin one humid August morning.

As she sat across the booth from the olive-skinned woman with dark eyes and a broad nose, Danica blew the surface of her hot coffee. "I understand your reluctance, Carmen," she said, "but this isn't about hurting people's feelings."

Carmen Flores, whom Danica had already learned was fifty-three and who'd been employed as an administrative assistant by the Travis County District Attorney's office for seventeen years, fidgeted in her seat and fingered the gold cross on her necklace. "I can't lose my job."

"You're doing the right thing. Just tell me what you know."

"My daughter stays with me. And my *nieto*, Luis."

"And they're going to be proud of you for telling the truth. It took a lot of courage to make that call. But now I need your help. *Por favor?*" She hoped that tossing in a little Spanish would help forge a bond with this woman, even though Danica couldn't speak the language to save her life.

Carmen dropped her head and sighed. "I only tell you because you are Mexican."

Danica didn't bother correcting her but pulled out her notebook. "You said something about drugs?"

According to Carmen, it was an open secret that the county's second assistant district attorney, a man named Blaine Wiesler, was using cocaine. Everyone in the office talked about it in hushed voices, but no one wanted to call him on it. "Mr. Wiesler," Carmen said, "he works long hours, sometimes all night. I've come in the morning and he's still there from the day before."

"Have you actually seen him do drugs?"

Color drained from the woman's face, and it looked like she might pass out. "Never mind," she said, fidgeting. "It's probably all rumor."

Danica nervously chewed the cap of her pen, afraid that Carmen was going to backtrack her way out of the story. "I understand," she said reassuringly. "Maybe he really isn't an addict. But that's not why you called."

When a waitress appeared next to their table to refill their coffees, Carmen jumped. "I've said too much already. I must get to work."

"Please, Carmen."

The woman slid out of the booth, clutching her purse to her stomach. She stopped and seemed to weigh her words. "Mr. Wiesler's a very bad man. He lies. And so many people he puts in jail. *Inocente*."

Danica wanted to be more sympathetic but figured she didn't have much time. "I need specifics."

Carmen edged close and dropped her voice to a whisper. "Stephon Hendrix. Russell Polistini. DeAndre Jones. That *comadreja* lied to put them away."

Over the next few days, Danica couldn't reach her source, no matter how many times she called. That's when she contacted her old college roommate, who worked for an oil and gas firm in Houston. She gave Sam the lowdown on the Waffle House conversation and said, "I don't know if I can get this Carmen woman to talk again. She was scared to death."

"She's worried people will think she's a snitch. You sure you want to jeopardize her job?"

Danica considered Sam's words. But Carmen Flores *was* doing the right thing, and she was surrounded by public servants who worked on behalf of the people. Carmen would be fine.

"She mentioned a few names. Men that had been sent to prison because of this Wiesler fellow. I'm gonna try to dig up some more facts."

"Be careful."

Within the week, armed with information from Carmen and more interviews, Danica discovered that Blaine Wiesler had compromised multiple criminal cases. He regularly lied to grand juries about evidence he didn't have. He forged lab results—Stephon Hendrix's fingerprints hadn't actually been found on that convenience store counter. And he hid exculpatory evidence—convicted murderer DeAndre Jones had security video proof that he was in a Louisiana casino the night he supposedly set a fatal fire at his supervisor's home.

In the Hendrix case, a store clerk had been shot by a pair of unknown assailants, one black and one white according to the grainy security footage. The next morning, police apprehended a homeless man named Russell Polistini, whose clothing and forearm tattoo matched the suspect's description. When Polistini claimed to have spent the night drinking with Stephon Hendrix, his junkie pal from the shelter, police arrested him too.

Danica could hardly believe the extent of Wiesler's corruption. First, he never should have been assigned to the case—he and the dead store clerk had been neighbors. Then he tried to get Polistini to roll on the other suspect. When that didn't work, he lied to crime lab personnel about circumstantial evidence that didn't exist and convinced a newbie to confirm a false identification.

Polistini and Hendrix—and many more—were sitting in prison because Wiesler had conspired to frame them. She thought about all the reporters who investigated and broke scandals, people who went to jail for failing to reveal their sources, war correspondents who died trying to tell a story. She had to do whatever it took to secure freedom for these prisoners.

Bolstered with documents from Carmen, she reported the story live at the top of the newscast for a full week, from the arrest of Blaine Wiesler to the resignation of the lead District Attorney to the judge's dismissal of thirteen separate cases. When she heard that DeAndre Jones, Stephon Hendrix, and Russell Polistini had finally been freed, Danica let out a whoop, satisfied in the knowledge that she'd made the world a slightly better place.

Because the story broke during sweeps month, the station's

ratings spiked through the roof and Danica earned kudos from her peers. The next week, management named her a substitute anchor for morning broadcasts. Three weeks later, she received a nomination for the Lone Star Award for excellence in investigative journalism, and then another from the National Association of Hispanic Journalists.

And two weeks after that, she filed the most painful report of her life.

Career criminal Russell Polistini—the man whose cause she campaigned for, the man she sprung from prison—went on a crime spree. He knocked over a few convenience stores. He knifed his accomplice. And he murdered a bunch of folks, including a police officer named Andrew Quinn.

As Danica stood in the crowded room of St. Luke's Episcopal Hospital, she kept coming back to the one irrefutable truth: if she hadn't helped free Polistini, his victims would still be alive.

For over a decade, she hadn't been able to shake the guilt. It was her fault that Carmen Flores lost her job. It was her fault that all those people got murdered. It was her fault that a cop's widow had to raise two kids by herself.

The worst part was that she ended up capitalizing on the whole ordeal, landing an anchor job and becoming famous. All for telling the truth about Blaine Wiesler.

A murmur spread through the throng of reporters, and a set of double doors opened. Two men in medical coats entered and took a seat at the dais. Then Senator Hartwell appeared, sitting in a wheelchair being pushed by a nurse, his left leg sticking straight out. For a man who'd endured a plane crash and undergone recent surgery, he appeared in good spirits.

But for some reason, the sight of Hartwell in a wheelchair bothered her. She thought about Mario and Zoey, how although their wheelchairs didn't define them, their confinement to a chair was still their most visible characteristic. For years, she'd considered a wheelchair the mark of someone special, a sort of rolling throne for royalty. And here Hartwell sat, a pretender to the throne.

She couldn't wait to expose him.

Doctor Number One, the physician who initially treated Hartwell in the ER, sat in front of the microphones and detailed the senator's injuries. Doctor Number Two was St. Luke's Chief of Orthopedic Surgery, the man who'd installed a titanium rod in Hartwell's leg. He described the complicated surgery and discussed future physical therapy. Nothing they said was new, except the part about the recovery schedule.

Then Hartwell was led to the center of the dais and guided to the bank of microphones. "I feel embarrassed," he said. "I didn't expect all this."

Which was a huge lie since his office had arranged everything in the first place.

He offered his thanks to the hospital and doctors. He spoke about his travel plans for Arnie Fletcher's funeral. And then he choked up, talking about the five men who died on the plane.

This was perfect, she thought.

"I only have time to take a couple questions, and then I have to leave for the airport." He looked to the front row and pointed at Barb Edwards. "Did you have a question?"

A pang of jealousy tore through Danica. That was supposed to be her.

Barb stood slowly, and Danica could see the deer-in-the-headlights look on her face. "How does it feel to be alive today?" Barb asked, and Danica could only shake her head.

"Feels good!" Hartwell replied, obviously thrilled with the softball question. "And allow me to take this opportunity to thank you again, Miss Cortez, for your bravery."

"Uh . . . I'm not Danica Cortez."

He appeared confused, nodding at Barb while looking

around frantically. A man rushed up to the table and placed a glass of water in front of him, then whispered into his ear. In an instant, she could see Hartwell transform back into self-assured politician. "What I meant to say . . . is that I'm feeling healthy and grateful, especially to the woman who pulled me from the plane. Any other questions?"

Danica's hand shot into the air, along with everyone else. "Senator!" she shouted. But a CNN correspondent grabbed the next question, something about whether his position on health care had changed given his recent hospitalization.

While Hartwell blathered some rubbish about the United States having the best medical care in the world, Danica realized she wasn't going to be able to do this the way she wanted, to engage him in a lengthy conversation that she could get on the record.

". . . and I plan to continue this fight in the Senate," he said. "Because the American people deserve—"

"What the American people deserve is the truth, Senator," Danica said, stepping forward.

"I'm sorry, but I was still answering this man's question. Let's show a little decorum, shall we?"

Danica took a breath to steel herself. "Can you explain why you've been lying about the plane crash?"

The mob of reporters began to buzz. Senator Hartwell motioned to an aide and said, "I think we're done here."

Reporters shouted: "Why are you leaving?" . . . "What is she talking about?" . . . "Senator, just a few more questions!"

Emboldened, Danica pushed forward to speak with him but was blocked by the crowd. All she wanted to do was look him in the eyes. But with everyone pressing toward the dais, she knew this wasn't going to work. Sensing he was about to mount an escape, she ducked under the outstretched arms of a reporter and rushed to the double doors.

A couple of seconds later, a wheelchair turned to where she stood. Senator Hartwell's face was beet-red, and she could see a vein pulsing along his temple. "Move!" he growled.

She leaned close. "I saw her."

"You didn't see anything," he huffed. "You don't know what you're talking about."

"I saw her," she repeated through gritted teeth. "Who was she?"

He grabbed the metal rims of his wheelchair and pushed hard, lurching forward and striking her knee, knocking her to the ground. As he rolled past, he muttered, "Get this bitch away from me."

Chapter 24

Garrison ran a crown of broccoli under the faucet, then gave it a good shake in the sink. "I'll make dinner when you get back from tennis," he told Zoey. "Stir-fry okay?"

"Yeah, yeah. I don't care. But can we talk again about getting a dog?"

"Hand me the cutting board," he said, knowing full well he didn't stand a chance of distracting her, like he used to do when she was a child. Last night, he had been in such a good mood after Danica's visit that he had made the mistake of not shutting down Zoey's dog talk completely. He'd been regretting it ever since.

She reached down into the cabinet, pulled out a glass cutting board, and held it up for him. As he grabbed for it, she pulled it back. "The dog, Dad."

"Honey, I totally get why you want a companion. But don't you remember how awful you felt when Sirius died? And Rigel?"

"Don't treat me like a kid. Did you ever hear anything from that organization?"

He pretended not to hear the question, because he knew how badly he'd dropped the ball. A year ago, he'd investigated the prospect of obtaining a service dog for Zoey, some Lab or Golden Retriever that could help pull her wheelchair or pick up things for her. Frankly, it didn't make a lot of sense to him, as he was able to provide all the help she needed. But she had gone on about it, had searched the Internet for various agencies, and had even sent a few emails to request information.

Surprisingly, the largest service dog organization, Canine Companions for Independence, turned out to be a nonstarter. Because Zoey didn't have cerebral palsy, muscular dystrophy, autism, or Down syndrome, she would have to wait until she was eighteen to apply for a CCI dog. Other organizations weren't as restrictive, but since Zoey wasn't as disabled as most candidates, she was lower on the waiting list.

Zoey didn't like to wait for anything.

Her latest scheme was to adopt a dog that had undergone training but had failed its final exams. It couldn't officially be a service dog and wear the colorful vest, but it had the potential to aid Zoey in doing daily tasks. The key word was *potential.* With their luck, Garrison figured they'd end up with one that was more trouble than it was worth.

"I'm gonna email that lady again," Zoey said. "I remember she said some dogs might be available in May. What did she call them, 'career changers'?"

He grunted. "I think she means rejects. Go get your tennis stuff. Danica should be here soon."

She left the kitchen in a huff, and Garrison began chopping the broccoli into florets. This idea of getting a dog was a bad one, he was sure. He remembered how horribly the experiences with Sirius and Rigel had turned out.

Zoey had been eight when they rescued Sirius, a mix of German Shepherd and Chow Chow, from the animal shelter. Tall and slender, with a curled bushy tail, he had a friendly disposition . . . but nothing between his ears. Named after the brightest star in the sky, the "Dog Star," Sirius couldn't have been considered bright by any measure.

Sirius barked whenever the clock rang the hour. He chewed baseball-size gravel in the landscaping bed. He once ate an entire throw pillow when left alone for an hour. And he loved to chase: squirrels, backyard birds, his tail.

And cars.

It was a frigid February afternoon, and Garrison had decided to take the dog for a walk along the greenbelt. Because of the low temperature and biting wind, he made sure to bundle everyone up before they left the house. He helped Zoey put on her heavy coat, the pink one with a hood and white fur accents, and he was wearing the North Face ski jacket that Celeste had bought him long ago for their Aspen ski trip.

They'd barely started, but Sirius was already full of himself, the brisk weather seeming to make him more hyper than usual. After half a mile, with Garrison pushing the wheelchair and Zoey holding the leash, the greenbelt narrowed as it approached a quiet street. Suddenly an SUV flew past from left to right, and the dog took off. Zoey held onto the leash for an instant, but Sirius was too strong-willed and ripped the leash from her hand.

She screamed as her chair leaned on two wheels. Garrison caught her before she tumbled to the ground.

"No!" she yelled.

The dog, a frenetic flash of brown and black, raced after the speeding vehicle, which was disappearing down the street. Garrison shouted his name. Sirius didn't stop.

"Dad, get him!"

He wasn't sure what to do: follow the dog or stay with Zoey.

Just then, a car backed out of a driveway and into the street. Garrison cringed as he heard the *thud-yelp* and saw the dog—Zoey's dog—fall lifeless under the tire.

They rushed him to an animal clinic and waited nervously for news, but all Garrison could think about as he sat with two blood-stained coats on his lap was of an even worse day of his life, sitting in an Austin hospital and wondering what was going to happen to Celeste and Zoey.

It was another two years before they got Rigel.

Another rescue dog, a miniature poodle that Zoey carried around in her chair, Rigel lived only three months before being savaged by their neighbor's pet mastiff, which had broken through several fence pickets and apparently shaken the poodle in its powerful jaws. Although Zoey didn't witness the actual attack, she had discovered Rigel's body at the edge of the patio.

That had been three years ago, and Garrison vowed that he'd never allow Zoey to endure that kind of pain again.

The best-case scenario for him would be for Zoey to get her energy focused on something other than dogs, which was why her tennis lesson with Danica couldn't have come at a better time. And while they were playing tennis, he would get dinner ready.

He finished chopping the broccoli and tossed a piece into his mouth. He ducked into the refrigerator and came out with an onion, a stalk of celery, and some fresh mushrooms, then dumped them on the island. All he'd have to do is toss everything into the wok, sprinkle in some chicken and garlic and soy sauce, a little ginger . . . man, he could practically taste it.

The doorbell rang.

It's her, he thought, and a nervous rush came over him. He had been waiting for Danica all afternoon, had de-cluttered the living room, had even showered and changed shirts just to look his best. No way was he going to be as unprepared and tongue-tied as he'd been the previous day.

He popped another piece of broccoli into his mouth, then threw all the vegetables back into the refrigerator and rushed from the kitchen. As he rounded the corner, he slowed to a pace that projected *casual stroll* instead of what he really felt: abject panic.

"Hi, Danica," he said, opening the door. "Great to see you again. Zoey's almost ready." In his head, the words sounded friendly and welcoming. Not bad for someone out of practice with proper houseguest protocol. He decided he was off to a good start. "Are you going to Clear Lake Park?" he asked, grinning broadly.

She seemed to suppress a smile. "Yeah. Those courts are perfect for Zoey."

He pulled a blue plastic rectangle from his back pocket and handed it to her. "Okay, here's the handicap permit. Hang it from your mirror. You sure you can handle this? Because I can drive her in the van."

"Trust me, Garrison. I'll take good care of her." She pointed at him and said, "Um . . . you've got a—"

"If you're not busy tonight, I'm cooking up some stir-fry."

"That's nice, but I've got a bunch of phone calls to make and emails to write. I've had a crazy day. Not sure if you heard. Lots of stuff about the plane crash."

"Not really. I don't watch the news." That was true to a point. Garrison didn't tune in to cable news programs, didn't view local afternoon or evening broadcasts, didn't browse news sites on the Internet. Hadn't for years. The only news he watched—a habit begun only yesterday—was Eyewitness9's morning broadcast with Danica Cortez. "Come on," he told her. "Eat dinner with us."

"I really shouldn't."

He found himself confused and conflicted. For years, he'd done everything he could to keep a distance from people. Now here was a woman he hardly knew, and all he wanted was to spend time with her. "Zoey wants you to stay," he blurted.

She smiled, but he knew it was one of those patronizing *I-want-to-let-you-down-easy* smiles he'd seen back in high school. Danica wasn't buying his story. Which left only the truth.

He swallowed hard. "Yesterday you wanted me to be honest

with you. Okay, here goes. I'm the one that wants you to stay for dinner. I'd like to talk and get to know you better."

Did I really say that?

"Uh . . . wow," she replied. "I'm sorry if I gave you the wrong idea."

"I mean . . . look, I'm making dinner anyway. I just want to say thanks for helping Zoey." He shuffled his feet. "Please don't say no."

The bedroom door closed, and Zoey came wheeling up the hall. "Dad, I sent an email to that lady. Why didn't you tell me Danica was here?" She squeaked to a stop and looked up at both of them. "Ew, Dad, you are so gross."

Great. Not only had he blown it with Danica, but Zoey had apparently heard his foolish talk, too. "I was just being polite."

"What are you talking about?" She pointed at him like Danica had. "It's just gross."

He looked from Zoey to Danica, who was biting her lip. "I tried to tell you."

"What?"

Danica was laughing now. "We'll be back by six, six-thirty at the latest. And yes, Garrison, I'll stay for dinner."

"You are?" Zoey said. "That's awesome!" Then she turned to him. "Can you not embarrass me when we get back? Two words, Dad. Mirror and broccoli."

While Zoey navigated her chair between orange cones that ran from deuce court to ad court, Danica checked her smartphone for messages. Five voicemails and an inbox stuffed with emails. Ugh.

Pissing off a U.S. Senator was definitely not the easiest way to uncover the truth. Now that he'd gone into full lockdown, except for one press release about rude reporters and inflammatory innuendo, she'd lost any chance of landing an interview.

"Don't roll so far past the cone!" she called.

Zoey nodded and rotated her wheelchair, her forehand stroke driving through an imaginary ball with great force. Then she blasted hard toward ad court, executed a backhand, and turned her chair away from the net, continuing her momentum back toward the other side.

"Much better."

"Yay, me!" Zoey replied, beaming.

She watched Zoey sprint from one side of the court to the other, never once rolling over a cone, never once dropping her racquet as she pushed. It was hard to believe she'd been playing for only a couple of days. The girl was a natural.

Back when Danica taught Mario to play tennis, he tended to lose his grip on the racquet and turn the wrong way after striking the ball. She used to think those mistakes had been her fault rather than his, since she'd never coached anyone before . . . and since he was the bravest and toughest person she knew. It took a year to realize that Mario didn't love tennis—he simply wanted to spend time with her before she left for college.

She tried to push back the memories from that freshman year at UC Santa Barbara: waving goodbye to him at her dorm, receiving those worried phone calls from Mom just before finals, rushing back home to visit him in the hospital. But she'd been too late. Three hours too late.

God, how she missed him.

Maybe that's why being on a tennis court with Zoey and basking in her zest for the game—and life—felt right. In a way, she could feel Mario's presence.

Zoey sped across the court into another practice forehand. As she spun into the shot, her wheels gave a shudder. The wheelchair lurched sideways, became motionless for an instant, then settled back onto the concrete.

"Stop!" Danica shouted. "You're gonna flip that thing."

But Zoey just tipped her head back and laughed.

"Take a break. Now. We need to talk."

Shrugging her shoulders, Zoey rolled to the net and squeezed a stream of water into her mouth. "This is so fun."

"You don't have a sports wheelchair, do you?"

"No."

"Well, you need one. I'm not going to have you fall while you're out here with me." She pulled out her phone. "Let me show you what I'm talking about." She launched the Internet and searched for a photo of the sports wheelchairs used in Mario's tennis league. Anyone who was serious about the game owned the kind with large cambered wheels for better turning and stability and a rear "fifth wheel" to prevent backward falls.

Danica wondered why she hadn't thought of it before. Playing all-out tennis in a regular wheelchair was too dangerous. It was a good thing Garrison hadn't been here. "You need to talk with your father about getting another chair."

"Dad's not gonna buy me anything new. He's already pimped out this one."

"We'll need to convince him."

"Good luck with that. He's kinda stubborn if you hadn't noticed."

"No, really. It's a safety issue."

"Okay, now you're talking his language. If it's something to keep me safe, he'll be all for it. I swear, if he could find a giant plastic ball, I'd be rolling down the hallway at school like a hamster."

"A little overprotective, huh?" she said, tossing a towel to Zoey.

"Don't get me started." Zoey shook her head. "He won't let me do anything."

From what Danica knew about Garrison, he would move heaven and earth to make his daughter happy. "I find that hard to believe. He's letting you play tennis with me, isn't he?"

Zoey crossed her arms. "That's different."

"Oh, really?"

"I've seen how he's been acting. He's even weirder than usual. There's only one reason he let me play tennis today." Zoey wiped her sweaty face with the towel, then dropped it beside her chair. "He likes you. A lot."

"You're crazy. Now get back out there and show how awesome you are. Just go slow and concentrate."

As Zoey wheeled away, Danica reflected on what she'd said. *He likes you.*

Those were the sort of words that could set a little girl's heart aflutter. She'd been that girl back in elementary school, when her best friend passed her a note that said BRANDON LIKES YOU and then she'd gone on to draw pages and pages of hearts and flowers in her binder. She'd fallen for it in high school, too, when painfully shy Spencer Brooks sent his twin brother to deliver the news that "Spencer likes you . . . and he really wants to take you to Homecoming."

But Danica was no longer a little girl. She was a college graduate, a woman living on her own in the nation's fourth largest city, a respected news anchor. She didn't need a man's approval.

He likes you. The words swirled in her head.

"Okay, Zoey," she called. "Let's practice some volleys. No side-to-side movement. Just toward the net." She tossed probably a hundred balls, and Zoey returned almost all of them cleanly.

When they were done, Danica bent down and hugged her. "I'm proud of you, Speed Racer," she said, using the same nickname she'd once had for Mario. "Let me take your picture. I want to have proof that I knew Zoey Sterling before she became a famous tennis player."

She snapped a couple of photos, and Zoey grinned from ear to ear. "Be sure to tell your dad how well you did today."

"What do you mean? You're eating with us, right?"

A loud gong sounded in Danica's head. Why had she agreed to stay for dinner?

"You're gonna love his stir-fry. It's so much better than takeout. He usually only makes it for special occasions."

Danica's breath caught. Special occasion?

After Zoey transferred into the front seat, Danica carried her wheelchair to the trunk, pausing to examine all the thoughtful customizations Garrison had added: a holster for a cell phone, a bracket to hold accessories—from a swiveling table to an umbrella, according to Zoey—plus a concave backrest fashioned from some flexible polymer.

She thought about him, the way he was both completely confident and utterly unsure of himself, the way he was dedicated to caring for Zoey. A real nice guy.

He was certainly television-friendly, as they said in her profession, with a strong jaw and steady smile and a touch of grey at his temples. The type of guy who usually ended up as a company CEO or movie actor.

And someone she wanted to learn more about.

Standing in the kitchen with Garrison while Zoey showered and changed clothes, Danica couldn't believe how nervous she was. She'd interviewed newsmakers for years: former President George H. W. Bush, Governor Perry, Brad Pitt, even the notorious Andrea Yates, the Clear Lake mom who drowned her five children not long after Danica moved to Houston. It didn't matter how famous or infamous a person was—Danica did her job and probed for the story. But as Garrison tossed chicken and vegetables in a wok on the stove, she found herself more nervous than she'd ever been.

"That smells . . . amazing," she said, fumbling for her words.

"Wait 'til you taste it. This is one my favorite dishes."

"You make dinner every night?"

He shrugged. "Cooking's no big deal. You just prepare everything ahead of time. I like it. It relaxes me." He spooned the stir-fried chicken and vegetables onto a platter and set it on the table next to a bowl of brown rice. Opening a drawer and pulling out six bamboo chopsticks, he said, "Could you set these out?"

"Uh . . . sure." She took them from his hand as if they were exchanging vials of nitroglycerin.

Please, not chopsticks, she thought, remembering the humiliation she felt whenever she attempted to wield the clumsy utensils. For years, she'd avoided Chinese restaurants and Japanese steakhouses out of fear of embarrassment. When she did get the occasional craving for moo goo gai pan or kung pao chicken, all she had to do was pick up the phone, wait for the food to be delivered to her house, and then tear into it with a fork.

"Wait," Garrison said. "I forgot. I've got these two pairs of really nice chopsticks. Blackwood with silver tips. I want you and Zoey to have those. I'll use the bamboo."

She gulped, then took all the chopsticks and placed them on the table, one on each side of the plate, hoping that was the correct way to arrange them. As she stood there, one hand on her hip and the other rubbing her chin, Garrison asked, "Would you rather have a fork?"

Her mind screamed *Yes! Absolutely!* but her mouth wouldn't cooperate. Instead she said, "No, chopsticks will be fine."

"I'm starving," Zoey said when she entered the room. "Did you make egg rolls?"

"I thought about it," he said.

"What about soup? Or Szechuan Green Beans?"

He gave a deep sigh, and Danica found herself wishing Zoey would give it a rest. For the past half-hour, Garrison had done nothing but prepare a meal that looked and smelled wonderful. And that didn't count all the time he'd spent chopping the vegetables.

"Go ahead, Danica," he said. "Dig in."

"O-okay." She lifted the chopsticks and placed them between her fingers as if she were trying to sign a document with two pens. Start with a piece of chicken, she thought, since it was the largest item on the plate. She exhaled, then began manipulating the chopsticks awkwardly. After a few seconds of chasing the chicken around the plate, she stopped to reassess matters.

When she looked up, she saw Garrison studying her, a smile creeping at the corners of his mouth. "So, how was tennis?"

Zoey rolled her eyes. "Why do you always have to ask so many questions? Can't I do anything on my own without you prying?"

"I was just asking."

"Danica says I need a new chair."

He lifted an eyebrow. "Oh, she does?"

Danica quickly raised a hand to her forehead, shielding her eyes. She didn't want to get involved in this conversation.

"Remember those funky wheelchairs from that video? Danica says I shouldn't play tennis without one."

"And why's that?"

"So I don't fall over. Don't you know anything?"

"Maybe you shouldn't play tennis if it's so dangerous," he muttered.

"There you go again! Tennis isn't dangerous. Tell him, Danica."

This was not what she'd bargained for, sitting between these two bickering with each other. She saw both sides, of course, Zoey wanting to be treated like an adult and Garrison wanting a little respect and gratitude for his sacrifices. "This food's really good," she mumbled.

"Well, is Zoey exaggerating?"

"I don't know."

"Come on, Danica. Tell him what you told me."

She began lightly drumming a chopstick on the edge of her plate. "If Zoey's going to be driving around the court, she probably needs a chair with better balance."

"Appreciate your advice," he said, enunciating each word slowly, then cleared his throat. "Maybe if she was more advanced or playing tournament-level tennis . . ."

"Frankly, Garrison, she's already good enough to play tournaments."

Zoey emitted a happy squeal. "You really think I'm good?"

She nodded, making eye contact with Zoey and letting her know they were in this together. "But even if she plays recreationally, a sports wheelchair is better for her. Certainly more efficient for moving around the court. And much, much safer."

Garrison scooped a helping of vegetables onto his plate. "You're not hungry, Danica?"

"I'm a slow eater," she lied, reluctantly taking the chopsticks in her fingers again. "You ought to look into getting a sports chair. Seriously."

The room was silent for a moment, except for clicks coming from the chopsticks. "I'm not saying we're gonna buy one," he said, "but any idea how much a sports wheelchair costs, roughly?"

"Beats me. My brother Mario had one. Used, I think. He loved it." In a moment of clarity, she grabbed both chopsticks in her fist and stabbed the chunk of chicken, then brought it to her mouth triumphantly. "Biscuit loved it, too."

"Biscuit?"

"Oh, that was Mario's service dog."

Zoey gasped. Garrison groaned.

"Biscuit used to pull Mario's regular wheelchair as part of his training. And occasionally his sports chair. Mario wasn't supposed to, but sometimes he'd let Biscuit run while pulling his Big Wheel. I mean, his sports chair. We called it Big Wheel."

"I want a service dog, but my dad won't let me have one."

He shook his head vigorously. "That's another evening's conversation, Zoey."

"I want to hear about Biscuit."

"I'm sure Danica doesn't want to talk about—"

"Biscuit was a sweetie," she said, remembering the gentle helper Mario had been partnered with for five years. "A black Lab. She pulled Mario's chair, picked up stuff off the floor, carried things for him. She was his best friend." Danica winked at Zoey. "I hope you get a chance to have a friend like Biscuit one day."

"One day," Garrison echoed. "Remember, CCI said you'd be eligible when you turn eighteen."

"But I don't want to wait four years! I want to be able to do things on my own. Now."

"We'll talk about this some other time. Don't be so dramatic."

"Don't . . . call me . . . dramatic!" she yelled, and pushed away from the table and stormed off to her room.

"Sorry about that." He tugged at the collar of his shirt. "She's a full-fledged teenager. Don't worry, she'll come back in a few minutes. Until then, let's enjoy our meal in peace."

Danica watched as he set about eating again, brandishing his chopsticks like some sort of ninja, plucking items off his plate and deftly placing them in his mouth. When he lifted a heaping of rice without dropping a single grain, her mouth fell open in amazement.

"I saw your news story while you two were out. Sounds like you're not gonna be on the Senator's Christmas list this year."

She chuckled. "Probably not."

"I don't get it, though. He survived a plane crash and you're giving him the third degree?"

"It's not what you think." This was exactly what Danica was worried about. A casual TV viewer wouldn't know what was crystal clear to her. She needed to get ahead of this story, get all the facts on the record and let the public know the truth.

Garrison shoveled in another mouthful of rice, paused to swallow it, and said, "I'm just glad you saved the guy. We were talking about it at work."

"NASA, right?"

"Yeah. You know, if Senator Hartwell had died, I'd probably be looking for a job right now." He tipped his glass of iced water toward her. "So, thanks."

She shrugged and began poking at the food on her plate again. Garrison wasn't going to be thanking her if she exposed the senator's string of false statements. Lying to the public about an affair was bad enough; covering up a woman's death and not allowing her body to be recovered would be unforgivable. "Can we talk about something else?"

"Tell me about you. All I know is that you play tennis . . . you had a brother . . . and you're the famous Danica Cortez. Well, I do know one more thing. No one ever taught you how to use chopsticks."

Staring down at her fingers, she could see one chopstick pointed at the plate, the other at the ceiling. She felt her face flush.

"It's not that hard. Want to learn?" Without waiting for an answer, he slid his chair next to hers. "See how I keep this one steady? And how I make small movements with the other?" He wielded the utensils with a practiced dexterity, demonstrating how to pick up chicken, vegetables of varying sizes, even rice. "Now you try."

As he guided a slender dark chopstick between her middle finger and the base of her thumb, she held her breath. His hands were strong, confident in their movements. "Now the other one," he said gently, sliding the companion chopstick in place by her index finger.

"What do I do now?" she asked, realizing the question could just as easily have been directed to herself.

With his lean, long fingers still encircling hers, he

whispered, "Go for it."

A clattering sounded from the back of the house, and Danica flinched, pulling her hands away from him. The silver-tipped chopsticks tumbled from her fingers and clinked against the plate.

Garrison scooted back to his original position and drew a glass of water to his lips. His eyes locked onto hers as he drank. When he was done, he flashed a mischievous smile.

Zoey was right, she thought, a thrill racing through her. *He does like me.*

Garrison couldn't believe what had just happened.

Up until Saturday, his world had revolved around the here-and-now, caring for Zoey and helping her navigate her teenage years. His life was consumed by the present and haunted by the past. But after sitting beside Danica, caressing her hands and inhaling her lilac fragrance, he wondered if there was something more out there. A future?

His mind spun with possibilities. If Danica spent more time with Zoey, he'd have a chance to get to know her better. He'd be fine as long as Zoey didn't change her mind about wanting to learn tennis.

Maybe he'd even ask Danica on a date.

More noises sounded from Zoey's bedroom, and her door banged open. "I don't believe it!" she hollered.

"Everything okay back there?"

Zoey barreled down the hallway and into the family room, breathing hard. "Oh, my God. Oh, my God."

Garrison and Danica answered simultaneously. "What?"

"The lady. From the email. She says I can have a dog!"

Chapter 25

Stepping out of her shower in the pre-dawn hours of Wednesday morning, Danica should have been exhausted. After all, she normally slipped into bed by eight or eight-thirty at the latest, and last night's dinner with Garrison and Zoey had gone on longer than expected. Danica had slept barely four hours. Yet her energy level was sky high.

Because today she was going to get to the bottom of the Hartwell story.

She applied her makeup in record time as she tried to map out a plan. First, she'd anchor her two morning newscasts, and then she'd have the rest of the day to investigate matters. She'd borrow an editing room and view all the news footage, even the stuff that hadn't made the air. She'd perform Lexis-Nexis searches on the computer system. She'd place some phone calls. All thanks to the resources of Eyewitness9, one of her favorite perks of being a TV journalist.

After donning her broadcast clothes, Danica crawled into her car with the knowledge that she'd bought herself another forty-five minutes, meaning she could get started on examining the Hartwell story before her broadcasts. She checked the rearview mirror and nodded to herself. *Let's go.*

Cruising along the empty boulevards, Danica could feel the
tautness of the muscles in her neck, arms, and legs as she
ruminated on Senator Hartwell. It had taken all her self-
control at the press conference not to blurt out accusations
about the affair he was desperately trying to conceal. She had
gone to propriety's edge, of course, by calling him a liar, but
she hadn't ventured over the line by publicly divulging the
details of her still-unverified theory. She knew better.

She'd wanted to let Hartwell have it with both barrels,
though, and she knew that's why her body was so tense. What
kind of man shows such callousness to his own wife? Did he
even think about how such betrayal can ruin his family, scar
his kids?

Suddenly an image of her own father surfaced, lugging
suitcases out to the car, waving goodbye but not offering a final
hug, fishtailing away down the street. That man couldn't wait
to get away from them. Away from her.

An uncomfortable tingle began to form in her lower right
leg. The tingle quickly gnarled into a knot, and she knew what
was coming next. Scanning the road and mirrors for traffic, she
braced herself for the all-too-familiar spasms. She switched to
manipulating the pedals with her left foot as she steered the
car into an empty strip center lot, then threw it into *Park* as
the charley horse hit her full on.

The pain was blinding. Her calf was in full rebellion,
contracting and cramping. She clambered out of the car, falling
onto her knees in the parking lot, and then slowly rose to her
feet. From her tennis experience, she knew what to do—stretch
it out—but nothing she did worked. Tears welled in her eyes.
Relax, she told herself.

And then she remembered Garrison.

To her surprise, just thinking about him gave her an
immediate sense of calm. Breathing slowly and deeply, Danica
could feel her leg muscles unwind—it was as if he were right
there with her.

But why Garrison? she asked herself, flexing her toes and wondering why this guy was stuck in her head. After all, she'd just met him. They didn't have a history together or anything.

In a flash, the past few days rolled through her mind, and she recalled the moments they'd already shared. Garrison was still a bit of an enigma to her, because there were so many facets to him. *Intriguing*, she'd thought at the tennis court, when he'd run around haphazardly throwing tennis balls to Zoey. *Awkward*, she'd thought on her first visit to his home. *Loving*, she'd thought each time she'd seen him with his daughter.

Before she knew it, her pain had completely gone away.

After massaging each of her legs, Danica got back in her car. "Well, that was fun," she said to the mirror, then pulled out onto the empty street.

The delay hadn't cost her much time, but she was no longer fired up to get into work. Maybe she was taking this Hartwell story too personally. She needed to maintain her objectivity on this, lower the stress in her life. She took a long, cleansing breath.

At a traffic light, she had to stop for an approaching car making a left turn. Waiting for her green, she gazed out her window to the right, where the NASA campus lay asleep. That's where Garrison worked, she thought. A few windows in distant buildings were lit, and they looked like little stars in the blackness.

To her left, she saw the still, dark void that was the lake for which the area was named. Most of the time, Clear Lake whizzed by without a second thought. But occasionally Danica would see the shimmering reflection of a fingernail moon—"a smiling moon" according to her mom—and marvel at the beauty of it all.

Maybe that's what she needed to do more of.

By the time she reached Beltway 8, her mind was clear. Unfortunately, the highway wasn't. There were red brake lights as far as she could see, the traffic diverted into a single lane from the usual four, and she saw what looked like road construction activity in the distance. She let out a big sigh and flipped on the radio for a traffic report.

Twenty minutes later, she'd all but forgotten about the traffic as she listened to the music she grew up with: Alanis Morissette, the Goo Goo Dolls, Sheryl Crow. Danica cranked up the volume and sang along with Jewel on *You Were Meant for Me*, the song she always associated with her senior year of high school.

She finally cleared the construction just as the radio station relayed news about the backup. "Other than that problem on the Belt, it's clear sailing into work this morning," said the traffic reporter, adding with a chuckle, "But why is anybody on the road this time of morning?"

"Tell me about it," Danica replied, hoping that Kathy's prediction of a prime-time promotion would soon come true.

"And in national news," said the radio DJ, "Senator Joe Hartwell appeared on CNN last night and blasted local Houston reporter Danica Cortez for her actions at yesterday's press conference."

It was a good thing her steering wheel was securely attached or Danica would have ripped it from the dashboard. The station played a brief recording of the incident, and she was surprised how angry she had sounded.

"Here are the Senator's comments about the confrontation at St. Luke's Hospital, which left many reporters shaking their heads."

"Obviously Ms. Cortez thinks this story is all about her," Senator Hartwell said, his voice dripping with indignation. "Five people . . . decent people . . . died in that field, and she's out there grandstanding in front of the camera. I don't know why she's spreading such malicious falsehoods, unless it's some pathetic attempt to draw attention to herself."

"Why, you arrogant prick," she told the radio and clicked it off.

By the time Danica reached the TV station, she was seething. Hartwell had fired a public salvo in her direction, and now it was going to be her turn. She needed to get her side out, convince her producer to let her deliver a rebuttal during the broadcast, tell the public she could prove the senator was a lying scumbag.

Unfortunately, she couldn't prove a damn thing. Because she had no clue about the identity of the dead woman.

She rushed through the Eyewitness9 building entrance and flashed her employee badge to the security officer. "Ms. Cortez?" the guard said, puzzled. "I thought you weren't coming in today."

"What do you mean?"

"Tami Jacobs came in half an hour ago. Real excited. Said she's anchoring her first-ever broadcast this morning."

Danica's stomach lurched, the top-of-the-rollercoaster feeling that instantly told her something was terribly wrong. When she entered the newsroom, the few employees that were gathered there saw her and scattered. She found news director Jerry Tomlinson's cubicle and banged on the padded fake wall. "Why does Tami think she's doing my broadcast?"

"Let's go step inside the War Room."

"No, we're gonna talk about things right here. This is about Hartwell, isn't it?"

Jerry cleared his throat. "Kathy tried calling last night, but you didn't answer. Everyone knows the guy's a blowhard, but he's right. This story has become about you."

"Are you kidding me?"

"You've gone through a terrible ordeal. I'm not sure anyone here really appreciated how traumatic that morning must have been. We shouldn't have put you on the air while you were dealing with all this stress."

"Jerry, it's me. I'm fine." She didn't mention her constant nightmares or the recurring muscle spasms. Stress was something she could handle—she always had before.

He blew a measured breath. "Here's what we're thinking. You've got some vacation coming—"

"I can't believe this."

"Why don't you take some time off, clear your head?"

"I'm talking to Kathy when she gets in," Danica replied, her hands trembling but her voice rock-steady. "I was doing my job. That's what the station pays me for."

"The truth is we're catching a lot of heat."

"That's what this is about? Who's applying the pressure, Jerry? Station management, your precious advertisers, Washington, who?" She paced around the cubicle and could sense colleagues turning in her direction. "Here's the way I see things. No one around here has the balls to stand up for what's right."

Jerry started waving his arms, like he always did when he became agitated. "This is exactly what I'm talking about, Danica. You're losing perspective here. Don't throw away your whole career over this."

"So now I'm throwing away my career?"

"All we want you to do is lay low for a few days, maybe a week or two."

"Am I being suspended?" She couldn't accept what she was hearing. Her job was actually hanging in the balance over this?

"Maybe you should find someone to talk with."

She wagged a finger at him. "Screw you, Jerry. Senator Hartwell is lying. I'll prove it." Then she stormed out.

When the sun finally rose, she called Sam. "I need to talk."

"What time is it?"

"Six-fifteen. Aren't you up yet?"

Sam yawned. "Still sleeping. Wait, six-fifteen? Aren't you supposed to be doing a broadcast?"

Danica gritted her teeth, trying to not think about Tami Jacobs, who was now sitting in *her* chair behind *her* desk. In less than a year, Tami had miraculously parlayed a traffic girl internship into a fill-in anchor position. Yet the closest thing Tami had to journalistic credentials was her recent profile of spring breakers at South Padre, reported with all the gravitas of a woman who herself had been named Miss Spring Break Cancun only three years earlier.

"Come on, I'll buy you breakfast," Danica said.

"Okay, that'll work. Can we meet at Denny's? My arteries could use some plaque to toughen 'em up."

"Good grief, Sam. Have a little self-respect."

"Waffle House?"

A vision of sitting across from Carmen Flores, the woman who'd worked with that corrupt assistant district attorney in Austin, leapt into Danica's mind. "No, not Waffle House. How about that little French bakery near you?"

"Belle Brioche? Sounds yummy."

Danica beat her friend to the restaurant by a good thirty minutes and sat nursing a latte underneath an arched window as the morning sunlight streamed through. When Sam arrived, Danica quickly gave her the lowdown and even managed to do it without cursing.

"How could they suspend you?" Sam asked, shaking her head.

"They're cowards, that's how."

Sam lifted a croissant from a basket in the middle of the table and waved it absently. "I don't understand why they're kissing Hartwell's ass and throwing you under the bus. Shouldn't it be the other way around?"

"You got that right," Danica replied, squeezing a dollop of honey onto her plate and then dragging a warm croissant through it. This was her favorite kind of breakfast, gooey and high-calorie, but she rarely allowed herself the indulgence. The sweet croissant didn't soften her anger, but at least it took the edge off. "Thanks again, Sam. I knew I could count on you."

"Of course. So, what's next?"

Danica shrugged. She'd been pondering that very question ever since Jerry dropped his bombshell this morning. The only silver lining to her suspension was that now she had plenty of time to investigate Hartwell and dig into the identity of the other victim, and she could do it without Eyewitness9's interference. But there was a corresponding, bitter reality: she wasn't allowed to use any resources from the station. She was on her own. Unless . . .

"Are you up for some research?" she asked Sam. "I could use some help. It'll be just like grad school, working on papers together."

"Sorry, Danni. Wish I could play Nancy Drew with you, but I can't. I have deliverables due Friday, and— " She checked the time. "I need to leave for work now."

"But—"

"You're Danica Cortez," Sam said, standing up. "You'll figure things out. I have total faith in you."

Danica managed a weak smile, but she was crestfallen. She really was going to have to do this on her own.

Sitting cross-legged on her living room couch, Danica was filled with a singular purpose: expose Hartwell's lies so she could clear her name and get her job back.

She used her personal laptop to pore over the news accounts of the ill-fated plane, whose trip records seemed to read like a travelogue. The private jet, a Gulfstream, had initially flown Hartwell and his Chief of Staff from Washington to Las Vegas on Wednesday. The senator attended an energy conference on Thursday morning, met with representatives of Genetechnologix Corporation that afternoon, then flew back to Texas the same evening.

Wait a second. She scanned the reports again. If the flight plan showed them leaving Las Vegas at seven o'clock at night, how come they were landing in Houston at four in the morning?

Then she saw it: El Paso International Airport. They'd stopped there to refuel. Was that where the woman boarded the plane? Or did she get on in Vegas?

Danica felt a surge of adrenalin. *I'm getting closer.*

She shifted again on the couch. This wasn't working, she thought, unfolding her legs for the hundredth time and trying to stave off another charley horse. She needed room to spread out. Standing abruptly with the laptop in her hands, she hurried without thinking toward the kitchen table.

She never saw the computer bag lying in the middle of the floor.

What happened next played out in brutal slow motion. Her foot caught the strap of the bag. Her arms flung out in response. The laptop flew from her hands.

It hung suspended in the air and, for a moment, Danica thought it might skid across the table's surface. But to her horror, it struck the table on its corner, spun, and plummeted toward the floor, like an airplane caught in a death spiral.

She closed her eyes. Then she heard the awful crash.

Chapter 26

Garrison wiped a towel across his forehead and increased the inclination of the treadmill, causing his quads to burn in response. Five miles in forty minutes—not bad for a guy years removed from completing the Houston Marathon in a shade under four hours.

He settled into a steady rhythm, his running shoes striking the treadmill's rubber surface. A current of cool air washed over his face from the fan he'd fastened to the side wall of the workshop. This was so much better than running outdoors, he thought, because this way he didn't have to deal with uneven sidewalks and stifling humidity, didn't have to deal with bicyclists and dogs appearing out of nowhere. Didn't have to deal with people.

As he ran, his mind began clicking off the day's to-do list: buy groceries, assemble the shuttle model's main engine, and figure out some alternatives for the problem with Zoey's binocular chair.

By the time the mileage counter rolled past six, a familiar runner's high began to kick in, endorphins coursing through Garrison's body as his task-oriented brain slowly disengaged. His head bobbed and his eyes drifted to the dark swath of stars covering the upper half of the front wall, a mural poster of the spiral-shaped Triangulum Galaxy.

Slowly he began to slip into a dream-like state, floating free in deep space, performing the spacewalk he was destined for. He imagined himself drifting untethered in the wide void, away from the orbiter, toward a universe where the laws of gravity were permanently suspended, with Celeste and Zoey flying alongside him. That's the universe he longed for, a place where loved ones didn't die and children didn't suffer because of his own shortcomings.

At the thought of those two precious people, something throbbed inside his chest, not lungs aching for air or muscles begging for relief. This was a hurt deeper and crueler than physical pain.

He slammed his fist against the stop button and glided off the rear of the treadmill, then leaned over to gather himself, gulping in big breaths of air. Even though he wanted to collapse onto the floor and curl into the fetal position, he understood he needed to do the same thing as when he'd hit the wall at mile twenty-one of the marathon years ago: just keep going. No matter how much it hurt.

After a sip of water and another wipe of the towel, he was on the treadmill again, its speed dialed back to a brisk walk, his runner's high gone. He stared ahead at the starfield, black and empty and far away.

It was bad enough that Celeste was gone—those dark days in the aftermath of her death were the worst he'd ever endured. But somehow the presence of Zoey, trapped in her grotesque wheelchair, seemed even worse, a permanent reminder of his deep failings.

He remembered their argument this morning, the latest battle over the animal that had become available through the service dog organization. How could he convince Zoey that she was wrong, that he knew what was best for her?

She was holding firm to this fanciful idea that she could

train the dumb thing, transform her life by having a constant companion that would do whatever she wanted. Hell, she had that already.

Of course she promised to take care of it, and part of him understood that taking on additional responsibilities had some merits. But he'd seen this movie before—one day she'd get all excited for something new and then days later get distracted or bored. If they brought a dog home, he knew who'd end up carrying the load. Again.

His cell phone rang, and he figured it was one of two people. Chip he could ignore. Zoey, on the other hand . . .

He muted the stereo and picked up the phone. Danica Cortez's name appeared on the display. Just then, his feet ran into each other and he stumbled forward. The phone fell onto the treadmill and shot backward, still ringing. He hit the machine's stop button and lunged for the phone, almost stepping on it.

"Are you okay?" Danica said. "You sound different."

"Fine," he stammered, trying to catch his breath. "Just . . . getting some exercise. Give me a second."

"I should call some other time."

"No, no. What's up?" Garrison covered the mouthpiece to conceal his heavy breathing.

"I know you're some sort of engineer. How are you with computers?"

"Uh, pretty good, I guess."

That was an understatement. He'd been working with computers for twenty years, could have pursued a career in software engineering or information technology if NASA hadn't changed his future by selecting him for the astronaut program. During grad school, he'd developed routines using bleeding-edge software to model the tensile and compressive strength of high polymer materials. But his greatest computer accomplishments had occurred closer to home: building his own web server, configuring a wireless network with multiple access points, integrating three astronomy applications with his telescope. Not to mention teaching his mom how to use the Internet.

"Something's wrong with my laptop," Danica said.

"Do you know if it's a hardware or software problem?"

"Well, I dropped it on the floor, so I'm thinking not software."

"Ouch. What happens when you turn it on?"

Danica didn't reply for a moment, and then she said, "None of the little lights are on, and the screen is totally dark." Another pause. "I'm screwed, aren't I? And of all days for this to happen."

He could hear the strain in her voice and figured she had more than computer problems on her mind. But at least he was qualified to help with something technical. "If you want, I can check it out."

"Only if I'm not bothering you. Sounds like you're at the gym or something."

"Actually, I'm at home, working on a project."

"Me, too." She sighed. "At least, I was."

"If it's any help, I have a spare notebook computer. You can borrow it."

"Really?"

"But let me take a look at yours first. It might be something simple."

Garrison carried an open cardboard box into his workshop as Danica trailed after him. Like the kind veterinarian who once tended to an injured bird that Zoey found beneath the kitchen window, Garrison carefully lifted what was left of Danica's laptop from the box. One of the computer's hinges had snapped off, and the display was almost completely detached from the CPU and keyboard. He grimaced as he listened to the sound of fragments moving around inside the unit. "You sure you didn't use a sledgehammer?"

"I was kinda hoping the problems were cosmetic. Maybe something's just loose?"

He turned the unit upside down and gently shook it. It sounded like a maraca. Something tiny fell off the computer, dropped onto the floor, and clicked across the tiled surface. When he slowly turned the unit back over, the letter Q was missing from the keyboard. He was about to make some sarcastic comment about not needing that key anyway but saw the worried look on Danica's face and thought better of it. "I can try a couple of things," he said. "Take out the battery. Reset the machine."

"Think it'll work?"

Mustering a smile, he said, "I'll try my best."

By the time Garrison finished examining the laptop, the other display hinge had broken off and two more keys—the X and the C—had fallen away. With a sigh, he accepted the inevitable and looked solemnly at Danica.

"So I've lost everything?" she said.

"I don't think so. The motherboard is cracked, but your hard drive is probably intact. You should be able to transfer data."

"Oh my gosh, you don't know what a relief that is."

She pressed a hand to her heart, and he found himself gazing at her wonderfully feminine features: the delicate shape of her fingers, the graceful arch of her neck, the fullness of her breasts. He'd seen attractive women before, but Danica possessed a beauty that seemed to transcend the physical.

Kiss her.

The thought came out of nowhere, and Garrison immediately wondered if he'd overheard the words from a TV in the other room. But the house was quiet. Which meant that his subconscious had delivered the message. What a preposterous idea, he thought. Sure, she was gorgeous and interesting and kind and amazing . . . but they'd just met.

"This is the first time I've ever dropped my laptop," she said, tucking a strand of chestnut brown hair behind her ear, "and hopefully my last."

He picked up what was left of the video display. "Sorry I couldn't do more."

"I just didn't know who to call. If this had happened before breakfast, I could have let my friend Sam look at it."

In an instant, Garrison's mind assembled the information as if it were a child's first puzzle. Danica, Sam, breakfast. It was so obvious—Danica had a boyfriend. Which meant Zoey had been wrong. Now he'd never get a chance to see if his attraction to Danica was mutual.

"Of course, Sam wouldn't know how to fix it," she said. "Or even how to take it apart. She's as clueless about technology as I am."

"She?"

"She who? You mean Sam? She's my best friend from college."

Kiss her, the thought came again, more urgently this time, and he raised his eyes to hers, wondering if she was having the same thought.

Instead she was crying.

"What's wrong?" he asked.

"Everything. This stupid computer. My job. I got suspended today."

"Suspended? What did you do?" He realized how accusatory that sounded, so he added, "I'm sure you didn't do anything wrong."

"I didn't. I was just trying to get some questions answered from that sleazebag Hartwell."

"Oh, the press conference. I can't believe they suspended you for that." He'd seen far worse behavior from reporters after Celeste was murdered, genuine predators who seemed to care only about landing an interview with him.

"Can we sit down?" Danica said. "I need to tell you something."

"We can go back into the living room if you want. It's more comfortable."

"No, I like this space. There's something reassuring about it. Or maybe it's just you." She smiled warmly. "You know, when the laptop fell on the floor, you were the first person I thought to call."

"That makes sense, I guess."

"But I didn't even remember you were an engineer until your phone started ringing. Funny, huh?"

"Yeah." A light flickered on the other side of the room, just over her shoulder, and he could have sworn it came from the starfield, a little star glimmering out of the emptiness.

When he returned from inside the house with another chair, she was standing in the area reserved for his shuttle and rocket models. "This is really beautiful," she said, pointing at the large model of the orbiter.

He gave a sheepish shrug. "You wanted to tell me something. Is it about Zoey? I'm sorry about last night. She can be a real handful."

"That's not it." Danica sat down and the old chair seemed to sag beneath her as if she were carrying a heavy load. "The plane crash," she mumbled. "I need to tell you everything."

She proceeded to relate what had happened to her on Friday: driving through thick fog, watching the plane fall from the sky, climbing over a dead woman before dragging the senator from the downed plane.

"That's why you were so tough on him in the press conference," Garrison said.

"He's up to his neck in all of this. That's why I need to figure out who that woman was." Danica pointed at her broken laptop. "Even if I fix that, it won't be of much use. My station won't allow me back in the building for a week. Which means I can't look at any videotape. And I'm shut out of news databases like EBSCO and Lexis-Nexis."

"Lexis-Nexis? I have access to that."

"Seriously?"

"Yeah. Through NASA. I was searching some stuff on it the other day."

"That's great! Show me how to log in."

"Um . . ." Helping her diagnose a hardware problem was one thing; allowing her to use NASA resources was another level altogether, because he'd be breaking his computer utilization agreement, not to mention violating all sorts of security policies.

"It's the only way I can find out who that woman was."

What Danica didn't understand was that he wasn't a person who challenged rules, especially because breaking them came at such a steep cost. Don't speed or risk receiving a ticket. Don't hack into NASA or risk losing your job. Don't drive late at night or risk running into a psycho with a gun. "I'm sorry. I can't. They might fire me."

"No they won't. We can sit at your computer together. It would be like you doing it. You said you're already authorized, right?" She chewed nervously on her bottom lip, and Garrison noticed she wasn't wearing any lipstick.

Maybe Danica was right. He was an authorized user and could oversee everything she did. It would be like sitting in the passenger seat while someone else drove the rental car.

Except that wasn't allowed either.

He ran a hand through his hair, weighing his options. Everything came down to a basic choice: help Danica and find himself in deep trouble, or stand pat and watch Danica lose what was important to her. When he looked at things that way, the answer was easy.

He reached over and powered on his computer. "Just tell me what you need."

"You're a nice guy, Garrison. Going out of your way for a person you don't know."

But that wasn't true—he did know her. In only a few days, he'd discovered she was not only a determined news reporter on some quest for justice, but also someone who made time to connect with a girl in a wheelchair. Someone who'd lost a brother to muscular dystrophy. Someone who wasn't afraid of a powerful politician.

Someone he was falling for.

"I'll help you," he told her, "but on only one condition. Don't ask me to reprogram a satellite to spy on Senator Hartwell."

"You can do that?" she said, smiling broadly.

"I'm an engineer."

"So my fate lies in the hands of a super nerd."

"You want my help or not?" he said, laughing.

"I do." She rose and paced across the room, pausing in front of the star mural. "There used to be a window here, right?"

He followed and stopped behind her. "How did you know?"

She gestured to the ceiling. "All these fluorescent lights. They're not good for you. And this huge poster—it's too dark and doesn't reflect anything. You need some sunlight in here."

As he edged forward, she turned around and they bumped into each other. "Sorry," he said, gulping nervously, "I was just going to show you where that old window was." He traced a finger along the poster, revealing a hidden rectangle that spanned the breadth of stars known as the Pinwheel Galaxy. He turned and shrugged. "I hadn't really thought about it. I guess this room could use some natural light. Maybe I'm just used to the darkness."

They faced each other, only a few inches apart, and gazed into each other's eyes. She moistened her lips and cleared her throat. "I guess we should get started."

He'd never made the journey NASA had selected him for, never got strapped into the seat of a shuttle orbiter, never felt its engines rumble beneath him as he took off into the great unknown. But he'd heard the tales from Chip and other astronauts. They said launching into space was the most profound moment of their lives.

Just one flight.

Just one kiss.

The thought both electrified and terrified him. What if Danica didn't feel the same way?

She lifted a hand and placed it on his shoulder, as if reading his mind. "I feel like I've known you forever."

"Me, too."

Slipping an arm around her waist, Garrison's hand found the small of her back and pulled her toward him. His other hand met hers and their fingers curled together. The scent of her perfume, layers of blackberry and jasmine and vanilla, wafted over him. He took a deep breath and readied himself for the journey.

Then she reached up and kissed him.

He wasn't sure what shocked him more, the fact that they'd shared a kiss or that she'd acted first. It all happened so fast.

"I don't know why I did that," she said quickly, pulling away. "I'm sorry."

"I'm not."

"You're not?" she said, her eyes widening.

Garrison whispered, "I should have done this sooner." Now certain what he wanted, he drew Danica tightly against him. He lightly stroked her face, tracing a finger along her cheek, around her mouth, and down her neck. She sighed softly in response and parted her lips.

He tilted his head and leaned down, closing his eyes. When he met her lips—those lovely and delicious lips—he found himself in the starfield once more, no longer drifting but soaring, as a brilliant star burst out of the darkness and illuminated his universe.

Chapter 27

As Zoey waited for her dad to pick her up from school, she tried to map out a strategy for Friday. There was no sense in telling him about the party Cara was throwing—the one everyone was talking about—because she knew his reaction. Rather, his overreaction.

She could soft-pedal things, tell him that she could go directly to Cara's house once classes were over. After all, Cara lived less than two blocks from campus, and Zoey would only have to cross one major road: the one in front of the school. Her dad would never need to know that it was going to be a pool party . . . or that both boys and girls would be there.

Her plan was foolproof except for one thing: he'd still have to pick her up.

That hitch, that perpetual and annoying hitch, had plagued her since she could remember. Just once, she wanted to do something on her own without him butting in and ruining all the fun. It was bad enough that she wouldn't be able to join the other kids in the pool—but if he showed up and created a scene in front of everyone . . . well, she'd probably have to quit school out of embarrassment.

The only way this would work, she figured, was if she could find someone else to drive her home from the party. Cara's folks? Not if they were chaperoning. Danica? Zoey perked up at the idea but quickly realized Danica was likely too busy to help even if she wanted to. Then a thought flashed—was Lucas coming to the party? She sure hoped so. And if his parents were anything like him, they'd certainly be willing to lend a hand.

With each possibility, Zoey grew more excited. One of those options was bound to work out. And then it hit her—the hardest part would be convincing her dad to stay away. Because no matter who offered to drive her home, even if the entire Clear Lake police force volunteered to escort the vehicle with their lights flashing and sirens wailing, her father would stare back at her unblinkingly and reply, "No, really, I'd prefer to drive you myself."

She blew a big sigh, wishing that Cara would show up so they could chat about options. She hadn't talked much with her best friend in the past few days, not even today at lunch, although that was because Cara had to discuss a U.S. History project with someone from her class. Zoey scanned the students still waiting for rides, knowing that Cara sometimes hung out and talked with friends before walking home. But Zoey didn't see her . . . or anyone else she knew, except Tiffany McAdams, who was lying on a concrete bench with her eyes closed like some Disney princess.

That's it! Maybe she could sleep over at Cara's on Friday. Her dad probably wouldn't give her too much grief; after all, he'd already agreed to that plan last weekend. Then he could pick up her up on Saturday morning, after everyone had left. That would work.

She took the phone from her holster and texted a message to Cara: *OK for me to slp ovr Friday?*

A few seconds later, Cara sent a reply. *Sry. Busy. Talk later.*

Zoey groaned in frustration. She really wanted to nail down the plans right away, before her dad showed up. Her fingers flew as she texted another note: *Check with ur folks. If I can stay with u, dad will let me go.*

A *beep-beep* sounded from her left, and Zoey looked up. "You ready?" her dad called through the open window of the van.

"Yeah, just a second." Zoey checked her phone again—nothing. Deciding she didn't want to come off as annoying, she suppressed the urge to shoot Cara another message and re-holstered the phone.

The van came to a full stop, and her dad practically skipped out to greet her. He gave her a peck on the head. "Great to see you, sweetie! How was school?"

"You're in a good mood," she said grumpily, her arms crossed.

"I'm in a *fantastic* mood. Get inside and I'll tell you about my day."

That was the last thing she wanted, to hear him drone on about one of his computer programs or his latest engineering marvel. She'd heard more than she ever wanted about resin casting, gyroscopes, and gas chromatographs, so she made the quick transfer into the van and shut the door behind her, closing her eyes and trying to fade away into her own world.

She heard the van's rear doors open, then listened to the sounds of her dad grunting as he lifted the wheelchair up and the clanking of metal as he secured it down. Then she heard something else—he was humming. He never did that.

He hopped back behind inside the van, bobbing his head and lightly drumming his fingers on the steering wheel as if music were playing in his head. "You ready to blow this popsicle stand?" he said.

Wow, he really was in a good mood.

Maybe she'd been getting herself worked up over nothing. Dad wasn't an ogre. Sure, he meddled too much, but he always had her best interests at heart. All she needed to do was explain how much this party meant to her and ask him straight out for permission, without resorting to some complicated plan involving a sleepover that Cara's folks might not even support. What was the worst that could happen? Oh yeah, he could say no.

"I saw your friend again today," he said as they pulled out of the parking lot.

"Cara?"

"Huh? No, silly. Danica came by this morning."

"I thought you were supposed to be working on that shuttle." Zoey bit off the words as soon as she said them. *Don't piss him off.* "I mean, you've been working really hard. It's looking excellent. So, Danica came by?"

"She just showed up. We talked for a long while."

"Oh no, is this about tennis? She's gonna bail on me, isn't she?"

He chuckled. "No, I helped her with a computer problem. And then we had a nice chat. Nice. Really nice."

Zoey heard her phone vibrate from the rear of the van and knew Cara had finally found time to reply. Hopefully, Cara's parents would sign off on her plan, although from what Cara had been saying, those two couldn't agree on anything. If the sleepover was a no-go, Zoey needed to ask her dad's permission now, while he was in such high spirits. "My phone," she mumbled.

"Oh, I think I left it in back."

"I'm waiting for a text."

"It can wait until we get home, right?"

Her stomach tightened. "I guess."

He turned onto a boulevard that ran alongside a bayou and greenbelt, the same greenbelt that she would have used to travel back and forth to school, except the mile-and-a-half trip from home was a total pain to drive in a wheelchair. Across the greenbelt, she could see Cara's backyard through wrought-iron fencing, a formation of moss rock boulders arranged on one end of a massive swimming pool, a hot tub on the other, and a pavilion where Zoey imagined drinks and snacks would be served.

"Um, Zoey?" her dad said. "Tell me what you think about Danica."

"Other than she's awesome? I definitely want to keep playing tennis with her." Zoey's voice trailed off as she studied him. He looked different somehow. Normally he drove with his hands clenched around the steering wheel, and his eyes were always darting to the mirrors. But he was looking, well, relaxed. It was almost as if he were—oh, my God. "You like her, don't you?"

He turned his head and smiled, then waggled his eyebrows at her.

"I knew it!"

"What do you mean, you knew it?"

"Give me a break, Dad. I see how you act when she's around. Like uber-goofy. You're even recording her program on the DVR. I thought that was weird, seeing as how you don't like news people."

"It's just that . . ."

She placed a hand on his arm. "It's okay, Dad. I'm glad you like Danica. I like her, too."

He sighed. "She's so easy to talk with. When she's not around, I'm always thinking about her."

"You are?" she replied, believing this must be the strangest conversation they'd ever had. "Does she feel the same . . . you know?"

He didn't answer but had a spacey, faraway look on his face. "We kissed today."

"No. Way."

"It was amazing." He swallowed and moistened his lips. "Don't tell her I told you."

They didn't talk the rest of the way home, but this wasn't one of their strained silences. The Beatles were blasting from the stereo, and her dad was humming along with them, once even joining in on the chorus of *Love Me Do*.

Zoey stared at him and tried to process this unbelievable news. For years, she'd hoped to match her father up with single women she'd come across: her third-grade teacher Ms. Archer, who was the nicest teacher she'd ever had; the woman at the astronomy store, who seemed interested in their ranch and checking out his telescope; plus all the divorced moms of her friends. But he'd always seemed resistant, as if he were afraid of something.

What had it been, a week since the two of them had met? And they'd already kissed? This wasn't like him at all.

In some ways, the whole idea of her dad falling for Danica—and vice versa—was weird and nauseating. But that wasn't what Zoey was feeling. In her heart, she knew that those two belonged together . . . like Romeo and Juliet.

When they reached their house, Zoey noticed Danica's car in the street. She cleared her throat and said, "Dad, it's cool how you two like each other."

"Thanks, honey."

"I want you to be happy."

"Me, too," he said, his voice almost a whisper.

She felt as close to him as she had in a long time. Suddenly she thought about Lucas and wondered if she ought to tell her dad about him, how nice he was, how smart he was, how she looked forward to school just so she could talk with him. And she wondered what it was like to be kissed. Instead, she said, "I'm glad you told me about Danica. It means a lot."

As her dad got out of the van to retrieve her chair, she wondered why their conversation couldn't always be like this, open and honest. No arguments, no fighting, just the two of them sharing the special moments of their lives.

He opened her door, and she swung out to position herself in the wheelchair. "Just to let you know," he said, "Danica and I are going on a date this Friday."

"Friday?" She couldn't believe her luck. Now she could attend the party without him getting in the way. "That's great,

Dad."

"I was thinking you could order a movie. Make some popcorn. I think you're old enough to stay home by yourself for a few hours."

I'm fourteen, she wanted to snap, but instead she said, "Remember how Cara went out of town last weekend? She's having a small get-together on Friday."

"A party?"

"Just a couple of friends. What do you think about me sleeping over?" She could see the gears turning in his head, so she added, "You wouldn't have to worry about me while you're on your date. You could stay out as late as you wanted. Please?"

"Let me think about it."

Normally, "let me think about it" was his way of prefacing a sure-fire rejection, but she could tell he was actually giving the idea some consideration. He muttered quietly, as if debating the merits with himself, then finally said, "I don't see why not. Just let me know when I need to pick you up on Saturday."

Zoey didn't recognize the man who was wearing her father's clothes and talking with his voice, but she was thrilled that he'd shown up. Following him as he rushed toward the house, she could only hope that this new agreeable guy would stick around.

When her phone buzzed again, she rotated her chair ninety degrees so it wouldn't roll down the driveway and paused to read all of the incoming messages. There was only one, and it was from Cara.

Sry but the party is private. u r not invited.

Chapter 28

Garrison had been gone less than twenty minutes, but Danica was already looking forward to his return. She knew that pursuing the story about the woman on the plane was important, but after reading the same accounts over and over, she wasn't any closer to solving the mystery. That's why she was wandering around his workshop and thinking about what had occurred between the two of them.

Kissing him had happened out of the blue. She certainly hadn't planned it, although if she were honest with herself, she'd been thinking about Garrison ever since they'd met.

Normally she seemed to attract guys who were flashy and flirty, but Garrison was the polar opposite. There was a quiet confidence about him, like how he knew his way around a computer or how he knew his way around a kitchen. When his van had that flat tire two days ago, he'd simply slipped into some old clothes and changed it out with the spare. He hadn't drawn attention to himself like so many others would. Like her old boyfriend. Like her dad.

She scanned the room and tried to make sense of the eclectic group of furnishings and decorations, hoping to learn more about the man with whom she'd shared a kiss. In one corner sat his computer desk, complete with docking station and two oversized monitors and a Mister Spock bobblehead, all a testament to his nerdiness. In another corner, she saw a treadmill and a set of weights and dumbbells, organized and clutter-free, confirming what she'd already suspected—he liked to work out.

Curious about the large space shuttle under construction on the other side of the room, she crossed to an area apparently dedicated to space memorabilia. Three model rockets, mounted on wooden bases, rested on a wide bookshelf beside his workbench. Arranged from largest to smallest, the Apollo Saturn V, Gemini Titan II, and Mercury Redstone rockets didn't seem as if they'd been made from a kit or bought from a store. Fascinating, she thought. He must have designed and built those himself.

Next to the rockets was a framed photo of a woman and a little girl, walking hand-in-hand at what appeared to be a Fourth of July picnic. Danica didn't need her reporter skills for this one—the picture was obviously Garrison's late wife and his daughter. Before Zoey ended up in a wheelchair.

Danica lifted the photo from the shelf and ran a finger across the glass. No wonder he was a homebody. Losing so much—his wife, his perfect little girl—would put anyone's priorities in order.

Danica hadn't known Garrison long, but it was obvious he was a loving father. Yet that was only part of the reason he'd been occupying her mind. There was something *right* about him, a core of decency and self-sacrifice coupled with a deep yearning.

She looked to the far wall, which was covered by that beautiful poster of a swirling galaxy. In some ways, the starry poster reminded her of the bedroom ceiling in her old home, where a pale blue sky and wisps of lacy clouds had appeared one weekend soon after Dad had taken off. As a teenager, Danica used to stretch out on her comforter and stare up at her mom's creation, pretending she was a bird flying above the earth, free from the troubles of high school and of a family trying to cope with the twin disasters of illness and infidelity.

She picked up the Redstone rocket and held it out in front of her, the star-filled galaxy in the background, and swung it slowly, as if steering the ship through the stars, like she used to do with a falcon figurine above her bed.

Just then, the tiny red tower positioned on top of the rocket fell off and bounced onto the floor.

"Oh, crap," she said, looking down to find the missing piece. She dropped to a knee, still holding the fragile rocket in one hand while sweeping the other beneath the treadmill.

Then she heard the front door.

For years, she'd had to conduct ambush interviews, barge in on unsuspecting people and pepper them with embarrassing questions and accusations. Their wide eyes and slack-jawed expressions would say it all—sudden realization and abject terror—and that's what always ended up running on the air. If Garrison walked through that workshop door and saw her fumbling with his stuff, he'd see the same look on her face.

With no time to think, she hurriedly placed what was left of the rocket on the shelf and dashed over to the computer desk.

"Danica!" Garrison called, and her heart practically stopped. "We're back."

She gulped. "Just working on the computer," she replied, hoping to sound cheerful. Her eyes darted back and forth across the floor, searching for the miniature tower. But it was nowhere to be found.

"Come on out here. Zoey wants to say hi."

Feeling as guilty as a three year old caught stealing cookies, Danica exited the workshop, not afraid that Garrison would yell at her or anything like that, but worried he'd think less of her for being so nosy.

When she walked through the door, Garrison's face spread into a big smile. "Hey, there."

"Where's Zoey?"

"Right behind me. She was messing with her cell phone a minute ago. I gotta tell you, I was pretty nervous telling her about us."

Us? For some reason, that pronoun seemed anything but comforting. "You told her?"

"It's okay, isn't it?"

"I-I don't know."

Her feelings were all jumbled now. Maybe this relationship—or whatever it was—would have been fine if it just involved the two of them, a brief romance they could blame on close proximity or on her heightened emotions from the plane crash. But there was a third partner on this dance floor, and the last thing Danica wanted to do was hurt her.

Reading her mind, Garrison said, "Don't worry. Zoey's going to be thrilled."

She swallowed hard. Why was Zoey already in the loop on this? Everything was happening so quickly.

Danica heard the sound of wheels rolling and turned her head down the hall. A shadow spilled onto the wood flooring, and a moment later Zoey rounded the corner.

"Hi there," Danica said, trying to manage a casual smile.

Zoey took one look at them and burst into tears.

Before Garrison had a chance to react, Zoey blew right past him, running over his feet and knocking him and Danica against the wall. The old Winnie the Pooh photo, the one with him dressed as Eeyore, got jostled and fell off its hanger, knocking Danica in the head and then crashing onto the floor.

"Are you hurt?" he asked, then shot a glance at the bedroom door that Zoey had just slammed shut.

"Oh, my God," Danica replied. She reached up slowly to touch her forehead, above her left eye. When she lowered her hand, there was blood on her fingers.

"You're bleeding. Let me look."

"It's okay. We shouldn't have . . . and now she's . . ." Danica moved backward and fumbled her way into the workshop, and he rushed after her.

"I swear, Zoey was fine on the way home." He examined the laceration above Danica's eye and felt a sense of relief when the injury appeared superficial. "I don't know what got into her."

"Sure you do."

He shook his head. "No, I don't." Then in a flash of clarity, he said, "You mean us?"

"There is no *us*, Garrison. Today was a mistake."

"Hold on. Listen to me." He grasped her hands, which were trembling. "What happened between us was definitely not a mistake. You and I had . . . have . . . something special. I'm sure of it."

"I should leave."

"Let me talk with Zoey and straighten this out." He gazed into her eyes. "Trust me, Danica, everything's gonna be okay."

She stared up at him, her eyes searching his, and he held his breath. Slowly, her jaw unclenched and the muscles in her hands relaxed. "Be gentle with her, Garrison. I remember being pretty emotional about my family when I was her age."

He nodded and exited the room, leaving Danica to return to her research. Listening outside Zoey's bedroom, he could hear muffled sobs, so he rapped on the door. "Can I come in?"

"Leave me alone."

Tentatively, he cracked open the door and stepped inside. Zoey hadn't even bothered to switch over to the bed. She had parked herself at the desk, head down, her face tucked into the crook of an elbow.

He cleared his throat. "You hurt Danica's feelings. I want you to apologize."

Zoey lifted her head and looked at him, tears staining her

cheeks. "What are you talking about?"

"You know very well what I'm talking about. Throwing a fit when you saw the two of us standing together. You need an attitude change, young lady."

"What I need is time alone instead of you barging in here and jumping my shit."

"Excuse me?" he said, his voice rising. He couldn't remember the last time Zoey used a profanity. "I will not have you talk that way in our home."

"Why?" she yelled. "Because I'm supposed to be Miss Perfect? Newsflash, Dad, I'm not perfect. Neither are you."

He could feel rage boil up inside him, and nothing would have felt better than to yell it out of his system. But this wasn't the time, especially with Danica across the hall. He simply said, "Stay here and think about the way you're acting. Come out when you feel better."

He waited for her to respond, but all she did was bury her head in her folded arms.

"I can promise you one thing, Zoey," he said, his neck muscles tightening. "If your attitude doesn't change, you can forget about going to that party with your friends."

In response, her shoulders shuddered and her body shook. She let out a desperate wail he'd heard only a few times in his life, when she was feeling completely sorry for herself. He wasn't sure what was wrong, but he'd obviously picked at some wound of hers. He stood and watched her, concerned and confused, then decided maybe it was best to leave.

As he turned the doorknob, he heard Zoey mumble, "I don't hate Danica."

"What?"

"This isn't about her."

"Then why are you crying?"

She lifted her head. "You wouldn't understand."

"Try me."

"Dad, you're always trying to fix things for me. This is

something you can't fix."

He studied her and realized she was harboring dark pain behind those eyes. Perhaps seeing him with Danica surfaced too many emotions: sadness at her mom being gone, jealousness of the new woman in his life, even loneliness or emptiness—feelings he understood all too well. Afraid he'd only make matters worse, he told her, "Feel better, Pookie. I love you." Then he left the room, wondering if getting involved with Danica had been a big mistake.

"Everything okay?" Danica asked when he returned to the workshop. Her lips were pressed tight, and he knew she was worried.

"Zoey's upset about something. I don't know what, but she assured me it's not about me and you. I think it's best to just let her cry it out."

"I'm sure this is very overwhelming."

"Yeah." His mind was spinning. He'd never seen Zoey so distraught. Kissing Danica had clearly complicated things.

"I want you to know something, Garrison. I'm not upset. Maybe a little unsettled, but that's okay."

"Maybe we shouldn't have kissed," he said, suddenly feeling guilty for having acted so impulsively. "That was a little too eager on my part."

A smile teased the corners of her mouth. "I think I kissed you first."

"Oh yeah," he replied with a smile. "I forgot." He could feel himself wanting to kiss her again but held back, knowing Zoey could barge in at any second. Instead he said, "How's your research coming?"

"Bleh. All dead ends." She patted the chair beside her. "Join me? I could use some moral support right now."

"You bet." He cleared papers off his computer desk to give her more room, then placed Mister Spock on the shelf behind the monitors. "Sometimes at work we bounce ideas and problems off each other, even when the other person doesn't know anything about the subject. And trust me, I don't know jack about politics."

"I'll try anything at this point. Okay, so this trip started in Nevada. I guess what they say is true—what happens in Vegas stays in Vegas. Anyway, Hartwell talked at a conference, and Arnie Fletcher was with him. The Genetechnologix guys were out there, too."

"Whoa. Can we start at the crash and work backward? It's the way my mind operates."

"I guess." Danica went on to explain the basics of the plane crash, how it had occurred while the plane was landing in heavy fog around four in the morning. She talked about how the plane split into two pieces, the front section containing the five dead men and the back section containing the senator and the mystery woman.

"They shouldn't have been trying to land in fog," Garrison said. "There are all sorts of protocols around that."

"Are you a pilot or something?"

Back during astronaut training, he'd had the opportunity to take the stick a few times, always under the supervision of an experienced pilot, never during a landing. He'd heard horror stories about how weather was a pilot's worst enemy. Weather and overconfidence. "The pilot should have known better than to attempt a landing."

"Maybe someone told him to land anyway. Maybe Hartwell. Does that make any sense?"

"Hmm," he said, pondering her theory. "Could be. Do you remember when the Polish president died in that plane crash?"

"In Russia? Yeah, I remember. I was with my friend when the news broke. Sam was pretty upset. She grew up in Warsaw."

"That crash happened in heavy fog, too. They believe officials on the plane forced the pilots to try and land."

"Look, even if Hartwell is to blame, I'd never be able to prove it."

"Unless the plane had a black box. What kind of plane was it?"

She checked her notes. "A Gulfstream G550, owned by Genetechnologix Corporation. It was their business jet."

"Yeah, that's pretty fancy. I'm sure it had both a flight data recorder and a cockpit voice recorder. The NTSB should have already found them."

"But it'll take months before they issue a report. By that time, Hartwell will already be re-elected and able to bury the findings." She shook her head. "Forget the crash. I'm trying to figure out everywhere Hartwell was in Las Vegas. That's the key. He must have picked up this woman there. She was late-twenties or early-thirties, maybe Hispanic, wild tattoos down both arms, another under her ear, and she had a huge rock around her neck. I told you about the necklace, right? I'm thinking Hartwell met her in a casino." She shook her head and scoffed. "Knowing him, it could have been a strip club. I doubt she boarded in El Paso when they stopped to refuel."

"What did you say?"

"She could have been a stripper that he smuggled on in Vegas. She's not listed on any manifest."

"No, you said they refueled in El Paso."

"That's right."

"I'll bet a hundred bucks she got on there."

Her head whipped around. "How can you be so sure?"

"You said it was a Gulfstream G550. That has a range of something like six-thousand-plus nautical miles."

"I don't understand."

"They didn't stop to take on fuel. They stopped to take on a passenger."

Chapter 29

Garrison saw Danica's eyes light up at his comment, and he marveled at how animated she'd become. Her skin was practically humming.

"You're right!" she said, circling a fist in the air. "That woman must have boarded the plane in Texas. Garrison, you're a genius!" She reached over and kissed him on the cheek.

He felt a blush rise in his face. It wasn't the kiss that embarrassed him, but rather the way she'd reacted to his theory, like he was some kind of rock star for applying a little rational analysis to the situation. He saw the Spock head bobbing in agreement.

"What now?" he asked.

"If that's true, Hartwell didn't pick her up out of the blue like I'd been thinking. She must have had a reason to sneak on that plane from some out-of-the-way airport at some godforsaken hour. I bet she was afraid she'd be recognized."

Danica was getting pumped up, and Garrison could only watch in amazement. For him, solving such a mystery was a logic problem—gather the facts and the answer becomes obvious. But she was acting like a bloodhound that had alerted on a scent, obsessed with the chase and oblivious to everything around her. She began spouting random thoughts: maybe the woman was Hartwell's mistress, El Paso was on the Mexican border, the jet was owned by a high-growth bioengineering company, Senator Hartwell was in the middle of a reelection.

Danica was just like Zoey, he thought, their minds both racing a mile a minute.

She opened her computer bag and riffled through a stash of papers in the side pocket. "Can you run some searches for me?"

Garrison nodded. "What am I looking for?"

"Start with *Mexican bioengineering.*"

He typed the search terms into Lexis-Nexis and waited for the results. "Two hundred thousand hits."

"Now add *Hartwell.*"

He clacked a few keys. "Seven hundred, give or take. Where are you headed with this?"

"I'm not sure." She buried her head in the open laptop bag. "Any articles with Hartwell in the title?"

"No." He sighed. "What was the name of the company that owned the plane?"

"Genetechnologix Corporation."

He tried a few different combinations of terms, but nothing of interest popped up in the search results. Out of ideas, he began to tinker with the search interface, when he suddenly realized the default option for news sources was English-only. "Let me try something," he said, clicking the dropdown box to indicate *Foreign Language News.*

Reentering the search terms and then limiting the articles to the past six months, he pressed the search button. Twenty-five articles came back. "Here's something. Looks like some articles from *La Prensa,* the newspaper out of Mexico City. Check out that first one."

Danica clicked the link and stared at the article on the screen. "You're kidding."

"What's the matter? You speak Spanish, right?"

"Um . . . not so much."

"I just assumed, you know, with a last name like Cortez. Sorry, dumb assumption. Let me look at it. My Spanish is a little rusty, but I did spend a summer in Barcelona back in college." He didn't bring up the fact that he'd also worked side-by-side with two Spanish-speaking astronauts, Pedro Duque from Spain and Ellen Ochoa, the second Hispanic woman to fly in space.

He began reading the article and quickly discovered that Hartwell was a vocal proponent of Genetechnologix's proposed expansion into western Texas and into Mexico, going so far as to insert a nineteen-million dollar earmark into the latest Senate budget for constructing an advanced bioengineering center in San Antonio. Plus, the article seemed to indicate that Hartwell was cozy with Mexican officials as well. "Hmm," he said. "It's interesting, in a policy wonk sort of way. But I don't think there's anything here that will lead us to that woman. Looks like another dead end."

Danica was fiddling nervously with her hair, twisting the ends around her index finger. "The station tries to pass me off as a Latina," she said, her eyes cast down. "The way they pronounce my name, the way they tell me to wear heavy makeup."

He looked long at her, noticing the features that made her appear Hispanic: raven hair, exotic lips, and eyes the color of coffee beans. Now that he had a chance to study her more closely, her skin did seem lighter than it looked on TV. "I don't think it matters."

"It matters to me. I mean, I'd be proud if I was Hispanic. But I'm not. I feel like I'm lying to everyone about who I am."

"Don't be so hard on yourself."

She scoffed. "I think I know about fifteen words of Spanish. It's an open secret at the station. Dah-nica Corrrrrrtez. God, I'm such a fraud."

He wasn't sure what to say.

Just then, Zoey knocked on the door and opened it. "How's it going?"

As glad as he was to see Zoey in a better mood, she had the worst timing in the world. "Could you give us a few minutes? I'll start dinner pretty soon."

"That's okay," Danica said. "Come on in, Zoey. We're not getting anywhere anyway."

"What are you doing?" Zoey asked, wheeling up and inserting her wheelchair into the space between him and Danica, nudging his chair aside to make room.

"I'm trying to find a woman," Danica replied, shrugging her shoulders. "Maybe Hispanic. Real pretty, with long tattoos down her arms."

"Cool. Why are you looking for her?"

"Please, let Danica work," he said, tapping his foot and growing unhappier with every moment Zoey was interrupting things. He looked over at Danica. She was grinning.

"If she's an actress, just look her up on IMDB," Zoey offered. "You know, Internet Movie Data Base? Oh, if you're looking for her, she probably did something wrong. Check out TMZ—"

"Zoey," he cut in, exasperated. "The woman's not an actress."

"Wait, I've got it!" Danica said, snapping her fingers and pointing at Zoey. Their eyes met and they nodded in unison. "Google Images!" they said simultaneously.

Danica moved the keyboard in front of her and typed in a search. "Let's give it a shot. Tattoo sleeve, tiger, skulls, Hartwell. And the answer is . . ."

He heard the click of the Enter key being depressed, and a second later, a low whistle from Danica's mouth. "Oh, my God, it's her." She pointed at the screen and yelled, "It's her!"

"Seriously?" he said, thinking Danica must be pulling his leg.

"Who is that?" Zoey asked.

Danica jumped up and shook Zoey by the shoulders. "That is Senator Joseph Hartwell's worst nightmare. Some woman named Celi Montalvo. We did it, guys!"

Garrison couldn't believe what he was seeing. On the screen was an olive-skinned woman sporting a long colorful tattoo down each arm and a dark tattoo that ran along her neck below her right ear. In her early thirties, he guessed, she was wearing an expensive gown and talking with three men in suits. One of the men was Hartwell.

"So, who is Celi Montalvo?" Garrison asked.

Danica darted back into her chair. "That's what I'm gonna figure out. Can I work here?"

"Of course. You want me to start dinner? I was thinking steamed sea bass over rice. Maybe a little asparagus. Might take an hour or so."

"That sounds amazing. Can I call if I need some help with Spanish?"

"Hold on, Dad," Zoey said, throwing up her hands. "You know Spanish and didn't tell me? It's, like, my hardest class!"

I found her, Danica thought, staring at the photo of the woman with the brightly colored tattoos, the woman who had been haunting her dreams since that terrible morning less than a week ago. But a photograph wouldn't be enough—she needed to assemble the pieces of this puzzle, determine how Hartwell figured into all of this. Only then would she be able to reveal the truth about the senator. Only then would she be able to reclaim her reputation as a serious journalist and not as some crazy reporter trying to steal the limelight. Of course, a little limelight wouldn't necessarily be bad.

The first order of business was to find out more about Celi Montalvo. Danica started with the blurb she'd found. Running the website's text through a crude Spanish-to-English translator, she learned that the year-old photo was of a businesswoman discussing economic development with several Americans. The men standing next to Hartwell were identified as *empresarios*, entrepreneurs or businessmen, but they weren't named.

Was this Montalvo some mover and shaker from Texas, maybe a contributor to Hartwell's campaign? Even if she was, how come she'd snuck onto his plane in the dead of night? That didn't make any sense.

Danica went back to Lexis-Nexis and searched for Celi Montalvo among the English-only articles. There were only three hits, but they were all articles about some woman from East L.A. who had raised six kids on her own, four who eventually became doctors and two who passed the bar exam. That Celi Montalvo didn't have a yellow-and-black tiger tattoo down her arm, a sea of skulls down the other, or an ornate scorpion winding up her neck and reaching below her ear . . . or a pair of breasts that were clearly not organically grown.

Danica scanned the photo again. Would this be enough to expose Hartwell's dishonesty? Probably not.

Absentmindedly, she jiggled the computer mouse, and the cursor responded by performing tight circles on the screen. One lousy picture, she thought, of a woman who looked like that. Danica propped her head onto her hand and stared at the screen. The cursor was circling the woman's name: Celi Montalvo.

Of course. It had to be a nickname. But for what?

She rapped her knuckles against her forehead, frustrated that the only similar words she could come up with were ridiculous: celery and celebration. One look at the tattooed woman—more of a biker chick with nice clothes—Danica knew that her other thought was equally ludicrous. Celi wasn't short for celibate.

Suddenly the answer cleared through the haze. Humming the opening strains to Paul Simon's *Cecilia*, she searched

Lexis-Nexis for Celia Montalvo. If that didn't work, she was going to try Cecilia. She pressed the Enter key, and more than a thousand articles were listed. Elation turned to disappointment as each new article turned into another blind alley. When she searched for Cecilia Montalvo, the results were even worse.

"How's it going?" Garrison asked, poking his head inside the door.

"Slow. Nothing on Celi Montalvo, but now I'm thinking it's a nickname. I found a bunch of articles about Celia Montalvo or Cecilia Montalvo, but so far they're all false leads. It's a long slog wading through them."

"Good luck. You can solve this. I believe in you."

She brightened at his encouragement. This was what made her tick, running down stories and sorting rumors from facts, and then being recognized for bringing the truth to light. Looking up into his kind blue-grey eyes, she desperately wanted to shut down the computer and spend the rest of the evening alone with him, but she also knew better. "Well, I guess I ought to get back at it. Someone's gotta find Celi."

"Huh," he muttered, "I don't know if this helps, but I once worked with a woman with the first name Araceli. She was from Puerto Rico. Celi? Araceli? I don't know if those names are related."

"Araceli?" She spelled it back to him. "I'll give it a try."

Once more, she returned to the news database, this time performing a search for Araceli Montalvo. She held her breath as she waited for the results. When they came, she could hardly believe what they said.

According to the handful of articles, Araceli Montalvo was a businesswoman from Ciudad Juarez, the city across the Rio Grande from El Paso. A real estate mogul. The most powerful woman in the state of Chihuahua. And the heavily tattooed daughter of Enrique Montalvo, the purported head of one of Mexico's most violent drug cartels.

"You think Hartwell was having an affair with her?" Garrison asked.

"I don't know that it matters. Look at who she is. Whether or not Hartwell was screwing her, he had to know her history. Seriously, how is he going to explain this drug cartel connection? And then he sneaks her onto his plane and lies about her being there?" She waved to the computer screen. "Bye, bye, Hartwell. Enjoy your retirement."

Chapter 30

Sitting in Sam's apartment, Danica couldn't help but feel giddy. She'd spent the previous day tracking down the facts around Araceli Montalvo, figuring out the woman's unseemly connections to Hartwell, and planning how she would tell the world.

"It's been a while since I've seen you this happy," Sam told her. "I like it."

"I just wish we could put a camera on Hartwell when he hears the bad news." Danica checked the time—only an hour before she'd head to the studio to announce her findings live on the Eyewitness9 six-o'clock broadcast.

"So you're done with weekday mornings?" Sam asked.

"Oh yeah. I am so looking forward to sleeping in." Danica had called Kathy Hammett last night to arrange a secret early-morning meeting, where they discussed the likely end of the senator's career, the definite end of Danica's suspension, and the start of her new responsibilities as the sole Eyewitness9 weeknight anchor, effective at the end of the month when Melinda Parris made her move to St. Louis.

"You don't have to tell me, but did they give you a raise? Weeknight anchor is super-high profile, I know."

"Obviously I have to get my agent involved, but Kathy was

pretty upfront about wanting to keep me, especially with Melinda basically dropping them to leave Texas. You probably heard that her husband signed with the Rams a couple of weeks ago."

She didn't want to tell Sam that she still hadn't committed to Kathy's deal. First, there was no deal unless the Hartwell story panned out. Second, she was still trying to figure out a way to do more investigative pieces while balancing Kathy's desire to lock her in the anchor chair five nights a week.

"I'm jealous, Danni. I'm not afraid to admit it. Next thing you know, you'll be in Rockefeller Plaza, shooting the breeze with Matt Lauer and Al the weatherman. What's his name?"

"Roker."

"See, you already know all the movers and shakers in New York. And I'm serious, I think you could parlay this deal into a network gig. Imagine your face on a poster over Times Square. It's what you've always wanted."

"Yeah," Danica said dreamily.

"It's not like you have any ties to Houston."

"Just you. And uh . . ." She trailed off, as an image of Garrison pushed its way into her mind, coming into sharp focus like a developing Polaroid snapshot. In her thoughts, she could see him there, standing in the kitchen cooking last night's sea bass, the warm mist from the bamboo basket curling around his head, his delight as he recalled how a young Zoey used to call the meal *steamed bad ass*.

"Earth to Danica," Sam said. "What was that?"

"Nothing."

"Don't lie to me. You fuzzed out there. Something's rattling around in your brain."

She sighed, trying to decide whether she should tell Sam the truth. They'd never kept each other in the dark on matters such as these, but she also didn't need Sam's cheerleading about her love life. Or worse, her opposition.

"I really like living in Houston," she said.

"Because? Come on, Danni, don't make me beat it out of you with this walking boot."

She took a big breath. "Okay, it's Garrison."

"I thought so! Are you telling me you'd give up a career in New York just to be with someone you met a week ago?"

Danica smiled mischievously. "Guess we'll never know. By the way, I won't be able to go to the movies with you tomorrow night. Garrison asked me on a date."

"Now we're talking, chica. Where are you two going?"

"I'm not sure. Somewhere local. He also wants me to visit their place in the country sometime."

"Ooh, I like it. A little outdoor sex. Sounds kinky."

"You've got a filthy imagination," Danica replied, shaking her head. "Garrison's not like that. He's very respectful."

"Wow, I'm surprised a tree hugger like you would go for an uptight Boy Scout. Does this guy even know he's dating a big star?"

"Please."

"Do you remember when you broke that story where all those people in the district attorney's office resigned?"

Of course she remembered. It was the story that launched her career. "What about it?"

"The public wouldn't leave you alone. They'd always come up to you in restaurants and the grocery store, asking for your autograph. Is this Garrison secure enough to have people fawn all over you?"

She thought of what Zoey had told her, how her dad hated being in crowds and around strangers. What if this relationship did blossom? Was it fair to make him endure that kind of discomfort?

"And this Hartwell story will be even bigger," Sam continued. "Once you bust a sitting U.S. Senator, it'll eclipse anything you've ever done. Even that story in Austin."

Clenching her fists, Danica tried to fight away the memories of eleven years ago. But they came rushing back, from the thrill of basking in the limelight of the biggest news story in town to the utter despair of learning that the man she'd helped free, Russell Polistini, had slaughtered all those people.

She didn't think anyone could ever forget her role in that debacle, let alone forgive her. Not Sergeant Andrew Quinn's wife. Not the loved ones of the others who died.

Not even herself.

After spending all morning and afternoon on the shuttle model, making steady progress toward assembling its pieces, Garrison decided to spend some time whipping out a solution for Zoey's binocular chair. He'd already found a heavy-duty cotter pin for the base, but he still wanted to improve the swivel mechanism. Of course he could mull over a design here in the workshop, but he couldn't implement a fix until the weekend, because the darn chair was sitting in the garage up at the ranch.

He stepped to his workbench and began piling all sorts of connectors, bearings, and scrap metal into a box. After a few minutes, he was no longer considering the pros and cons of each piece but simply tossing them in. When he realized he could probably construct a new binocular chair from all the junk, he gave it a rest and plopped down in his office chair, utterly exhausted.

Eyeing the clock, he realized he'd been holed up in his workshop the entire day. And if he counted yesterday, when he'd been working alongside Danica at the computer, he hadn't been outside—except to chauffer Zoey—in almost three days.

Normally that wouldn't have bothered him. After all, he'd spent years trying to fortify his home into a place where he and Zoey could feel comfortable and safe. And just like an ancient stone castle built to keep out its enemies, his home had a place that served as final refuge from invasion: his workshop.

He should have felt secure here, but he felt uneasy.

And he thought he knew why. He was allowing himself to dream again.

In those depressing weeks and months and years following Celeste's murder, when his life's plans were altered and his dreams for spaceflight were crushed, he'd found a degree of peace by focusing on what was immediately in front of him. But these past few days had marked a turning point. Now he was looking at the world with a new perspective, one where the here-and-now wasn't sufficient anymore.

Getting to know Danica was the best thing that had happened in a long time. She'd breathed new life into him.

That's why he was uneasy. This feeling of hopefulness was foreign to him.

Leaning back in his chair, he began to think about Danica. The funny thing was how different the two of them were. If a dating website had considered their personality profiles, its sophisticated algorithms would never have matched them up. He was methodical; she was instinctive. He preferred to work alone; she shared her job with millions of viewers. On top of that, he was pretty sure she was a liberal . . . with a capital L.

But none of that mattered.

He stood and paced the room, allowing himself to contemplate a life outside this workshop, a life that wasn't a constant stream of mundane rituals and caregiving chores, one filled with the vibrancy of Danica.

Gazing at the starfield poster, he sighed heavily. Who was he kidding? He was fated to the life he already had. Surely, he was imagining everything about their fledgling relationship. It had just been a kiss, after all.

Besides, the two of them couldn't possibly be destined to end up together. He was a damaged widower. And she was about to become a national star, blasting off on her own fantastic journey. She deserved to soar and not be weighed down by his baggage.

That's right, his inner voice jabbed at him. *Danica needs a real man. Like you used to be.*

He turned, and his foot struck an object that skidded across the floor and bounced off the baseboard. His first thought was that he must have dropped a bolt.

On the floor lay a red miniature latticework tower, the fourth resin-cast version he'd produced for the Redstone rocket and the only one that hadn't fallen apart after he'd removed it from the mold. The needle-like tower, with its escape mini-rocket and three canted nozzles, was supposed to sit atop the bell-shaped astronaut capsule at the apex of the Redstone. His eyes whipped to the bookshelf, where the model rocket still stood. Its escape tower was missing.

What was it doing on the floor? Had he accidentally knocked it off when he was gathering materials? He didn't think so.

His eyes traced a path from the rocket to where he'd kicked it. No, he would have noticed doing that. Zoey must have messed with it.

He pocketed the tower, then ran a hand through his hair, his tense fingers rubbing along his skull. *This is my room*, he thought. Scanning the rest of the workshop and wondering what else Zoey had messed with, he found himself growing more agitated—with her, with himself, with the entire situation.

Other than the red tower, he didn't see anything else out of place. Everything was as he'd left it yesterday . . . and the day before . . . and the day before that. He scowled at the items in the room: the treadmill, where he was destined to forever run in place; the computer, which had locked him into a virtual world; and the space shuttle, which would never transport him to the stars.

Looking around the windowless room, he began to realize that maybe this situation wasn't healthy. A man shouldn't have to feel cooped up like this in his own home. The odd thing was that he'd built this place to be a refuge from the evils of the outside world. But it wasn't a refuge—it was a prison.

It's what you deserve.

Garrison blinked his eyes. He could have sworn that the voice came from the stone-faced Mister Spock, whose angled eyebrows flashed a disapproving glare at him. "No," Garrison said, and reached out and whacked the figurine with the back of his hand. Its head wobbled side to side, mocking him. *Live long and be miserable.* Something snapped inside Garrison, and he grabbed the figurine by the head and twisted until the spring broke and Spock's head came off in his hands.

He couldn't live like this anymore.

Crossing the room, he stood in front of the starfield poster and ran a finger along its swirl of unreachable stars. He yanked it down from the top, tearing it into two pieces. Behind the poster was the room's original window, now covered with pieces of cardboard and a layer of black plastic, all duct-taped together to keep out the light. That definitely had to go.

His fingers began working at the duct tape but couldn't pry it apart. He remembered the rocket escape tower and pulled it from his pocket. Then he began to saw at the tape with the pointed end. Once he loosened a corner, he ripped the remaining duct tape and jerked down the plastic and cardboard.

Light from the afternoon sun pierced through the window.

Now I'm free, he thought, before spying the old photo of Celeste and Zoey on the table.

He clutched it to his chest and felt his knees buckle. Dropping to the floor, he began to sob. Because as long as the man who'd murdered his wife and injured his daughter was still alive, as long as Garrison still held onto the guilt from that fateful night, he'd always be a prisoner to his past.

He would never be free.

Chapter 31

Celeste saw the gun in the man's hands, and her insides turned to ice.

The man standing above Javier, who was writhing on the floor and moaning, had a crazed look. Celeste figured he must be high on drugs. She stood there, stock-still, praying the guy would just grab his money and get out. Suddenly a squeal sounded from her right—*Zoey!*—and the man turned in their direction. His lips peeled back, revealing a set of black, rotten teeth, and he leered at her.

Out of the corner of her eye, she could see Zoey playing in the ball pit. *Please, God. Save us.*

The door to the restrooms flung open, and the other customer came out, the silver-haired man who'd brought food to her. He was rubbing his hands together as if drying them. He made eye contact with her, and a quizzical look crossed his face. Then he looked over to where the gunman stood.

"Stop!" the silver-haired man shouted, although Celeste wasn't sure if he was shouting to her or at the gunman. His hands slid to his waist, and then she saw his shirt move up. Something dark was tucked into his waistband, and his hand twitched toward it.

He has a gun, too. Oh, my God, they're in this together.

Suddenly a loud pop sounded, and the silver-haired man lurched backward. He teetered for a second, looking down at his chest through glasses that had been knocked askew, then slumped to his knees.

Celeste screamed.

The gunman laughed and said to the fallen man, "No one screws with Rusty." He waved his gun and pointed at the lady at the register. "Now empty the cash drawer or you're gonna end up like that asshole."

Why hadn't she listened to Garrison instead of venturing out on her own? The only thing she wanted was for this horrible ordeal to pass. Then she would rush straight home to be with him, to melt into his arms.

Another shot rang out, this time from the man on the floor, whose t-shirt was stained dark in the middle of his chest. His arms hung limply at his sides, and his fingers curled around a small handgun. His lips were moving, possibly involuntarily, and then he coughed up blood.

Celeste took a step back and toward the ball pit. *Whatever happens*, she thought, *I must protect Zoey.*

The gunman was now grabbing under his left shoulder and cursing. He brandished the gun in front of him and took several steps toward the customer, who was still on his knees, his weapon no longer in his hands but lying on the floor. The gunman shoved the barrel of his own gun into the man's face, pushing up his cheek. Without saying a word, he squeezed the trigger and fired a shot directly into the eye of the man, who immediately fell to the floor, lifeless.

Celeste felt a warm rush of urine. "Hail Mary, full of grace," she mumbled. "The Lord is with thee. Blessed art thou amongst women, and blessed is the fruit of thy womb, Jesus."

"Momma!" Zoey called from the ball pit.

"Shut up!" the man shouted.

Celeste urgently shushed Zoey to be quiet while keeping her eyes focused on the gunman. She knew what she had to do:

distract his attention. Inching away from Zoey, she raised her hands. "Please. Take your money and leave us alone."

He threw back his head and uttered a wicked laugh, his ugly teeth giving him the illusion of a corpse. Javier moaned from the ground, and the gunman kicked him in the face. "I ain't going back to prison."

Then he leveled the gun at her.

Detective Carl Curtiss lifted the yellow caution tape and stepped through the door of the Burger King in the foulest mood. He'd investigated murders in the past, mostly domestic disturbances that had escalated to the point of violence, sometimes a murder-suicide, but never with this body count.

And never with a dead cop.

He stepped around a pool of blood and looked at the crumpled man on the floor. "I worked with this guy for eight years," he told the uniformed officer, who was scribbling information onto a log sheet. "Andy Quinn was the best officer—no, he was the best man I've ever known. You find the shooter yet?"

"No, sir. We've alerted the hospitals. You saw the trail of blood out the door. We don't think he got far."

"Get CSU out here. I want prints and DNA. I'm gonna see to it that this son of a bitch gets the needle."

"They're on their way."

Detective Curtiss grimaced at the carnage. "How many?"

"Three dead, one on her way to the hospital. Not sure she's gonna make it. You got Sergeant Quinn here plus a couple of employees, that boy over there and a woman behind the counter. A couple of teenagers called it in. They were on a first date."

"Well, they'll have something to remember it by." Detective Curtiss turned and walked through the restaurant, careful not to disturb the scene but trying to get a feel for what had happened. "Two customers, right?"

"The sergeant just got off duty. And the woman, she's from the Houston area."

"Hmm." Years of training and real-life investigations had taught him that not all cases were as they first appeared. Maybe this was a robbery, maybe not. Maybe it was a love triangle. Detective Curtiss knew the importance of keeping an open mind.

He surveyed the restaurant and noted that all the tables were empty and clean except for two. In a booth beneath a large plate glass window, a cold cup of coffee sat on a tray, two open sugar packets flanking the cup. Just the way Quinn used to drink it.

At a table on the other side of the restaurant, he noted the contents of the other customer's tray. A little hamburger and French fries that been hardly touched. A couple of sodas. And a piece of pie, probably for the woman on her way to the hospital.

He took a few steps past the table, then spun around. Two sodas? "Hey," he shouted to the officer, "are you sure about the number of victims?"

"Yeah. I was first to arrive on scene. There's four vics. Three dead here, plus that lady we transported. What about it?"

"Something's not right."

"I don't understand."

Detective Curtiss rubbed his temples and tried to visualize what had occurred. The suspect would have been standing by the front counter. He must have gotten the drop on Quinn and then taken everybody else out. It didn't make sense that this extra drink was his. But whose? "You checked the bathrooms?" he asked. "Walk-in cooler? Storage room? Parking lot?"

"Of course."

He went back to the table with the two drinks. Two cups. Two straws. He plopped down on an empty chair and scratched his head.

Looking around the room, he studied each table and booth, from the drink station to the children's play area. Nothing seemed out of the ordinary—

"Holy shit!" he called, and began running toward the ball pit. As he drew closer, he saw a tiny, round hole in the plastic wall. *No, not a child.* With an ache swelling in his chest, he peered down into the sea of multicolored balls, afraid to discover what he knew must be there. But no one was inside, thank God.

"False alarm," he called to the officer. "I was worried that a kid might have—"

His eyes caught the diaper bag lying next to the ball pit entrance. His stomach seized. Darting his gaze back to the colored balls, he suddenly saw something move beneath them, nudging them around. A tiny arm came into view, its fingers moving slowly. He gasped.

"It'll be okay, little baby," he whispered. Then he turned and shouted, "Call an ambulance!"

Chapter 32

Danica cruised into the newsroom on Friday morning, unable to stay away from the rush of the place. The previous night's broadcast had been a bombshell, its repercussions still rattling across the country as the sun rose. All the morning shows had led with the shocking story—her story—of a Mexican national who was allegedly another victim of last week's plane crash in Houston.

Danica had laid out the lurid details in her report. Araceli Montalvo, a powerful figure in the drug trade of Northern Mexico, had secretly boarded a plane containing Senator Hartwell during a late-night stop at the Texas border a week ago. Danica herself had witnessed the woman on the downed plane and went into great detail about what she'd seen after the crash—the tattoos, the necklace, the proximity to Hartwell—but she skipped the part about the woman's almost-decapitation.

Barely able to contain her contempt, Danica had gone on to list Hartwell's misdeeds: violating FAA policies by sneaking Montalvo onto the plane without logging her on the manifest, covering up her presence to ensure she wouldn't be discovered, concealing her unseemly and possibly unlawful relationship with his reelection campaign.

"Senator Hartwell continues to insist these claims are baseless," Danica had said in a closing on-air commentary, "but I can assure you I'm telling the truth. Certainly, many questions remain unanswered. How did the senator meet Araceli Montalvo? What was the nature of their relationship? Why did he lie?" She stared straight into the camera. "The citizens of Texas deserve answers."

As Danica stepped off the elevator, she was filled with excitement. She couldn't wait to dig into the rest of the story. But making her way to her desk proved impossible, as she kept getting bombarded with congratulations and high-fives from seemingly everyone at the station.

When she passed Kathy Hammett's office, she considered asking what was shaking on the promised anchor position, but then decided against it. *Whatever happens is supposed to happen.* Then she had a fleeting hope about a possible eventual rise to executive producer, just like Kathy had accomplished. Could something like that be in the cards for her one day?

Kathy looked up and saw her, then beckoned her in by waving a Snickers bar. "You're here. Good. Have you heard the latest?"

"Hartwell?"

"No, no. Bob Woodward. He was on CNN this morning talking about you."

Danica's pulse raced in response. "He was?"

"Yeah. He gave you major props for standing your ground while everyone was bashing you."

"He did?" She could hardly believe it. Bob Woodward, one of the legendary reporters who broke the Watergate scandal, had said nice things about her.

"You sure seem to have a knack for being in the middle of the story. Hurricane Katrina. Now Senator Hartwell. Didn't you live a street over from where Andrea Yates killed her kids? You're like our own Forrest Gump."

Danica couldn't wait to find the video on the CNN website and see Bob Woodward's interview. "What did he say exactly?"

"Ask him yourself. I just got an email from Anderson Cooper's people. They want you and Woodward to do a joint interview tonight."

She gasped. "Really?"

"Danica, it would be easier to hate you if I thought you were lucky. But you've earned this." Kathy bit into the candy bar and said with a mouthful of chocolate, "Just don't forget the little people on your way up."

Don't forget the little people. The remark triggered a sick sense of déjà vu for Danica, as her news editor in Austin had said the same thing after she broke the Wiesler story. For six weeks she'd been the toast of the town, lauded by her peers and commended by her bosses for her instincts and tenacity. Of course, once Russell Polistini went on his killing spree, all of those accolades vanished overnight.

She mumbled goodbye to Kathy and headed out of the office, her mind preoccupied with thoughts of the Austin disaster. She tried not to be pessimistic about it, but the parallels between Wiesler and Hartwell were too similar to ignore: the corruption, the lack of contrition, the eventual public shaming. When the Wiesler story had unfolded, her world seemed perfect. Then everything fell apart.

Would the same thing happen again?

After putting the final touches on his shuttle model, Garrison exited the workshop and came into the family room. At least he was feeling better—yesterday's semi-meltdown had been a definite low point—and he figured his new sunlight-drenched workshop had something to do with his brighter mood. Plus, it was hard to be pessimistic when he was only hours away from going on his first date in a long time.

"What are you watching?" he asked Zoey, who was parked in front of the TV. When she gave him the cold shoulder, his parental radar immediately went up.

He lay back in the recliner and pretended to watch her television program—some reality show about brides searching for the perfect wedding dress—but couldn't take his attention off his little girl. For the past two days, she'd been an emotional wreck, shutting down any conversations about school and crying at the drop of a hat. Now she was supposedly watching her show, but she kept sneaking glances at her cell phone.

"Is your headache getting any better?" he asked, and she grimaced at his question. "Isn't tonight your sleepover with Cara?"

"I don't feel like going."

He cast a worried look at her. This didn't sound like her at all. She was always champing at the bit to do things on her own, especially anything that involved hanging out with friends. That headache of hers must have been a doozy. "Maybe I should stay here and take care of you. Do you need some Tylenol?"

"Oh, my God," she snapped, "are you ever gonna frickin' leave me alone?" Then she clicked off the TV and wheeled away.

He shook his head as she disappeared into the piano room. This new aspect of her personality, disrespectful and antagonistic, was getting to be a real pain in the butt. He'd been dreading her adolescent mood swings for a long time, having read parenting books that compared the teenage years to the terrible twos, but what surprised him more than anything was their intensity.

He heard Zoey begin to plink out notes on the piano in the other room, and he allowed himself a comfortable sigh. Three years of music lessons from an elderly woman in the Methodist church hadn't turned Zoey into a concert pianist, but it had turned her onto music. Although he never had an aptitude for anything musical and barely knew the difference between a sharp and a flat, he was sure of one thing: when Zoey played *Au Clair de la Lune* and *Twinkle Twinkle Little Star* at the third-grade recital, she was definitely the most talented one there.

Now her fingers were dancing across the keys, playing the distinctive intro of *Come Sail Away*, his favorite track from Styx's *Grand Illusion* album. That song always seemed to relax her.

He heard her stumble over a couple of notes, repeat the phrase, and then slam her hands down on the keys. A moment later, she came back into the family room and glared at him.

"I'm not going to Cara's house because she didn't invite me."

"What?"

"She hates me."

"She didn't invite you?" he asked, incredulous.

"Cara's all popular now. She's hanging out with Tiffany and her crowd." Zoey sniffled and wiped the back of her hand beneath her nose. "All of them are going to her party."

He sprang from the recliner and ran to her. Dropping to his knees, he threw his arms around her. "You listen to me, Zoey. Don't let someone like that get in your head. Cara's not your friend."

"I know. I don't have any friends."

His heart flinched as he recognized the pain that once drove him to crawl into a whiskey bottle for escape. "Look at me, sweetie. You are the strongest, most amazing girl I know. If the kids at school don't see that, then that's their problem."

Her head dipped. "I need to be by myself for a while." She started toward her bedroom, seemed to reconsider things, then rolled slowly into the foyer and stared out the leaded glass of the front door.

He wanted to follow, but he didn't. He wanted to say

something, but he didn't. He wanted to change everything and make her happy again, but he couldn't.

These were the times he missed Celeste the most, not only for her steady hand—she'd always been able to soothe Zoey's tears—but for her reassurances that he was doing the right thing as a father. Lord only knew how powerless and unqualified he felt. From his perspective, his relationship with Zoey was getting worse and not better.

He left her alone for ten minutes and then reappeared with some chocolate chip cookies that he'd taken from the freezer and warmed in the microwave. "I'll call Danica," he said. "She'll understand."

Zoey shook her head. "That's the last thing I want. Don't stay home on my account. That's not fair to either of you." She smiled up weakly at him, as if the sadness was dragging down the corners of her mouth, and shrugged. "At least one of us should have a friend."

In that moment, Garrison felt his love—and respect—for Zoey grow more than he ever could have imagined. Through her pain, she was showing something he'd rarely seen: a certain sense of maturity, caring for someone else in spite of her own heartache. She was truly like her mother.

He kissed her forehead. "I'm gonna need you to do something for me before I leave."

"Let me guess. Alphabetize the emergency contact list?"

"Very funny. No, hang on." He dashed away into his bedroom. A moment later, he reappeared holding a blue button-down shirt and two striped ties: one in navy and cream, the other in navy and red. "Which one looks better?"

She rolled her eyes. "It's not a job interview. Wear something nice."

"Aren't these nice?"

"I like the shirt. But no tie. Where are you taking her anyway?"

The question—one he probably should have entertained

himself during the past two days—just hung there unanswered, as frantic thoughts began to race through his head. "Um . . ."

"Seriously, Dad? You're supposed to tell her where you're going. That way she knows what to wear, too. Haven't you ever watched *The Bachelor*?" She sighed. "Okay, let me tell you everything I know."

A half-hour later, he was feeling pretty confident. Zoey had chosen his outfit, and he had showered and shaved. A little splash of cologne from the bottle he hadn't opened in over a decade, a gargle of mouthwash, and another layer of deodorant—he was good to go.

He stood in front of Zoey and spread his arms. "How do I look?"

"Not bad for an old guy," she said, grinning. "Don't forget, drop by the grocery store and buy her some flowers. Not roses. Something colorful. Girls like that."

He nodded and took a couple of deep breaths. "Thanks, honey."

By the time he'd started the van and driven out of the subdivision, he'd formulated a plan for the evening. As a compromise for his aversion to crowds and Danica's willingness to being seen in public, he was going to suggest an evening of bowling, because he figured he could rent a lane far away from the league bowlers and still gain a measure of privacy. They could eat at the bowling center, or he'd suck it up and take her to a restaurant after the crowds had thinned out. As far as date plans went, he worried that Danica might be a little disappointed, but it was the best idea he could come up with on short notice.

Seven o'clock was the time they'd agreed to a couple of days ago, and he pulled into her driveway at five minutes before the hour. As he walked to her front door carrying a colorful arrangement of carnations, daisies, and miniature roses, he wondered if she'd even want to go bowling. He'd spent all those years as a teenager in the youth leagues, had even rolled a 224 when he was fifteen, so he knew his way around a lane, but if this was her first time—well, he sure hoped they wouldn't need the gutter bumpers. They were so humiliating.

He rang the doorbell, then blew into his hands, trying to detect if he had bad breath. He waited. Then he rang the doorbell again.

The chime was working, as he could tell by holding his ear against the glass, but he went ahead and knocked anyway. "Danica?" he called.

She didn't answer.

Repeating the push of the doorbell and the rap on the door, Garrison waited for her to come out. Suddenly he realized he must have shown up at the wrong house. What an idiot, he thought. He jogged out to the street to check the street name, the house number, and the directions she'd given him. No, he was in the right place.

But she wasn't.

He opened his cell phone and called her. It rolled to voice mail. He texted her and waited for a reply. Nothing.

Maybe she was working, he thought, knowing that hadn't been the plan. She'd already told him that she was taking a break until Monday. As he trudged back to the van, the little voice in his head began whispering to him. *She forgot about you, Garrison.*

He crawled in the front seat and stared at her house for another half-hour. Finally, he started the engine. *That's what you get for trusting a stranger.*

That couldn't be true, he thought, arguing with himself. Danica couldn't have forgotten. She had seemed as excited about their date as he was. And that kiss—there was nothing more real, more honest, than that.

He dropped the transmission into reverse, keeping his foot on the brake, then cast a final gaze at the front door. The voice that haunted him in the middle of the night sneered at him. *No, she didn't forget you. She knew you were coming.*

There it was, the unvarnished truth. If Danica really cared about him, she would have been here. There was only one explanation: she must have changed her mind.

He cursed under his breath, and then he drove away.

Chapter 33

G arrison drove around aimlessly for half an hour, finding it hard to believe that Danica had stood him up. He was kicking himself. Had he been so naïve as to think a busy celebrity like her would make time to be with him? He pulled his van into a small pocket park on Clear Lake and walked to the water's edge. Sifting sand through his fingers, he stared out at the dark water, remembering all the times he used to come here after Celeste was killed, questioning why his family had been torn apart.

A terrible thought flashed: maybe Danica hadn't shown up because something bad had happened to her as well. Instantly, gooseflesh formed on the back of his neck, and he could feel the tiny hairs stick straight out. He grabbed his phone and left another message for Danica, a plea for her to contact him. It couldn't happen again, he thought, not to another woman he cared for.

By the time the sun was sinking on the horizon, his logical self had wrested control from his emotional self, so he headed home, still concerned about Danica but no longer consumed by panic. Drawing on the theory he'd learned in college physics— his professor called it Occam's razor—he decided the most likely answer was the simplest. Danica had remembered the date wrong.

When Garrison arrived at the house and told Zoey what had happened—actually, it was less a recitation of facts and more a rambling mess of conjecture and rationalization, with a dollop of self-pity—he expected her to commiserate with him, another Sterling who'd been let down by a supposed friend.

"I know Danica," Zoey said. "She wouldn't do that on purpose."

"You're probably right," he replied, not sure if he believed it anymore. He checked his phone again for any text messages. "Oh well," he said with a shrug. "I guess it's just the two of us again. How about we settle in and watch some TV?"

"I've got a better idea." Zoey reached into the pouch attached to her chair and extracted some color printouts. "So I've been researching how to train my new dog."

Not the dog again. "Come on, Zoey, you're jumping the gun on this. We're not ready for a dog. I've been trying to tell you."

"What the crap, Dad?"

"It's a bad idea."

"Danica's brother had a dog, and she said it was awesome. She thinks I should have one, too."

"I don't care what Danica thinks," he said, storming toward the kitchen. "She's not here, is she?" He was done arguing, because he could feel his blood pressure rise each time the subject of the stupid dog came up. He opened the refrigerator, wishing it contained a beer.

"How is it a bad idea?" Zoey demanded, rolling into the room.

He ignored her and began to scan the shelves inside the fridge. He saw the Diet Coke and wondered if he had really thrown away all that booze. Nine years sober with not a single sip of alcohol, but there were times when all he could think about was the way the stuff tingled on his tongue and burned warm in his throat, the way it deadened his pain.

"Talk to me, Dad! Why won't you let me have a dog?"

He whipped around and shouted, "Because you're fooling yourself, Zoey! You think a dog will solve your problems? Well, it won't." He slammed the refrigerator and muttered at the closed door, "I'm damn sure not gonna take care of something else around here that needs my total attention."

When he turned around, Zoey was staring up at him with wide eyes. "You think I'm a dog?"

"Of course not. That's not what I said."

"You think I'm helpless, don't you? Just like everyone else." She threw the papers at him, and they cascaded around his feet. "Screw you, Dad. I'm not as helpless as you think."

"Honey—"

"One day I'm gonna leave this house and find a place of my own. Get a job and travel around the world. I have big dreams."

He sighed heavily. Don't dream, he wanted to say, because disappointment always comes to dreamers. He'd been a dreamer himself once, with his eyes fixed on the stars, his imagination brimming with hopes for a grand future. Yet all those dreams had been dashed in a hail of bullets.

"I don't want you to get hurt again," he said quietly.

Zoey scoffed. "Isn't that what life's about?" She threw up her hands. "I want to feel pain. I want to feel joy. I want to feel love. Stop trying to protect me."

But that's my job, he thought, even if it was one he sucked at. "Zoey, I know we both had plans for tonight and they fell apart. We shouldn't take it out on each other."

"You have no frickin' idea how tired I am of not being able to go places."

"I know." The worst part was that this whole situation was his fault—he should have done the right thing back when she was a little girl, shielding her from harm instead of allowing her to suffer at the hands of that animal. "I'm so sorry you're in that wheelchair."

She shook her head. "Big deal. I can work around that."

"If only I'd done something different . . ."

"Take a look around, Dad. You don't go anywhere. You don't try anything new. Yeah, I may be in a wheelchair," she said, and pointed an accusatory finger at him. "But you're the one who's paralyzed."

When the interview with CNN's Anderson Cooper was over, Danica yanked out her earpiece and sat back in the studio chair, exhausted by the experience. Over the years, she'd met most of the news folks in Houston, but now she was rubbing elbows with titans of the industry. Last week after the plane crash, it had been the anchors from the morning network shows. Tonight it had been the prime-timers. With Anderson Cooper and Bob Woodward together in CNN's studio in New York City, and she and Nicholas Kristof chiming in over the satellite uplink, they'd discussed the state of journalism in America and the importance of a determined free press.

She pulled out her smartphone, which she had silenced three hours ago, half-wondering if Oprah might be trying to track her down for an interview. When she saw the text message, she gasped.

Where are you? Garrison had typed.

With a hand clasped to her throat, she played his three voicemails. The first message contained more confusion than anything, with Garrison wondering if he'd remembered the details correctly and apologizing if he'd screwed up. On the second message, she could tell he was really frustrated and disappointed. But the last message really tore at her heart, because she could hear the strain in his halting voice. "I hope you're okay," he had said with gulping breaths. "If you're, uh, going to be much later, call me. Or if you're having car problems, call me. I'm really worried about you, Danica."

How could she have let this happen? She'd been so wrapped

up in talking about herself that she'd forgotten their date. Forgotten *him*.

She checked the time—a little after nine. Maybe they could still go out. With her heart pounding in her chest, she rang his number. If only she had called him earlier and told him how important the interview was to her. He would have understood.

"Danica? Is everything okay? I was worried."

"I'm fine. I'm so sorry."

"Where are you?"

"At work. It's a long story."

"I was afraid you'd had a car accident, that you were at a hospital or something."

Danica knew exactly what he was feeling. After her father walked out on the family, she used to hold on to the belief that the reason he wasn't coming home was that he'd been found injured and taken to a hospital, where no one knew who he was. In her heart, she always knew she was weaving an elaborate lie for herself, preferring to pretend her father wanted to come home but couldn't instead of facing the truth that he'd abandoned them.

"I'm so sorry," she repeated. "This is all my fault."

"What happened?"

Danica was sure there was nothing she could say that would be acceptable. So she took a deep breath and went straight with the truth. She explained how she'd come into work in the morning and basked in everyone's adulation, and then she proceeded to relate the details of the conversation with Kathy and the satellite interview with her heroes. "I'm embarrassed," she told him. "Can I make it up to you? It's not that late. I think I can get us in at Brennan's. My treat."

"No, I can't."

There had been a few times in her career where working a story had caused her to change her plans, even reschedule the occasional date, but she'd never left someone standing alone at her front door. "I know you're mad at me. And you have every right to be." *Please forgive me*, she thought, afraid to say the words.

"I'm not mad. I do want to see you, but I can't leave Zoey alone right now. We just had this huge argument."

Danica winced, not wanting to hear the details. In her mind, it was clear that they had fought about her and Garrison going on a date in the first place. She knew Zoey must be struggling to hang on to her dad, afraid she'd lose him to someone else. Boy, could Danica empathize with that.

"I should have known better." Creating a rift between father and daughter was something Danica wanted to avoid at all costs. Yet she knew that if this budding relationship with Garrison happened to blossom into anything more serious, she'd find herself caught in the middle of their family and become the focal point for all their tension. She'd cause the very rift she was afraid of. "Maybe we shouldn't go out," she told him.

"What are you saying? I thought we liked each other."

"I do like you, Garrison." The word *love* popped into her head and she quickly pushed it away. "I care about you, both of you. That's why I don't want to hurt either of you. Maybe tonight was a sign. Maybe we're not supposed to be together."

"But—"

"Please forgive me, Garrison. I didn't mean for this to happen." Over his protests, she mumbled an awkward goodbye and ended the call.

She trudged out of the studio, no longer wanting the bright lights and attention, then slipped past her colleagues in the newsroom without saying a word. When she reached her house, an empty shell of a place that was as dark as her mood, she let the tears flow.

She'd ruined the one good thing in her life.

After Danica hung up on him, Garrison didn't know what to do. He thought about driving straight to her house, but going there would be fruitless since she was still at work. He thought about holing up in his workshop, but returning to the same place that felt like prison a day ago wouldn't bring him any peace. He thought about spending time with Zoey, but talking with her was going to do nothing but lead to more arguments.

Instead he went into the kitchen.

He wandered the room, staring into the pantry, the refrigerator, the freezer. He opened the spice cabinet and began straightening the tins, then stopped and decided to stack them by color. It was a trick his mom had taught him, applying different colored labels to the various types of spices: blue for the general ones such as ground cumin and cayenne pepper; green for the herbs; and pink for the sweet spices, his favorites being star anise, ginger, and cardamom.

Before Celeste died, his culinary expertise had been limited to grilling burgers and hot dogs over charcoal, but then he'd been pressed into service under the worst possible circumstances. Under his mom's patient guidance, he had learned to boil eggs, braise meat, steam vegetables with a double boiler, even debone a chicken. Then when Zoey turned four and he'd baked her birthday cake from scratch, creaming the sugar and the shortening, separating the yolks and the whites, and folding everything together—all by himself— his mom had pulled him aside and told him how proud she was.

"There's a difference between being an adult and being a man," she said. "You've been an adult for a long time, able to make your own decisions and take hold of your future."

"Thanks, Mom."

"But I've seen how you sacrifice, how you set aside the things you want in order to care for Zoey. I know you love her, just like I love you." She wiped a tear from her cheek. "You're not just an adult, Garrison. The way you practice sacrificial love—agape love is what our pastor calls it—that's what makes you a man."

It was the last conversation he ever had with his mom, and he could still remember the way she'd lifted him up even as she was in the midst of that unforgiving chemo. At her funeral a month later, which resulted not from her fight against bladder cancer but from a backwards fall off a porch swing, the one thought running through his mind was gratitude for sharing that tender moment with her.

"I love you," were the last words he'd spoken to his mom, a far cry from his thoughtless remarks to Celeste years ago. "Go to hell," he'd told her in the driveway that fateful night. And in one of life's crueler ironies, he'd passed the trait on to another generation. "You're the one who's paralyzed," Zoey had told him in that disdainful tone.

He couldn't understand why people always hurt the ones they cared for the most.

What he and Zoey needed right now was a break from all the drama, an opportunity to get on better speaking terms. Fortunately, he'd already planned a weekend trip to the ranch, which always seemed to work wonders.

He filled a large pot with water and set it on the stove, then pulled the chicken meat from the refrigerator. Tomorrow, he figured, would be a good time to enjoy one of their favorite family meals. Crunchy chicken casserole took some prep time—he had plenty of that tonight—but he was willing to do anything to restore good feelings between the two of them.

As he chopped a green bell pepper on the cutting board, he contemplated what Danica had told him, that she didn't want to come between him and Zoey. What Danica didn't understand was that this family divide had been growing for a long time, like tectonic forces tearing continents apart. Zoey was steadily pulling away from him, and he was afraid that the mounting tension would eventually cause a rupture.

But would Danica be the trigger that ripped them apart? That was hard to imagine, especially considering how supportive Zoey had been about them seeing each other.

He diced an onion and added all of the veggies to a pan, then began sautéing them in olive oil. No, he decided, it was impossible for Danica to come between them. So it didn't make any sense to not see each other anymore. In fact, even after she'd left him hanging, he wanted to see her again, as soon as possible, to convince her she was wrong to worry.

Smelling the fragrant aromas coming from the stove, he realized tomorrow's dinner needed one more thing to make it perfect. And it wasn't a spice. He wanted to invite Danica to the ranch.

As he continued to combine the casserole ingredients, he found himself dreaming about the next day. He couldn't wait to share this meal with Danica, on the picnic table near the star shack, as they watched the sun slowly set in the west. Later they would try out Zoey's new binocular chair and fire up the telescope. And with the moon now a waxing crescent, the night sky wouldn't be flooded with light, so he'd be able to share the stars with her.

Spending time with Danica, far away from the distractions of the city, might be just the thing to launch their relationship. They wouldn't be alone, of course, but that was okay, too. All three of them could hang out, and Danica could realize she wasn't a third wheel.

He found himself smiling—he had a plan.

The microwave read ten o'clock as Garrison placed the final touches on the crunchy chicken casserole and set it in the refrigerator. Now he had plenty of time to chat with Danica. When he strolled into the family room to retrieve his cell phone, he noticed the TV was on. The late-night news was just starting, and there was a video of Danica on the screen.

He dropped into the recliner and listened as the news anchor reported the latest on the Senator Hartwell scandal. They showed a brief video clip of Danica talking on a split-screen with Anderson Cooper, and he found himself thrilled for her, knowing how much that moment must have meant. As uncomfortable as tonight had been for him, at least she'd been doing the thing she loved.

When the segment was over, he looked for the remote control, ready to power off the TV and give her a call. He leaned forward to pick up the remote from the coffee table, when the screen suddenly flashed a photo that made him collapse back into his chair.

"Today the U.S. Supreme Court rejected the appeal," the news anchor said, "of notorious killer Russell Polistini, convicted of capital murder for a deadly crime spree across Central Texas eleven years ago. Polistini will face execution by lethal injection in Huntsville on Monday."

Garrison's hands began to shake. Then his arms. Then his entire body. He could hardly believe it—his wife's killer was headed to the death chamber. Garrison was finally going to see justice served on the man who'd destroyed his family.

From a cold, empty place in his soul where despair and depression seemed to flourish, a dark thought gurgled up and infiltrated his mind. *Good riddance, you piece of shit.*

Chapter 34

Zoey woke up grumpy on Saturday morning, frustrated that she was stuck at home instead of hanging out with the other girls at Cara's sleepover. She went to the bathroom to get ready, going through the tedium of showering and putting on her clothes, a task that took more time than the average person. But that, as her father always liked to tell her, was because she was better than average.

Back in her bedroom, she fired up her computer, hoping she could find a bit of peace and quiet away from her dad. Last night's argument had been terrible, and although she was sorry she'd hurt his feelings, it didn't change the fact that she was ten-thousand percent correct: she needed her freedom and he needed to stop blocking her.

What really pissed her off was the way he'd acted when she talked about getting her dog, the one she wanted to call Scout as a tribute to her favorite novel. Everything she'd read said that Scout could help her become more independent. Why couldn't her dad see how important that was? Heck, if she became more independent, that meant he could get out more, be more independent himself. That's what he needed.

But no, Dad was getting cold feet again. It seemed as if he was afraid she would spend all her time with Scout and ignore him. *Good grief. He's jealous of a dog.*

She glanced to the doorway, making sure her dad wasn't there, then fired up her email. A couple of years ago, when her dad outfitted their house with wireless Internet, he'd also arranged with the cable company to set her up with a personal email account, although she rarely used it these days, ever since she learned that each incoming message was being secretly copied to his account as well. When she discovered it—he'd casually asked about a homework assignment on *The Diary of Anne Frank* that Ms. Pettigrew had accidentally sent to the wrong class—she'd simply obtained a private email account instead of calling him out and getting into a big fight.

She wasn't expecting any email this morning, although part of her still hoped Cara would have the common decency to offer an apology about the party. But of course, her inbox was empty. Then she logged onto Facebook—her dad didn't know about that either—and cocked her head at a new friend request on her home page. Who would be friending her? She'd already linked her account with Cara, plus three girls from Band. Both aunts and all five of her cousins were her other friends. This new person, whoever it was, would make twelve. Unless it was a mistake.

When she rolled over the icon to see who had sent the invitation, she giggled at the thumbnail photo. Lucas Hardesty's profile picture was some jokey Halloween snapshot, him dressed in a Harry Potter t-shirt and a pair of nylon shorts stretched practically to his armpits, wearing black plastic glasses and a helicopter beanie.

Then she read the message attached to his friend request. *Hey, Zoey! So I went to Cara's party tonight. Where were you?* Instantly, her chest tightened—she didn't want to read another word. What she wanted to do was wheel down the concrete path behind her house and go straight to Cara's and demand to know why she was being such a bitch. After all, they'd been close for three years, had been friends in real life and not just on Facebook, and now Cara was acting like they'd never even met.

Then Zoey reread the first part of his message. Lucas went to the pool party? How did he score that? Not that Lucas wasn't complete awesomesauce, but Cara hadn't even seemed to know his name until a few days ago. Shaking her head, Zoey read the rest of his note. *I hoped you'd be there. That's the only reason I went to the stupid party. I thought about you the whole time. Anyway, be my FB friend!* He ended the note with a smiley face.

She propped her chin in her hands and stared at the screen, at his silly outfit, at his message. *I thought about you the whole time*, he said. Wow.

If she could have danced around the room, she would have, but instead she pushed away from the computer, rocked her wheels back and forth with unbridled joy, and rushed from the room to share the exciting news with her dad.

She couldn't find him.

Rolling through the house, she checked the family room, his bedroom, and the kitchen, not locating him anywhere. When she opened the door of his workshop, she did a double-take, as it looked as if the place had been transformed. Rolling through the room, she noticed the fully assembled space shuttle in the corner and the decapitated Mister Spock figurine on his desk. But the oddest thing was how the morning sun streamed in from outside, brilliant rays of sunlight flooding the workshop, illuminating the dust motes, and reflecting off the treadmill's metal frame into her eyes. *When did he put in a window?*

"Dad?" she called.

Not hearing a reply, she circled back to the kitchen. This wasn't like him.

She heard the sound of laughter outside the kitchen window and turned her head to see her dad standing barefooted on the patio, wearing maroon shorts and a Texas Aggie t-shirt. He had a cell phone to his ear and happily waved one arm as he chatted with someone.

Because she couldn't hear what he was saying, she tried to use context clues to figure out what was going on. She studied him carefully as his face contorted with varying emotions, from surprise to seriousness to glee, but she could tell that even when he furrowed his eyebrows—that was his focused scientist look—he wasn't unhappy.

He mouthed *Bye-bye* into the phone and turned toward the house. She felt an instant alarm, concerned he'd think she was spying on him.

"Hey there, Pookie!" he said, using the endearment she'd grown tired of. "Isn't it beautiful outside?"

"Uh . . ." She'd come to tell him about Lucas, how he was this boy at school that she liked, but after looking at her dad's exuberant expression, she wasn't sure she wanted to ruin his mood. The more she thought about it, she also wasn't sure he was ready to hear that his little girl—his Pookie—had a boyfriend. Not that Lucas was her boyfriend, she quickly thought. Of course not. He was a just a friend. *I thought about you the whole time.* She felt a shiver down her neck.

"Great news," Dad said. "Guess who's coming with us to the ranch?"

No way, she thought. There's no way that Lucas called him and landed an invitation.

"I was just talking to Danica," he said, smiling. "She's gonna spend all day with us. We're calling it our make-up date. Turns out last night was a huge misunderstanding." He winked at her. "We've had some misunderstandings ourselves, haven't we?"

Zoey slowly nodded.

"Last night was pretty rough," he said. "Sorry about that."

She played back their argument in her head, but with the benefit of hindsight, she now realized his crankiness had been due to some big mix-up with Danica. Maybe he really wasn't against getting a pet. Maybe he was simply lashing out, using the dog as a substitute target for his frustration.

Which meant this might be a good time to bring up the dog again. "Hey, Dad," she began, and then realized there was a better way to play this. If she could just get Danica to talk to him . . . he would listen to her. "Never mind. That's great about Danica. When are we leaving?"

"Soon. Have you packed?"

"I will," she said. "Promise."

"We're staying through tomorrow."

"I know."

"What about homework? Do you need to bring your computer?"

Her computer. She could see it in her mind's eye, the screen still displaying Lucas's welcoming message, the Facebook application still awaiting her answer. *Are you going to be my friend or not?*

"I gotta go, Dad!" Zoey wheeled out of the kitchen and tore down the hall. When she reached her doorway, she executed a sharp left turn like Danica had taught her on the tennis court and then flew to her desk.

She clicked on the Facebook post and enlarged Lucas's profile picture. Did she really want to be friends with a nerdy guy who dressed like that and didn't care what other people thought?

Yes, she thought, clicking the *Accept* button. Absolutely.

Garrison pulled into the cabin's driveway and checked the clock. Only one hour to get ready for Danica's arrival. He rushed out of the van and retrieved Zoey's chair from the back, mentally reviewing the list of everything he needed to do, chores that included tidying up the cabin and making sure the star shack wasn't a total disaster.

"Anything I can do to help?" Zoey asked, sliding into her

seat.

"How do you feel about cleaning the toilet?"

"Yuck. Seriously?"

"Someone's gotta do it. The countertop and sink need to be wiped down, too. The bathroom's not gross, but I want the place to look nice." He slung two duffle bags with NASA logos over his shoulder and lifted an ice chest from the back seat as a wasp buzzed past his head.

Zoey sighed, then shrugged. "I'll do it. But you can't tell anyone."

"That's the spirit. Thanks, Pookie."

"And stop calling me Pookie!"

While Zoey set about taking care of the bathroom, Garrison wielded a broom and a duster and did a quick once-over on the rest of the house. He stepped outside and beat their *Cabin Sweet Cabin* welcome mat against a tree, knocking off all the dirt. He wanted everything to be perfect for Danica.

Returning the welcome mat to its place at the front door threshold, he looked up and noticed an umbrella-shaped, papery nest hanging underneath the eave, its honeycomb-like cells instantly recognizable as the unique construction of a red wasp. He frowned at the nest—almost the size of a baseball— and knew he had to get rid of it.

A long time ago, he and Celeste had driven to Johnson City to help her dad clear mesquite and cedar trees from their Hill Country place. If it had been up to Garrison, he would have skipped the trip altogether because he worked better with his mind than his hands and because he'd spent the whole journey there squabbling with his wife about his long hours and how he wasn't pulling his weight with the new baby.

The foreman of this lumberjacking operation was Celeste's dad, a sixty-year-old bear of a man who had the burliness of Paul Bunyan and the stamina of his blue ox. Garrison never knew what to call his father-in-law—both Dad and Robert sounded odd to his ear—so he'd settled on Mr. Gurgenmeyer, even though the name sounded funny each time he said it.

The two of them started at sunrise, chainsawing a stand of old junipers and scrubby mesquite, then running the gas-powered log splitter on the limbs and trunks, pausing only to eat lunch and drink Gatorades. As the afternoon sun beat down, they loaded the split logs onto Mr. Gurgenmeyer's rickety trailer and hauled them back to the house.

He could feel the sweat soaking through his long-sleeved work shirt and the ache from muscles that weren't used to so much activity. He peered into the trailer and saw all the firewood they'd chopped and split, finding it hard to believe how much they'd accomplished since morning. Exhausted, he couldn't wait to call it a day.

His father-in-law unhitched the trailer from the pickup and cleared his throat. "Celeste said you might be flying soon."

"Yes, sir. Supposed to hear something in the next couple of weeks. Looks like either Endeavour or Columbia."

"I don't mean to get in the middle of y'all's business, but don't you think this astronaut career is a little dangerous? I've got this new grandbaby and I sure don't want her daddy . . . well, I remember Challenger."

Garrison swallowed hard. Of course he'd considered the risks of spaceflight, but he also knew the Challenger explosion had been caused by a series of failures, which wasn't likely to happen again. He would be around to look after his family. "NASA has come a long way since Challenger," he said.

"Not far enough. Promise me you'll be there to take care of that little girl."

"Yes, sir," he said solemnly. "I promise."

Garrison gathered up the empty Gatorade bottles and turned toward the house, longing for a shower to wash off the grime and sawdust before the women returned from town with Zoey.

"Where are you going?" Mr. Gurgenmeyer asked, picking up a log from the trailer bed. "We've still gotta stack all this."

A groan vibrated through Garrison's chest as he watched his father-in-law carry away an armful of firewood. Afraid of disappointing him, he sighed and reached into the trailer. "Where do you—" he began, but a sudden buzzing and then a sharp pinch on the back of his hand silenced him. He retracted his arm, and a red wasp flitted away.

"Son of a bitch!" He lurched back from the trailer, his skin on fire, the back of his hand already swelling. From the trailer, three more wasps rose from the wood and began circling. Panicked, Garrison waved his arms.

Another jolt of pain hit him in the neck. And then another.

By the time he'd run inside the house and stripped off his shirt, he'd been stung four times in all, one on the hand, two on the neck, and one on his chest, right above his heart. Garrison's skin began itching uncontrollably.

"What am I supposed to do?" he asked when his father-in-law opened the screen door.

"Hold still." The old man went into the kitchen and brought back several bags of ice, then applied the cold compresses to the sting sites. He grasped Garrison's wrist and began kneading a stinger between his index finger and thumb. "You're not allergic to wasps, are you?"

Garrison shook his head and grimaced. "Shit, shit, shit."

"I know it hurts," his father-in-law said sympathetically, "but you've got tough it out. You don't have a choice."

As Garrison stared up at the empty wasp nest below the cabin's eave, his father-in-law's long-ago words echoed in his mind. He could still remember how much he hurt that day, all the itching, all the swelling. Mr. Gurgenmeyer had been right back then—Garrison hadn't had any choice except to grit his teeth and suffer.

Those wasp attacks had been merely a prelude to the heartache he'd soon face: Russell Polistini's assault on his family, the Columbia disaster that took his friends, the accident that killed his mother. And each time, he'd endured the insufferable pain.

Screw pain, he thought. The only way to stop it was to prevent it from ever occurring.

He grabbed a can of Raid and the broom. With one swing, he knocked the paper nest from the eave and drenched it with bug spray. Feeling a rush of satisfaction, he inspected the remainder of the porch, eliminating two more nests and crushing them under his heel.

As he dropped into a rocking chair on the porch and waited for Danica, he thought about how much he hated wasps, the way they always blindsided their victims, attacking people at their most vulnerable. He knew that although he'd exacted a measure of revenge today, the wasps would eventually return.

They always did.

Chapter 35

Garrison sat on the front porch, rocking in his chair and staring out at the crescent-shaped pond to his west. He watched as a sandpiper with long, gangly legs waded in the mudflat on the far shore, intermittently probing its bill into the soft earth to forage for food, instinctively fighting for its survival.

What he wouldn't give to spend another day talking with his mom about shorebirds, listening to her tales of birding along the Texas Gulf Coast. What he wouldn't give to spend another day hoisting beers with his astronaut buddies instead of grieving their last moments over the skies of East Texas. What he wouldn't give to spend another day . . . another hour . . . another minute with Celeste.

Whenever he'd fall into a deep melancholy like this, the power of nature was the only thing that seemed to console him. He just needed to walk under the canopies of ancient oaks, smell the musty fragrance of damp pine needles, lie back and dissolve beneath a star-filled sky. Then his soul would be restored.

Closing his eyes, he found himself swaying with the breeze, inhaling the fresh air. He listened to the tweeting of the sandpiper across the water and the soft rising chip of a songbird, probably a painted bunting by its thin, high-pitched call. When he heard the sound of tires rolling across gravel, his eyes opened to see a car coming up the road.

Danica.

The nervous anticipation he'd been trying to ignore suddenly vanished, leaving his spirit lighter and filled with a certain hopefulness. He quickly ran a hand through his hair and rubbed his dusty hands on his shorts, then strolled out from the porch to greet her. "You made it," he called.

"Did you know you're in the middle of nowhere?" she called back.

"That's the way I like it."

She maneuvered her car down the narrow road and parked it behind the van. When she got out, he was struck by how beautiful she was. Dressed smartly in a teal blouse and khaki shorts—a shade lighter than her skin—Danica turned her head side to side, scanning the scenery, her raven hair looped over the top of her shoulders. "You sure have a lovely place out here." She reached into the car and retrieved a white bakery box. "I brought you some cupcakes. Strawberry amaretto. Wish I could say I made them, but they're from this wonderful little French bakery near my house."

"Sounds amazing. Come on inside."

When he opened the front door, she exclaimed, "Wow, it's beautiful."

A sense of pride welled in him, and he showed her around the small cabin, pointing out the touches that made the place feel like home: hand-painted tiles of Texas wildflowers behind the stovetop, the lamp that he and Zoey had built together from an old stoneware jar, black and white photos of trees and ducks that Celeste had taken.

He knocked on Zoey's bedroom door. "Danica's here."

"Awesome. I'll be out in a minute."

He led Danica back to the kitchen and set the box of cupcakes on a platter. "I thought we'd have some lunch and then I'll give you the nickel tour."

"I want to see that star shack you were telling me about." She laid a hand on top of his. "Thanks for the invitation. Thanks for giving me a second chance."

He gazed at her face, remembering the kiss they'd shared in the workshop, and felt an urge to touch those lips again. He leaned across the corner of the island to savor them one more time.

"Hey, Danica!" Zoey called as she popped into the room, and Garrison flinched back. "Ooh, I love your sandals. And your nails. Are they pink or orange?"

"Iced coral. I can paint yours later if you want."

Zoey nodded happily. "Congrats on your big story."

"If wasn't for you and your dad the other day, there might not have been a story."

"Yeah," he said. "That was a good day."

Danica smiled at him. "A very good day."

"Is that man gonna get fired?" Zoey asked. "He should."

"I can't believe he's still denying everything." Garrison had seen that on last night's news, another press release from the senator's office, this one stating that national security issues prevented him from commenting further. That had been the moment Garrison rolled his eyes and reached for the remote control, just before Russell Polistini's face appeared onscreen along with the news that his last-gasp court appeal had failed.

"I guess you haven't heard the latest," Danica said. "A jeweler from Vegas confirmed Hartwell purchased an emerald necklace just like I described. He told them it was for his wife."

"What a jerk."

"They released the security footage this morning. But that's not the best part. CNN was able to trace the money trail to his political campaign. They found proof of a connection with the Montalvo drug cartel. An hour ago, Hartwell resigned."

"Whoa, that's fantastic!" he said and gave her a hug.

"Mega fantastic!" Zoey added.

"If you need to do one of your interviews, we'd understand." As soon as he said it, he wanted to take it back. He had been looking forward to today after last night's misunderstanding, and hoped her job responsibilities wouldn't pull her away again.

"I'm not going anywhere. I've already turned off my cell phone. No one even knows I'm here. Well, except for my girlfriend Sam. She wants to meet you, by the way. And you, too, Zoey. I've told her what a beast you are on the tennis court."

Zoey beamed back at her.

"Sounds like a celebration is in order. Let's throw a picnic. Who's hungry?" He opened the refrigerator and pulled out a couple of covered bowls. "I've got sandwich stuff. Nothing fancy. Just some chicken salad and—"

"Ooh, effobee!"

He gave her a quizzical look. *What did she say?*

"Tuna fish," she said sheepishly. "It's an old family recipe."

"Oh, okay. What about you, Zoey? What kind of sandwich do you want?"

She scowled at him. "You didn't bring any ham or turkey? Whatever. Give me a PBJ. But let's not go outside. It's too hot."

He wanted to scold her, but suddenly realized he'd be able to spend time alone with Danica, which was exactly what he wanted. "You're right," he said, quickly opening a loaf of bread. "It's no problem if you want to stay here." Afraid that Zoey might change her mind, he prepared the sandwiches in record time, then packed a picnic basket with their lunch, the cupcakes, and a jug of lemonade. "Text me if you need anything," he called to Zoey as they prepared to leave the cabin. "We'll be back later."

"What do you mean, later? I want to hang out with Danica."

"Trust me, we'll be back soon," Danica said. "I want to spend time with you, too."

He knew that if they didn't get away now, Zoey was going to

insert herself right in the middle of their date, and he'd end up being the third wheel. He opened the front door. "Ready, Danica?"

He led her toward the star shack, avoiding the decomposed granite path—the one he'd put in for Zoey—in favor of simply wandering through the meadow. They serpentined between loblolly pines and post oaks, bypassing knee-high tufts of prairie grass at the forest's edge, and paused to watch a nine-banded armadillo shuffle through the field in front of them. When the armadillo reached a scrub of yaupon, it lowered its head and rooted beneath a blanket of dead leaves.

Garrison felt Danica's fingers curl around his, and then she leaned into him. Her scent, a combination of jasmine and blackberry, with a hint of vanilla, wafted over him.

"I'd forgotten how magnificent nature can be," she said.

"It's one of the reasons we like this place."

"I used to take walks with my mom when we lived on Puget Sound. It was so beautiful. We'd always see something interesting, an eagle's nest, harbor seals, a black fox. There was a bluff where we sat together and looked for orcas." She quieted and a pensive look crossed her face.

"Is she . . .?"

"Yeah. Last year, right after my birthday. Heart attack."

He squeezed her hand and strolled alongside her in silence, feeling their strong bond and contemplating their common past. He thought about his own mom, how absurd it was that she'd fallen down on her own porch, how senseless her death had been. How senseless all death was.

They hiked around a copse of pines to where the fence separated his property from the neighbors, admired a scissor-tailed flycatcher perched on the barbed wire, and then snuck up on the star shack from the south. "Here she is," Garrison said, "my little sanctuary."

Danica peered in through a window. "It looks like a full-blown observatory in there. Are you sure your last name's not

Hubble?"

He grinned. "I guess you could say I like astronomy."

"That's an understatement." She gestured toward the picnic table. "Let's go eat lunch and talk. I want to know more about you."

Opening himself to others was clearly outside his comfort zone, but there was something about Danica that made him feel safe, a surety that he could allow himself to be vulnerable without fear of being hurt. As they took their seats across from each other at the picnic table, he handed her a tuna sandwich and took one with chicken salad for himself. "What do you want to know?"

"Gosh, I have a million questions flying through my head. Start with the star shack. How long have you had it?"

"Five or six years, I guess. I built it with Zoey."

Danica raised an eyebrow.

"You'd be surprised what she's able to do," he said, pouring lemonade into a plastic cup.

"Nothing Zoey does surprises me. There's not much that can hold her down."

"Just me." He shocked himself with his reply, but maybe Zoey's complaints had embedded themselves in his subconscious. "At least that's what she thinks. How about you? Is there a star shack in your life?"

She contemplated the question, twisting her hair around a finger. "I don't have much time for anything beyond work."

"At least you enjoy what you do." He knew she loved her career—she talked about it with such passion—but he also knew there was more to life than work. He'd learned that the hard way. "You should be proud of yourself for that report on Hartwell."

She demurred. "Six people died in that plane crash, not five. As imperfect as Araceli Montalvo was, she didn't deserve to die in anonymity. I needed to tell her story."

"And you did a great job."

She shrugged. "There are always regrets."

"What do you mean?"

"Well . . . I remember how pumped I was after the ambulance left with Hartwell. I was reporting live and breaking all this big news. Everyone was paying attention to me." She lowered her eyes. "I didn't tell anyone about the woman in the plane. She was undoubtedly dead, but if I'd just said something, maybe her family would've had a body to bury."

"You did your best."

"Maybe." She took a long drink of lemonade and set it down with a sigh. "What about you? Any big regrets?"

As innocent as her question was, all he could hear was his accusatory inner voice. *Of course you have regrets, Garrison. Profound regrets. Unforgivable.*

"I had to change careers after my wife passed," he said, looking toward the sky. "I guess that's a regret."

"Oh, my God, your wife. I'm so sorry!"

"It's okay." He shut his eyes as images from that horrible time forced their way to the surface: a clock that read 4:07, a sheet-covered gurney, a girl's first wheelchair.

"I don't mean to intrude, but what happened to your wife? How did she die?"

This wasn't how he wanted to spend the afternoon, discussing details of Celeste's death. What was he supposed to do? Tell Danica that an animal named Russell Polistini murdered his wife in cold blood? That Polistini was about to be executed by lethal injection? That he couldn't wait to hear the news that this guy was finally going to pay for destroying his family? Those weren't subjects to be discussed on a first date.

"I'm sorry," she said. "I'm being rude."

"It's not rude. You see, there was this guy—" He caught himself, realizing that if he divulged the details, he'd sound like a real-life Eeyore wallowing in his grief. Besides, Russell Polistini wasn't the only person to blame in this ordeal. *That's right, Garrison. Look in the mirror.*

"You asked about regrets," he said and heaved a deep sigh. "The night my wife died, I should have kept her home, kept her safe. But I didn't. Every time I see Zoey in that chair, I blame myself."

"It's not your fault."

"That's not the worst part," he replied, shaking his head, thinking about his last painful words to Celeste. "Never mind, forget I said anything."

"I didn't mean to upset you."

He had never told anyone his darkest secret and was terrified that Danica would look down on him, decide he wasn't worthy of her. But when he stared into her eyes, he saw nothing but compassion and reassurance. He took a deep breath. "My greatest regret? The last thing I said to Celeste before she died . . . I stood in that driveway and told her to go to hell."

They finished eating their lunch, but Garrison didn't want to go straight back to the cabin. He needed time to decompress. They went on a long walk, meandering through the woods, along a dry creek, and toward the pond. As they leaned on the rail of the dock, watching a flock of mallards swim lazily on the water, he wrapped an arm around her.

"Don't mention that stuff about my wife to Zoey, okay?" He knew he was treading a fine line these days and didn't want to make matters worse. If Zoey learned about the unkind words he'd spoken to her mother, he'd lose her respect. And if Zoey blamed him for everything that had happened to her, he might lose her altogether.

"Sure, it'll be our secret." She leaned her head on his shoulder. "I love how relaxed I feel out here. It's very pretty."

"Just wait 'til sunset. The colors are so vivid. Clouds will go from pale peach to the color of your fingernails and then looking like a glass of merlot in a span of minutes. I've taken pictures just after the sun disappears on the horizon, and you'd swear the sky was on fire."

"You make it sound poetic."

"Nature is a kind of poetry, don't you think? The rhythms of planet rotation, the varying wavelengths of light, the refraction of the atmosphere, all working in concert to create the perfect moment."

"I've never met anyone like you."

"What do you mean?"

"You're all smart and sciencey, a real-life Mister Spock. But then you have this whole Zen thing going on in the kitchen and out in nature. It's a little contradictory, you know? Plus you and Zoey are so close."

He blew a sigh. "Things aren't always great."

"She's a teenager, Garrison. One minute she's all sweet and caring, and the next her head's spinning around and pea soup's everywhere."

"Oh, you've met her," he said with a chuckle.

"Met her? I've been her. I *am* her."

"You're a teenage girl?"

"Sometimes," she said, pressing her lips together the way Celeste used to do. "I fret about whether I look pretty or whether I'm too fat. I wonder if I'll make friends. And I dream about a future that's better than what I have now."

He brushed a lock of dark hair from her face and gently ran a finger along her cheek. "I think we worry too much."

She smiled, and he leaned forward to kiss her. Her face felt cool against his; he recognized the heat pulsing through his own body. He breathed in her fragrance, could taste her on his lips. Her mouth parted slightly and their tongues touched, tentatively at first. She leaned back against the railing and he pressed close, his fingers combing through her hair, pulling her toward him.

I'm falling in love with you, he thought, but didn't want to say the words out of fear that Danica might become another painful regret in his life. Instead he held tightly to her, hoping he could be part of the future she dreamed about.

His cell phone chimed and he startled, recognizing the special ringtone. "I'm sorry," he said, breaking their embrace. "I should check this. It's Zoey."

"I understand."

"Everything okay?" he asked into the phone.

"I'm bored. Are you two ever coming back to the cabin?"

"Hang on." He covered the mouthpiece. "She says she's bored," he whispered through a smile.

"Maybe we should head back."

"Or maybe we could stay out here a little longer." He reached across to kiss her, but Danica turned her head, offering her cheek instead.

She gave a wan smile. "I don't want to get hurt. And I don't want to hurt you."

"No one's gonna get hurt," he replied, as a red wasp flew between them and hovered, before it circled upward and disappeared.

Chapter 36

As Danica strolled back to the cabin with Garrison, she felt exhilarated. There were times when the rush of doing live television or interviewing newsmakers would trigger a sense of elation, but those emotions faded after the camera went dark. With Garrison's arm wrapped around her, she could practically sense the endorphins coursing through her system, and all she could do was smile, bathed in the warm glow of his affection.

You'll meet the right man one day, her mom had promised her, and Danica wished that Mom had lived long enough to know Garrison, size him up, make some pronouncement about his worthiness. Of course, she would have been impressed by his intelligence and kindness, the way he sacrificed for others. But her mom was wary as well. Maybe she would have said, "Watch yourself, Danni. A man is never as he appears," jaded thoughts from a woman abandoned by her husband and left to fend for herself, a woman who'd lost her faith in the institution of marriage and the vows made between a husband and wife.

"Something on your mind?" Garrison asked as they reached the front porch.

What could she tell him? That she, like her mom, had a hard time trusting men? That she worried Garrison might be like her father and ex-boyfriend, someone who'd dump her when times got hard? That she pondered these deep thoughts only because she was falling in love with him?

Deflecting his question, she said, "I was going to paint Zoey's fingernails. Want to join us?"

"Can we brush each other's hair and have a scavenger hunt?"

"After the pillow fight."

He gave a mock squeal. "That sounds so fun!"

"Seriously, if you want to play a game with us or something."

"That's okay. I've got a few things to do to at the star shack. Enjoy yourselves."

When Danica came inside, she was concerned Zoey would grill her about Garrison, but that didn't happen. Zoey was much more interested in getting her nails painted and having another woman-to-woman conversation.

"Remember me telling you about Lucas?" Zoey asked, waving her hands to allow to the base coat to dry. "He friended me on Facebook."

"Have you told your dad yet?"

"No way. I thought about it this morning, but then I totally bailed. You know how dads are."

Danica nodded, but the truth was that she had no idea what it was like to be in Zoey's shoes. Her dad had barely been around when she was growing up, and then completely out of her life by the time she was a teenager. He'd never even met her first boyfriend. She dug the coral nail polish from her purse, hoping to change the topic. "You ready for the top coat?"

"Do you think Lucas will like it? Because my friend Cara wears a lot of makeup, and I think it looks tacky. I want to look classy."

"You're very classy, Zoey. I'm sure Lucas sees that."

Zoey giggled nervously. "He said he was thinking about me

when he was at Cara's party. That's a good sign, right?"

"You bet."

"I want him to like me."

Danica gave a deep sigh. "Here's my opinion, if it counts for anything. Don't go through life worrying about whether a boy likes you or not. Happiness starts with liking yourself. You have to be content with who you are, not what someone else wants you to be."

"I'd like to be more, you know, womanly."

"You will." Danica painted a long stroke of the orangish-pink color down one of Zoey's fingernails. "Just love who you are right now. Tomorrow will take care of itself."

"It's hard."

"I know," she said, reflecting on how hard it had been for herself, dealing with the guilt that wended around her heart like a choking vine. For years she'd blamed herself for her father's leaving, Russell Polistini's brutal murders, and Mario's lonely death. "It's hard to love yourself if you harbor regrets."

"I don't think I have regrets."

"Then that's good." She finished applying the nail polish to Zoey's fingers, satisfied with the results. "Now blow on them. They'll dry faster."

Zoey alternated between blowing on her fingernails and holding them out in admiration. "I wonder what my dad will say. He doesn't let me wear makeup."

"I think he'll like it. You look sophisticated."

"Not to mention classy," Zoey said, grinning. Then her smile disappeared. "No, Dad will hate it."

"Now why do you say that?"

"He doesn't want me to grow up. He wants me to stay his little girl so he can take care of me. Where is he, anyway?"

"Out at the star shack." Danica's thoughts drifted to Garrison and how devastated he was by his wife's death. The trauma still haunted him, that much was clear. And she knew that's why he had such a hard time loosening his grip on Zoey.

"Could you do me a favor? Will you talk with my dad?"

"Me?"

"You know what it's like to be a teenage girl."

Danica remembered what she'd discussed with him, how she was able to empathize with Zoey because all women, at some level, were still that scared teenager. Even now in her early thirties, she felt as confused as when she was in high school.

She cared deeply for Garrison but wasn't sure if the feelings were mutual. When he kissed her out on the dock, it seemed they had truly connected. But it was just as possible that her imagination was running wild, projecting emotions on him that he didn't share. Maybe he was like the other guys, more interested in being with Dah-nica Corrrrrrtez than getting to know the real her.

"You didn't answer me," Zoey said. "Will you talk with my dad?"

Danica shrugged. She seemed to have a knack for screwing up a good thing, forgetting their first date, talking about his dead wife, rejecting his kiss. Would acting as Zoey's emissary mess up his relationship with his daughter?

"Come on, I know you like him."

She scoffed. "Yeah, but I'm not sure he likes me."

"Seems like I heard something about that recently," Zoey replied. "I believe I was told not to worry about whether a boy likes you or not."

"The person who told you that was an idiot."

"That person is my friend."

In that moment, Danica could sense the bond between them growing even stronger. They weren't simply two people with complicated families, each lamenting a mother and struggling to accept a father—one absent, one omnipresent—they were kindred spirits searching for purpose and understanding.

"You're a remarkable young lady, you know that?"

Zoey smiled, then picked up her right leg by the back of her ankle and slung it across her left knee. She unlaced her shoe and removed it, along with her sock. Then she repeated the process with the other foot. Danica watched in awe at Zoey's graceful movements.

"Well, what are you waiting for?" Zoey asked. "Aren't you going to paint my toenails?"

With thin, wispy strands of cirrus clouds trickling across the expanse of a fading sapphire sky, Garrison flicked a switch to illuminate the concrete pad with a soft red light. He knelt in front of the binocular chair and spun it slowly counterclockwise, inspecting the way it moved, listening for any kind of catch. The final repairs turned out to be easy; the hard part had been transporting the unwieldy thing from the garage to the star shack without killing his back, an achievement made possible only by using a six-wheel mover's dolly.

Satisfied that the swivel mount was working as intended, he set about affixing Zoey's new astro binoculars to the chair. Binoculars were often the best way to view the night sky, but this oversized pair was too heavy to hold for long. After mounting it to a moveable bracket above the head of the chair, which would keep it steady, he lay down and peered up through the lenses.

What a sight, he thought, focusing the binoculars on the reddish Arcturus, one of the first stars of the evening. He couldn't wait for dusk to slip into nightfall, when other longtime friends would gradually make their appearance: the twin brothers Castor and Pollux, little King Regulus, the Seven Sisters. They'd eventually slide across the sky from east to west, part of a grand zodiacal parade that included a lion and bull, a crab and scorpion, the hunters, even a swan named

Cygnus. And he couldn't wait to introduce them all to Danica.

For years, he doubted whether he could ever love again. His marriage with Celeste had been wonderful and intense, the kind of love poets write about, so when it ended suddenly—like a collapsing star—he'd been sucked down into a great void of emptiness. A black hole where nothing could escape the darkness, where powerful forces kept all light from penetrating.

Then Danica came along, and he knew love might be possible again.

He headed back along the path toward the cabin, flashlight in hand, thinking about how he wanted tonight to be special. When he opened the door, he was surprised to see the girls lying on their stomachs in the middle of the floor, propped up by their elbows. Tissue threaded between Zoey's brightly painted toes. A pile of playing cards lay between them.

"It's called Crazy Eights," Zoey said. "Want to play?"

"Why are you on the floor?"

"I felt like it, okay?"

"You should've seen her, Garrison. She's like a ninja getting out of that chair."

Danica and Zoey exchanged knowing glances and gave each other a high-five, then executed a choreographed series of handclaps punctuated with a fist bump.

He stood there staring at them, shaking his head. "You two are nuts."

Zoey made a goofy face at him.

Danica rolled onto her back and laughed. As she lay there, her dark hair spreading on the floor behind her, he noticed the swell of her breasts underneath her blouse. An image of an old Saturday cartoon popped into his mind, the one where the hero's eyes widen and bug out of his head. *Don't ogle her*, he told himself.

She was indeed beautiful but not because she was perfectly formed. He hadn't noticed it before, but her right leg bore a scar at the knee and small moles dotted her other leg. They obviously didn't bother her since she was wearing a pair of shorts.

A natural beauty, he thought, and he was glad she hadn't succumbed to modern pressures and tried to change her body with implants or heavy makeup. Then he remembered that she used a bronzer to look more ethnic on TV, which meant she had the same foibles as everyone else. For some reason, that made her more appealing.

She tilted her head and looked up at him, meeting his gaze. An innocent smile crossed her face. "What are we looking at tonight?" she asked, and he practically dropped his flashlight in response.

"Yeah, Dad. I don't want to waste my time outside if the sky sucks."

Hearing Zoey's voice snapped him back to reality, and he forced his eyes away from Danica. "The moon," he said, "should be up for a few more hours."

"I hate the moon," Zoey said. "It's boring."

He frowned at her. She was going to spoil everything with her attitude. "Then stay here. I don't care. Come on, Danica. You've never seen stars like we have out here in the country. Tonight we'll even be able to see the rings around Saturn."

"Sounds lovely. Zoey, join us."

Say no, he thought.

Zoey gave a dramatic sigh. "Fine. I'll go."

After walking with Garrison and Zoey along the darkened path, Danica arrived at the star shack. The building, nestled in a tree-lined meadow, had resembled a storage shed earlier in the day, but now in the dim light, it seemed more like a church. A holy place.

She followed him into the star shack and stared slack-jawed

at the room, which glowed red from the special lighting. Spanning the length of one wall was a narrow desk containing a laptop computer, a pair of monitors, and a variety of astronomical charts. The telescope, sleek and black—obviously high-end—sat in the middle of the room, mounted to the floor by a thick concrete pier. If a tornado happened to strike, she wanted to be attached to that telescope—it wasn't going anywhere.

"Here she is," Garrison said with a sweeping gesture, and she wasn't sure if he was talking about the telescope or his whole setup. "Ready?" Before she could answer, he pressed a switch, and the star shack's roof began to rumble. The ceiling, which was covered with plywood instead of sheetrock, vibrated and then shifted toward the other side of the room, disappearing at the wall's edge.

She looked up to where the ceiling had been and could see the night sky. "Wow."

"Never gets old," he said, gazing skyward alongside her. He stepped over to the telescope and removed its eyepiece, then babbled something about f-ratios and field of view. "I'm thinking Orthoscopic since we're gonna look at Saturn and the moon, but we can always switch over to the Plossl. It's higher mag."

She nodded even though she didn't have a clue what he was talking about. "So everything's good?"

He smiled at her. "Everything's perfect."

Unsure if he meant something more but hoping he did, she decided not to press matters. She picked up a laminated star map and turned it over in her hands. "Where did you learn all this stuff? Are you an astronaut or something?"

"Do I look like an astronaut?"

As a matter of fact, yes, she wanted to say. When he'd first mentioned that he worked at NASA, she'd imagined him dressed in an orange flight suit, waving to the cameras as he was loaded onto a spacecraft. Smart and confident. Calm, cool, and collected. Garrison could have been an airline pilot or an astronaut . . . except for that whole *afraid-to-try-something-new* mindset. "Actually," she said, "with all that red light, you look like an alien. I guess I probably do, too."

His face turned serious. "You'd look beautiful in any light."

"Maybe I should tell my bosses they ought to shoot me with night vision."

He slid his arms around her waist. "I know it sounds corny, but beauty doesn't come from the outside, how pretty you look. You've got this powerful inner light." Then he kissed her, more tenderly than before. "Danica," he said softly. "You're very—"

"Dad?" Zoey called from outside.

"Shit," he muttered, and then called out, "Just a second."

Their eyes met, and she knew they were sharing the same thoughts, that they needed to be together. And they both knew it couldn't happen, shouldn't happen, with Zoey around. Danica kissed him back with a simple peck on the lips, afraid to reveal her true emotions. "Go. She needs you."

They exited the star shack and stepped out onto the concrete pad. Zoey sat beside the binocular chair, slowly spinning it. "Show me how it works."

"First I have to move you—" he began, but seemed to catch himself. "Or . . . you can do it on your own." Danica watched his muscles tense and jaw clench, and she was sure it took every bit of restraint for him to allow Zoey such a measure of independence. She was sure of two other things as well: that he was ready to spring forward in case of trouble and that Zoey would never realize the magnitude of his gesture.

Zoey slowly lifted herself from the seat of the wheelchair so that her bottom was hanging at the chair's edge, and Danica was reminded of how Olympic gymnasts performed L-sits on parallel bars, supporting their full body weight on their hands. It was a feat that required tremendous upper body power, but that was one thing Zoey had plenty of: strength.

She pushed herself forward and fell safely onto the padded

binocular chair, then methodically lifted and spun herself until she was oriented correctly. She slung her legs into place and lay back. "That was easy," she said, panting from the exertion. "But it's comfortable. I like it."

"Check this out," Garrison said, lowering the binoculars to her face. "They're much stronger than our regular ones. Try looking at something."

Zoey adjusted the position of the binoculars and turned the focus ring. A wide smile spread across her face. "That's frickin' cool."

"What do you see?" Danica asked as she tied her hair back into a ponytail so it wouldn't fall into her eyes.

"You know the Big Dipper? The second star in the handle? That's actually two stars, Alcor and Mizar. I can see both of them."

"Usually we have to break out the telescope for those kinds of details," he explained. "What about Saturn? Can you see her rings?"

"Where is Saturn? I can't find it. I must be in the wrong part of the sky."

He placed a remote control in Zoey's hand. "Right button is clockwise. Left is counter."

She depressed a button and her chair began to rotate. "Oh yeah, this is so frickin' cool."

Garrison figured that Zoey would quickly tire of the binocular chair, but he was wrong. For an hour, she scanned the sky for objects of interest, her excitement growing with each discovery. She noted the isosceles triangle formed by the moon, Saturn, and the bluish star called Spica. She used a green laser pointer to explain to Danica what comprised the constellations of Ursa Major and Ursa Minor. And she marveled at the vast swarm of stars known as M13, the Great

Cluster in Hercules.

He'd taken Zoey stargazing many times, but she'd never been engrossed for so long. It figured that the one night he wanted her to beg off, to allow him and Danica time alone, she had to start channeling Copernicus and Galileo.

"Aren't you getting tired?" he asked.

"No, Dad. That's what's awesome about your chair. I could lie here for hours."

He groaned and looked over to Danica, who was stifling a laugh. "I think I'm gonna show Danica how to use the telescope."

"Didn't you already do that? Wow, I wish I could see Saturn's rings."

"How about you get back in your wheelchair and look through the telescope? I looked at the rings earlier. They're sweet."

"Later, Dad. I want to stay out here a while. I love these binoculars."

He cocked his head at Danica, signaling a desire for her to follow him. Inside the star shack, he closed the door and whispered, "I'm sorry."

"It's okay. She's having fun."

"I know. I was just hoping . . . well, that we could have more time alone." He leaned down to kiss her, but she raised a hand to block him.

"Not now, Garrison. You know it's complicated."

"What do you mean, complicated?" A thought flashed that there was someone else in her life, but he knew that wasn't true. Maybe she meant that he'd crossed a line with her, gone too fast. After all, it was only their first date.

"I'm not mad or anything," she said, reading his mind. "We just have poor timing. You gotta admit, Zoey's in a really good mood."

"Yeah."

"Be thankful she likes spending time with you."

"You're right," he said, wishing the night would have turned out differently. But he was willing to wait.

When they returned to the porch, Zoey had rotated her binocular chair again, facing away from them. "What are you seeing now?" he asked.

"I'm just thinking," Zoey said.

"About what?"

"I don't know, how infinite the universe is. I've never seen so many stars."

"They seem so close," Danica said. "But then I think about how far away they really are."

"Unreachable," he said.

She laced her fingers with his. "Not unreachable. Just complicated."

He knew Danica wasn't talking about the stars anymore. Of course she was right—their relationship was complicated, mostly because he was a single dad focused on his daughter.

"I'm cold," Zoey declared.

How was he going to balance the needs of his daughter against his own needs? Maybe that's why he hadn't dated much.

Danica nudged him. "She said she's cold, Garrison."

"What? Oh, she's cold! I'm sorry, sweetie, maybe you ought to go back to the cabin."

"I'll go with her," Danica said, picking up the flashlight.

After thanking him again for her birthday gift, Zoey completed the transfer from binocular chair to wheelchair, then headed north with Danica along the path and disappeared into shadows. He heard giggling and laughing and finally the distant sound of a door closing. He couldn't wait for Danica to return.

Ten minutes later, he was still alone. For as long as he could remember, being by himself at the ranch was the greatest feeling in the world. Now he couldn't stand it.

He went into the star shack and wandered around. He

arranged his star charts into squared piles; he powered off his laptop. *She's not coming back*, his inner voice said, and the truth hit him hard. He'd been fooling himself to hope for a more magical end to the evening. With a shrug, he hit the button to close the roof, activating an unseen garage door opener and flooding the room with a grinding clatter. Slowly, the stars—the only things he could count on in his life—disappeared behind the roof.

When he turned around, Danica was standing in the doorway, backlit by moonlight. He'd witnessed the most amazing sights from this room, star clusters and ring nebulas, double stars and galaxies, but those had all been light years away. Danica was the most heavenly object he'd ever seen . . . and she was near enough to touch.

"You came back," he said, the words sounding more like a question.

"Of course."

He moved to where she stood, and the hint of vanilla in her perfume seemed stronger. Her hair was no longer tied in a ponytail, and her blouse was no longer tucked into her shorts. He ran his hands down her bare arms and felt goose bumps form on her skin.

"Do you have a blanket?" she asked.

He nodded, mesmerized by the sight of her standing there. He found a blanket and an old comforter in the closet, then led her outside to one of his favorite places, a patch of soft grass with an opening in the tree line to the west. The crescent moon was setting on the horizon, its vague reflection shimmering on the pond. He could hear the croaks of bullfrogs and the chirps of crickets echoing around them.

He spread out the comforter on the ground, then draped the blanket around her shoulders. *This is supposed to happen*, he thought, and somehow he knew she felt the same way. He kissed her, more urgently this time. The blanket slipped from her shoulders, but she made no move to catch it.

He pulled back to look at her, to gauge her reaction, not wanting to cross the line. But she didn't turn away. Reverently, he unbuttoned her blouse, revealing the supple curves of her breasts. He traced his finger along the scalloped edge of her bra and then, reaching behind her, tried to undo the clasp.

"Let me," she whispered, and unhooked the clasp below her cleavage, causing her bra to fall open. In the moonlight, her dusky breasts rose and fell with her quickening breath.

He pulled off his shirt and then, forcing himself to be patient, lifted one of her breasts to his mouth, kissing, teasing, tasting. Her fingernails scratched against the back of his neck, and she drew him closer.

They lowered themselves onto the comforter, sitting on their knees and staring into each other's eyes. They breathed in unison. Her hands ran across his bare chest and then brushed, feather-light, across the front of his pants. She reached up to touch his face, but he captured her hand, then guided her down onto her back as if they were performing ballet.

More sure of himself now, he ran kisses along her hot, flushed skin, radiating the scent of jasmine and vanilla. He looped his fingers inside the hem of her shorts and tugged, sliding her shorts and panties down her legs. Then he stood and shed his own clothes, conscious—but not self-conscious— of his nakedness.

He glanced upward and inhaled, wanting to savor the moment. *I've waited for this a long time*, he thought, as a meteor streaked across the sky.

Breathless, he watched her shift gracefully on the comforter beneath him. She smiled. And then he bent down to meet her.

Chapter 37

When Garrison woke on Monday morning, his first thought was of Danica. The weekend at the ranch had proved to be everything he'd hoped. She had slept over on Saturday night, the two of them in separate rooms, and then sometime before dawn, she had padded naked to where he was sleeping and beckoned him to join her.

After making love, they strolled to the pond to watch the conjunction of Mercury and Venus in the morning sky. The rest of the day was spent with Zoey, playing card games on the porch and talking about everyone's hopes and desires. For the first time in a long while, he was able to imagine a future filled with joy instead of fear.

He rolled out of bed, still thinking about Danica and wanting to call her after he drove Zoey to school. In the kitchen, he pressed a button on the coffee maker, yawned, and then stepped to the refrigerator to retrieve some creamer. He glanced at the calendar to check what was on their schedule.

When he saw the circle around Monday's date, he thought he might throw up. The date bore a single notation: RP.

Russell Polistini.

Garrison had been ignoring it all weekend, not wanting to

let that ghost from his past ruin everything. But he couldn't—wouldn't—ignore him today. Later this afternoon, Russell Polistini would be strapped to a gurney and wheeled into the death chamber. IVs in his arms would flow with a saline drip until the warden signaled for the lethal cocktail to be administered.

Yet Garrison wasn't driving to Huntsville, wasn't going to look through the open curtain and into the cold-blooded killer's eyes, wasn't going to listen to the man's final statement. And he wasn't going to watch him die. Because in another cruel twist, Polistini had not been tried for, let alone convicted of, Celeste's murder. The Travis County District Attorney's office, which had been in some sort of turmoil when the crime happened, had chosen to prosecute Polistini solely for the capital murder of a police officer named Andrew Quinn, ignoring the killing of Celeste and two restaurant workers.

That's what angered Garrison most: the way everyone seemed to forget her after she died. The public and the news media had focused initially on the slain cop and, once he was laid to rest, talked incessantly about the killer. Celeste was but a footnote in the saga, and even though he would have hated to see the grisly details of her death splattered over the media, he wished there had been a proper way to share how wonderful she was.

He sipped his coffee, trying to calm his trembling hands while thinking about the living victim in the ordeal. For more than ten years, he'd been able to shield her from knowing her assailant's name, but that would change today. Once Polistini was executed, he'd finally tell Zoey everything. So he needed to steel himself for the day because he had to protect her one last time. It took all his strength to act normal as he cooked breakfast, drove Zoey to school, and waved goodbye.

At nine o'clock, while he was listening to highlights about the previous night's Astros game, the home phone rang. He tried to ignore it, figuring it was a telemarketer, but anxiety got the better of him. Hoping the call wasn't about Zoey, he picked up the receiver.

"Of course, I'm aware of it," he said. "No, I'm not going to Huntsville."

He listened carefully to the caller's question. In times past, he would have slammed down the receiver and told them to stop bothering him. But this was about Celeste and her memory, about the justice he never saw delivered for her inside a courtroom. "Okay," he said, "I'll do it."

When the school bell rang, Zoey rolled down the hall and through the exit doors, trying to avoid the crush of students hurrying home. She wasn't in a rush herself, as Dad had said he was running an errand and might be late. But she hadn't talked with anyone all day and hoped she could hang out with a friend until Dad picked her up. Not Cara, who had been busy talking to other people every time Zoey saw her, and not Lucas, who hadn't been in English class this morning.

She still hadn't learned the details of Cara's party, although she'd been hearing whispered conversations about it all day. In his Facebook message, Lucas had declared the party "lame," but she still wanted confirmation from someone else so she could feel better about missing it.

Zoey sat in her chair on the sidewalk, watching kids board buses and crawl into cars, when Reshma Kumar strolled past. They weren't friends, but at least Reshma never called her names. "How's it going?" Zoey asked.

Reshma turned around. "Um," she mumbled, shuffling her feet.

"What did you do this weekend?"

"Not much," Reshma said, but she wouldn't meet Zoey's eyes.

"Did you go to Cara's party?"

"You mean you heard?"

"I couldn't make it," Zoey lied. "Cara said everyone had a good time." That was a lie as well, since Zoey hadn't talked with her supposed best friend all day.

Reshma's eyes widened. "I can't believe you're not pissed off."

"It was just a party." The truth was that Zoey was still hurt by her exclusion, but she figured if she acted cool, she might show everyone that Cara didn't have complete power over her.

"Hey, Zoey!" a voice called, and she turned to see Lucas Hardesty coming up the sidewalk.

A jolt of excitement hit her, and her fingers began to tingle. "I missed you in Ms. Pettigrew's class," she said, now wishing that Reshma would move along.

"Who's your friend?" Lucas asked. "Wait, you were at the party, right?"

Reshma paled. She stammered some excuse about leaving a new box of reeds in the band hall and rushed away.

"That was weird," Zoey said.

"All your friends are weird," Lucas replied, smiling. He pointed to his open mouth, revealing metal latticework that covered his teeth. "Check it out. Mom made me wait until our last band concert was over. What do you think?"

You're handsome, Zoey thought. Instead she blurted out, "Have you ever looked at stars?"

"Huh?"

"You know, stars and constellations. The Milky Way. I was thinking maybe we could go stargazing together sometime."

"Okay, sure. That might be fun." He rocked back and forth on his heels, holding on to the straps of his backpack as if he were a first-time parachutist. "Um . . . I heard you had a birthday last week."

It hadn't been much of one, she thought, remembering the disaster of her birthday. No decorations on her locker, no special treats at lunch, and no happy birthday wishes from anyone at school.

Lucas removed his backpack, then reached inside and pulled out a package that looked like someone had wrapped it in the dark. "I got you a present. Not really for you, I mean." He shrugged. "Just open it."

She smiled, happy that he'd cared enough to learn of her birthday and then to get her a gift. She tore open the wrapping, which consisted mostly of Scotch tape, and the package's contents fell into her lap: a box of dog biscuits, a retractable leash, and a bright red collar.

"I don't get it," she said flatly, remembering how hurt she'd been when Dad called her a dog. Was Lucas making fun of her, too?

"You were talking about getting your new companion dog. What's his name? Scout?"

She forced a smile, trying not to cry. Dad was never going to get her a dog. "It's very thoughtful, Lucas."

"Wait, there's more." He withdrew another present, a tiny box wrapped in silver paper. A purple ribbon encircled the box and was knotted in a tight bow. He handed it to her. "This one's for you."

When the wrapping fell away, Zoey's fingers ran along the velvet surface. She'd seen commercials from jewelers before, so she recognized it right away, but in her wildest dreams she'd never imagined receiving something like this. "For me?" she asked, and flipped open the lid to reveal a heart-shaped sterling silver necklace with some sort of engraved message on the pendant. Lifting it from the box, she held it by the chain and tried to read it, but a gleam of sunlight flashed against the twirling silver charm and reflected into her eyes. She held it between her fingers and said, "'To thine own self be true.' Isn't that Shakespeare?"

He nodded. "It's from *Hamlet*. When I saw it, I thought of you."

"I love it."

Just then, a car pulled to the curb and beeped its horn. Lucas glanced over his shoulder. "Dang it, it's my mom. I gotta go. See you tomorrow?"

She clutched the velvet box tightly in her hand. "Can't wait."

Before she knew it, Lucas was gone and she was sitting there alone, contemplating what had just happened and wondering if she'd even remembered to thank him. She gazed at the necklace—it was shaped like a heart!—and slipped it inside the zippered pocket in front of her backpack. She may not have had many friends, but Lucas was a keeper.

When she saw Cara exiting the building, she decided now would be a good time to talk things through, hopefully hear an apology and get back to being friends. She quickly stuffed the leash and treats into the side pouch on her wheelchair, then rolled toward Cara, who was joined by a group of blondes with tresses that were flat and chests that weren't.

Cara saw her and flashed a look that was part contempt, part shame, then clutched her books to her body and pivoted, leading her posse of Populars in the opposite direction. Zoey rolled more quickly, trying to close the gap, but she was cut off by Tiffany McAdams, who was the caboose in Cara's little train.

"Where are you going, Bulldozer?"

"I want to talk to Cara."

"Well, she doesn't want to talk to you," Tiffany said, stepping in front of the wheelchair. "And you know why."

Heat rushed up Zoey's neck as she tried to pretend she wasn't embarrassed. She searched her memory for what she might have possibly done or said that had insulted her friend. But she was drawing a blank.

"Dammit, Bulldozer, get your fat ass off my foot!" Tiffany gave her a shove and sneered at her. "You and your stupid wheelchair."

And that was the answer.

No matter how many books she read, no matter how many

A's she earned, no matter how many kind words she had for everyone, she would always be the girl in the wheelchair. That would never change. That's why Cara had dumped her.

She unconsciously rolled backward, feeling sorry for herself, before remembering Lucas's gift. *To thine own self be true.* Screw Cara, she thought. If she wants to surrender her identity to become one of the Populars, let her.

"What are you still doing here?" Tiffany said.

Zoey gritted her teeth. She used to roll her eyes at Populars, thinking they were like cats, sashaying through the halls and preening, filled with delusions about how significant they were. But she had underestimated them. They were more like pack animals—wolves or hyenas—who attacked anyone who didn't conform to their perverted social order.

"I'm tired of girls like you acting as if you own this school," Zoey said.

Tiffany's nostrils flared, and she yanked on Zoey's wheelchair pouch, ripping it from the frame and dropping the contents onto the ground. When she saw the box of dog biscuits, which had broken open and spilled onto the sidewalk, she chortled. "You dropped your snack. No wonder Cara doesn't like you. Your breath smells like dog food."

Zoey shoved forward. "Out of my way, bitch."

"You want to talk to Cara? Go ahead, it's your funeral. I'm sure you know what happened at the party."

"Of course I do," she replied, not knowing what Tiffany was talking about.

"Everyone was thrilled you weren't there. Especially Cara. She really enjoyed her seven minutes in heaven."

"Seven what?"

"God, you're pathetic. You don't have a clue, do you? Spin the Bottle? Seven Minutes in Heaven?" Tiffany scoffed. "Cara showed your little boyfriend what a real woman is like."

Nausea swelled in Zoey's stomach as the clues suddenly fell into place. She really hadn't been imagining all the whispered conversations and weird looks at school. Everyone was in on it, she was sure, talking about her and laughing at her behind her back. "Hey, did you hear? Bulldozer thinks Lucas likes her. She's such a loser."

She darted her eyes to Cara, who was standing in the distance with her new friends, and wanted to rip out her heart.

Just like Cara had done to her.

Danica pulled into the parking lot at the news station, more excited than she'd been in a long time. She was finally done with those early morning shifts, and soon she would be in the big chair for evening newscasts. For the next couple of weeks, she would have carte blanche to run with any story she wanted to pursue. All it had taken was her blistering report on Hartwell and his subsequent resignation.

Yet her excitement was based on more than a career on the rise. After visiting Garrison at his ranch, coming to know him more intimately and confirming her feelings about him, she believed she was finally in a good place in her personal life. Simply watching the stars with both him and Zoey and getting caught up in their enthusiasm had allowed her a chance to reconnect with nature and recapture a part of her youth. Thanks to him, she'd entered a world that was vastly different from her own, where chaos always seemed to reign. This new world was better because it included him.

As she came through the newsroom greeting the handful of reporters and editors, Rocky Campbell stepped out of an editing bay and gave her a high-five. "I still can't believe I was this close to reporting your story. Next time a plane crashes, I'm taking it."

She laughed. "Your time is coming, Rocky."

"So how does it feel to be the most talked-about journalist in the country?"

"It feels great!" This was the pinnacle of her career, she knew, becoming a prime-time anchor and getting courted by national media. Roger Ailes of Fox News had already promised her a guest position on *Fox and Friends*, and Terry Gross wanted to conduct an in-depth interview for NPR's *Fresh Air*. "I'm looking for Kathy. Seen her?"

"I think she's on set."

"Thanks, Rocky." Danica walked up to the thick frosted glass that separated the broadcast set from the newsroom and peered through it. When she used to be a reporter, she often wondered what life was like on the other side of the glass, the brightly lit stage where anchors delivered the news. That's where she had wanted to be.

When she had eventually crossed the threshold and took her seat at the anchor desk, she discovered that reading a teleprompter containing a script written by someone else wasn't what she'd dreamed about when she was taking Journalism classes at Berkeley. Even though the money was great and the recognition was rewarding, she often felt the stage was more like a cage.

Kathy pushed through a heavy door made from the same frosted glass. "Oh, there you are," she said, looking frazzled. "Hurry up and finish your makeup."

"I thought I had forty-five minutes."

"You don't. Aren't you the one who begged to do this story?"

"Yes, but—"

"Why do you even care about this Polistini character?" Kathy asked. "He's just another murderer."

"I've followed this story a long time," she replied, irritated by Kathy's blasé attitude, one of the side effects of the news business that Danica hoped to avoid. "Since I was in Austin. Remember?"

She blew a sigh and pondered on the difficult path she had traveled with Russell Polistini. A dozen years ago, she hadn't even heard of him. At first, he was a rumor and then eventually a name, courtesy of Carmen Flores. Then he became her cause célèbre, a minor street criminal who'd been railroaded by an unjust legal system. As she publicly took down the county's corrupt Assistant District Attorney, his victim—Polistini— became the symbol of her idealism and tenacity. But then he'd gone and done the unthinkable. In one hate-filled night, he'd destroyed the lives of four families.

Even though her Q Score never sank among viewers and she ended up landing a job in Houston's big TV market, she still had to live with the fallout of championing a victim-turned-villain: ridicule from her peers, disdain from law enforcement, and the guilt. Oh, the guilt.

So she had to see things through to their conclusion, even if it meant facing a family member of one of Polistini's victims. "I have to do this," she said somberly, knowing that conducting this interview would be another step toward forgiving herself.

"Okay, Danica, I guess I should trust your instincts. The guy you're interviewing should be done with makeup now. Brooke's gonna get him situated on the sofa set. Who is he?"

"Husband of one of the victims. Her name was . . ." Danica checked her notes. "Celeste Gurgenmeyer. She lived in Clear Lake. Looks as if her husband still does."

"Just like you."

"Yeah," she said, thinking it strangely coincidental that this widower lived near her. She might have stood behind him at the grocery store or passed him at the dry cleaners without even knowing it.

"I talked with him," Kathy said. "He's real edgy. I guess that's why he wouldn't let us go out to his home. And by the way, his last name's not Gurgenmeyer." Kathy rolled her eyes. "What kind of woman keeps a maiden name like that?"

Danica dashed away to finish her makeup, then pushed through the heavy door and headed to the "sofa set," which Eyewitness9 used for its soft news segments. It was appointed with a curved leather sofa and glass-topped coffee table to give the place a less formal feel.

She thought it odd that in all the years since the killings, she'd never met this widower who'd maintained such a low profile. Maybe her uneasiness stemmed from the fact that she knew seemingly everything about Russell Polistini and Andrew Quinn, but hardly anything about the others. She could detail Polistini's life history: his formative years as the child of a prostitute, his reputation as a low-level street thug, and his descent into violent crime after becoming hooked on crystal meth. And she could recite the particulars about Andrew Quinn's family, including the wife who'd been his high school sweetheart and the two gap-toothed kids—Andy Jr. and Abigail—who would soon be old enough to attend college.

But she hadn't known—hadn't cared?—about the other victims. For her, the story had always been straightforward: Quinn versus Polistini, good versus evil. Not about the two employees whose families came from Central America and couldn't speak English. Not about the Houston woman whose husband refused to speak with the media.

At least she wouldn't have to sit across from Mary Quinn and face her scorn. The man she was supposed to interview, Gary Gurgenmeyer, wouldn't know her at all.

When she rounded the corner, she was astonished to see Garrison standing there. What a thoughtful surprise, showing up at her station unannounced. "Hey, stranger," she called, "What are you doing here?"

He turned, and a peculiar look crossed his face. "I thought you were off today."

"No, I came in to do an interview. Why are you at the station?"

Garrison's eyes darted around the room, and he began to shift restlessly. "It's a long story."

He's trying to surprise me, she realized, quickly scanning the set, half-wondering if he'd brought a bouquet of flowers. But she didn't have time for romantic gestures—she had work to do. She surveyed the area, looking around for the man she was set to interview, the victim's husband from Clear Lake.

Clear Lake—her breath caught when she made the association, and she snapped her eyes to Garrison. No, she told herself, that's just a coincidence. Lots of people live in Clear Lake. Her interview subject was someone else. An astronaut. A widower.

Oh, my God.

Chapter 38

A wave of nausea hit Danica, and she had to close her eyes to keep the room from spinning. It couldn't be. She let out a long breath and slowly opened her eyes, praying she'd been imagining things. When she saw Garrison standing there, not crossing his arms or clenching his fists like an accuser, but rather staring at his phone and paying no attention to her, she felt a momentary sense of relief. But then she recognized what he was doing: checking his studio makeup in the phone's reflection.

She gasped and tried to wrap her head around the disaster she'd created. And there was no doubt—this was her fault.

Now she had to find a way out of this mess before things got worse.

"Hurry up, Danica," Kathy said, barging onto the set and pointing at the digital clock that hung above them. "You've got less than an hour, and you haven't even started."

"What is she talking about?" Garrison asked.

Everything was crashing in on her. She wrapped her arms around herself, wishing she could escape the situation, wake up from the nightmare. But the nightmare was all too real.

"Danica?"

Tell him the truth, she thought, falling back on the principal canon of her profession, but she knew doing that would destroy him. Destroy them. Instead, she swallowed hard and decided to strike a middle ground, continuing forward but without offering full disclosure. "I'm the one doing your interview, Garrison."

"What?"

"Trust me, I had no idea."

"I can't do this," he said.

Kathy pulled her aside and whispered, "I talked with Rocky. That Polistini guy is being executed today."

"I know," she whispered back.

"Finish this interview and get your editing done. I want this story on the air tonight."

Before Danica knew it, she and Garrison were sitting side-by-side on the sofa, studio lights in their eyes and lavalier mics on their lapels, hurtling toward disaster as if they'd been chained to a runaway train. She received a signal from the control room, cleared her throat, and automatically recited the introduction she had written. "Your wife was killed more than eleven years ago," she said to Garrison, seeing him wince as she delivered the words. "Can you tell me about that day?"

His fingers dug into the sofa. He looked mournfully at her. "I received a phone call in the middle of the night, a little after four. The officer said there had been a shooting."

"You weren't with your wife?" She knew the answer but felt powerless to do anything except follow the script she'd already drafted.

"Her dad was sick. She drove her car to Austin. I didn't go. It was just her and . . . our daughter—" His voice broke and his eyes welled up with tears. "She was only two and a half."

Sweet Jesus, what was she doing to him?

"Let's take a break," she said and ripped the mic from her blouse. She wanted to tell him—what? that his wife had been killed by the man she'd helped free? that she was filled with deep regret?—but the words caught in her throat. He was sitting there with a stunned look on his face, his eyes blinking rapidly like a war veteran reliving an enemy attack.

When she rose, Kathy was glaring at her, obviously annoyed she'd stopped the interview just as it was turning emotional. Danica didn't care. Kathy could fire her if she wanted.

She turned and marched toward the studio's exit door that led to the newsroom. "Where are you going?" Kathy called. "Get back here." But Danica didn't stop. She figured she might as well open that door and keep walking.

She knew it was over.

Garrison couldn't understand what was happening. It was horrifying enough talking on camera about Celeste, but sitting beside Danica and answering her questions? He should have stuck to his original plan: stay home and follow the execution details from the safety of his workshop. He'd let down his guard, and now he was paying for it.

"What's going on?" he asked the heavy-set woman who'd been overseeing things.

"A minor glitch," she replied, seemingly preoccupied with something else. "We'll get it taken care of."

"I don't understand why Danica was here. You see, we—"

"Normally we'd use one of our reporters. However, this is Danica's story. Trust me, sir, she's the best." The woman waved over the makeup artist to touch up his face, then pulled out her cell phone and started yelling at someone on the other end.

After waiting on the sofa for a good five minutes, Garrison stood and dug the body-pack transmitter from his pocket. "Forget it," he said, realizing that Danica must have found things ridiculously awkward as well. He wasn't going to wait around for these people to locate someone else to conduct the interview.

"Hold on, sir. Give us a few minutes."

"I don't think so."

The woman threw a reassuring arm around his shoulder and tried to guide him back to the sofa. "Please don't go. Danica's just upset right now. Probably because she's been so close to this story for years."

He froze in mid-step. *She's been close to this story for years?*

As Danica steered her car onto the freeway, she wasn't sure where she was headed. The only thing she was sure of was that she needed to get away.

The image etched in her mind was that of Garrison sitting next to her on the sofa, a thousand-yard stare on his face as she waylaid him with questions about his dead wife. As soon as he put the pieces together, he wouldn't be able to look at her without blaming her.

When Sam didn't answer her phone, Danica frantically tried to figure out who else she could call. Not anyone at the station—she'd be lucky to still have a job. And certainly not Garrison.

Then a crazy idea popped into her head: maybe she could talk to Zoey. The girl was level-headed enough, plus she understood what her dad was like when he became upset. Yeah, she thought, Zoey might have some insight.

Danica exited the freeway and cruised along the frontage road, stopping at the traffic light. To her right, an eighteen-wheeler belched diesel smoke, and the acrid smell made her queasy. When it finally rumbled forward and turned at the red light, she figured things would be better, but then she saw the building on the corner—a Burger King—and her head pounded in response.

Instantly she was transported to the dark night of eleven-plus years ago, when she had stood in a Burger King parking lot and reported on the four victims of a mass shooting. She could still remember the flashing police lights reflecting off the glass entrance, the distant view of a bloodstained floor, and the close-up of a bullet hole in a plastic playground wall.

That's where they had found the fifth victim.

Her throat tightened at the thought of that little girl, bloody and barely conscious, and at the young woman she'd become, a teenager with a bright aluminum wheelchair and bright coral fingernails. Danica buried her head in her hands.

She was going to lose everything.

Garrison left the studio in a daze, then climbed into the front seat of the van and whipped out his smartphone. He plugged the terms *Danica Cortez* and *Russell Polistini* into an Internet search engine and couldn't believe the results.

Danica and Polistini. Polistini and Danica. Every article said the same thing, that she'd fought a public battle to release him from prison, that their history was intertwined. Why hadn't she mentioned it before?

Isn't it obvious? She's been playing you.

He had no answers to quell his inner voice, to stop the second-guessing and the I-told-you-so's. Maybe the voice was right. After all, problems that appeared the most complex often had a simple answer. So did this one.

She knew.

She knew that Polistini had killed Celeste, yet she hadn't said a word about it. Then she'd found someone to convince him to go on camera and spill his guts. Danica was just another TV vulture picking at his family's carcass.

That's not true. She loves you. And you love her.

"Bullshit," he said out loud, deciding that his long-time inner voice—his practical, defensive voice of reason—had more credibility than this new lovesick one.

He was kicking himself for not seeing it in the first place. Why would a famous news anchor like her fall for a guy like him? Because she had an agenda, he realized. Danica had masterminded this sting, tracked him down, and inserted herself into every aspect of his life.

How long had she been planning this? Days? Weeks? Years? He wouldn't put anything past her. Take down a senator and ambush a widower, all in a day's work for the famous Danica Cortez. She was slick, he had to give her that. Acting like she didn't know who he was. Acting like she enjoyed hanging out with Zoey.

Zoey.

Garrison was seething with anger now. It was one thing to screw with his emotions, but to pretend to be Zoey's friend . . .

He grabbed his phone and dialed Danica's number again. He didn't care how many times she let it roll to voicemail, he was going to get some answers.

Normally Zoey hated it when her dad picked her up from school, but today she couldn't wait for him to arrive. Ever since she'd learned the news about Cara and Lucas, she'd felt the stares from students walking by and heard their mocking whispers. Needing a place to hide, she had barricaded herself inside one of the band hall's practice rooms.

If she hadn't been so shocked by Tiffany's revelation, she would have raced up to Cara and told her off. She could still see the smirk on Cara's face as she stood there with her gang of Populars, hanging on Tiffany's every word. How could her best friend do that to her?

And what about Lucas? Was he in on it, too? *Of course he was.* How else to explain the embarrassment of the dog biscuits and the total humiliation in front of everyone?

Zoey heard footsteps clicking along the hallway, so she rolled backward against the inside wall in order not to be seen. Dad was right. Strangers weren't to be trusted.

The door swung open and her band director poked his head in the room. "I'm locking up, Miss Sterling. You waiting for a ride?" When she nodded, he said, "Sorry, you need to wait outside."

She slowly rolled out of the practice room, listening for the sound of voices, ready to change direction if she had to. When she reached the exit doors, she took a deep breath and pushed them open. The sidewalk was empty. She was all alone.

In the sky, the puffy clouds she had seen at lunchtime were gone, replaced by a low bank of dark thunderheads gathering in the west. A gust of wind picked up loose debris from the parking lot and spat it at her. *What time was it?* she wondered, suddenly feeling more exposed than ever. Dad was never late.

Just as she was pulling out her phone to call him, she saw Danica striding toward her from the parking lot. "Were we supposed to play tennis today?" Zoey asked. "I must have forgotten."

"No, Zoey. I need to talk to you."

"Where's Dad?" A chill raced down her neck as she saw the tension on Danica's face. "Oh, my God, did something happen to him?"

"Can we go somewhere private?"

"Not until you tell me what happened to my dad."

Danica scanned up and down the sidewalk as if she were worried about someone overhearing their conversation. "I'm sorry, Zoey—"

"My dad! What's wrong?" she screamed.

"No, no, nothing's wrong. Your dad's fine. But we need to talk."

Zoey slumped her head and began to cry. "You don't understand. I've had the worst day."

"Me, too."

"My friend is so mean."

Danica bent down on her knees and looked into Zoey's eyes. "I'm sorry you had a bad day. I really am. I wish things could be different."

"What are you saying? Is this about tennis?"

A strained, forced smile crossed Danica's face. "I can't play tennis with you anymore."

"What?" This day was getting worse by the minute. "God, why does everyone hate me?"

"I don't hate you, Zoey. I care about you a lot. It's just . . . well, your dad and I won't be seeing each other after today."

"But—"

"Which means I can't see you anymore, either. I needed to tell you in person. I'm sorry."

Zoey heard a door slam, and she looked past Danica to see her dad running toward her.

"Stay away from my daughter!" He raced up and positioned himself between her and Danica, then thrust a finger in Danica's face. "You keep away from her, you hear me?"

"Dad?" Zoey had never seen him so angry—the veins in his reddened face were actually pulsing.

"Get in the van." He crossed his arms and waited.

"I don't understand what's going on," Zoey said, shifting her eyes between both of them, fully aware of their body language, fearful of what was happening. "Why is everyone upset? Is there a problem?"

He glared at Danica. "You're damn right there's a problem."

As Garrison secured Zoey inside the van, he kept looking over his shoulder at Danica, wondering what kind of scam she was trying to run by showing up at his daughter's school. He gave Zoey a peck on the head, then marched back to where Danica stood. "I can't believe what you did," he growled.

"It was a coincidence, I swear. I thought I was interviewing a guy named Gary Gurgenmeyer." Her eyes were wide, pleading.

"Gary?" he scoffed. "That's the best you can come up with?"

She reached for his hands, but he shook her away. "Garrison, I give you my word. I did not know you were going to be at the station."

"You're lying."

"Excuse me? How dare you. I'm no liar."

"Really? Then tell me about Russell Polistini." At the sound of that name, she recoiled, and he knew he'd nailed her. "And don't give me any of your bullshit."

"I . . . I . . ." She was on her heels now.

"Polistini," he repeated, his mind swirling. He was no longer listening to Danica but thinking about the sociopath who was on his way to the death chamber, the son of a bitch who had ruined so many lives and deserved what he had coming to him. Garrison couldn't wait to see Polistini gone, only wishing he had the chance to push the lethal drugs himself.

". . . and then a judge released him," Danica said. "Because of some corrupt District Attorney . . . Look, I'm not lying to you. I didn't hear Polistini's name again until last Friday."

"Uh-huh."

"I know that doesn't excuse what I've done."

You're right, he thought. It didn't excuse her at all. At least Polistini had committed a random act of violence; Danica's crime was personal.

"I'm done listening to this nonsense," he said, turning toward the van. "We're leaving."

"Seriously? Then you're a coward." When he whipped back around, she said, "You're too chickenshit to face the truth."

"Oh yes, the mighty Danica Cortez. Angel of truth. It's all a con, isn't it?"

"What?" she snapped.

He pointed back at the van. "You lied to Zoey. You lied to me. You go on TV and pretend to be someone you're not. You do whatever's convenient for Dah-nica Corrrrrtez. Your whole life is a big lie."

"At least I have a life."

"What the hell's that supposed to mean?"

"You know, I could understand it if your wife had died last year. But it's been a decade, Garrison." She spread her arms. "You've built this fortress around your life. You're afraid to try new things. What kind of life is that?"

The kind that keeps out strangers, he thought, the kind that protects his family. His greatest failure had been allowing Danica to cross the moat in the first place.

"You know the worst thing about it?" she said. "The way you pulled Zoey into this garbage."

"Don't you dare bring up Zoey!" Lightning flashed in the sky, followed by low, rumbling thunder, and Garrison vaguely recognized the storm that was building.

"Blame me all you want for what happened to her," Danica said. "Trust me, I blame myself more than you can imagine. But it's not the wheelchair that keeps Zoey in chains. It's you. Frankly, I think you prefer it that way."

"Oh, go to h—" The same words he had fired at Celeste almost escaped his mouth again, and he suddenly felt the weight of his guilt. He didn't want to say anything else he would regret.

"By the way, if I was so fired up to get my big story, how come I left in the middle of the interview?"

She's trying to trick you, his inner voice told him, but there was a deeper part of him that understood the logic of her argument. If there was anything he knew to be true, it was that news reporters would cut off their own arms to land a story. In his mind, he tried to assemble what had happened and compare it to her explanations. Could this really be some horrible coincidence?

He could see tears welling in Danica's eyes, and an image flashed of his final argument with Celeste, when she'd cried in anger and frustration. That image was burned indelibly into his memory, and he didn't want the same thing to happen with Danica. "Hold on," he said, raising his hands palms up. "Let's talk about this."

"I don't want to talk to you anymore. You called me a liar."

"Help me understand—"

"I thought you were different, Garrison. But you're not. You're just as selfish as everyone else." She shook her head in disgust. "And to think I fell in love with you."

As she turned on her heel and ran toward the parking lot, he stood there paralyzed. Had she been playing him for a sucker, another stranger taking aim at his family? Or had he misread the entire situation? He could feel himself sliding sideways, magnetic poles shifting, the laws of gravity compromised.

Danica was climbing into her car. He took off in a full run. His mind was riddled with confusion, but he was certain of one thing. He loved Danica, had known it from the moment they had met. He couldn't imagine his life without her.

Her car engine suddenly roared to life, and her tires squealed as she backed out of the parking space. Just as it had happened with Celeste. He stood there helpless, watching the woman he loved leave him in anger. He stared in horror as she peeled out of the parking lot.

He couldn't believe it. She was gone. Forever.

Chapter 39

This is awful, Zoey thought as she watched Danica sprint across the parking lot. She'd watched their argument through the van's closed windows, seen them point and yell at each other, and although she hadn't been able to hear what they'd said, their message was clear. When Dad had pointed at the van, she'd read his lips: *Zoey.*

Their argument was about her.

Raindrops splattered against the windshield, and soon Dad trudged her way, not appearing to care that he was getting rained on. As he drew closer, she panicked, unsure of what to say to him.

Why had they been arguing about her in the first place? Did this have anything to do with Cara and Lucas? No, her dad and Danica wouldn't care about that. Maybe they'd been arguing about tennis, how much of a sacrifice it would be. Maybe Dad didn't want Danica to spend so much time with her. Or maybe Danica didn't want to spend any time, period.

Zoey groaned, believing her life couldn't be any worse. All the kids at middle school hated her. Now her only grown-up friend was yelling at her dad . . . about her. And the only thing she had to look forward to was high school, where bitchiness and cruelty could be Olympic sports.

The van door swung open, and her father climbed in. "Looks like it's going to rain for a while," he said with no emotion in his voice. "There's a big storm out there."

"Dad?" She tried to read his face, but it seemed as if he'd shut down.

"You have homework tonight? Because I have stuff to do in my workshop."

It was clear he wasn't going to bring up whatever had sparked their argument, so she kept her mouth shut during the drive home. She couldn't understand why everybody was so angry all of a sudden. Everyone had seemed happy at the ranch—especially Dad. Obviously something had changed.

Even though Zoey didn't know what she had said or done wrong, she still felt an overwhelming sense of guilt and shame, knowing there must be some basic flaw in her character that caused people around her to become upset. Dad. Danica. Cara. Lucas. Maybe the Populars were right—she was a loser and no one wanted to be around her. She shielded her eyes, afraid to look at her dad, afraid to be seen by him.

By the time they arrived home, the rain was falling in angry, angled sheets. She waited while he exited the van and went around back to open its rear doors, which jutted out into the driveway. She could hear him muttering under his breath as he wrestled her wheelchair free. When he finally opened her door, he was drenched and clearly pissed. "Let's go."

"Um . . . could you maybe dry it off? You know, the rain?" She watched him close his eyes and rub a hand across his forehead, which always signaled he was fighting a major headache. "Never mind, Dad. It's not that wet. I don't want to be any trouble."

And that, she realized, was the core of it. She hadn't said something wrong, hadn't done something wrong. Her very existence was wrong. The reason he and Danica were having problems was because he was always having to care for her instead. The both of them didn't have time for each other.

Which meant their breakup was her fault.

"Come on, Zoey," he said, giving the seat a halfhearted swipe with his bare hand. "Get in."

She made the transfer, then darted a nervous glance at him when she felt water seep into the back of her shirt. Part of her wanted to discuss what had happened at school—not just concerning him and Danica, but also with Lucas and Cara. But another part figured she should step aside and give him time alone. She rotated her chair and followed him inside, maintaining a clear distance between them, then breathed a sigh of relief when he disappeared into his workshop and shut the door.

"Now what?" she said to herself. With a shrug, she rolled to her own room, slid from her still-damp chair onto the bed, and hugged her favorite body pillow, the one with pink flowers that Gran-Gran gave her for Christmas years ago. Lightning flashed through the window, followed by a low groan of thunder maybe five seconds later. When the neighbor's fence gate slammed open from a wind gust, she jumped at the sound. Trying to ignore the gathering storm, she pulled the sheet over her head.

An hour later, she woke in her darkened room and peered out to the backyard. Rain was still falling, more gently now, but the wind had died down. Two limbs from an oak tree had broken from its trunk and fallen onto the lawn. *That's going to be a lot of work for Dad*, she thought, then remembered the reason she'd holed up in her room in the first place: he needed a break from looking after her.

Zoey stared at the wheelchair, her reliable partner all these years, and wondered why it was such a big deal to everyone. Sure, there were times when she was frustrated by not being able to walk like other people, but she had long ago accepted what had happened. For her, the wheelchair was merely an inconvenience. But for him, it had always been the reason she couldn't go to a friend's house, couldn't go on a field trip, couldn't go anywhere. *Oh, my God*, she thought. *He doesn't just think I have a disability—he thinks I'm handicapped.*

She winced at her sudden insight and felt an urge to rush into his workshop and give him a piece of her mind. How dare he treat her like a kid. No, not a kid. A cripple.

When she reached for her chair, her anger subsided, replaced by a wave of sadness. No matter what he thought about her, she still had to face the undeniable truth: she would always be dependent on her chair.

Which meant she would be dependent on him. And he'd be forever bound to her needs.

For years, she'd fought him for small measures of freedom such as going to a birthday party or chilling with friends. But the stakes were higher now. Maybe she'd always need that chair, but she had to stop relying on him, not just for herself but also for him.

He deserved to not be confined to the same wheelchair. He deserved a chance to follow his dreams. He deserved to be happy.

With her body still shaking, Danica gazed numbly out the rain-pelted window of Sam's apartment, heartbroken from everything that had happened with Garrison.

"Let me get this straight," Sam told her, handing her a fork and a slice of cheesecake. "That guy from Austin—"

"Russell Polistini." She felt a shiver when she said the name.

"One of those people he killed was the wife of your boyfriend?" Sam shook her head in disbelief. "That's messed up."

"Yeah."

Danica twirled her fork in the gooey dessert—Sam's homemade Polish *sernik*—and wished they could go back to their carefree college days, when the two of them used to snack in their cramped apartment while working on school projects or discussing international affairs. Back when they were young, in a time before the world felt the gut punches of 9/11 and global financial uncertainty, life had been simple.

But life wasn't so simple anymore.

In her mind's eye, Danica could still see Garrison's anguished face and hear his harsh words. She knew that he'd been muddling his fury at Polistini with his frustration about her involvement, but there was also a certain clarity that had revealed itself. "His wife would still be alive if it hadn't been for me. And Zoey wouldn't be paralyzed."

"You didn't do anything wrong, Danni. You're not the one who pulled the trigger."

"But—"

"And you're not responsible for Polistini getting out of prison. I remember that story. You reported about a bad guy in the D.A.'s office. Then the courts threw out some convictions. I'm sure a few of those folks were innocent."

Remembering Garrison's stunned expression, Danica felt a swell of nausea. How could she have done this to him? "You should have seen how hurt Garrison was. He thinks I set him up. We said mean things . . . terrible things . . . to each other."

Sam studied her closely. "You know what I'm gonna tell you, don't you?"

"Yeah, that I have to suck it up and go talk with him."

"No, that's a stupid idea. What I was going to say is that if Garrison really cared for you, he wouldn't have believed the worst. Danni, you're a journalist. You've got a chance to take your career to the next level. NPR? Another interview on *Good Morning America*? Guest-hosting *Fox and Friends*? Fox does know you're a bleeding heart, right?"

She shrugged. "Maybe they're only interested because Hartwell was a Democrat."

"That's my point. You took down a sitting U.S. Senator.

Who does that? I'll tell you who," Sam said, waving a fork at her. "A damn fine reporter, that's who. You better not blow your big break pining away for a guy you hardly know, who yelled at you for doing your job."

Danica sat back and frowned, confused by Sam's response. She didn't want to hear Sam's thoughts about her career. Shouldn't a true friend tell her to search her heart and chase what's important? Or maybe that's exactly what Sam was doing. After all, the reason Danica had pursued journalism was so she could make a difference in people's lives. So jerks like Hartwell couldn't cheat on their wives and ruin the lives of their kids.

And Garrison? Even if there wasn't this Sword of Damocles hanging over the two of them, how was their relationship ever going to work? They'd known each other for little more than a week. They'd barely scratched the surface of discovering what made the other person tick. Then there was his daughter—Zoey was obviously where his priorities rightfully lay.

"Maybe you're right," she said. "Garrison should have believed me. He shouldn't have had such a meltdown."

"Exactly. Don't throw your future away because of some guy."

"Garrison is not *some guy*," she said, the words coming out more defensively than the way they sounded in her head.

"Okay, fine. I'm not saying you should burn bridges. If you and Garrison are meant to be in love, you two will figure it out."

"Hold on, I thought you were too cynical to believe in love."

"I am. But you deserve to be happy. If Garrison makes you happy . . ."

He does, she thought. Most of the time. She felt a deep yearning to be with him again, to restore things back to the way they had been before.

Sam cleared her throat, and Danica looked up. "Are you trying to piss me off?" Sam asked.

"What?"

"When you called, I knew it was important. That's why I made sernik. Just like old times. Now stop playing with your food and eat it."

Danica lowered her eyes, smiling at Sam's comment out of habit. As she lifted the fork to her mouth, she noticed that her plate was adorned with the UC Berkeley seal. Between the image on the plate and the signals from her taste buds, long-dormant memories sprang to life. Suddenly she was back on her old college campus. Berkeley was where she became best friends with Sam. Where she fell for that creep Kevin Taggert. And where she took to heart the university's motto: *Fiat Lux*. Let there be light.

That's what journalism was, she believed, shedding light on the dark places of the world. If not for journalists, cockroaches like Blaine Wiesler and Joe Hartwell would continue to scurry around undetected. Through all her confusing emotions, the one constant had been the vocation she'd been called to.

"I'm a journalist," she blurted, but the words weren't directed to her friend.

"That's what I told you. So you'll be doing those interviews?"

She nodded. "You know, I heard Dan Rather got his big break after covering some hurricane in the Sixties. Woodward and Bernstein weren't anybody important before Watergate. Maybe this is my opportunity. You really think I could land a national job?"

"ABC, CNN, MSNBC. Pick any letter combination you want." Sam took a bite of her cheesecake. "I have a hard time imagining you on Fox News, though."

"Because I'm not a conservative?"

"No," Sam said, smiling. "Because you're not a blonde."

Garrison sat at his computer desk and examined what was left of the Mister Spock bobble head, trying not to think about how badly he'd screwed things up with Danica. He must have pored over the situation a dozen times, and each time her explanation made more sense. She hadn't set out to deceive him.

Their chance meeting on the tennis court had been real. Their attraction had been real. Their lovemaking had been real . . . and amazing. But their miserable TV interview, conducted in a fake living room under the glare of false room lights, had simply been a cascade failure of the highest magnitude.

It was no one's fault, yet it was everyone's fault.

He remembered the old proverb that had guided him in his career as a mechanical engineer, reminding him to pay attention to the details or suffer the consequences. The proverb began with the line "For want of a nail the shoe was lost" and went on to describe the catastrophe that ensued: losing the shoe and then the horse, the rider and his message, the battle and the kingdom. All for the want of a horseshoe nail.

Or an O-ring . . . or a piece of foam insulation, he thought, looking at the space shuttle model and acutely feeling the immense void again.

His hands began to shake, and the figurine fell onto the desk, the Spock head rolling away until it came to rest beside the computer monitor. In that moment, Garrison comprehended the worst part of cascade failure: the immeasurable loss.

Seven astronauts had perished on Challenger, seven more had died when Columbia broke apart, and another three had burned to death as Apollo 1 sat on its launch pad. Those NASA tragedies never should have happened, but someone— everyone—hadn't been paying attention to the details.

Tears streamed down his face as he thought about Celeste, who had also lost her life through a fateful string of events.

He'd spent all these years looking back, trying to determine causality and assess culpability. But it didn't matter where the blame lay, because Celeste was gone forever.

Now he'd lost Danica as well.

If only he hadn't taken that phone call, he never would have gone to the TV station. And he wouldn't have run into Danica. Then everything wouldn't have erupted into such a hateful confrontation, with him calling her a liar and her calling him a coward.

Lightning flashed like a strobe into the room, and he cursed in response. Uncovering the window had been a bad idea. Tonight it was lightning; tomorrow the hot sun would stream through. Now he remembered why he'd blocked the damn window in the first place.

He rummaged through the trash and found the torn piece of cardboard he'd ripped off days earlier, then taped it back onto the glass. He had kissed Danica right here, in front of the starfield poster that had covered the window. Now the starfield was gone, torn to shreds and tossed away.

He sat down and buried his head in his hands. They were past the point where apologizing would do any good. The damage was too great. It was hopeless.

You need a drink.

He recognized the voice, clear and urgent, that same inner voice he'd first heard after Celeste died, and then again after Columbia, and then again after Mom. That voice may have led him to dark places, but at least it had offered direction when he wasn't sure where to turn.

You need a drink. How about a beer?

No, he thought, shaking his head, trying to gain control of his senses.

Or maybe something stronger. Why not? You're all alone now.

He picked up the pieces of Mister Spock and tossed them in the trash as if they were radioactive. He needed to get out of here.

There's a convenience store around the corner.

He rushed from the workshop and into the kitchen, praying that the voice wouldn't follow him but also smacking his lips at the prospect of a little something that might take the edge off. What was the harm, really, with having one drink?

"Hi, Dad," Zoey said, sitting in the family room watching TV. "Are you going somewhere?"

"Uh . . . no. Of course not."

"You've got keys in your hand."

He stared down at his fingers, which were curled around his NASA meatball-logo keychain. "I was looking for a USB stick," he lied, licking his parched lips. "It's almost ten o'clock. Why aren't you asleep?"

"Can we talk?"

"You know, I think I will run up to the store." Fifteen minutes was all it would take for him to drive over there, buy some liquid companionship, and slip back before Zoey missed him. Too bad it was after nine. Man, Stoli would taste so good over ice. At least he could still buy beer. "Are you okay to be by yourself for a bit?"

"That's what I want to talk about." She gave a deep sigh. "It's really important."

He could picture that six-pack in the cooler and imagine how good it was going to taste, but he also knew he'd have to wait a little longer. After Zoey went to bed, he'd have plenty of time to get reacquainted with his old friend. His fingers loosened around the key chain, and he placed the keys back on the wall hook. "I don't want to talk about Danica."

Zoey muted her TV show and gave a deep sigh. "It's not about her."

"Is it school? Friends?" She cringed, and he knew he'd hit a nerve. "Has someone been calling you names again?"

"That's just part of growing up."

"I can talk with someone at your school. A counselor or

principal."

"No, Dad. Stay out of it. You'll only make things worse."

"Then what do you want?" He knew the answer as soon he asked the question—Zoey wanted that dog. This was not a battle he could fight today.

"Never mind," she said. "I'm sorry for what happened between you and Danica."

"There's something bothering you."

"Look," she said, and pointed at the TV. "The news is on. They're talking about the storm."

He sighed. If she didn't want to talk about what was troubling her, that was fine by him. He didn't have the energy to deal with her issues tonight. *Then go to the store*, his inner voice said, but there was no way Garrison could leave his daughter alone, unhappy like this.

He sat back and watched the remotes from reporters describing the storm's extensive damage, then listened as the Eyewitness9 weatherman forecasted isolated thunderstorms over the next few days. When the screen returned to the woman at the anchor desk, the lady that Danica was going to replace, Garrison realized he'd have to stop watching the news again. He couldn't imagine seeing Danica's beautiful face every night and knowing he'd blown his chance with her.

"Here's an update on the story we brought you on Friday," the anchorwoman said, "concerning convicted murderer Russell Polistini."

"Turn it off," Garrison barked, remembering his disastrous interview with Danica.

"No, I want to see this."

"Right now. Give me the remote."

"It fell on the floor."

He rushed toward her wheelchair and dropped to his knees, searching for the remote control. He couldn't let her watch this.

"Earlier this evening, Polistini was put to death by lethal

injection in the Huntsville Unit. His death marks the five-hundredth inmate to be executed by the state of Texas since 1982."

Garrison gasped. He had dreamed of this moment for years, believing that his life—their lives—would be transformed when justice was finally served. Yet the moment had arrived, and he felt surprisingly empty. Because nothing had truly changed. Zoey would always be paralyzed. Celeste would always be dead.

"Eyewitness9 reached out to the spouse of one of his victims earlier today."

Oh shit.

"Dad?"

Turn it off. Turn it off!

He spied the remote control beneath the sofa and dove for it. As he grabbed the remote, he heard the anchorwoman say, "The wife of slain officer Andrew Quinn issued the following statement. 'Andy was a good man, a loving husband and father, and a dedicated police officer. I hope everyone will remember the names of the victims in this senseless tragedy and forget their brutal killer.'"

The screen went black as Garrison powered off the TV. The last thing he saw was footage of some car wreck. He laid his forehead against the wood floor and exhaled. They weren't airing his interview. Thank God.

"What's going on?" Zoey demanded. "That man they were talking about . . ."

The police officer, he thought. Quinn. The cop's wife was right—everyone should remember the names of the victims. Perhaps now he could tell Zoey the truth after shielding her from it for so long. After all, Polistini couldn't hurt them anymore.

Garrison rolled onto his side. When he looked up at Zoey, he saw her pounding her fists against the arms of her wheelchair and staring at the blank screen. She snapped her head down at him and gave him an icy stare. "Why didn't you tell me?"

"What do you mean?"

"I know that name," she said, her voice rising. "He's the man who murdered Mom."

Chapter 40

Garrison could hardly wrap his head around what Zoey had told him. She already knew who Russell Polistini was. "How?" he asked.

"You must think I'm an idiot. Haven't you ever heard of Google?"

He clambered to his feet and moved in front of her wheelchair. "I didn't think . . . I didn't want you to . . ."

"What? Know the truth? Guess what, Dad. I've known about Russell Polistini, about everything, for years. I'm glad he's dead."

Although he'd long ago told Zoey she'd been injured in a shooting that had also killed her mother, Garrison had always clung to the belief that keeping Zoey in the dark about the brutal facts of the case would protect her. She certainly hadn't needed to learn the gory details about how her mom and three others had been gunned down. "I guess I should have told you sooner, but I was waiting for you to get old enough to handle it."

That seemed to set her off. "You know, I'm so tired of this crap. I'm fourteen. You act like I'm still the kid you had to push down the hallway to kindergarten."

With sudden clarity, he realized she was right. She wasn't a helpless little girl anymore. She was a woman, fierce and strong . . . just like her mother. He gazed at Zoey, finally able to see how much she favored Celeste in so many ways. Why hadn't he noticed before?

Because you're not a good father.

"If I could change things," he told Zoey in a pained voice, "I would. But I can't." Lacking the energy or desire to continue arguing, he walked past her toward the kitchen.

"You're leaving? How dare you ignore me."

"Please, I've had a long day."

She followed after him. "Why were you and Danica fighting about me at school? You still think I'm too young to play tennis, don't you?"

"It wasn't about you. Trust me."

"Oh, so now I should trust you? How about one of these days you learn to trust me?"

He slammed the counter. "Dammit, Zoey! Leave me alone!" He slowly lifted his hands, which were trembling, and knew exactly what he needed to do to stop the shakes.

"Sure, I'll leave you alone. I can manage just fine without you."

"Good," he said, spying the keys on the wall.

As Zoey rolled away, she paused and glared at him once more. "No wonder Danica yelled at you. You're a real jerk."

Her words sliced through him. No matter how hard he tried, he always ended up ruining everything. Now he understood the bitter truth: he was the cause of all the carnage in his life: Celeste, Danica, and now Zoey.

Just one flight.

Just one drink.

That was the answer. All alone now, he grabbed the keys and reached for the door, his inner voice urging him on. He could feel his whole body shuddering.

But something was holding him back, trying to steady his compass and offer him guidance to somewhere other than the bottom of a bottle. He stared at the keys and after a moment set them on the counter. He wandered through the house, unsure where he was headed, until he ended up in the bedroom closet. An old box of family photos seemed to call to him, and he pulled it down from the shelf. He sat cross-legged on the floor, reviewing each picture with a growing sense of comfort, each one reminding him why life was too precious to toss aside.

Just one drink?

Never again. He needed something much more important.

Just one more chance.

Zoey woke the next morning and stared at the ceiling, wishing a new day would change things but knowing in her heart that it wouldn't. She didn't want to go to school and face everybody, didn't want to hear how badly Cara and Lucas had duped her, didn't want to hear the Populars mocking her again.

Still dressed in her pajamas, she transferred onto her chair and rolled out of the bedroom and through the hallway, not particularly wanting to talk to her dad either. She found him sitting at the kitchen table, dunking a slice of French toast in his coffee. "Dad?" she croaked, and ran a hand across her throat. "I don't feel good."

"Do you have a fever?"

"Maybe."

He kissed her forehead. "Nope, no fever. Go back to bed and get yourself some more sleep," he said a little too easily.

"Don't you know what time it is?"

He waved a flippant hand. "It's not a problem."

Not a problem? Uneasiness prickled at the back of Zoey's mind. This wasn't like him. She scanned the room, thinking this was how celebrities must feel when they're getting punked.

"I cooked breakfast," he said. "French toast and bacon. Do you feel up to eating? Let me pour you some orange juice."

It's a trap. She barked a couple of coughs. "I don't think I can go to school today."

"Well, you sure picked a lousy day to get sick. The school sent an email this morning. They're closed."

"School's closed?"

"Apparently, yesterday's storm damaged the cafeteria roof. They expect to be open tomorrow, though. You know, you don't look that sick. I bet you won't even miss a day."

Her shoulders slumped. "Great," she muttered.

He returned to the table with a plate full of her favorite breakfast items, and she had to force herself to pick at the food as if she were really sick. "About last night," he said. "I want to apologize for not telling you about the man who shot you and your mom."

"Russell Pol—"

"Let's not say his name anymore. Okay?"

She nodded.

"Look, I have to go into NASA today. Some big meeting about the project."

It was then that she noticed he was wearing a pair of nice slacks and a button-down shirt. "Does this mean you won't be working from home anymore?"

"Just today. It shouldn't go past noon. But if you're feeling bad, I'll stay here with you."

"I can take care of myself." She realized she sounded somewhat hostile, so she added, "I can be responsible. Let me prove it."

He seemed to consider what she'd said, and after a moment replied, "You're right. I can trust you. I'm gonna have to work harder on that."

Astonished by his new attitude, she found herself speechless. Then she managed to utter, "Thanks, Dad."

He slid a box toward her along the kitchen table. "After you went to bed last night . . . well, I wasn't thinking straight. So I dug in the closet and found this. It helped me feel better."

"What is it?"

"A box of old family photos. You and your mom. The three of us. Some from our college days. If you're bored while I'm gone, you might like looking through them."

She opened the lid and saw a photograph she had never seen before, one of her as a baby with her mom and grandma. Her eyes welled with tears.

"I love you, Dad."

Garrison trudged into the NASA building, weary from last night's battle with his demons but satisfied that he'd gone a long way to mending the strain between Zoey and him. The rift with Danica, however—well, that was something that couldn't be fixed. He yearned to call her and hear her voice once more, but he was sure she would hang up on him and officially seal their doomed relationship.

Instead, he went straight to the conference room, which was packed with everyone from his project, and found an empty seat alongside the wall. It didn't take long for the bad news to be displayed on the screen: his team in Houston was being de-staffed off the project.

"Don't worry," Chip told the group as Garrison stared out the window, trying to comprehend how he was going to deal with yet another disruption in his life. "There's a place for everyone here at NASA."

That was easy for Chip to say. He already had his new job lined up at Goddard Space Flight Center.

After the meeting, Chip ushered Garrison into his office. "So I saw the news," Chip said cavalierly. "Were you there when they gave him the needle?"

Garrison found it best to ignore Chip when he acted

obnoxious, so he tried to change the subject. "When are you getting transferred to Goddard?"

"I was on a jury trial once," Chip said, ignoring the question. "A woman slit her boyfriend's throat while he was sleeping. Seems he was slinging his sausage around the ol' neighborhood. I was the only one who wanted to give her the death penalty."

"Can we not talk about this?"

"I think the public ought to be able to kill a certain number of people a year. You know, murderers, rapists, child molesters, psycho women with butcher knives. And if we're still under our quota for a given year, toss in a few do-gooders, like the ones who want to keep me from smoking." He laughed. "Sounds like a plan, right?"

"Um, how's Janet?" Garrison asked, hoping he'd correctly remembered the name of wife number three.

"Well, she hasn't threatened to slice off my pecker. That's a good sign. But to answer your first question, I'm leaving for Goddard in two weeks. That's why I wanted you to meet with you today."

"Do you want me to pull together some reports for you take to Washington, D.C.?"

"Better than that. I want you to come with me."

As soon as her dad left for work, Zoey rushed to her bedroom and changed into an old t-shirt. With hours to herself, she wanted to get the most out of her day, and that included exercising, cleaning her room, and cooking lunch. By the time Dad returned, she wanted to show him how independent she could be.

Her first goal was to get a good workout. If she were ever to be fully self-sufficient, she needed to improve her stamina. She backed her chair against the wall, set the brakes, and performed tricep pushups, each time holding her body off the seat for a count of five. The muscles in her arms and shoulders burned with every lift, along with her abs, but she would never complain, knowing how lucky she was compared to others she'd met.

On her seventh set of pushups, her right elbow buckled. Her full body weight slammed onto the chair arm and she almost tumbled out, falling onto the seat instead.

Be safe. She could hear Dad's words echoing in her mind. She knew she ought to have a spotter, but it could never be her father. The whole idea was not to be dependent on him.

She shifted from pushups to arms-only jumping jacks until her arms wore out, then collapsed into her seat. That was enough for one day. She rolled over to her desk, opened her journal, and jotted down what she'd accomplished. Tomorrow, she vowed, she'd do even more.

After enjoying a long shower, she donned fresh clothes and returned to her room, intent on cleaning it so thoroughly that he'd have to notice. She started with her desk, which was littered with old homework and printouts about the dog she'd never get, and tossed the papers into the trash, pausing only to wistfully reread the information about dog adoptions.

She brushed against the wireless mouse, and her computer display flickered on. Glancing at the clock—plenty of time before Dad would get home—she decided to go online and see if anyone else was bored by having to stay home.

She logged into Facebook and began reading the statuses in her news feed, but it took a minute to realize there weren't any recent updates from Cara, which was totally out of the ordinary. That girl practically lived on Facebook. A few clicks later, she learned the reason: Cara had unfriended her. *What a bitch.*

Just then an alert box flashed onscreen, indicating she had a new message, and she clicked on it without thinking, still fixed on Cara. The note was from Lucas—the guy she used to like.

Don't believe the rumors, his message said, followed by a request for her cell number. She hesitated, but curiosity won over, and the next thing she knew, her cell phone had rung and Lucas Hardesty was on the other end of the line.

"You're friends with Cara Reynolds, right?"

Well, I was, Zoey thought, remembering her unfriended Facebook status. "What did she say now?"

"I'm so frickin' pissed. Apparently, Cara has been telling people she made out with me at her party. Have you heard anything?"

She remembered how Tiffany had basically shoved the gossip in her face and laughed about it. "I might have heard something. That was you?"

"It's not what you think. Cara and her friends were playing some stupid game. I was standing by the door, and all of a sudden Tiffany what's-her-name told me Cara had something important to tell me."

"Was it about me?" Maybe she would finally learn why Cara had been acting so mean.

He blew a deep breath, and she could hear him struggling to maintain his composure. "I only went in the closet because I thought the same thing. She got angry when I asked about you."

"So you two didn't make out?"

"No! And I don't know why she started this nasty rumor."

"It's not your fault. Cara's mad at me." Although for the life of her, Zoey didn't know the reason. But she was going to find out. "Let's talk later. I have to go do something."

Zoey opened the wrought iron gate that led to the driveway and rolled through, then swung the gate closed behind her. The only way she was going to get to the bottom of things was to speak face-to-face with Cara, far away from the meddling girls who'd poisoned her heart.

She drove down the sidewalk past their neighbor's house, then turned right onto a winding concrete path that cut through to the greenbelt. She'd gone this way to Cara's house twice but this was the first time she was driving solo, and she figured it would take half an hour.

Pushing her wheels hard, Zoey had to avoid fallen branches and rain puddles as she went along, but she wasn't going to let a few obstacles deter her. It was one thing for her former friend to go after her—she was used to getting picked on. But how dare Cara attack Lucas? He was the kindest person Zoey knew.

She thought about the gifts he'd given her. He'd gone out of his way to learn about her birthday and hand-wrap all the presents. A guy like Lucas never would have hooked up with someone like Cara. She felt ashamed for thinking he had.

After ten minutes, she rolled to a stop, tired from all the pushing. She shook out her arms, feeling the strain from her earlier exercise, and then pulled each arm firmly across her body, trying to stretch out the muscles. It was going to be so satisfying to tell Cara what she thought of her and then watch her ex-friend try to spit out an apology.

She stared down the path in front of her and realized she hadn't seen a single person during her journey. A rumble of thunder sounded, and she quickly understood why no one else was out. Another storm was coming. She got her second wind and pressed on.

As the greenbelt curved along the edge of a tree-lined golf course, she gazed out onto an unoccupied fairway and wondered if wheelchair golf was something she could try in the future. Yeah, she thought, that might be fun.

Staring past the sand traps and manicured green, Zoey noticed she could see straight through to her middle school. Which meant that Cara's house was closer than she'd thought.

If she took a shortcut through the golf course, she'd definitely get there before any rain started.

She veered off the greenbelt and down the concrete cart path, past a pond with some ducks, and then to where the next tee box was located. She rested her arms while she coasted downhill and took a quick glance back over her shoulder to spot where she'd left the main sidewalk.

Her chair began to rattle, and the wheels vibrated under her fingers—she was picking up speed. She snapped around and saw the bottom of the concrete path ahead of her, covered with water and flanked by a massive tree. Squeezing the rims, she tried to slow herself, and then she pulsed the brakes. The chair tilted sideways and her right wheel slipped off the concrete. Suddenly she was airborne.

She raised her arms to her face. As she tumbled forward, the ground rushed toward her, and her last thought was of Dad.

Chapter 41

S taring through floor-to-ceiling windows at the jet parked outside her gate, Danica hugged her arms across her chest. She couldn't help but be bombarded with mental images from the last time she'd been this close to an airplane: the roiling smoke, the burning fuselage, the tattooed body of Araceli Montalvo. The lady from Fox News had assured her that traveling to New York City would be a luxurious experience, a trip complete with limos and five-star accommodations, but Danica was anything but comfortable right now.

It wasn't as if she were worried that her plane would crash— she'd developed a fatalistic view of death anyway after seeing how it touched so many lives. She simply understood that when the cabin doors closed, there would be no turning back. Just like when she boarded those planes in Seattle and Los Angeles. Just like when she drove the U-Haul out of Austin.

She was going to hand her boarding ticket to the agent, walk through that jetway, and say goodbye to the Bayou City, the flat, hot landscape of the Gulf Coast she'd called home for ten years. Goodbye to mosquitoes and humidity. Goodbye to Eyewitness9.

Goodbye to Garrison.

Her throat tightened at the thought of him, how kind and intelligent and quirky and, well, how wonderful he was. Garrison was the only man she'd ever truly fallen in love with. And now she'd allowed her own thirst for telling the next big story to come between them. That's why she had to leave Houston, she knew, not to chase money or fame but to make a fresh start.

Danica pulled her cell phone from her purse. She wanted to call him, hear his voice again. But with her fingers poised over the call button, she froze, unsure of what to say to him. That she was sorry about the pain she'd caused? That she would never forget their time together? No, there was nothing she could say that would make things better. Even the death of his wife's killer wasn't going to change the situation.

Maybe the best thing to do was push Garrison out of her mind completely and move on to the next adventure in her life. Blinking back tears, she cancelled the phone call and peered out at the airplane, her stomach churning.

"Excuse me," a voice said, and Danica jumped. She looked up to see a young blonde—perhaps a college coed—in hip-hugger jeans and platform sandals. "You're Danica Cortez, aren't you?"

"Uh-huh."

"My name's Ashley. I think you're, like, awesome." She giggled nervously. "I'm sure you hear that all the time."

For years, Danica had lived for these moments, being approached and complimented by a stranger, perhaps signing an autograph or posing for a picture. Today she just wanted to be left alone.

"I'm gonna be like you someday," Ashley went on. "I'm majoring in broadcast communications."

Danica studied the girl's eager face and remembered how idealistic she'd been at that age. Back at the start of her career, filled with unbridled energy and a journalist's healthy skepticism, she'd been ready to take on the world. But years of doing the same thing, reporting on endless tragedies and enduring the drudgery of live broadcasts—not to mention discovering that everyone she covered seemed to be lying about something—had congealed her honest skepticism into hardened cynicism. "Are you sure you want to be in the news business?"

"Absolutely. I can't wait to, like, go on TV and do reporting and stuff."

"Well, good luck," Danica told her, noticing how much this Ashley girl reminded her of her nemesis, Barb Edwards over at Channel Five. Danica craned her neck to see whether passengers had begun lining up to board, but no one had.

"I'm flying to visit my dad. Are you going to New York, too?"

"Yeah," she replied bleakly.

Ashley unwrapped a stick of gum and popped it into her mouth. "It sure sucks that we're gonna be late."

"What?"

"They made an announcement a few minutes ago. Something broke on the plane. Didn't you hear?"

Danica whipped her head to the agent desk and confirmed the news on the monitor. Her flight would be delayed for two hours. Ugh.

"So, do you have any advice for an aspiring journalist?" Ashley asked.

"I'm sorry. This isn't a good time."

"No, it's perfect. I'm here all by myself. I can chat until we take off."

Danica rubbed her eyes and sighed. "Okay, here's some advice. Don't go into the news business."

The smile on Ashley's face faded. "Wow, you don't have to be rude."

Danica's cell phone went off in her hand, and she startled. She gazed down at the phone, the screen pressed into her palm, the instrument vibrating. *Answer me*, it urged. But she was afraid to turn it over, sure that more disappointment lay in wait on the other end of the line.

"Look," Danica said, "if you want to be a journalist, forget about the news business. It's an illusion. Real journalism is about finding the truth."

Answer me, the phone insisted in her hand. *This is important.*

"What do you mean?" the girl asked. "Find the truth?"

As Danica tried to form an answer, she was distracted by the buzzing phone. An odd sixth sense, not her reporter's instincts but some primal intuition, was telling her that for once in her life this wasn't bad news. It wasn't someone sending her on a reporting assignment in the middle of the night or urging her to hurry home to "be with your brother before it's too late."

Suddenly Danica understood things perfectly. She'd been searching for years to figure out what was false and what was real. And her reality—her truth—was literally in the palm of her hand.

She squeezed the phone and flipped it over. It was Garrison.

Her hands began to tingle. She drew a breath, afraid to let it go.

"Danica?" he said, and her heart lifted at the sound of his voice. "I was wrong about everything. I'm sorry."

"No, I'm the one who's sorry. Yesterday at the TV station—"

"It was a misunderstanding. Where are you? I need to see you."

I need to see you, too. "I'm at Hobby Airport. I've got this audition in New York." She winced, feeling so shallow for talking about work instead of the things that really mattered. "I'll only be gone a couple of days," she said, trying to convey a sense of hopefulness. "Can I see you when I get back?"

When he didn't speak for a few seconds, she knew she'd messed up again. "Wait, Garrison. I'll reschedule my trip." Her mind raced with the people she would need to call, not sure if it was even possible to reschedule at this late date.

"No, this is important for you. Go to New York."

"But—"

"You deserve this, Danica. I hope everything works out for you." Before she could say anything, he hung up.

She clutched the phone to her chest and began to shake uncontrollably. Tears flowed freely down her face as she came to grips with what she'd done. Then she folded into sobs.

Zoey spat out a mouthful of mud. *What just happened?* She lifted her head from the muck, coughed, and tried to take stock of things. She was never going to forget how it felt to hurtle through the air and slam against the ground, all the while praying she wouldn't strike the trunk of that huge tree. She had missed it by less than a yard.

What she needed to do was get out of this mess. Diverting her route onto the golf course had been a dumb idea, so the best thing now was to climb back into her wheelchair. Wherever that was.

She gathered her hands beneath her chest and pushed herself up, spitting out more mud, and spied the wheelchair. It was maybe six feet behind her, toppled onto its side in the grass. Hoping her chair wasn't broken, she mapped out a path to it, believing she could right it and climb back on.

As she peered at the wheelchair, her vision suddenly blurred. The chair, the cart path, and the trees all disappeared behind a murky film. Blinking to regain her sight, she quickly realized the sludge that filled her throat was also running into her eyes. She raised a hand to wipe her face, clearing it momentarily, but cringed when she pulled her hand back.

It was covered in blood.

The crimson smear on her hand confirmed this hadn't been one of her typical falls, the kind that featured her slipping off the seat and being sent sprawling onto the floor, the kind that mostly annoyed her but sometimes made her laugh, the kind that always freaked out her dad. This fall was different.

Bright red drops began to stream from her forehead, causing a rivulet of blood to swirl in the muddy water. She wiped off her hand and touched a finger to her forehead, probing for the source of the leak. When she found it, just above her left eyebrow, she pressed her hand against it, remembering the concept of direct pressure she'd learned in Health class.

This was no time to panic. But her vision was getting worse, her left eye closed and bloody, her right eye covered with mud. She could feel the panic coming on anyway.

"Hey!" she called, "Could I get some help?" She waited for a reply, sure that a passerby would hear her, but the only response came from a rumbling sky. She hollered a few more times but soon decided it was a lost cause. The golf course had obviously been closed due to the storm, and she was too far from the main path on the greenbelt to be heard.

That left her with only one option: call Dad. But that would mean admitting she'd broken his rules about going out alone and then enduring his obsessive worry in the future. She needed to do this on her own.

She flipped herself onto her butt and crabbed backwards toward the chair, dragging her limp legs behind her. She had no idea if she'd fractured a leg, but she didn't see any exposed bones. That was a good sign.

When she reached her chair, she pulled alongside it and tilted it back up. She inspected the wheels—the left one was perfect, the right one was bathed in mud but seemed okay— and set the brakes.

She wiped an arm across her face. *I can do this*, she told herself, fighting the quivering fear and forcing herself to think about all the times she'd transferred from chair to floor and back again. She took a deep breath. Allowing her muscle memory to guide her, she wriggled up from the mud and clung to the footrests. With a series of pushes, she lifted herself up and maneuvered onto the chair, heaving a sigh of relief when she was finally positioned on the seat.

Now to get home. She certainly wasn't going to Cara's looking like this, all covered in mud and blood. No, she needed to drive home before her dad got back and realized she was gone.

She grasped both hand rims and pushed. Nothing happened.

What the heck?

She checked to make sure the brakes were disengaged, then pushed again. Again, nothing happened. When she looked down, she saw that her tires were sunk into the muddy ground.

This couldn't be happening. She wasn't going to be able to free herself on her own. She was going to have to call her dad after all. "This sucks!" she yelled, and reached for the cell phone holster.

It was empty.

Chapter 42

Go to New York.

Garrison sat in Chip's office, hardly able to believe what he'd told Danica. What was he thinking, encouraging her to leave to pursue her dreams? Of course she was going to be happy there, doing exactly what she wanted, while he was going to have to stay here and be miserable without her.

"Here's the bottom line, Garrison," Chip said as he leaned back in his leather office chair. "If you follow me to Goddard, you'll be set for the rest of your career."

"I told you, I don't want to move to Washington."

"You'll love it. Zoey enjoys museums, right? She can go to the Smithsonian anytime she wants."

"It's not that."

"I guarantee you'll work on challenging projects. And you can have the same flexibility with your schedule as you have now. If you stay in Houston, you're going to end up on some shitty project and they'll force you to work on campus every day. You'll hate it."

Chip was right—Garrison was going to hate staying in Houston. But he couldn't just drop everything and move to Washington D.C. He wasn't like Chip, who could feel comfortable anywhere. And he wasn't like Danica, who had all these plans for her future and could realize them somewhere else . . . without him. No, his life was here. Zoey was here.

"I'm gonna need you with me. You're my secret weapon."

Isn't that the truth, he thought. The only reason Chip's projects had been successful in the first place was because Garrison had always shouldered the heavy load. "Sorry. Can't go."

"Then you're an idiot. Stay here in this armpit of a city. I don't care."

Garrison shook his head. For years, he'd put up with Chip's bad behavior and passive-aggressive comments, all in the name of friendship. Maybe Chip's transfer to Goddard would be the best thing for Garrison. He might not even miss the guy after he moved to the East Coast. Then a thought flashed. "Wait, how far is it from Washington to New York?"

"Oh, they're real close," Chip replied in the same loose way he reported that his projects were on-schedule and on-budget. "You want to show Zoey the Big Apple? Great idea. Empire State Building, Statue of Liberty, Rockefeller Center. Everyone loves New York."

"Uh-huh," he muttered, trying to plan how he could see Danica up there. Maybe there was a glimmer of hope after all.

"But you wouldn't want to live in New York City," Chip continued. "Terrible place. Everyone who moves there regrets it. Well, you know, everyone except the illegals."

He tried to ignore Chip's boorish remark, but he'd heard that preceding line before. *Everyone who moves to New York regrets it.* Danica had once said the same thing to him.

"Where do you think you're going?" Chip asked as Garrison began packing up his laptop.

"I have to see someone."

"See, this is what I'm talking about. You're a guy who needs a flexible work schedule."

"Good luck in Washington." Garrison zipped up his

computer bag and slung it over his shoulder.

"If you leave now, you'll be making the biggest mistake of your life."

Garrison suppressed a smile. "That's funny, I have to tell someone else the very same thing."

Garrison buckled his seatbelt and called Zoey's phone, needing to tell her that she would have to go it alone a little longer. When her phone rolled over to voicemail, he didn't immediately turn the steering wheel to rush home, like he would have done in the past. Instead he left a calm voicemail, asking her to call him back. She was probably preoccupied with something, that's all. She was old enough to take of herself.

As he sped up the Gulf Freeway toward Hobby Airport, the troublesome voice in his head appeared again. *Don't bother. You can't change her mind. Danica doesn't love you.*

But this voice wasn't trying to protect him. It was telling him to run away and hide, just like all the times he'd had the urge to drown his troubles with alcohol. He understood perfectly now. If this inner voice got its way, his nagging doubt would metastasize into full-fledged fear. And fear would produce the paralysis he'd lived with for eleven years. *Life's too dangerous. Don't risk it.*

Yet he'd struggled with doubt and confronted a series of what-ifs all his life. What if I send in my application and NASA turns me down? What if I propose to Celeste and she says no? What if I try to be a good father and my own daughter rejects me?

Doubt wasn't the problem. Fear was the problem.

He saw the exit for the airport and turned on his blinker. Screw fear. He was going to face the truth, no matter how it turned out. If Danica was at the airport, he was going to tell her how much she meant to him. And if she rejected him . . . well, he'd be devastated, but he also knew he would find a way to move on, just like he'd done before.

He was no longer going to let his life be ruled by fear.

At the airport, he pulled into one of maybe twenty empty handicap parking spaces and jumped out. He dashed through the garage toward the terminal. At the entrance, he sidestepped an elderly couple and a lady with a stroller, then passed through the automatic doors.

He looked left, then right. He drew a breath, gaping at all the people. The strangers. The concourse seemed to spin around him. He stumbled forward.

Not a panic attack. Not now.

Squatting on the tile floor, he leaned over and dropped his head between his knees. He ran a hand across his forehead and wiped sweat from his brow. Look at me, he thought, the tough astronaut who set the class G-force record, about to puke.

Crowds—he hated them.

Remembering what a therapist once told him, he closed his eyes and tried to imagine himself in another place, relaxed and in control. But where? Someplace where he could be alone, that was for sure. He thought about his college days at Texas A&M, how he used to rest under the massive oak near the Academic Building and dream about his future. He'd been happy then, a time of innocence when everything in his life was in perfect alignment. He pictured Celeste—*a stranger killed her*—and panic swelled again in his chest.

He squeezed his eyes shut and concentrated on finding some other place of calm. An image of his workshop began to form. He breathed slowly through his nose and could feel the stress begin to recede. Running on the treadmill and building rocket models—those things always relaxed him.

Then suddenly he was inside the star shack. He could practically hear the chirps of crickets and the hum of his telescope's autofocuser. He could see the puffs of white vapor that he'd breathe on a winter night. And he could smell the clean air. Yes, he was safe here.

He recalled his last visit to the ranch, that perfect weekend with Danica, the night the two of them made love. When that wonderful memory surfaced, the roof of the star shack in his mind began to slide open, revealing a deep dark sky, empty except for one little star that twinkled in the expanse. Growing in size and intensity, it suddenly exploded into billions of glimmering fragments, flooding the sky with light.

Garrison blinked open his eyes. Everything was clear to him now. He didn't want to languish in a dark void anymore.

I have to find her, he thought, rising to his feet and surveying the crowded concourse, which suddenly didn't seem as scary. He saw a bank of monitors and rushed toward them. Had she already left?

He scanned the departure board and found a flight bound for New York. He noted its gate number and flight status: *Delayed.* Putting his trust in the accuracy of the information, he bolted away, filled with hope as he headed for gate forty-two.

Then he reached Security.

"Boarding pass and ID, please," the TSA screener said, her hand outstretched. After a moment, she peered up at him over dark wire-rim glasses. "Hurry up, you know the drill."

The truth was that Garrison hadn't flown in years, not on a space shuttle and not on an airplane. The only thing he knew about airport security was that it was notoriously bothersome. "I need to see my girlfriend," he told the woman, whose looks reminded him of Sarah Palin. "She's about to fly out. I'm supposed to take off my shoes, right?"

The TSA agent shook her head. "Only checked-in passengers are allowed through to the gate area." She gestured to the line of people forming behind him.

"Wait, there's gotta be something you can do."

"Sir, you need to step aside. Next."

He fell back, stunned. This wasn't right. He was supposed to stop Danica from going to New York, catch her as she was handing her ticket to a flight attendant, whisk her up in his arms and kiss her as fellow passengers erupted in applause. He wasn't supposed to have some airport security officer go all Barney Fife on him.

Garrison marched forward to the checkpoint. "Can I talk to a supervisor?"

"Trust me, sir. You don't want me to call my supervisor."

She rested her hand on the walkie-talkie on her hip, like a cop posturing with a grip on his holster, and Garrison understood he wouldn't get anywhere with her. "Then I'm calling someone," he muttered, turning away. When he pulled the cell phone from his pocket, he quickly realized he'd been fighting this the wrong way. All he had to do was call Danica and ask her to wait.

He dialed her number. She didn't pick up. He dialed it again. No answer.

Terrified of what that meant, he ran to the monitors and located her flight again. This time the status flashed *Boarding*. There wasn't much time.

At the Delta check-in desk, he flagged down the first agent he saw, a grey-haired woman who was changing out ticket paper in one of the kiosks. "I need your help," he said, gulping air. "I have to talk to my girlfriend before she gets on her plane."

"What flight number is that?"

"I don't remember. Oh, God."

"Then what's the destination? Look, I can't help you if you're gonna hyperventilate on me."

"New York. Gate forty-two. Hurry." The lightheadedness he'd felt earlier was back, this time with a vengeance. His chest felt as if someone were squeezing him in a bear hug.

The agent studied him, shook her head, and then typed something on her computer. "You said New York? Yeah, that plane's already left."

"It's gone?" The reality of what that meant struck him, and he slumped against the counter. "She's gone."

It was the same gut-wrenching feeling he'd experienced after learning Celeste had died, the sense that every nerve in his body had lost the will to live. Only this time it was an airline agent delivering the sad news instead of an ER doctor. Garrison's face began to tingle and his vision tunneled grey, as if he were pulling double-digit Gs on the centrifuge.

It would have been so easy to succumb to the blackness, to slump to the floor and slip into unconsciousness. But he couldn't. The stakes were too high. He had to tough it out.

He pushed himself up off the counter, now sure of what he needed to do. If Danica was moving to New York, so would he.

"Like I said," Danica told the Fox News executive producer on the phone, "I do want to come to New York. All I'm asking is that we push things back a day."

"That's not how things work," the man replied, obviously annoyed. "You're scheduled for a live interview in the morning, and then we can discuss how best to move forward. It doesn't help if you're being difficult."

"I'm not trying to be. It's just . . ." She glanced at the airplane parked on the tarmac and decided telling the truth was best left for another time. "My plane has a mechanical problem. And the weather's really bad. It's only been a couple of weeks since I was involved with Senator Hartwell's crash. Frankly, I'm afraid to get on this plane."

"Are you telling me you have PTSD?"

"I just need one more day."

The executive producer took a long pause and then finally said, "Your hotel and limo are all arranged. Be in the studio by six-thirty tomorrow morning."

She swallowed hard. "And if I'm not?"

"Then this will be the last conversation we ever have."

After hanging up with the guy, Danica powered off her phone in disgust and stood there frozen, unsure of what to do. She absently twirled her fingers in her hair, frustrated that her work life was now as screwed up as her personal life. She understood this New York opportunity was something that came around only once in a lifetime. Even though it meant joining forces with the ultra-conservatives at Fox News, she finally had the chance to become a national anchor. It was what she'd always dreamed of. She would be stupid to turn her back on them.

The other thing wearing on her was how she'd left things at Eyewitness9. Kathy Hammett was still pissed about the Garrison interview and had gone ballistic after hearing about the call from New York. Danica hadn't meant to burn bridges with the station she'd called home for a decade, but it was clear she had. If this trip didn't pan out, her career was ruined.

"Flight fourteen-seventeen to New York LaGuardia is now boarding," a voice called over the loudspeaker. "We appreciate your patience during our delay."

I need more time, she thought desperately. She removed her boarding pass from her carry-on bag and re-read it to see whether there had been some mistake. But her destiny was painfully documented in black and white. She trudged toward the gate agent desk, pulling her luggage behind her, as if she were on some crazy moving sidewalk that led to doom.

"New York, here we come!" squealed the blonde coed, sidling up next to her. "I can't believe it. When I get there, I get to meet my father for the first time in eighteen years."

"Really?"

"Yeah! He's apparently been searching for me a long time. You know, there's, like, a million Ashley Smiths out there. He just called out of the blue one day and told me how much he regretted not being part of my life. Isn't that awesome?"

"Good for you." Danica knew her own father would never seek her out, considering that he had already skipped the funerals for Mom and Mario.

"Group number two," the agent announced.

"Oh, that's me," Ashley said. "Wish me luck."

"I hope it works out for you."

"My dad's taking a week-long vacation. And he's in the middle of some big merger. Cool, huh? He told me that sometimes you have to stop what you're doing and chase what's important." Then she breezed away.

Danica took a sharp breath at Ashley's words, an echo of Sam's sentiments yesterday. *Chase what's important.* For years, she had set her sights on the next great promotion. Reporter to anchor. Small-market to large-market. Local news to national news.

If she listened to conventional wisdom, her future lay in the bright lights of New York City. There was nothing more prestigious, more important, than that. But every cell of her being didn't want to go.

She closed her eyes and could immediately sense him, all of him. The tenderness of his hands, the trace of Southern drawl in his voice, the scent of his body as he made love to her under the stars.

Chase what's important. Was that really to be found in New York?

Of course not. Everything was in sharp focus now. If she got on that plane, she would regret it forever. Because what truly mattered was here in Houston.

She crumpled the boarding pass in her hand. *I love him*, she thought, the excitement washing over her. She pushed through the crowd of passengers. When she reached the concourse, she sprinted down the hallway.

Garrison telephoned Zoey again and frowned when she didn't answer. It wasn't as if he was worried about her—okay, maybe just a little—but he ached to talk with her about Danica and their future.

He jangled the keys in his pocket and headed for the parking garage. He had no clue what moving to New York would involve, but he had three hours to consider matters before Danica's plane touched down. He knew that NASA ran a research lab at New York's Columbia University that operated under the Goddard umbrella. Could he transfer there?

As he walked toward the terminal exit, an Indian woman in a long flowing sari came through the doors pushing an overfilled luggage cart with one hand and guiding a small wheelchair with the other. In the wheelchair was a black-haired boy about four years old. Remembering Zoey's childhood days, Garrison felt a keen sense of empathy for the woman, who was obviously struggling to handle things on her own.

Then her luggage shifted.

"Watch out!" Garrison rushed to the woman, his arms extended, afraid everything would crash down on her and the child. She must have sensed it too, as she released the cart.

In an instant he was at her side, just as two suitcases slid from the top of the cart. He blocked one with his arms, but the other struck him square in the back and drove him to his knees. He heard the woman scream.

"Your son," he said, stumbling to his feet and ignoring the sharp pain below his shoulder blades. "Is he hurt?"

She looked to the child in the wheelchair. "Raj?" Her son, whose thin arms and legs seemed to dangle from his trunk, gazed up at them and smiled. A mirrored smile appeared on her face. "You saved my boy. I don't know how to thank you."

Garrison exhaled a sigh of relief. "Just glad I could help." He tousled the boy's dark hair and smiled, but another jag of pain caused him to wince. He dropped to a knee and rubbed a fist along his back. A crowd of people appeared, and he watched stranger after stranger offer assistance to the woman, repacking her cart and helping with the baggage she couldn't handle. As she departed with her son, Garrison marveled that they had escaped without injury and wondered if this was the reason fate had led him to the airport.

Throughout his life, he'd witnessed tragedies that were culminations of oversights and missteps, cascade failures resulting in immeasurable harm. But he'd never particularly noticed the positive outcomes around him. Life seemed so random—but was it? Maybe there really was a master plan for the universe, a truth he couldn't yet grasp.

Closing his eyes and breathing slowly, he allowed his imagination to take him to the only place where everything seemed to make sense: beneath a sky that held the answers to all of life's mysteries. The world moved in cycles, he'd learned. Sun to moon, east to west, day to night. And when the world turned its darkest, stars would appear.

He inhaled deeply, calming himself, and a scent wafted into his consciousness. After a moment, he began to recognize the familiar aroma of blackberry and jasmine, with a touch of vanilla.

Danica's fragrance.

He opened his eyes. She was standing in front of him.

"Garrison?" she asked incredulously.

"You didn't go," he whispered. He rose and reached out to touch her face, hesitant to believe what he was seeing. But there she stood, the woman who'd restored joy and meaning to his life.

Gazing into each other's faces, they exchanged glances of apology and forgiveness. He slipped his arms around her, drawing her close. He could feel their hearts begin to beat in unison, and she laid her head on his chest.

Gone was all doubt. Gone was all fear. Holding her tightly against him, he was more certain than he'd ever been. He lifted her chin and brushed a lock of raven hair from her face, awed by her beauty.

Nothing mattered except her and Zoey.

"I love you," he told her, using the most profound words he knew.

She traced a finger around his mouth, her touch like that of an angel. Her face spread into a wondrous smile. "Me, too."

They pressed their lips together, and suddenly they were no longer in a busy airport surrounded by strangers but alone in their own starfield, sharing a kiss amongst the heavens.

Chapter 43

Zoey frantically ran her hands along her wheelchair, digging through its many pouches, but she didn't find her phone. She did, however, find a purple gel pen she'd forgotten about, plus what was left of Lucas's gifts: a dog collar, retractable leash, and a handful of dog biscuits. Even though she hadn't eaten lunch, there was no way she was ever going to munch on those, no matter how hungry she became.

And she was hungry.

She should have at least tossed a granola bar into one of the pockets before she left. But no, she had to rush away in a huge hurry, all keyed up to confront Cara, who was the person responsible for getting her into this mess in the first place.

A clap of thunder sounded and Zoey flinched. At the same time, a torrential rain began to pour down. Large drops splatted around her like meteorites.

She inspected the ground for her phone—it must have flown off the chair like she had—but she couldn't find it anywhere. The rain was fierce now. Zoey could no longer see her school building in the distance through the wet, grey shroud.

Knowing she didn't have any time to waste, she scooted to the edge of her seat and prepared to do her "Ninja dismount," as Danica called it. She lifted her limp legs out straight, placing them slightly off to one side so she would slide instead of buckle, and placed a fist on the ground to use as a pivot. Then she pushed off, like she'd done thousands of times. But whether it was due to her bloody hand or the wet chair, she slipped and rolled her wrist, dropping all her weight onto it.

She shrieked at the pain. "Stupid-ass frickin' wheelchair!"

Lying on the grass, she flexed her wrist, and bolts of pain ricocheted up her arm. "I am so screwed," she muttered and looked around again for the phone, hoping it was still in one piece when she found it. Dad was going to give her grief, but she didn't have any other choice. She even knew what he was going to say, that this wouldn't have happened if she weren't so impulsive. Which was true. Dad never would have bolted from the house just because of what someone told him on the phone—

The phone.

Oh crap. It was sitting on her desk—Zoey could see it clearly in her mind—left there after talking with Lucas. She swallowed hard and tried not to cry.

Dad couldn't help. Lucas couldn't help. This was up to her.

Just one flight.

As Garrison stood in the middle of Hobby Airport's bustling terminal, holding Danica tightly against him, he wondered if she was going to harbor doubts about not boarding her plane to New York. He'd faced the decision himself—abandoning a shuttle ride into space—and had second-guessed himself for years. What if Danica regretted not getting on her flight and pursuing her dreams?

"I want you to be sure," he told her, "because I'll support you no matter what."

"The truth is I don't know what I want for my career. Maybe

it is a network job one day. Or maybe my destiny is here in Houston . . . or somewhere else. All I know is that I want to be with you, Garrison."

He bent down and kissed her again, the pain in his back still present but muted. "Let's go home."

She gave him a lopsided smile. "I, uh, took a limo to the airport. You think I could catch a ride?"

"Hmm, I think we can work something out."

From her position on the ground, Zoey gave her wheelchair an angry shove, trying to free it from the mud, but it wouldn't budge. *Think, Zoey, think.*

She glanced around, trying to take stock of her situation. The chair: stuck but seemingly in one piece. The weather: getting worse by the minute. Her own body: except for a bum hand, bloody face, and useless legs, she was in perfect shape. She laughed at the absurdity of it all.

When she pulled on the chair again, she heard a metallic clinking and cocked her head at the sound. What was that? She shook the chair and heard it again. Oh, it was just the dog leash.

Then she had an idea. Maybe she could forge her own escape. She unbuckled the side pouch, letting it drop onto the ground, and then ran an inventory of what she had. Leash, collar, gel pen, the pouch itself. They had to be useful somehow.

She scratched her head. She'd already yanked on the chair without success. How could anything in this pile change that? As an experiment, she wrapped the end of the leash around both footrests and hooked the metal clip back onto the nylon lead, forming an anchor knot. Then she crabbed away from the chair, tugging on the leash as she grimaced in pain.

The chair moved a bit . . . but not much. *I need leverage,* she thought, knowing she was slipping far too much where she was. Then she spied the tree she'd almost slammed into. She recalled her dad's boring explanations of simple machines—levers and pulleys and inclined planes—and wondered if she could use the tree as the fulcrum for some sort of makeshift pulley. It was worth a shot.

She tried to backward crab away from the chair again, but her wrist balked when she put her weight on it, forcing her to halt. There had to be another way—she wasn't going down without a fight. She fastened the dog collar through the leash's hand loop and attached it around her belt. Then she flipped onto her stomach and army-crawled on her elbows to the tree, lugging the lengthening leash with her.

The rain was coming down in sheets now and pooling in the low area around the tree. An image emerged of waters rising around her, but she had come too far to end up drowning in a flash flood. She wrapped the strap around the base of the trunk and crawled onto the concrete for better traction. She set the switch on the leash so it wouldn't release any more tether.

"Let's do this," she said, and began shuffling herself back away from the tree. Her wrist was on fire, but she concentrated on the task at hand. Pull. *Pull.*

Just when she thought the leash might break, her wheelchair drew free of the mud with a loud *slork*. She yanked it a few more feet, disconnected the hand loop from her belt, then army-crawled back to the chair and guided it onto the sidewalk.

"Yes!" she hollered, pumping her fist.

A recoil of pain shot up her arm. She rolled onto her back and clutched her wrist, hoping it wasn't broken. As she looked up into the sky, the driving rain blended with her tears. Sure the chair was free, but how would she ever push herself home?

Driving to Clear Lake through a lashing rainstorm, Garrison tried to figure out how he was going to explain things to Zoey. Her last impression had been that everyone was mad at each other. He knew he needed to approach this delicately, telling her of his feelings for Danica while reassuring her that he wouldn't love her any less.

"Let's stop by your house first," Danica said, reading his mind. "I can tell you're worried."

"You mean Zoey not answering her phone? It's probably on silent. Or maybe she's taking a nap. She wasn't feeling good this morning." The traffic light turned red, and he braked to a stop, wishing he could erase the parental doubt that always seemed to nag at him. He sighed. "I've spent my whole life worrying about her."

"Isn't that what parents do?"

"Sometimes I wonder if I'm holding on too tight, you know?"

Danica placed a hand on his leg. "What you've done with Zoey is wonderful. I don't think I've ever met a teenager as poised or full of life as her."

"Full of life?" he chuckled. "Zoey drives me nuts. But she's a good kid."

"And you're a good father."

A lump rose in Garrison's throat. *A good father.* No one had ever told him that, or if they had, he hadn't believed them. He wished Mom and Celeste were still alive so they could see how things had turned out, how Zoey was growing into such an independent young woman, how he'd done his best to raise her.

A little before three-thirty, Garrison padded into his home, Danica behind him, both trying to keep quiet. "I'm just gonna look in on her," he whispered, thinking the best thing would be to let Zoey sleep and allow her body to recharge.

"Want me to do anything?"

He gave her a sly grin. "Later."

Then he walked down the hallway, thinking about how happy he was for the first time in a long while. When he reached Zoey's bedroom, he peered inside. She wasn't there. He turned back to Danica and gave her a confused shrug.

"Is she not in her bed?" Danica asked, coming up the hallway.

"She's not in her room," he replied. "Zoey," he called, "where are you?"

But the house was silent.

"I'll go look for her," Danica said.

A hollow formed in Garrison's gut. Something was wrong. He rushed through the house, throwing open all the doors and examining all the rooms. He ran back to her bedroom and looked for signs of where she might be. His hands were trembling. This was his worst nightmare come true. *She's gone. My daughter's gone.*

Danica appeared in the doorway. "I can't find her anywhere."

Garrison dropped onto the edge of the bed and rubbed his temples. There had to be a logical explanation for this. He pulled out his cell phone and dialed Zoey's number. Suddenly the room filled with music. He stared at the phone lying on the surface of her desk. "Why doesn't she have her phone?"

"Oh, God."

"Don't worry. Everything's gonna be okay." He wasn't sure if he believed it himself, but he had to in order to preserve his sanity. Then he had an idea. He grabbed Zoey's phone and checked the call history. Her last call came at eleven-thirty. Over four hours ago.

Unsure of what else to do, Garrison called the number. "This is Zoey Sterling's father," he said. "Who is this? . . . Lucas who?"

Danica gently squeezed his arm. "That's the boy from school she likes."

Garrison did a double-take at her. "Listen to me, young

man. Is my daughter with you?"

The boy denied knowing anything but told Garrison that some girls at school had been pestering Zoey. "Zoey said she had to go do something."

"Do something? What does that mean?"

"I don't know. Maybe she went to talk to Cara."

Garrison looked out the windows and could see heavy rain pouring down and ponding in the street. There was no way Zoey would have gone out in weather like this. "Do me a favor, Lucas. See if anyone from school knows where she is. Call me back on her cell phone."

When he hung up, Danica asked, "Should we call nine-one-one?"

"Not yet. You stay here at the house. I'll go look for her." He gave Danica a tight hug before leaving. "I'll find her."

"I know you will."

He rushed outside, and by the time he reached his neighbor's house, his clothes were soaked. "I'm looking for my daughter," he told Mrs. Wilhelm in a panicked voice, but she hadn't seen Zoey. Neither had Mr. Thompson at the next house or the young couple who had moved in a month ago.

He tried to quell his growing fear, but with each shake of a neighbor's head, it refused to let go. *Where can she be?* Zoey's last call had been at 11:30. Which meant she'd been gone . . . he checked the time. *Oh, no. Not 4:07.* The same heart-stopping time that had been on the clock when he fielded the phone call about Celeste.

Lightning flashed in the sky, followed by the low groan of distant thunder. The rain had tapered off somewhat, now falling as a steady drizzle. *Please, God. Let her be safe.*

He raced back home, wresting the keys from his pocket, then chirped the remote for the van's locks. Just as he was about to open the door, he heard a grunt behind him.

He spun to see Zoey pushing awkwardly toward him in her wheelchair. "Daddy!" she said, smiling weakly at him. *Daddy—*

the most precious word in the English vocabulary.

"Zoey!" He rushed toward her but froze when he saw her in closer detail. Her clothes were covered with mud and ripped at one of the knees. Then he saw the blood—on her hands and on her jeans, smeared on the wheel rims and down her face.

"What happened?"

"I'm sorry, Dad. I should have listened to you—"

"Where are you hurt?"

"I . . . I fell out of my chair. By the golf course. My wrist, I think it might be broken."

"Don't worry, you're safe now." He reached down to lift her out of the chair, but paused when he noticed how much she was shivering. "How long have you been out in this weather?"

"I'm so c-cold," she said, her voice quavering.

"Let's get you inside." The front door opened and Danica stepped onto the porch, her eyes darting between him and Zoey, her mouth agape. "I don't know the whole story yet," he called, "but can you find a blanket?" Danica nodded and ducked back inside as he stepped behind the wheelchair.

"What's Danica doing here? I thought you two broke up."

Garrison breathed a deep sigh. "A lot happened today, sweetie. But it's all good now." As he pushed her forward, he found himself pondering the complete unpredictability of life. He'd seen the dark, capricious side: death tearing apart his family and ripping away his friends. But now he'd learned how merciful fate could be. He'd almost lost Danica. He'd almost lost Zoey. Yet he hadn't.

It was as if angels were interceding on his behalf.

When they reached the door, he noticed the rain had finally stopped. "Wait a second," he said. "You fell off your chair over by the golf course? That's so far away. If your arm's hurt, how did you climb back in your chair? And how did you get home?"

She smiled up at him. "Like you said, a lot happened today."

Chapter 44

Garrison found it hard to believe that July was fast approaching. Houston was still reeling from the previous month's violent thunderstorms, including the EF2 tornado that had struck less than five miles from their home. An ugly swath of destruction had been carved into the landscape east of Clear Lake, demolishing the Kemah Boardwalk as thoroughly as Hurricane Ike had done years earlier. More than half of the buildings in the Johnson Space Center complex had broken windows, and the roof of Garrison's office building had been torn off by high winds.

He leaned over and tightened the laces of his running shoes, then peered out the window of the workshop. Bright sunlight streamed inside, bathing the room in a warm glow. *It's a good day to run*, he thought, hoping he'd finish before the temperature climbed to ninety degrees.

The wall opposite the window, where his treadmill had once been positioned, was empty these days except for posters of *The Right Stuff* and *Apollo 13*, two of his favorite movies. After selling the treadmill on Craigslist, Garrison found he liked how less cramped the workshop was. Besides, he rather enjoyed pounding the sidewalks of his neighborhood with a warm breeze in his face. It certainly beat being cooped up inside.

"I'm going running," he told Zoey as he came into the family room. "Back in a bit."

"Are you not going to tennis with me?"

"I thought you hated it when I—what do you call it?—invade your space."

She scoffed. "I do, but . . . Aren't you gonna miss seeing Danica?"

He smiled. For some reason, Zoey still thought she needed to play matchmaker for him. If she only knew how committed he and Danica were to each other, she wouldn't have to keep dropping hints. "I'll see you after tennis. Love you."

Five minutes later, after having stretched his calves, hamstrings, and quads, he pressed the lap timer on his watch and set out for a run. He'd been following the same path for weeks, two loops through his neighborhood and then an extended run north along the bayou, which allowed him the chance to view great blue herons and ibises poking along the shore and the occasional red-tailed hawk swooping overhead. Maybe he was a creature of habit, but that wasn't necessarily a bad thing.

After completing his usual two loops, his body felt strong and his mind clear. He passed the pocket park, still surprised no one had yet removed the uprooted pecan tree that lay across the children's play fort, and then reached the point where he always turned right.

Go the other way. It wasn't a thought, per se, but more of an impulse. *Try something different.*

He considered the idea and glanced down the path. It seemed crowded with people: a teenage boy on a bicycle, a few other joggers, and an old couple walking a pair of black dogs. What the heck, he thought, and veered left.

Soon he found himself returning to that magical flow state where everything seemed effortless and he felt like he could run forever. He could reach that runner's high on his treadmill, drifting in and out of the starfield, but running in the real world seemed to intensify the effect.

When the path reached another fork, he swerved right, not sure where he was headed but confident he could eventually find his way back. A few minutes later, the sidewalk led him beside a golf course. He slowed to a stroll and put his hands on his hips, gazing at the cart path that intersected his sidewalk. His eyes followed the path through the trees and then down a hill. This must have been where Zoey had fallen.

In his mind's eye, he could see Zoey cruising along the cart path and then tumbling out of her wheelchair. He imagined how alone she must have felt. And he could picture her crawling through the mud and eventually tugging her chair free.

A contented smile spread across his face. *That's my girl*, he thought. Even though it had taken him forever to notice, he now knew that Zoey was capable of handling anything life threw her way. She didn't need him holding on so tightly anymore.

He took a deep breath, turned back north, and headed home.

Danica stood in her kitchen, a wooden spoon in one hand and a bowl of cookie batter in the other, and checked the recipe book again. She didn't know the traditional one-month anniversary gift but figured she couldn't go wrong with chocolate chip.

As she poured in the semi-sweet chocolate nibs, she wondered why she'd never tried her hand at baking before. The whole process had seemed so intimidating, especially when she'd seen how much effort Sam put into it, but working alongside Garrison had shown her that cooking wasn't difficult at all. She spooned the batter into balls on a greased cookie sheet and then ran a finger along the inside edge of the bowl.

The best part about baking? Chocolate chip cookie dough.

After popping the cookies in the oven, she fired up the company laptop and checked her email, hoping her persistence might finally pay off. For days, she'd been playing phone tag with an employee of the Houston Port Authority, asking him for documents about Port executives who were possibly involved in ethics violations and conflicts of interest regarding international contracts for the new Turning Basin Terminal.

To her delight, her inbox contained more than ten messages from a Wayne Sweetwater, and she quickly scanned them to discover email chains of conversations between Port executives, plus PDFs of invoices and expense reports. Danica let out a low whistle. "Oh, this is gonna be fun."

It didn't matter that the story would never go national. She was back doing the work she loved, uncovering the seedy truth about corrupt public officials. "Chase what's important," everyone had told her. And that's exactly what she'd done.

Even though Fox News had been willing to give her another shot, she had declined their offer, instead attempting to rework her contract with Eyewitness9 to do more investigative pieces. But that hadn't panned out either. These days she was no longer sitting behind an anchor desk—although that was a good thing—because she'd parlayed her credibility and popularity into a new gig: leading *The Investigators* for Channel Five.

Which meant no more early-morning wakeup calls and no more heavy makeup. She wasn't looking forward to working at the same station with Barb Edwards but knew that wouldn't last long either. Rumor had it that Barb's recent "vacation" was actually spent in the office of her cosmetic surgeon, a sure sign that Barb had her sights set elsewhere.

When the timer went off, Danica moved the cookies to a cooling rack and changed into her tennis outfit. Although she enjoyed teaching Zoey the finer points of tennis, she was pretty sure Zoey's interest in the sport was waning. The last time they'd played, all Zoey could talk about was how she couldn't wait for high school to start so she could see Lucas every day.

Danica felt the same way about the man in her life— sometimes she found herself practically giddy when seeing Garrison after a long day. And then there were those feelings that only a woman knew: the trembling anticipation before making love, the peace and certainty when lying in his arms, the sheer joy of imagining their future together.

She broke a cookie in half and bit into the gooey piece. Oh yeah, life was sweet.

Sitting in the passenger seat beside Danica, Zoey couldn't wait to get back home. Although she enjoyed hanging out with Danica and actually *playing* tennis, practicing Danica's drills was a different story. Spinning in all directions had become tedious, and it wasn't as if she was going to turn into some tennis phenom. She wondered how she would break the news to Danica.

"Do I smell cookies?" Zoey asked.

"Chocolate chip. They're not for you, though." Danica paused and then chuckled. "I'm just messing with you. They're for all of us. Your dad and I are celebrating our one-month anniversary today."

"Has it been a month already?"

"In some ways I feel like I've known your dad my whole life." She pointed out the window. "Isn't that your old middle school?"

"Ugh. Hated that place." Near the front of her old school, a small group of girls sat in a circle on the grass. Zoey recognized Cara and Tiffany right away. "Danica, you remember high school. Do girls act mean there, too?" When Danica didn't respond, she said, "That's what I figured."

"You'll be fine, Zoey. You'll make new friends."

"Did I ever tell you what I found out about Cara? Why she was so mean to me?" She gazed out the window toward the girls, where the telltale curls of cigarette smoke rose above them. "Her folks are getting divorced."

"Oh. That can be tough."

"She wanted more than anything to be a Popular. That's what everyone calls them. Turns out I was too different for her new group of friends."

"Sounds like the kind of people you don't want to be friends with."

"Yeah, I guess," she replied, still half-believing that having crappy friends beat no friends at all.

When they arrived home, Zoey rolled up the ramp to the front door, opened it, and tossed her tennis bag into a basket inside the foyer. She wrinkled her nose at a new, strange scent that drifted in the air. It wasn't her father's cooking.

"Look who's home," Dad said, walking in from the kitchen. He turned and clapped his hands against his knees. "Come here, boy!" Thumping sounds came from behind him, and all of a sudden a chocolate Labrador bounded into the room. "Say hello to Gundo."

Zoey blinked her eyes, not believing what she was seeing. "I thought I couldn't—" she started to say, but the dog trotted over to her and licked her hand. "Is he mine?"

Her dad wrapped his arm around Danica's waist and stood there beaming. "I called the lady who emailed you. It took some convincing, but she let me pick him up early. And by the way, I know you wanted to call him Scout, but he already has a name."

"Gundo?"

"It means warrior."

"He's beautiful," Danica said, kneeling down and petting him.

Her dad rubbed behind the dog's ears, and Gundo craned his neck to look up. "He's very smart," Dad said. "You can teach him stuff, but he's not supposed to be a service dog."

"That's okay."

"Besides, you don't need someone to take care of you. But Gundo can certainly be your friend."

Her eyes welled up. A friend. That's all she'd ever wanted.

"Tell Zoey what the lady told you," Danica said, nudging him.

"So, he's a Lab, about two years old, and he's gone through all the service training. But he didn't graduate. Got too distracted." With a smile, he added, "Figured he was perfect for you."

She stuck her tongue out at him. "You think you're funny, don't you?"

Danica cleared her throat. "Garrison, tell her about his heart."

"What do you mean?" Zoey replied, feeling a stab of alarm.

"It's nothing dangerous, but Gundo was born with a condition called . . ." He extracted a piece of paper from his pocket. "Patent Foramen Ovale. PFO. They found it when he was a puppy. He was born with an opening between the chambers of his heart. The hole was supposed to close but it didn't."

"It caused a murmur," Danica explained.

"Oh, my God. Is he gonna die?"

"No, no, sweetie. It's just something to be aware of. It probably closed on its own. And it wasn't bad enough to keep him out of training. We should just pay attention to it, not run Gundo too hard, that kind of thing."

She looked into her dad's eyes and suddenly understood why he'd been so protective of her over the years. She'd known Gundo for only a couple of minutes and already loved him completely. And just like Dad, she would do anything to care for him.

Zoey ran her hand underneath Gundo's chest to gauge his heartbeat. It felt strong and steady. He cocked his head at her, then wandered away, sniffing the floor and the furniture. "I can't believe I have a dog," she told Danica.

"I'm glad. We all need someone we can count on."

"No!" her dad yelled. He was standing there with his hands clamped to his head, staring into the family room. "No, Gundo! Bad Gundo!" He turned to Zoey and shouted, "Your dog just peed on my recliner!"

Zoey shook her head and said the one thing she'd been dying to tell her father for years. "Dad, don't be so dramatic."

Chapter 45

W hen the movie credits began to roll, Garrison turned off the cabin's TV. It was after midnight—they'd started the film more than two-and-a-half hours ago, back when Zoey was happily chatting about the upcoming start of school. She'd lasted only an hour before zonking out.

Even though Garrison's eyes had adjusted to the dim light, now that the television was off, he couldn't see a thing in the pitch-black room. From his left, he heard the sounds of snoring—from Zoey, who was asleep on the couch, and from Gundo, who lay curled beneath her. Reclining against his chest was Danica, and he just lay there breathing in her scent.

Eventually she shifted against him. "Movie over?" she mumbled.

Garrison kissed her hair. "Let's go into the other room." When he rose from the sofa, Danica lay her head down and moaned softly.

"Okay, sleepyhead," he whispered, "I'll see you in the morning." He unfolded a light blanket and placed it on top of her, and she exhaled a contented sigh.

"I love you," he told her, his voice barely louder than the crickets outside.

"Love you, too," she murmured.

He stood there a moment, considering whether he should crawl into bed, then decided he'd take a stroll out to the star shack instead. Long before Zoey had pleaded to watch a movie, the plan had been to do some late-night stargazing, which meant her binocular chair was still outside.

Garrison padded to the door and opened it, and he heard the metallic chime of a dog collar behind him. "You need to pee, boy? Come on." He walked out onto the porch, and Gundo followed, stretching his entire body before walking up to an oak tree and raising his leg.

With no illumination from the cabin and no light pollution on the horizon, Garrison navigated his way to the darkened star shack like a blind man, shuffling slowly along the decomposed granite path, accompanied by his four-legged companion. Gundo had been to the ranch only a few times, but it seemed he already knew every square inch of the place. In fact, he seemed to have become part of their family with hardly any transition.

"You're a good dog, aren't you?" he said, and he could hear the swish of Gundo's tail and its echo in the jingling collar. "Want to go look at stars?" Garrison cast his eyes upward and surveyed the vast blanket of twinkling lights above him. There were times when stargazing seemed more an exercise in messing with his gadgets than appreciating the glory of nature, but tonight's sky was too beautiful to ignore. "Wow," he said, awestruck, more confident than ever that they'd made the right call to stay in Texas.

After buttoning up everything at the star shack, save the binocular chair, he went outside and found Gundo. He sat cross-legged on the ground and rubbed the dog's ears. "You like it out here, boy? This is a pretty place, isn't it?"

Gundo panted in response, and Garrison laughed quietly. The great thing about dogs was their optimism, and this buoyant Lab was no exception. Gundo didn't mind that he'd flunked out of dog school or that he'd been born with a congenital heart defect—he was full of boundless enthusiasm.

Garrison had seen that same zest for life in Celeste, the way she always lived in the moment and never dwelled on anything negative. He'd seen it in their daughter, who refused to allow her condition to define her or hold her down. And he'd seen it in Danica, whose passion for what she believed in had reinvigorated his own excitement for life.

He ran a hand along the dog's smooth, muscular haunches, amazed how Gundo had been able to thrive in spite of misfortune. He pressed on Gundo's chest and raised a hand to his own for comparison, feeling the steady pulses and contemplating how much they had in common.

Perhaps we all have a space in the heart, he thought, some tragedy or deep regret that shapes our lives. The secret to rising above it is not to dwell on the emptiness but rather to fill the space with meaningful things. Doing worthwhile work. Raising a child. Rediscovering how to love.

He climbed onto the binocular chair and lay back, staring up and soaking it all in. The scientific part of his mind immediately picked out the constellations of Cygnus, Delphinus, and Aquila, but as he lay there and allowed himself to disappear into the starfield, he swore he could actually see the swan and dolphin and eagle come alive.

What a privilege it was to be able to revel in the majesty of the night sky, to view the same tapestry of stars and planets that his ancestors once had, to commune with the heavens. He took a deep breath and closed his eyes. Maybe he was an astronaut after all. For he had truly journeyed to the stars.

Acknowledgments

When I write stories, I always try to approach them with a keen eye toward the reader, making sure I do my best to deliver a story that engages them. It's sometimes easy, sometimes difficult, but always rewarding. I want to thank so many who have supported and influenced me through the years, making this dream possible.

Let's start with family, because at the end of the day, that's what matters.

To my wife Susan, who has been my best friend for three decades and somehow doesn't take it personally when my story kills off the wife yet again, thank you for supporting my writing and encouraging me when I wasn't sure where the story was headed. I love you.

To my children, Lisa and Brian, who have completed the journey into adulthood and are knitting their own families, thank you for being proud of what I do . . . and for inspiring the children in my novels. May God continue to bless your lives.

Family is certainly a common theme in my writing, and I must thank my parents, whose 53+ year marriage has been an inspiration and an example. They've shown me that no matter what challenge presents itself, standing together is the only way to face it.

I consider it a great honor to work alongside other talented writers in my critique group. They share my passion for the craft and my love for the characters, and have helped shaped this story. My deepest thanks to John Oehler, Stacey Keith, Sarah Warburton, Bill Stevenson, Heather Shelly, and Vanessa Leggett. Their books are amazing, and I recommend them.

I also want to recognize you, dear reader, as I believe that a writer and a reader share a special bond. I consider it my job to deliver characters worth caring about, story that keeps you interested, and writing that doesn't get in the way. When you suspend disbelief and disappear into this world, described by the author but given full life in your own imagination, you join together on that journey. Thank you.

The publishing industry continues to undergo tremendous change, which has been a challenge for authors. Please support writers who truly serve their readers. The best way to do that is to spread the word when you find a story that engages you, that takes you into a rich world filled with complex characters.

If *Space in the Heart* has done that for you, I humbly ask that you take the time to tell a friend or write a spoiler-free review.

Of course, I'd love to hear from you. Drop me an email or contact me via social media. I enjoy working with book clubs, too! Please visit my website to read the latest news:

www.rodneywalther.com

Novels by Rodney Walther

BROKEN LACES

SPACE IN THE HEART

www.ingramcontent.com/pod-product-compliance
Lightning Source LLC
Chambersburg PA
CBHW050903250626
47155CB00001B/79